Praise for NEON LIGHTS

"You will literally sail through the wavy twists and reach an ending that is satisfying and astonishing. The comic elements in this book are gut busting. Zig Zag Claybourne is totally inventive and this piece of work by the writer is certainly original. The book will have you laughing till the end... its ins and outs are such that you will be left amazed."
JEFF RIVERA, best-selling author of *Forever My Lady*

"Zig Zag Claybourne is officially the funniest guy I know!"
SPARKLE HAYTER, author of the *Robin Hudson* mysteries

"If Douglas Adams and Chris Rock had a bastard lovechild and raised him on nothing but sweet potato pie and bourbon, this is what would ensue."
LANA WINTER, author and worldwide blogger

"Kudos to Zig Zag for... having both the audacity and the sense of humor in taking on urban lit in the first place."
S. J. HOUEN, super soul sister

NEON LIGHTS

Narmer's Palette Books

Edmonton, Alberta Canada

Published in the United States of America.

Print ISBN 978-0-9877039-8-9

Ebook ISBN 978-1-927081-05-1

First Edition, July 2013

Cover design by Nathaniel Hébert, www.winterhebert.com

"Everybody wants a piece of writing but we ain't seen nothing yet. If writing becomes sexy Victoria's Secret had better invent some new draws!" –SDW

I dedicate this novel to the lady behind me in the bank line who told me about her gynecological test results via the lively public cell phone conversation she carried on, of which I was in no way a part. Oh, and to Pam Grier, as she is a goddess.

Chapter One

Two weeks ago Barclay finally got a meeting with Jim Cross of Crosshairs Books, a small press publisher, to talk about *Onion Roll*. Hadn't wanted a meeting. Just sales figures. "No, no, we need to meet," he'd heard all of three times, but apparently they had two different understandings of the word "meet" because a promised date never crossed Cross' calendar. Barclay's contract stipulated a royalty increase from eight to twelve percent if sales passed twenty-five thousand units. *Onion Roll* was into its third printing, a blockbuster for a relatively literary novel by small press standards. The royalty checks were good but dwindling. An urgent email from Cross breathlessly mentioned "renegotiating" three times while telling of the company's battles to stay viable to the black community. "We're not going down without a fight," the email went on. "I know you've got concerns. Let's meet."

"Barclay Royse, sit down, man, sit down!" Jim Cross, founder and publisher, Crosshairs Books. Jim Cross had written three books about blue-collar brothers tightening up booshie women as only men with names like Payton Rent could, three best sellers showering him with brief fame and serious money.

It had been the third book signing eight years ago when Barclay met Cross. Marilyn wanted her copy of *High Voltage Below* signed by a real writer, calling her husband over when she reached the front of the long line.

Cross, head down, signed Marilyn's book. His plan had been to finish the signing with a roguish smile. Beautiful women always got the roguish smile. Royse was a tall mofo though. He nixed that. *Marilyn, enjoy everything I have to offer*, he wrote.

"My husband's a writer," she said to the author of *Duct Work, Copper Pipe*, and now the book guaranteed to blow the lid off what men really needed from a woman, especially when it wasn't his own, *High Voltage Below*. Hearing the word 'writer,' women behind her glanced unimpressed at Barclay, who dragged over.

No, I'm not, Barclay thought, and had a drawer full of manuscripts to prove it. He shook the man's hand and said, "Pleasure," with the nod that said that was the extent of their conversation.

James Cross, however, took cock-blocking—even if you had wedding ring receipt and proof-of-purchase—as slightly less offensive than clubbing baby seals. And while clubbing seals was theoretical, cock-blocking was not. It cut to the soul. Married men were damned annoying. "Maybe I know your work," he said. "You published?"

Barclay smiled as amiably as someone wanting to kick a priest in the nuts. "Not yet."

Cross pointed out the copy of *High Voltage Below* in Marilyn's hands. "I've got an email address in there. Keep in touch. Not yet can always become one day."

And butterflies will swirl my asshole atop a rainbow bidet! thought Barclay, complete with interior goofy smile. "Appreciate it."

"You ever…" Cross asked him with a slight nod toward the book in Marilyn's hand.

"No."

"A lot of men don't. Check it out though. Might be something you need."

I need, thought Barclay, enunciating his thoughts slowly and distinctly for this hack's benefit, *Morrison, Danticat, Shakespeare, and Marquez.* "I'll do that. Thanks."

"Thank you," said Marilyn. Barclay immediately headed off. Being away from a line of impatient black women was never a bad thing.

"Barclay, brother, sit down, please?" Cross stood. He'd

seen a movie where the classy host never sat first. Barclay swung a seat around. "You need anything? I can have Netta run across to the store. Listen, we don't have a lot of time," said Cross. Files lay open on his desk, along with a stack of manuscript packages designed to make him look busy.

"I want you to know *Onion* is doing great," said Cross.

"That's good."

Cross jumped directly to it. It was best to keep writers off guard. "I want to change your contract, though, to give you an opportunity to do another one, building off this first one."

"Another book."

"A sequel."

"Everybody dies."

"Shakespeare killed off people all the time and did sequels."

"No, he didn't."

"Know what, if we can back your percentage down on *Onion*, I can roll more revenue into marketing your next book, which is gon' fuckin' blow the hell up, am I right?"

"I'm poised?"

"You're poised. People know your name. Folks like you at the signings. You need one more book with us under this contract—"

"Which we're about to renegotiate."

"To bump you up to the next level with Crosshairs. Barclay, I can see a string of books by Barclay Royse under Crosshairs, and then in association with one of the major houses, 'cause they've been sniffing around my ass. I keep my ass clean, so it ain't shit they smell. Crosshairs publishes the best. I got the best literary—"

For unknowns.

"—drama—"

For unknowns.

"—urban—"

Barclay hated sales pitches.

"—and now I'm moving into street. I want you to stay with us, brother, and work to keep Crosshairs doing what it does best."

"Don't we need to talk numbers?'

"Yes! And I had them here—" He made a show of searching his desk. "Netta will bring in some figures. I want to make sure me and you are on the same page."

"James, we'll be on the same page. But I need to know what book you're reading. What's *Onion* sold, what is my next book likely to sell, and how do we go about moving up? I'm hearing what you're saying but..."

Cross held up a hand. "I understand. Matter of fact, wouldn't have it any other way. I'm pretty sure you're close to the bump point. Once Netta gets those numbers back in to me—you know, we had some computer problems, and then I was at that conference. Anybody tells you they don't get buck wild at book conferences, they lied. Then off to Atlanta— anyway, right now you're at eight percent. I want to cap you at ten. Royalties are one thing but we're talking about long term."

"Which I'm poised to blow up on."

"Baghdad style, man! We can rework the contract without lawyers 'cause it's straight and what I said. You're going to make the twelve percent mark. Hell, my own wife read *Onion* and asked me why can't I do like that. I mean, fuck! My ass has built a company up, gave authors a place to be seen and heard—'cause how many other urban publishers make sure their authors get book signings and publicity?—got three bestselling books under my belt, and at home I get asked why I'm not doing what Barclay Royse does. That's poised, brother."

Barclay nodded thanks.

"So you stick with me," Cross finished.

Barclay hesitated.

"You're not about to walk out of here without a check today," said Cross as though Barclay had protested against one.

"An advance?"

"No. It's not that much. But consider it a bonus in good faith. Free and separate of any contract negotiations. Just you, me, and thank you between the two of us. But then I wanna talk to you about your next book. If we can get it to drop by the end of summer..."

Barclay heard the words but the words became meaningless in the context of sitting in James Cross' office talking about having a book finished by the end of summer and it was already early May. All Barclay heard next was "Fuh, fuh, fuh fuh fuh duh" capped off with "You and Crosshairs are heading for a new dimension."

Barclay waited.

"Street, man."

Fuh fuh duh?

"Black romance and drama?" said Cross. "On lockdown! Not selling the way it was. Don't get me wrong, Crosshairs is still master of the game, but we gotta grow, you know, dance the dance."

"You've already got street."

Cross shook his head. "Nuh-uh, I've got urban. I ain't got *street*."

Fuh duh!

"And the street that's out there is absolute bullshit," he continued. "I got writers thinking they're Donald Goines' offspring, and I got females pumping out their sexual fantasies like suffragette *Penthouse*. I want street...but I want you."

Duh fuck?

"You write a street book, brother, and I guarantee you it...will...blow up. I wouldn't put this to any of my other authors. You got the skills to get in shit. It's like you're telepathic!"

The incredulous frown started hurting Barclay's face. "I'm not...cut out...for—Street? Street?"

"Shakespeare basically did street lit back in the day."

"No, he didn't."

"I'm sure he did."

"James, I can't write street lit."

"That's where Crosshairs is going. You've gotta come with us."

"Everybody and their mama is doing street lit!"

"Know what? You're selling. My other authors ain't. I couldn't see why at first, but, see, they're writing me. They're watering down my Kool-Aid. I take a chance on you, you give 'em sweet tea and they lose their minds. I get emails wondering when you're going to drop another book."

"They're not looking for street."

"They don't know what the fuck they're looking for; all they want is more tea. I know: you're an author; you don't write street. Street is utter bullshit."

"Yes, it is. And if you mention Shakespeare again I'll punch you in the nuts."

"That's street right there! You can write this shit in your sleep. I guarantee you will sell more units with this next book than all your other books combined. White women read your stuff! Not Oprah-level but maybe some that watch *The View*. Ok? You got black women, library black dudes, and enough white women to notice...reading your stuff. Write a street book."

"There's no way I'm writing a street book."

"It's all about the name. Let me take care of the details. Hell, write under a pseudonym. Once it gains momentum, I'll let it leak that it's you. Curiosity kills the cat, we scoop it up, shave it bald, sell the hair to some wig shops and sit back and blow up."

"I'm not a name author."

Cross played Publication Chutes and Ladders well enough to know that authors had as much gratification-control as a teen-aged boy. Now was the time—and the reason he'd needed a face to face meeting—to lean in and set the hook. Out of the thousands of names trapped inside a book store, maybe twenty-five were "name" authors. Maybe fifty. Generously, maybe a hundred. Out of a million books swirling the world at any given moment, a small group of a hundred individuals woke up knowing that their name on a cover meant another unit sold.

The Holy Grail...

Cross looked him dead in the eye and asked the question every dedicated writer pretended to ignore.

"You wanna be?"

Chapter Two

He stared at the computer monitor.

I can do this.

But didn't want to.

It's a pretend page on a computer screen. It's not real writing if it's not written down.

Eye of the tiger. Be a man, dammit!

Was Marilyn downstairs or was she in the garden? He needed more facial scrub if she was going to the store.

"Marilyn!"

No answer.

Barclay scratched his neck. He hated a beard in warm weather but also hated shaving in warm weather. The bastard hairs came back pissed and intentionally made his face itch. There had to be a better way, although that one time he'd convinced her to buy Nair hadn't worked out so well.

He stared outside for distraction. It looked nice. The flowers bloomed at full head under a bright sun. Somewhere out there a woman bent over using her back instead of the cool knee pads they'd bought—bent over being the operative visual, with her jean shorts and whistle-while-you-work buttocks shifting to and fro—while to Barclay Royse's left was a bookcase. Three books were stacked on a shelf eye level with him: *Rambeau Shakespeare* by Barclay Royse, *Not Unlike A Fairy Tale* by Barclay Royse, and *Onion Roll* by him again. The Work. The obscure, unknown work.

The Work. At hand. Today.

He faced the monitor. Normally it and the keyboard were his friends. Normally they behaved for him.

Not today.

Another glance outside. The office presented a cropped view of the backyard. Marilyn raced across the lawn spinning crazily and swatting at a bee that was likely already fifty yards away. She sprayed herself in the face with the water hose.

He typed "Dedicationz" with a Z... and stopped. That Z stopped him cold.

Get up and get out.

The backyard was full of greenery and other colors. Near the garage, oranges and reds. Bordering the privacy fence, greens and whites. Dripping beneath the patio canopy, one brown wife. Being married for more than two years meant a man knew when to keep his mouth shut.

"Nice out." Barclay sat on the swing lounger. The sun made him squint when he looked up at her. "Did you get him?"

Marilyn Rolls-Royse, when dry-haired, damn near approached regal. Wet, with dripping face and semi-transparent tee shirt, she looked skanky. He was turned on.

"Why are those planted so close to the faucet!" she demanded. Those being the buttercups she planted two weeks ago. She was the master of rhetorical accusation. She shook her hair out, raining on gnats and floaties.

"Grass needs cutting," he said.

She plunked beside him on the swing and kicked back. He immediately extended his legs. Noise from the kids next door ran along the wooden privacy fence. The Royse yard was wide open, not large but large enough for a sizable handmade planter that was starting to look a little weedy, a barbecue space, a hammock between two kissing pines, and the swing area reserved for afternoon raspberry tea or evening Tiki lamp relaxation.

"Damn bugs," she mumbled. Two myths of gardening: bees are necessary; if you leave them alone they will leave you alone. Bees annoyed the hell out of her.

"Bugs suck," he agreed.

"I hate summer."

It wasn't summer. It was May. Pointing that out to her

almost overrode the fact that she was wet.

"You look good wet." He admired the filled bra through the tee shirt. "But it ain't free."

"I could sell peeps to the kids and retire."

"That meeting I had? They want another book out of me."

"Want, need, and get don't necessarily make three."

"I'm contracted for two. He put out *Onion Roll*," he reminded her. "Now he needs another."

"You got out of your contract with your first crazy publisher."

"They let me out. On friendly terms."

"You should've stayed with them."

"I thought Crosshairs was better."

"Go back to them."

"Hell no. You just said they were crazy. And it's not that easy."

"When is it? You've got three books in stores and still don't have an agent. I'm not one to say, but..." She shrugged.

One of the kids on the other side shouted "Hey!" then a section of fence shook from sharp impact. This meant Wallace was about to knock the hell out of Terry.

Marilyn raised her voice. "Wally!"

"Ok!" But he was already on the chase.

"Ok then."

"Ran out of face soap last night."

"Why do you let it get so low? I keep four bottles in my closet."

"Your stuff lasts longer 'cause you've got delicate girlie skin. My stuff's gotta get through this," he said, ruffling the scrag.

"You use too much shampoo too."

"Not a lot of Indian in my family," he said. "Don't get the stuff you got last time."

"It's the same thing."

"No, it's not. Other stuff was bottled. They went to the tube 'cause it's probably cheaper than the hard squeezy bottle, so they probably cheaped everything. Leave the tubes be." He looked at her hair slowly poofing away. "You washing your hair tonight?"

"Yeah, why?"

Barclay shrugged.

The phone rang.

"You didn't bring the phone out?" she asked.

"No, babe."

A face appeared in the kitchen window. "B-Ball!"

Barclay got up. Three people called him on a regular basis: telemarketers, his best friend, and some nut named Marilyn who knew where he lived.

Had already talked to telemarketers.

Marilyn's brother Mario handed off the phone in the kitchen. Then disappeared. Marilyn's brother Mario lived in the house. Somewhere.

"Took you long enough, you fat old goat," Bela's voice greeted.

"Whassup?" Men of his age could still say whassup, even though the word was hopelessly outdated. Men of his age were hopelessly outdated.

"She letting let you play today?"

"I think so." The hoop was over Barclay's garage. "She's washing the car first."

"You in the middle of something?" said Bela.

"Writing."

"Good, I'll be over in fifteen minutes to pick you up."

Bela's car always smelled like fruit and cloves. "I need to make reservations at this restaurant."

"And I'm here why?"

"Moral support."

"One you met three weeks ago?"

"Yeah."

"Trudy," said Barclay.

"Her name's not Trudy."

"Big Booty Trudy." Barclay watched the restaurant come into view. Bela swerved into the valet circle. This restaurant had an outdoor fountain. Bela was dressed in basketball tear-offs. The valet and Bela did a quick exchange. The valet, now behind the steering wheel, looked questioningly at Barclay sitting beside him.

Bela bent in the driver's window and did the same.

"I'm not getting out," said Barclay.

Bela gave him the get-yo-ass-out-the-car head twist. Barclay exited.

"You don't spend this much money on three weeks."

"I like her," said Bela.

"You valeted to make a reservation."

"You see any parking spaces? Cars all up and down the street. This place is the shit."

"What kind of fool tries to get prime reservations in tear-off pants?"

Bela knew something about places like this. "Places like this respect doing business in person. My credit card is dressed right."

The lobby was full of plants that looked like they made more than you, and two flanking wall tanks featured tropical fish on a social level much too high to be bothered with you. They swam lazily in select groups and avoided any appearance of eagerness as pertained to bits of food swirling the tank.

Booshie Fish weren't included in McElligot's Pool, thought Barclay, crediting Dr. Seuss' omission to racial sensitivity.

"Bela, you got on basketball gear."

"Shut up." Matthew Bela Hills was about to work his mack.

"May I help you?"

It was a skinny white guy. Maitre'D's were never fat. They were always skinny white guys.

While Bela slid his hand into his back pocket (the universal male symbol for money talks) he said, "How far out you booked for reservations?"

"For the two of you?"

"No, just for two."

The skinny white guy gave the appearance of consulting something out of view atop his mahogany lectern. Etiquette prevented the men from peering over.

"Will three weeks do?"

"Oooh, can we do two weeks?"

The Maitre'D gave a frown of compassion.

"One week?" said Bela, tossing Hope Alive on the pile.

"Are you proposing?"

"Before he has to ship back out," Barclay said. "Command."

"Middle East?"

"Is there anywhere else?" said Barclay.

"We really don't have anything else," the Maitre'D said. Just that quickly, he was speaking solely to Barclay now. "Three weeks."

"What are the odds of a cancellation?" said Barclay.

"There's a list for that too."

"But they won't know if somebody cancelled or not." Barclay smiled as though he and the man were about to enter a compact. He moved a hair closer. "Please?" It helped that the Maitre'D was younger than them, not by a lot but noticeably so.

Bela became conciliatory. "Hit me with whatever you have," he acknowledged, bringing his wallet into view.

Barclay watched the man seek surreptitious hints of command off his friend. Maybe military commanders, like real men—which the Maitre'D needed others to see that he was—didn't need to carry masculinity in a holster in plain view.

Taking a back seat for them was probably a relief.

Bela handed over the card. "You'll look out for me?"

The Maitre'D swiped it, locking Bela's information into his schedule.

"Yes, sir."

Bela pocketed his things with a nod.

"Thank you," said Barclay.

Passing the bay of keys, well out of earshot of the Maitre'D, Bela asked, "You really think he's going to call?"

"I do."

"Why?"

"He shifted eye contact with both of us."

Bela smiled. "We're the Kings of Rock," he said, wondering how much to tip for a three-minute valet.

"I hope Big Booty Trudy appreciates this."

"What if I really like her? You gonna keep calling her that?"

"Yes. She's kind of stupid," said Barclay.

"You met her two times."

"So I know her as well as you do."

"Edit your thoughts, man."

"All right. Not to her face."

"Shut the hell up."

When Bela parked in the driveway Marilyn sloshed a bucket toward her car, her hair contained far from the water with a scrunchy.

"If I was supposed to be command," Bela brought up exiting the car, "why'd you do all the talking?"

"He's got family in the military," said Barclay.

"How do you know?"

"I know."

Marilyn called over her shoulder, "He knows, Bela. He always knows."

"Mario still inside?"

"Don't know."

"I'll risk it."

The men sat in the kitchen where they could watch Marilyn.

"I do like her," said Bela.

"I know."

"You think she's stupid."

"Bela, she is stupid. She stayed on the cell phone the whole time you introduced her."

"Could've been an important call."

"Nobody has important calls on cell phones."

"She's not stupid. She just ain't complicated."

"That what it's called now?"

"I'ma kick ya ass out there."

Barclay tapped the table and confessed, "I gotta write that book."

"The hoochie book? Ha! You can't get outta the contract?"

"Too much effort. I can get this done in two weekends."

"You got lucky with that second book. What was it, 'Potato Skin'?"

"Onion Roll."

"Made some money and got noticed," said Bela.

"I want to be Stephen King."

"Yeah, well Steve's seen your dead end job; I don't think he plans on swapping any time soon."

"Shut the hell up."

"Fucking artiste. Be funny if this is the book does it for you. Hell, that's all that's getting published these days, little hoochie books. Get in on it while you can. Boom won't last forever."

Marilyn sloshed sudsy water over the car.

"We should go out there and help her instead of sitting in here," said Bela, never one to pass up the surreptitiously respectful peep.

"What is it about this girl you like so much?" Barclay asked.

"Make it sound like I'm a pervert."

"How old is she?"

"Twenty-seven."

"How old are you?"

"Forty—"

"You don't even have to add the three. Ok, she ain't a girl, she's a tween."

"Why don't you like her?"

"It doesn't matter why I don't like her. What matters is why do you like her? Sex is sex, but come on, she's stupid. I gotta call it like it be."

"I'ma kick ya ass on the basketball court."

"That's what you keep saying. Come on, man, your standards were never that low. Now you're making reservations and acting like I gotta give you her hand in marriage. You better not be talking about getting married."

"Hell no. Ok, that didn't come out right. Not with her, not now. Maybe. I could. People grow."

"Stupid people don't grow."

"Shut up."

Twenty minutes after Marilyn finished up and moved the car, Barclay had his ass kicked. The men dragged back into the kitchen straight for the fridge.

"You are a complete waste of a tall man, you know that?" said Bela.

Both men wheezed.

"Didn't I take it to you though?" Barclay countered between wheezes.

"When I was getting chased by bees."

"Didn't I take it to you?"

"He did have that one good shot," said Mario of Barclay, then he disappeared.

They plopped back at the table. Cold water was a blessing to hopelessly outdated throats trying to play basketball.

Wallace and Terry had even come around the driveway to watch them in case of the comedy gold of grown-up injury.

Barclay watched sky and earth enjoying themselves out there. The grass was cut, the flowers blooming, and there was every indication that Marilyn planned on firing up the barbecue.

He liked his house.

What ill befalls a man to write one measly book when he already has the world in his hands?

"What're you smiling about, boy?"

"Nothing. Stay for dinner and ask Marilyn about your new lady." He stood slowly.

"Where're you off to?"

"I've got some writing to do."

"It's the weekend."

"Brother, I'm at work. Where are you?"

Bela shrugged. "I know where the TV is."

Chapter Three

Barclay watched the cursor blinking behind the word "Dedications" with a Z.

And sighed.

Z wasn't a bad letter. In Canada they called it "zed" as though it were some hillbilly Frenchman. Any letter with a name wasn't bad, not in itself. But to willfully stuff S's face in the mud... that was just wrong. S hadn't done anything to anybody. Granted slavery started with S, but so did Superman, Star Trek, sex and souvlaki. To willfully relegate the S to being under the thumb of the Man, that was just wrong.

But maybe it was a joke in itself now though. Even bangers knew how ridiculous it was spelling bangerz with a Z. West Hollywood bangerz, maybe. But authentic ones? Fuck no.

Barclay stared at the cursor. He hit the space bar twice, giving the letter enough breathing space to feel safe. The cursor waited. Go forward or go back.

Shall we go back?

Hell no.

He quickly typed, *In about a year from now Neon would have both of the Brothers Jetstream in love with her. They would sit her down on a palatial throne of glass in the Hall of Silences where beams of light crisscrossed the ceiling through two thousand tiny windows, and solemnly ask her to decide between them...*

"I see the book about a woman named Neon," he told Jim Cross over the phone. "Something bright, something colorful."

"Ok."

"I want to make her more than what readers and the characters in the book think she is."

"Ok."

"Young lady trying to make it through college without

sacrificing who she is."

"Oh, no. Have you read any of these books?"

"No."

"Road trip. Do some research. Get that girl the hell away from college."

"I know enough about them."

"No you don't. Get thee to a Barnes and Noble, then start writing. I like what you wanna do, but I want you to know what you're doing."

I am not going to the store to buy hoochie books! Men don't buy hoochie books! "Jim, can't you send me a packet?"

Cross laughed dismissively. "I just gave you a check, I know you can buy a couple books."

I'll take Marilyn with me, he thought.

Marilyn thoroughly left him to head to the humor section. She kept hope alive that one day she'd walk over there and find a completely brand new *Calvin and Hobbes* selection.

Being a man on a mission, there was no time to wait for the ring of teenaged girls (who, between them, had enough fabric for one pair of jeans, let alone the three that were so tight they didn't have buttcreases) to drift toward other sections of the book store. They weren't going to other sections of the store. These three had done a rotation around the African-American table for fifteen minutes (between calls and laughing at geeky customers perusing the history section across the aisle) without once looking with genuine curiosity anywhere else. And they were loud. Granted Barnes and Noble was to a library what a titty bar is to a daycare, but still.

"Don't get that one, it's about some fags," the one in faded jeans said.

The prettiest one wrinkled her nose and dropped the book. "Why I wanna read about men fuckin'?" She bent the rhinestone lettering on her jeans toward something else but hesitated. The dudes on the gay book were fine as hell.

"You don't."

"Unless they're in prison or some shit," the pretty one hoped. She picked it up again and read the back cover, then announced, "These motherfuckers ain't in prison. 'Hard Knocks: how does a gangsta keep it on the low when his rival's banging the back do'?' Excuse me," she said to Barclay as she reached across for a cover that was nothing but hard pecs. She dropped *Hard Knocks* atop *Triple X, Part Three*.

He'd purposely come after work thinking kids would have been gone by now. There was always somebody around these tables, but the younger they were the more annoying they were, and teenaged girls could annoy to the point of murder. Particularly if they were later teens and had decided they were as grown as they needed to be.

Barclay was effectively invisible to them. He wondered if it was his slacks or the shirt tucked into his pants.

The girls left with their picks.

Six books between them. He loved candy too but he also liked a good meal. The street-lit table—and it was always a table, the books laid flat so the covers were easy to see—was close enough to the information desk that employees could keep an eye on it but, thankfully, there was no one manning that station now. He sidled to the stacks of books.

Inwardly he screamed *THESE BOOKS SUCK*, but this was a research mission, so outwardly he studied the titles dispassionately. *The Thug and I. Hankty Bitch. Head, Part Six. Black Girl: Wet. Cash 4 Gold.* They were thin and malnourished. Somewhere in the world pennies a day could have prevented this.

He checked his surroundings. Still relatively alone.

Mama Cap featured a photograph of a middle-aged, slightly dumpy woman dressed in tight jeans and a wide lamé belt that hadn't been stylish even when it was stylish, hip cocked with a gun in one hand and a pile of cash superimposed at the right near a group of stonefaced black kids staring outward, eyes hard and mouths set in the perpetual frown of the legit.

Barclay had a suspicion this elder-hooch was not a model.

He read the dedication. D. (for Death) Row Price, authoress (what the fuck?), gave much love to everybody on the outside that still believed in her, especially mama.

That clinched it. She'd gotten her mama to pose for the cover of *Mama Cap*.

D. Row knew a lot of people. The dedication page stretched three strong, ending *And much love to God, for only He can judge me.*

No, apparently men too, 'cause you're in for five to ten, Barclay thought, finished with the defiant turn of her dedication-slash-confession-slash-introduction.

He flipped to page one. The first word was "Suck." Italicized and in caps. He closed the book, making sure there were no children present. He put *Mama Cap* down and went for one with ample brown cleavage pouting behind a hard, thuggish male model. *Digga Proof.* Wet body parts slapping together jumped at him off the pages.

He flipped randomly.

"How much more you want?" he shouted grimacingly.

"I want it all!"

"What?!"

"Stick that all—"

Page twenty-three: *Bitch thought she was fixing to get her hands on his money but pussy hadn't been made out of gold yet and this nigga could snatch it whenever he wanted to. Yeah, but she didn't know that. She believed sucking his thang and scratching his balls was her paycheck today.*

Page eighty-seven: *"You shot him!" she screamed out hysterically. He twisted the muzzle into her temple. "Shut the fuck up, bitch!" he hissed out menacingly. They heard Po-po*

noises through the window. He looked at the security bars.
They were just like jail cell bars. He couldn't get out the
window and if they catched him he couldn't get out of jail. It
was so ironic the bitch he was playing had set him up.

Paragraphs on page one-twelve were obviously out of
sequence:

She could suck all she wanted but she wouldn't get no love.
He steeled himself up. He wasn't gone come. Bitch could suck
for a day and he wouldn't come. Digga Proof! he told himself
angrily. These nuts outlast a tidal wave!

Mama was the proudest she had ever been of him. She
smiled so bright he broke down and smiled back. She took off
her apron and hugged him happily, and he felt something stir
that was held down for a long time—

"So?" Marilyn said, peering around his shoulder.

He held it for her to read.

"Oh my damn," she said.

"Yeah."

"So?"

"Grab three at random." She did. He did the same. He
faced her. "You gotta read 'em."

"I'll read it," she said, and said it willingly, which put him on
the defensive.

She knew her husband's frowns. "I'll tell you what I think of
them as a woman. I'm here to help."

"You better not start liking those. I'm just getting used to
you reading romance."

Her head was in the books as they walked to the checkout.
"Baby, Harlequin ain't never done this," she said. "I just might
have to read all of these."

"Oh my ignorant Jesus, this shit is terrible," he said. The
sheet made a hammock between their bodies. Books were
spread between them.

Marilyn leaned over and kissed the muscle of his shoulder. "Uh-hm," she said. Her book was *Ho Down*. Country hoes. Dirty South.

"This making you horny?" he asked.

"No. You are." Her hand closed.

He hadn't realized the circus was in town, tent pitched and everything. "Oh."

She moved her books aside. He prepared to do the same. "You keep reading," she said.

"Oh?"

"Don't let me stop you. You were saying this was terrible?"

"Yes...No..." Sharp exhalation. Then deeeep inhalation.

"Spelling errors?" he heard her say.

Head thrown back, he answered the ceiling. "Too many. Spell-check just... gave up." He made an effort to read again. "Listen to this."

"I'm listening."

She didn't listen very church-like. "'He suppose'—where the fuck is the D, baby?!—'to be passion and fire so why they acting like I ain't suppose to get none?'"

"That's terrible, baby," she said.

"I know."

"I think everybody should get some."

Books damn near flew to the floor.

He rolled out of bed without waking Marilyn and entered what six months ago had been unused attic space but now was an adjoining office. The desktop was already powered up, while the laptop waited patiently on the table. Owing to Marilyn being asleep, he bypassed them and went for the notepad. Under the lamp he sat to write.

The book would have to be about a woman, and the woman would wonder why men thought it was ok to look at her. He created this scene: Neon wiped fog from the bathroom mirror. She lotioned her upper body, cupped her full breasts to make sure they stayed in place, then drew her hands down the curve of her waist to the flare of her hips, and realized something: all her girlfriends either had stretch marks from kids or tattoos for men. She didn't. When she was naked she was naked. You couldn't tell anything more about her than she was beautiful.

She liked that. Thought for the day: *Be Beautiful When Naked.* Neon.

*

Savory Controls might have been a snack maker or infrastructure development complex. He had a knack for ending up at places whose names gave absolutely no indication what they did. Goodman Workspace. Rooter Inc. His jobs at these places were vague at best and nearly mythical at the praise-lord-Jesus-God I'm actually getting paid for this level. Working for Cena Brothers Outdoor Renewal— *The COBRA!*—straight out of college doing landscaping and brickwork was the only time his work life actually had clear guidance.

His cubicle at Savory Controls was one of the larger ones due to employee attrition. A few coworkers knew him, and he knew them. They knew his job title but had no idea what he actually did, which also summed what he knew about them. Everybody naturally assumed, however, that since direct deposit showed up every two weeks someone had to be doing something to keep Savory Controls moving along.

Barclay was TCP. Acronyms were big at Savory Controls. He'd written a TCP memo detailing the necessity of rearranging his workspace for optimal performance, seeing as he was tall and the left-facing wall was the longer of the cubicle, plus the window from two rows down sent afternoon sunlight directly onto his monitor, and that—while the company planogram was specific—it was actually more productive for him to face the corridor instead of sitting with his back or side to his approaching coworkers to minimize distractions.

His immediate circle of coworkers knew he wrote books. They just didn't know he wrote them at work.

To his coworkers he was Barclay Royse, the guy with a sissy name that nobody would say so to his face. It was understood: he wouldn't bring up the books, and definitely neither would they.

Of Savory's five floors, Barclay worked on four and Bela on three. The fourth floor, being snack stash paradise, meant Bela tended to loiter.

He loitered into Barclay's cubicle. Barclay, in the middle of a call from a potential agent, waved him off.

The friend sat down.

"...never about what you've done though, is it?" said Winona Medved on the other end. "What are you going to do next, that's the meat. One of the lines in your query stood out: 'I'm ready to work with someone on a long, slow relationship.' Your writing's good, there's passion—"

'But' is the worst word in any language.

"—but are you ready to be as marketable as you need to be? I wanted to call you personally because I've read your three books. I loved your three books. Not my cup of tea but I loved them. But I'm not sure you've answered what's a Barclay Royse book. Stephen King's not going to sell a chick-lit novel. Toni Morrison, sword and sorcery, no. The name has to associate. Your books were creative and thoughtful, a little heavy-handed—I'm going to be honest, you want me to be honest—and the plots were clearly secondary. That said, I definitely need to see more of your work. What are you working on now?"

Bela rooted through his candy drawer.

Footfalls signaled someone coming his way, but they

weren't managerial steps so Barclay didn't need to worry. His brain told him, 'Well, there's this girl who's this stacked hoochie who has these two idiot boyfriends and she decides to steal money from a drug lord...' Praises went to his mouth, though, for stepping in and saving him: "A drama about relationships in the urban jungle."

"Sex In The City urban or Stella Jamaica urban?"

"Stella Jamaica. Skewed younger. Something about real love as opposed to Hollywood urban."

It was very quiet on her end a moment. "Is that related to *Onion*?"

"Not really."

"Tell you what, if I call you back, let's see where we can go."

"Fair enough." *Fuck! Shit! Damn!*

"Put together another packet. Those emails you sent, include them. I want to review everything fresh after a week or so. Can you hold out that long?"

"Definitely."

"Lovely."

"Pleasure."

Bela had two candy bars in his pocket and sat there without shame. "You get it?" he said.

Barclay shook his head.

"Hard nibble?"

"Glad-handing. I'm not gonna hear back from her."

"Come to dinner with me."

"Brother, don't take this wrong. I got zero interest in your girlfriend. You don't need my approval. Screw her as though you're Pharaoh himself."

"Seriously, I think I'm picking up some subtleties from you?"

"She is unbelievably stupid. And you keep letting me say she's stupid so you know she's stupid. Her ass is too big and she keeps trying to make her tits pop out. She worries me."

"Bring your wife."

"I see that you've seriously lost your mind. You don't bring a wife around your boy's fuck buddy."

"You know a memo came out about language. Marilyn won't care, man. Dinner."

"Your treat."

"Hell no."

"Let me call her."

"Cool."

"How many Snickers you got in your pockets?"

"A man neither asks nor answers that question."

That book hung heavy on his mind as he left work.

He decided to detour through the old neighborhood.

Where he'd grown up, a small city called Stovey, was over five hundred miles away but its dope house fit perfectly—he slowed a bit to take in the details—over this one: a squat bungalow with weathered bricks and peeling roof, the bars on its windows and doors flawless. The houses beside it bit their tongues and stayed quiet.

In front of one an older woman tended a tiny square right off the front porch containing a single row of lettuce in dirt so black and fertile it looked edible. Plastic pinwheels flanked her porch like propellers hoping to take the home away.

The other neighboring house had given up. Not a single house plant was visible through its large bay window.

He drove two more blocks, parked, walked a bit, then decided to head home.

"I counted eighteen cell phones by the time I did four blocks. Eleven in cars. Who're all these deaf people that everybody's talking to so loud? If not for you I wouldn't even own a phone. Nobody even talks into the phone anymore, they talk at it."

"Kids have to be different," Marilyn said.

"I saw a forty-five damn year old grizzled up man talking to his phone as if it was a block of cheese. People looked at me weird when I checked my phone for the time then put it back in my pocket."

"You are weird."

"But they don't know that! Almost made me lose my appetite. You still wanna go to this dinner?"

"Bela called. Said you need to adjust the volume on your damn cell phone so you can hear it ringing. Dinner with Elaine is postponed till tomorrow."

"Big Booty Trudy."

"Dammit, Clay."

"What?"

"I'm gonna call her that now."

"She's got a huge ass, babe."

"Maybe she can't help it."

"Pass up McDonald's every once in a while she could. What're we doing for dinner?" He poked through the fridge.

"You'll know when you cook it."

He disappeared into the fridge again. "Leftovers with cheese?"

"Works for me."

Barclay Royse knew he wasn't good for anything but making mental noise. He needed to be a writer. Nothing else would do.

It was hot and the blinds were wide open. The night was clear and full of stars.

He told her about the agent.

"You think she'd represent you if she found out you were writing a hoochie book?"

He shook his head in the dark. "I don't think so." It was depressing to think that Cross needed it written in the first place. There was mental candy, then there was decay and gingivitis. "I don't want to write it, babe."

"I know you don't."

"I have to write it."

"And if it sucks?"

"I'm afraid of that."

Cross called him the next afternoon. "You probably been stressing over this?" he said.

"No, I'm—"

"No, I got this. I want you to hang with some niggas."

The chirping crickets even stopped to say *What the—*

"Not dangerous niggas, just niggas. You know. Niggas."

"I'm darker than you!"

"You're not hearing me. Are you a nigga?"

"No."

"Do you wanna be?"

"No."

"Do you want this book published?"

His mouth stepped in again to save him. "Of course, but—"

"Authenticity, brother. They know if you ain't keeping it real."

"You're the same age as me!"

"So?"

"Grown-ass men don't say 'keeping it real'! Let me call you back, I'm at work—" he grimaced and dinged himself a point for mentioning that to Cross, who was probably sitting back smiling and masturbating furiously in celebration.

"I'm just saying research your piece," Cross explained. "You're the King's English but we need Smitty Mofuck." He popped a cackling laugh. "Y'know?"

Barclay inhaled slowly, exhaled slowly. "Ok."

"We cool?"

"Definitely."

"My man!"

"And Jim? Thanks for not mentioning Shakespeare."

"Brother's sensitive to your needs."

"No Spooks? How you gonna keep it real without Spooks? Niggas is just the tip of the Titanic. We got whole subcultures gurgling."

"You're not helping, Bela."

They stepped up to Bela's shiny new car. He hadn't had a shiny new car yesterday.

"When the hell'd you get a new car?"

Bela popped the trunk. They loaded the office chair that someone had left for trash. It had a broken caster. Modern cars, worthless pieces of crap all, meant the chair only fit halfway in the narrow trunk. "Focus, man. Behave at dinner tonight."

"You've got a new car."

"Know what you should do?" said Bela. "Self-publish and sell books out of your car."

"And figure out the lotto's secret system while I'm at it. New car and new stupid girlfriend... Sexuality stable, brother?"

"Shut the hell up." Bela tested the tensile strength of the bungee cord tying the trunk down.

"Don't show up with a Jheri curl tonight," Barclay warned.

"Shit, I was sexy as hell with my Jheri curl," said Bela.

"I gotta get home, Google some niggas. Probably a local supplier."

"Everything comes from China, brother, don't act brand new."

"Babe, I gotta hang out with niggas."

She clipped another coupon. The box of expired coupons always needed more. "Got the ones down the street," she said. They tended to have too many people over and the husband thought he was young enough to look cool on a red and yellow sissy motorcycle. He also liked to stand outside in the morning shirtless while on the phone, probably, Barclay theorized, to air out his thick belly hairs. His seventeen-year-old daughter was a neo-skank, in that she went to trade school and gave up the draws with regularity, but hadn't turned her parents into grandparents yet.

"Nah, they're just Negroes. Niggas come in plain brown wrappers."

"Just keep 'em off the furniture. And whatever you do, don't feed them after midnight. Are you going to help me plant—"

"No." And in case she hadn't comprehended, "No. You'll forget where everything is then blame me next year for digging up stuff I thought was weeds. You'll cuss at me, babe, and cause me grief."

"We're planting before June."

He poured himself the sliver of orange juice Mario'd left and got the tip of his tongue wet. After a year of Mario living with them, he'd learned to take satisfaction in whatever amount he could get it. He planned to one day find Mario's coffin within the house.

"That agent call you back from yesterday?"

"No," he said. Then added, "They don't work that fast."

"Don't take it out on the girl at dinner. You're a vindictive cuss."

"I'm a writer."

"Same damn thing."

"No, I'm observant."

"Why does he want us to have dinner?"

"'Cause he's retarded and has no social skills."

"What does that say about you?" She smiled at him.

"Same thing it says about a woman that'd marry me."

The phone rang. Cross again. "Listen," Cross said, "You weren't offended by what I said?"

"Which part?"

"You are truly a funny sonofabitch. The niggas. Y'know? We cool with the niggas?"

"Oh yeah, I feel you."

"As long as you feel me."

"Feeling you up, man."

"I just want to make sure you're cool. You're 'bout to blow up."

Barclay covered the mouthpiece and whispered to Marilyn, "I'm about to blow up." To Cross: "I understand where you're coming from, man. Can't write a hood book from Bugfuck Heights."

"I didn't want it seeming like you weren't a nigga yourself."

"I appreciate that."

"You can boldly go. This book is gon' be the shit! Barclay Royse—get a pen name with the quickness, but—Barclay Royse coming at you from the street. *AuntiesWithSushi.com* pushed *Onion* like never before when it came out. You had everybody reading that book, from bitches to thugs to library bitches." He caught himself. "When I say everybody, not like *New York Times* everybody, but still..."

"No, I've got an IED in mind."

"You and I are gon' blow some shit up with this. All right, since you're cool, I'm cool. You're my man, though, right."

Barclay heard Whitney singing *And IIII-e-iiiii will always love Youuuuuuu.* "Thanks for the call, Jim."

They hung up.

"Does he call all his writers like this?" asked Marilyn.

"The ones that make him money."

"You really need an agent."

*

The restaurant wasn't as swanky as Bela's future reservation. It didn't have a valet but it did have a parking attendant way too old to still be a parking attendant. Plus he was checking Marilyn's ass out, but whatcha gonna do? Marilyn, in charcoal-grey top, black flare-leg slacks and an avocado green sash with matching jade-like earrings and her hair pulled into a ponytail, looked tasty.

Barclay searched for Bela and spotted him. He spotted the woman next to Bela on her cell phone. He wondered about the capricious nature of friendship.

Quick shot of Big Booty Trudy: every article of clothing a hair too small in order to accentuate a modest bust yearning to be chesty and a caboose capable of pulling freight. There was a variety of ass clearly visible even when a woman's back was against a wall. Bela's girl wore black jeans that made her legs look like drumsticks dipped in tar. Her stylishly straight hair was inky black and laser cut, not a lock out of place from the *Hair-Exxtasy* photo it had been recreated from. The hair was so black it glowed from the light around it. She'd worn leopard to her prom. She knew it. Bela knew it. Everybody knew it. Leopard print and silver goddess-heels. There were pictures of it online somewhere with the caption "Look at your relatives!" And it hadn't been that long ago. Well, the prom might have been, but she still owned that outfit.

As they closed ranks Barclay wondered if she had the traditional tramp stamp or the popular neck tat.

She seemed oblivious to Bela, and he, as he kept an eye out for his friends, to her. Later, after being around her for five minutes, Barclay realized it wasn't obliviousness, she subscribed to the belief that not blinking made her look intelligent. When Bela introduced her to Marilyn outside the restaurant, Marilyn unconsciously leaned forward into the woman's eye contact and spoke a little louder just in case the girl was slow.

Everybody knew this evening was going to hell. Elaine nudged it down that slope by never getting off her phone. She trapped the thin machine between head and shoulder and smiled and clasped hands. She wasn't saying anything on the phone, just listening. Barclay had watched her face, and it was a pretty face, the entire time he and Marilyn approached, with Bela looking one direction and Elaine the other, and her lips hadn't moved.

When they waited to be seated she told the person on the other end, "Let me call you back," then opened her purse. She dropped the slim phone in and pulled an earpiece out, sliding it on politely as though it went with blue earrings.

Seated, Bela beamed, "Barclay and I've been knowing each other since, damn, what?" he said, feeding the pass to Barclay.

"Forever and a day."

"'Bout that."

Elaine smiled at Barclay with insincere eyes.

"Best friend," said Bela.

"Former lover," said Barclay.

"Excuse me?" said Elaine.

"Ignore him, he's like that."

Bela gave a micro-glance to Marilyn hoping she'd come in off the bench.

She sat out for the moment.

Barclay smiled, giving Elaine the full benefit of his eye crinkles. "I'm as harmless as they come. I'm glad Bela got us together. It's nice to *meet you* meet you. The man doesn't date very often."

This restaurant, Crab's Galley, was famous for its crab cakes and smothered mushrooms, which Bela knew and hoped would lull Barclay into a good mood. Barclay Royse often whored himself for crab cakes.

They placed appetizer and drink orders before settling into

awkward silence pretending to peruse the ambiance. The restaurant was crowded for a weeknight. The susurration, clinks and rattles of dining seemed the perfect cover for date night espionage, which was the only reason Bela had thrown this together. He wanted information only trained operatives could provide. She didn't look pregnant, but Barclay would have to get confirmation from the wife on that.

Barclay didn't want to blurt *Why are we here?* except he did want to blurt why were they there. And it was too early to ask the *Where'd you meet?* questions. Instead, Barclay gave Marilyn his own micro-glance hoping she'd come off the bench.

She groaned inwardly, put on her pleasant face, and said, "That cut is perfect on you."

"Thank you!" said Elaine, immediately toying with her hair. "I wasn't sure at first, it took a little while to grow out."

"That's not a weave?" said Marilyn.

Bela and Barclay were shocked. The look on their faces said "We can ask that?"

"Nope, all me," came the proud answer. A lock fell over her earpiece.

"I tried growing mine out that long once," said Marilyn.

Barclay felt safe to jump in. "It didn't take," he said. Unspoken frigidity came off his wife. Safety was an illusion!

The earpiece's blue light popped on. "Hello? No, I'm at dinner. With friends. No, not now. Ok..." She paused. "Ok... Later. I used to have really short hair but everybody thought I was a boy," she said.

The hell they did, thought every other head at the table.

Her ass was like a rock. A rock that had been pounded on for years and years. But gave no ground.

Her ass contained enough packed meat to make the starving reconsider cannibalism.

It was a round ass, not huge, but large enough to shield

preschoolers from the rain. It was an ass that regularly jogged around a high school track with the word "sexy" stretched out to "sweet mother of Jesus" the width of its pink cotton sweat pants.

Elaine stood just below average height. Another six to eight inches and the ass might have seemed proportionate, but at five-six, thirty-two, thirty, forty-six, nobody in the history of the earth had ever thought she was a boy.

"Yours is a good length," she told Marilyn. "You work in an office?"

"Yes."

Elaine smiled at her powers of follicular perception. "That outfit is you. I couldn't get away with a sash."

"Your hips aren't—" started from Bela's mouth but stopped cold at the *Dammit-women-are-talking-shut-the-hell-up!* save from Marilyn. He snagged their waiter. "Could I get a round of water here?" He smiled at Marilyn. He smiled at Elaine.

He looked at Barclay to warn him against any hint of laughter.

The cell phone vibrated for attention. The blue laser scope diode lit up.

Her body language, which had very briefly opened up, bowed to her god. Her shoulders dropped, her arms moved closer to her sides, and her lids lowered to squints.

"Hello? Hey, Ok." Yadda. Yadda. Yadda. "Ok. No. No, he didn't. No. Because I was there." She stared without blinking at the space between Marilyn and Barclay while talking, unaware it was disconcerting to the others to pretend she wasn't actually at the table despite clearly hearing her voice. "Listen, can you call me back? Bye." Then she shook her head as if she couldn't believe the nerve. "Sometimes people just won't stop calling you! It's a shame I rent and don't go to movies anymore because my phone won't stop ringing. Sometimes I'd like to see a movie on the big screen, y'know?"

"Yeah, we stopped going too when there was more talking in the seats than on the screen," said Barclay, hoping the hint would take.

It didn't take.

He lobbed another one. "What would be good would be phones on vibrate that you couldn't feel."

"Yeah," she said.

Barclay stood and looked at Bela. "Come to the bathroom with me."

Bela didn't move because obviously Clay hadn't said that even though the man stood there watching him divide his cheese sticks into neat cutlets.

Marilyn nudged Bela under the table.

He frowned, told the cell phone he'd be right back, and followed Barclay at a comfortable distance.

"Give me her number," Barclay said once the door closed. Normally Barclay couldn't demand ice from a Swede. "You got that promotion you didn't want and you've been having sex for two weeks straight."

"I hate when you do that."

"You don't have to talk and she doesn't take up precious space since she's probably dressed and out before you roll over. Why'd you take the promotion?"

"It's two more letters! Now I'm not just GTS. I'm ECGTS. It's worth it for a two letter jump."

"Not if you gotta latch onto Big Booty Trudy to make yourself feel better."

The white dude at the urinal quickly zipped up and gingerly wedged between them, stopping to wash his hands since others were present. This was so cool! He'd never seen gay black men squabble (even though this was a moderately upscale restaurant). Seemed logical they'd refer to significant others in the feminine. "Trudy" was likely code for Truman.

He washed his hands a little slower. Gay dudes trying to act like not-gay, *and* black. They were both in conservative suits and ties, although the taller one seemed more ill at ease in his than the one with all the issues.

"You're not even qualified for the job," said the tall one.

"I knew you'd say that."

"You're not."

"I think the point here is you didn't want me having that job over you."

"*I'm* not qualified for that job."

"I think I've made my point."

Barclay unzipped on the way to the urinals. Bela waited.

The white guy dried and left. Before the door closed he heard the flush and the shorter one saying, "I like these sinks in here..."

"Yeah, they're sharp," said Barclay, heading for the glazed stone sinks per the same Men's Handwashing Code.

Then he pulled his phone out.

Bela gave him the number.

"Thank you." He wondered why the bath towels in his home didn't feel as good as the paper towels in Crab's Galley's bathroom. Marilyn was probably skimping on fabric softener.

Rejoining the party, he kept his phone in plain view, dialed the number of the blankly listening Elaine, rested the elbow of the arm holding the phone on the table, and waited.

Her phone beeped in her ear.

"Hold on," she said to the person on the other end of her conversation, smiling demurely at the group. "Hello? Hello?" Shrugging, she bipped back to the original listening.

"Think you're gonna want dessert?" Bela asked.

"Oh no—unless y'all are? No, that's not right, that's not what they said." The waiter brought fresh rolls. She batted sweet lashes at him and grabbed for one. "Ok." She went silent.

Barclay hit redial in his lap. She held her phone away and

looked at it as if the machine had gotten dirty. "I don't know this number," she said. "Hold on." She switched over. "Hello?"

Barclay disconnected. He sent a text to his wife: Text 555-7301.

Marilyn's phone beeped. She looked at it. "Excuse me." She pushed away to read the entire message. Barclay's face was nondescript except for the slight rise in his eyebrows toward Elaine.

Fifteen seconds later "One New Text" flashed across Elaine's screen with a musical trill. "I'm at dinner, I'll have to call you back." Then she read: "'Marilyn says Carpe Diem.' I don't know any Marilyn." She turned to Marilyn. "Could you pass me the salt?" She winked. "I definitely didn't ask for the heart healthy Margarita," she said and laughed, glancing hyperactively at each person in turn. "Carpe diem," she dismissed.

"Fish store on Hudson," said Barclay.

"I put myself on that no-spam list," she said. She pushed buttons to read the entire text: "'...Carpe Diem is not a fish store.'" Then she frowned.

"Anti-marketing campaign," said Barclay.

Marilyn smiled at Barclay over her pineapple Malibu.

Elaine placed her phone in clear view on the table. Her blue earplant seemed to be laser-sighting.

"Did you need to finish that?" Barclay said with a nod toward the tiny, stylish annoyance.

"No, no. Listen, I really think—"

Her phone chimed in her ear.

"—Hello? Hello?" She glanced. "That same number."

Barclay, holding the phone directly in front of him, disconnected but continued pressing random menu entries while staring intently at the tiny screen. He glanced up at her. "I had that happen to me all day once." He closed his phone and put it in his pocket. "What plan do you have?"

"TMI."

This restaurant served the best crab cakes in the city. Why would anyone waste precious chewing time talking to someone in no position to procure more? But then Barclay decided it was like driving. No one thought they tailgated anymore either. A full car length between you and the driver ahead was like an invitation to other drivers to dominate you, your wife, and your sad childhood.

Automatic action.

He was about to suggest she turn the phone off when she turned to him with that blue diode pinning him to the spot, and he realized that the insidious piece of hardware would not allow that thought through. She'd look at him as if he'd asked her to worship Satan. She'd wonder if she had heard him correctly. She'd wonder what kind of weirdo friend Bela had, which might put Bela in a bad light.

Bela didn't deserve that.

Instead he found himself saying, "You have the prettiest blue eyes," which was weird since she wasn't white. She was a shade browner than his wife but her eyes were glacial blue.

"Thank you! I wasn't sure if I wanted these or green tonight."

Noise swelled in the background from an old couple celebrating. "Is your ass real?"

"Pardon me?"

"He said they look so real," said Bela, nodding at the old couple. "Real love."

"That's not what he said."

"I asked were they from Israel. What do you think of that couple?"

"Those old folks? I think that's beautiful." She addressed Marilyn. "Y'all married too long? I meant, a long time?"

"Not yet."

"Marriage is nice."

The uncomfortable silence that follows more than two complete sentences among strangers settled.

"You've got a slight accent," said Barclay.

"I'm originally from New York."

"Were you there?"

"9/11? Yeah. Nowhere near the towers but I was there." The timbre of her voice wasn't pained, it was challenging. "Did you have people there?"

"No," he said.

That was precisely what she needed to hear. "You know we did that shit," she said.

"I think this is a conversation for when we're drunk," said Bela.

"That ain't nothing but a word," said Elaine.

"This ain't the time," said Bela.

"No, it's fine," said Barclay.

She glanced for ears then said, "Me and my girls figure this: It's common sense. They're supposed to hate us so much, right, that they're flying jets into buildings. So why the hell ain't they done nothing since? Don't give me that bullshit about vigilance and Homeland Security. Some crazy mofo could come out of Home Depot with the shit to make a nuclear bomb, so don't tell me Hassan is sitting around throwing his hands up saying 'Oh well, we can't use planes no more.' George Bush in a flight suit and suddenly we had the Justice League looking out for us? Come on now."

She rested an elbow on her chair back and leaned. She took a professorial sip of her drink and reiterated, "Come on now." She hit Barclay with a knowing nod. "White folks the only ones believe in Superman or the tooth fairy. That's why I like Barack. Barack says fuck Superman, I got John Henry for ya. Whatever happens, we gotta work."

"Right now all stories come out of 2001," said Barclay.

"Maybe the next decade will hook us up with something

brand new. Superman made Lex Luthor up so he could keep his job. Who'll toast to that?" she said, raising her drink.

Barclay, Marilyn and Bela took cautious sips from their glasses. It had never been historically profitable for black folks to exhibit sense, common or crazy.

The entire point of the dinner was for Bela to justify his lack of reasoning when it came to Elaine. Barclay needed to know why Elaine in the first place, and waited till the ladies broke for the restroom to find out.

Bela jumped the gun, challenging, "You still think she's stupid?"

"An asshole can be charming sometimes. And a conspiracy theorist? Brother, what, you going for the Guinness Book of What the Fuck?"

"She made sense."

"And a doofus got an A on a test last week! Look, stupid functions every day. That doesn't mean you should encourage it. Everything about her says she intentionally limits herself. That, my brother, makes me wonder what you're doing with her when you're wondering the exact same thing."

"Brother, you see that ass?"

"Like two elves working a pendulum saw. But you ain't that shallow."

"I wanna be! I've got two more letters, got a new car, bought a rug, brother, with swirly patterns—" (as a bachelor, floor covering tended to be whatever fell on the floor till the weekend cleaning)—"I've been good my entire life, man. I want to tap pure ass before I leave this earth!" He hadn't noticed the young waitress standing behind him, and she, to her credit, ignored him.

"Why the fancy restaurant then?" Barclay asked.

"I don't want her leaving me too soon."

Dating on the Incentive Plan.

"You Chrysler Employee Discount Mother—"

The waitress smiled.

There was loud clapping at the anniversary table. Marilyn returned while Bela and Barclay listened to the old man's celebratory speech. She said nothing.

She adjusted her napkin on her lap while the men waited for clues. She adjusted the angle of the fork on her plate.

She said: "She asked me to tell you she'd be a few more minutes handling business."

"She on that phone when y'all in the bed?" asked Barclay.

"She's not on the phone," said Marilyn.

The general mood at the table imploded just a little. "She's a nice girl, Bela," said Marilyn, the consummate diplomat.

"Got a kind of purity about her," said Barclay.

They heard the waitress snicker before she hustled off.

"Bela?" Marilyn said, waiting till she had his full attention. With it she told him, "Grow up."

He tried to act innocent.

"Bela." It didn't work.

And he knew it.

"Yes, ma'am."

"Ok then." She pushed her plate away. "I think I'm ready for dessert."

They ordered once the business woman returned.

Waiting for the desserts they'd tried talking politics but everything became cabal-related with her. Nobody saw a lot of women conspiracy theorists. She was strangely fascinating.

"Obama might be the anti-Christ but, come on, like white folks ain't been trying to summon hell on earth the last few hundred years. But let the anti-Christ be black and they lose their minds. Tell you what: Palin." She plopped her breadstick on her plate in triumph.

On the subject of martial arts movies: "Chuck Norris."

Bela choked a little. He hadn't known this about her.

"You know about Bruce Lee, right?" said Barclay. "Sammo

Hung? Jet Li? Sonny Chiba?"

She rolled right over him. "They had a two hour Walker rerun on last night," she said to Marilyn, whom she figured shared in the sisterhood of Chuck Norris lust, that rugged, kick-ass cowboy who could kick a man in the face without lifting his feet. Elaine had the website of Chuck Norris truisms saved in her favorites. When she was down she often thought of the best one: Chuck Norris lost his virginity before his father did. That was the kind of man she'd settle for ultimately. Bela simply filled the day because there were twenty-four hours in one. Nobody was expected to fill them on their own.

The token black guy on Chuck Norris's TV show was cute too, but he always got his ass kicked, so, again, right now she made do with Bela.

On the subject of music she mentioned *American Idol* and everybody shut up.

They hadn't touched on books yet but it was inevitable. The first mention of Oprah and it was on.

He hoped Bela wouldn't tell her he was a writer.

"Clay's a writer."

"Really?" She smiled broadly.

"Got three books in stores," said Bela.

"Oh?" She smiled. Broadly. Barclay was sick of that smile already. Nothing genuine came from crazy-wide, bright smiles. "Anything good?" she asked.

Barclay's cheesecake went down in a cold, hard lump.

Bela jumped. "Obama lifted the moratorium on wiretap lawsuits."

"They shouldn't have had immunity in the first place," said Marilyn. "That cheesecake good, babe?"

"Outstanding."

"What else do you do?" asked Elaine. "You look like you've got a lot of energy. Stuff with power tools and stuff."

"No, I work."

"Ohhh..."

The writer considered himself a serious writer. Not a great writer, but he was serious. Books being such an intimate form of communication, there was seduction in it, both in writing and reading, and that meant he had to be the literary equivalent of a playa playa, which meant this ignorant woman with a head, a neck and an ass—no body in between—needed to respect the skills.

She clearly didn't, because she still stared at him wide-eyed.

"You want to write a book, don't you?" guessed Barclay.

Elaine genuinely brightened this time. "Yes! I've been thinking about one of those websites, y'know, like the Black United Method Writers Crush. Bumwrush. Or the D-Town Writers Social Block. We've got something in common! I think I want to write a book."

"Son of a bitch," Barclay murmured.

"I didn't want to say this but he's got Tourette's," said Bela.

"Fuck I do!"

"See?"

Elaine made sure to slurp the last of her drink before slowly setting her napkin aside. "I think maybe you should take me home," she told Bela. "I feel very disrespected." She offered a weak smile in the general direction of the only other woman at the table with any sense. In the space where Bela's date was supposed to say "Nice meeting y'all"...she didn't. Instead, irritated that her writerly ambitions had been shot down, she mumbled, "What the hell kind of name is Bela? What, your mama liked old vampire movies? What if she liked lemonade?" This meant Bela wouldn't be getting any tonight. "Mrs. Royse," she said with a curt nod. Marilyn gave the half-nod in return.

On the way out with her Bela hissed, "That's my middle name. Why you wanna talk about my name?"

Marilyn tore into Barclay that night. She hadn't dressed up and done her hair (and he almost said "You didn't do your hair; you just pulled it into a ponytail"—but he didn't) to be nodded at as a rude cow. He wouldn't be getting any either.

"I think I want to write a book." He'd heard the words come right out of her mouth. As if it were that easy. Writing was like John Henry pulverizing his way through a mountain, as opposed to some twit who merely broke a nail. So the following day—he tore back. Only with paper. Paper that was soft. And a little wet. But irritating as hell when it crumbled. Because that's what a writer does. Dammit.

It was time to write this book.

And he'd get it done before the weekend.

NEON
Where the "Street" has no name

Word

by SDW

("What's that mean?" asked Marilyn.

"Sweet Dick Willie," he answered, knowing by the time the book hit print she'd forget.

"Oh yeah," she said, nodding. "We'll discuss later. And nobody says 'word' anymore."

"Haven't had a chance to hang out with niggas yet."

"This book supposed to be serious?"

"No."

"Niggas don't have much of a sense of humor."

"Yeah," he answered. "I know."

"Niggas laugh at what hurts 'em, not what's real."

"Babe?"

"Yeah?"

"Stop reading over my shoulder. That's bad luck.")

Dedicationz

All to God, the Father most high! Muhfagees can't do it You ain't in it, so big peace on the upstroke. Everybody best get that ass together before thousand foot Jesus brings the pain.

Thanks to Mama and Daddy 'cause, y'know, big peace on that broken condom. Don't laugh.

Big ass peace to Trudy, 'cause if it wasn't for you...

There's a bunch of other folks thought I was gonna mention them but nobody knows who they are and some of them can honestly kiss my natural ass, so instead let's act like something important happened and shut the hell up. SDW will make you smile a while.
NEON – everybody's got a little light...under the sun, under the sun...
...under the hot ass, broke down, low paid, tired and horny and ain't nobody around cancer-causing sun!
Got a little light.

Chapter One

A Book's Gotta Start

In about a year from now Neon would have both of the Brothers Jetstream in love with her. They would sit her down on a palatial throne of glass in the Hall of Silences where beams of light crisscrossed the ceiling through two thousand tiny windows, and solemnly ask her to decide between them.

But for now, she ground it up into Boo's face then dropped it down to his fat dick. Money came easy for a sexy bitch and she had the goodies strong niggas crawled for, titties like blinking lights and curves like road signs.

Her name was Neon Temples. Late summer in Day City.

("Isn't that a little too graphic so early on?" Marilyn asked. Being right there, her cleavage smelled like candy. Her presence at his shoulder diverted precious blood from his brain, but he proudly maintained focus.

"Go back to 'Ho Down'," he reminded.

"Oh yeah," she said.)

Granted, Boo was stupid as hell but Neon had three hours before Le'Mon was supposed to call. Neon prided herself on what she called her "home business": printing off graphics and flyers and stuff, and three hours was too long to ignore the fact that she needed that new expensive software upgrade available for a limited time at twenty percent off at the mall. One innocent call to Boo and he was like Pssht!—and dropped the money on her kitchen table while trying to figure out the best time to grab some. Neon knew two things for certain about men, and she bent over just enough to show him. She'd put on a deep V wrap just for this occasion.

"Looks like you plan on coming in those pants?" she said to the naughty boy. "You better hold that."

"Gott-tam!"

Boo wore jogging pants and she wasn't wearing anything under her wrap, so when she suddenly dropped and scissored her knees she could nip his thing between her—

"Godee-um!!"

And if she lowered a little more and rubbed forward—

"Dammit, girl!"

And turned around to bend in so he could whiff the perfume at her cleavage, her warm, cocoa-gold, downy fresh cleavage—

"Neon? *Neon?* Neon!"

("Neon's a stupid name."

"Babe?"

She backed away from his shoulder, shaking her head, saying, "Ok...")

Then put the entire wrap in his hands so quickly he didn't even know how she got naked, well, that was what they liked to call "added value." Give folks more than what they asked for, especially when it wasn't more than what they wanted in the first place.

She slipped his t-shirt and thin jogging pants off. On melting summer days like this the whole world should have been naked. Even with the window air conditioner chugging its best she felt the heat waves outside pressing steadily against the walls.

When Boo's lips closed over a nipple she closed her eyes to the delicious replay of every good memory she'd ever had. There sure as hell weren't a lot of them. The city sucked. Boo traced areola-land first, just barely touching her stubby mountain as it grew. When he swallowed the nipple the tip of his tongue tracked from base to crown. Boo might not have known diddly, but he knew serious titty.

A tight shiver let him know he was on point. She draped her arms around his broad, dark shoulders. He opened his jaw to suck as much flesh as possible, causing Neon to tighten even more. She loved what was about to come next.

He hummed.

Deep, penetrating, full baritone throat vibrations, like sonar bouncing around inside the boob and filling up the nipple with tingly ice.

She pushed close to his ear and breathed, "Boo? You wanna play or play?"

"Bes pay."

"Hm?"

He remembered he had *some* home training. He popped the titty out. "Let's play."

She pulled him to his feet, lowered herself to her knees, and didn't so much suck him as did back-up vocals on him, "Um"-ing and "Um-hmm"-ing so much anybody giving an amen would've fit right in at this church. It might have been hell on toast outside but that had nothing to do with the beads of sweat breaking out on his bald head. Neon's nails dug into his buttcheeks.

She pulled back to ask, "What you wanna do, Boo?"

"I'ma fuck them titties," he slurred.

(*"Oh you nasty bastard,"* Marilyn said, *reading with relish after an hour of puttering around the house.*)

"Oh, I don't think so."

"Come on, girl. Apple pie and hot dogs."

"You ain't never heard me sing the Star Spangled Banner."

"War on terror, baby. Negro's gotta search them thirty-six C's."

"For them WMD's?"

"You know it."

(*"Is it me or does a book like this seems better suited to George W.'s reign?"* asked Barclay. *"Street lit just doesn't seem pro-Obama, does it?"*)

"How 'bout I dick slap ya nuts with my titties?"

He hit the carpet so fast she thought he had a stroke.

"We still going to the movies next week?" she asked offhand, planting slow kisses across his abs.

He managed to squeak "Yep" between breaths.

She let him slide between her glossy breasts before settling both soft weights on his wrinkly boys and shimmying her shoulders a little. Then she did something quick that he couldn't see but that made his eyes shoot wide the hell open.

"You sure you don't wanna play?" she asked innocently.

"See, why'd you slip the juice on your fingers and rub it on the tip of my—?"

She did it again. He nearly fainted.

She studied her finger making lazy circles around the head. "What?" she said.

He tried maneuvering her by the shoulders. She resisted.

"Big strong Mandingo mofo like you can play for days," she told him.

"Poon!"

"That's what you need, huh?"

("Barclay."

"What'd Chynette do page one, Cash 4 Gold? Admitted she'd gotten so high she'd fucked her man's brother for a bag of Cheetos, then described in awkward detail the sensations of said buzz-fuck. I'm just a victim here, babe.")

"Neon?"

What happened next was wrong on a humanitarian level. She licked her juice off his tip.

"Fuck my mama!"

"Ooh, shit," she said, wide and slick enough to straddle and pump his dark dick inside her one quick time like a piston, paralyzing the veins in his neck before hopping off. "Boo? You made me wet."

"Neon?"

She moaned deeply.

"Neon?"

Then Neon Temples groaned.

"Neon?"

Then she plucked her fingers from the river and squeezed him hard with the moist hand. "Boo, you 'bout to get fucked up."

"Rise up Christian soldiers!"

"Hell yeah!" She stabbed down and rocked the hell out of Gibraltar till Boo started bucking so hard he almost threw her off. She rose to the tip, pinned him with a hand to the chest for a count of five, found a good, comfortable groove again, and finally made him come hard enough to break glass. Neither one moved afterward except for muscle ticks, spasms, and eye twitches.

She rolled off for a minute and listened to him struggle to stay awake. He'd come off an extra long shift, so she could see the need for a snooze. As soon as he started snoring she knew he was knocked out enough for her to get up. Passing the swivel fan she nudged it with her toe to angle it a little more toward him.

("Neon is going to be a complex woman," explained Barclay. "She's not a slut and she's not a doofus."

"She's Elaine."

"Not really."

"She had a huge ass, didn't she?"

"Like a hot air balloon," said Barclay, and should have stopped. But he rolled on, "Tight and lean."

"Tight and lean?"

He scrambled mentally. "Like good pork. Not a lot of fat."

"Um-hm. I plan to review this when you're through today," she said and left.)

Neon liked dancing for Boo. It gave her a good isometric workout. The layer of sweat covering her naked body pulled her to the shower where she took ten minutes to enjoy cool water plus a silkening shower gel that made her so smooth and fragrant she immediately wanted to fuck herself like Jethro must have done Ellie Mae: quick, goofy and wrong. *('Men are goofy fucks,' Marilyn later wrote in the margin of the printed rough draft; 'women are sensualists.' Barclay would get a kick out of that.)* She absolutely loved her body and especially loved the things that made her body feel good.

Neon scratched a nipple with a fingernail, leaned against the blue tile with the spray aimed between her breasts, and let the other hand flow with the water. But just for a minute.

When she padded naked to the kitchen she counted up Boo's gift then dropped it, went to where he slept, knelt, wrapped her lips around his limp thing and gingerly tugged it erect *('You wish!'),* keeping things light and keeping things slow so as not to fully wake him but making damn sure that whatever he'd been dreaming about now featured melting ice and geysers.

He stirred enough to prop on his elbows to try to watch her, but Neon proceeded as if she didn't notice him, playing her tongue along familiar contours as though she had nothing but time.

After he came she let him shower off. She picked his clothes up and draped them neatly over the sofa, making sure his wallet didn't fall out. Dumb men always had fits when a woman touched their wallet; *I can grip your dick but don't palm the leather.* Boo was usually mellow though. She even picked his draws up for him, then settled on the sofa and listened to some of the noise outside.

It had felt good on Boo but not good enough to break her off. And since she hadn't let her fingers finish in the shower, she let them do the walking now. By the time he stepped out dried and refreshed it was on one very mellow sista.

He grinned and reached for his clothes. None of his other bitch—Oh, shit. He stopped his brain cold. Sometimes he thought Neon was psychic and if she even caught a hint of that word floating the air he could kiss his ashy ebony ass Good-trifling-security car driving-negro-Bye! Nobody else he knew would bother to keep his personal stuff neat, even if they were just some old kicks, and she even let him keep a spare uniform in her basement.

She was sitting buck-naked on her sofa. Damn if she didn't make it seem the most natural thing in the world to do. She was who Boo wished he had enough sense to be with for real. ('Is Boo Bela?' Marilyn wrote, to which Barclay responded when reviewing her notes, "Baby, it's a book. Nobody is anybody.")

A shoulder-length perm held Neon's pretty face.

Boo swore patches of her tasted like caramel.

When she laughed her eyes were always watchful.

And her body was the truth, the whole truth, and nothing but the truth. She made men push their kids aside for a clear view of her. Her curves framed sex like *We The People* framed the Constitution.

("That's an obtuse reference," said the wife.

"That's the whole point," said the husband in later conversation. For now, Marilyn read in bed, Barclay watched Blade Runner *for the sixth time, and Mario ate the last slice of cheese.*)

The first time Boo saw her she was leaving a club he'd just let her in. He'd done a friend a favor and filled in as a bouncer. Nothing but titty and ass file by door-bouncers at clubs, so the first time he saw her it didn't register. But when she left not twenty minutes later—and definitely not looking happy—it hit: Damn. Not only damn, but "Wait." He stopped her long enough to tap her on the shoulder, say "Here," gave her a card with his number on it, then stepped back to the rope where hoochies glared at him.

He never found out why she'd left so soon. But, hell, that was a year ago.

"You heading out tonight?" he asked behind the sofa, kneading the muscles of her neck.

"It's too hot."

"That's why they air condition the clubs, girl."

"Why? You going?"

"Hell naw. Skeezes between checks this week."

"Don't forget I wanna go to the movies."

"I gotcha." He never knew whether she liked being kissed, since plenty of women he'd known didn't, but he did it anyway. Hell, if the only thing better than good pussy was new pussy and the only thing better than new pussy was Neon...well, do the math.

Sometimes you had to treat a bitch like a lady.

Chapter Two

"Nasty stankass mofo muhfuckah"

Her phone rang later that night. Boo had been gone several hours. "Hello?"

"Hey, girl." The voice had no confidence, no sense of time, and absolutely no sense of style.

"Well?"

"I'm in it, girl! I'ma be running some shit before two months is out."

She reminded herself again that Boo was several hours gone.

"Why'd it take you so long to call?"

"Time's an illusion, girl."

"Then you need to David Copperfield your ass a watch. I don't work CP time."

"Whatever."

You don't tell a black woman whatever. She tells you whatever.

Then makes sure you're in hell.

"You said you were calling at ten. It's eleven-fifteen and you're happy on the phone."

"And you gotta de-elevate a brotha's high?"

"Low flying monkey bastard," she mumbled.

"You just trying to make a nigga smile at your silly ass."

"Le'Mon—I hate waiting around for nothing."

"I know."

"And you're on your cell?"

"Right, right."

"Trifling!"

"Let me know when you're ready."

"Ready for what?"

"To listen, you crazy bitch!"

She hung up and rolled over on her lumpy bed.

Three minutes later her phone rang:

"Hello?"

"Ok, fuck the dumb shit. All right, I'm sorry. I shoulda called your ass."

"Ya ignorant bastard," she mumbled.

"Neon," he said holding up a finger as if she could see him. He was standing in a bus stop shelter listening to a crackhead snore.

"Hold on," she told him, "I got another call. H'lo? Hey, Boo. Naw, I'm not doing anything. Ok, hold on, let me check." She rolled out of bed and stumbled about. "Ok, I'm in the kitchen. I don't see anything on the floor. You think it fell out your wallet? Hold on, let me look in the living room. Oh, that was good to you? Ha, when it ain't good you let me know! Not under the sofa. Yes, I'm feeling under the cushions, yes. Naw—shit, is it that serious? Damn, Boo, don't act like you can't get another one. Naw, I ain't saying I got it. I'm not playing. I'm not playing. Boo? Ok, then. Backtrack your peoples 'cause you know it ain't me. Yeah, somebody's on the other line. A big meaty nigga, you don't want none of that. See, you're laughing now, it wasn't that serious. Lost shit either gets found or it doesn't. All right, I'll let you know. Bye."

"WHATDAFUK! I'm about to get paid all up in this shit and it's about to start raining out here and ain't no damn bus coming and talking to you is not mutha-fuckin' free! Don't act like I won't come up in there and lay dick all cross ya forehead-_"

"That's what I've been waiting for you to say."

"—I will unzip—what?"

"One: it's hot. Two: it's late. Three: I'm by myself. Four: fat dick."

"Naw, man—"

"Fat, long, sign of the beefcarver..."

"We about to get paid, baby."

"...dick ain't been sucked all day."

"Neon?"

"Hold on." She wet her lips. "You ain't heard me: Dick. Ain't. Been. Sucked. All day."

"Shit, girl."

"Think about that next time you call me."

"Bus ain't coming yet. Why'd I loan my car to them drunk muthafuckahs..."

"Don't get too wet out there. Call me tomorrow."

"Tomorrow you wanna pick me up?"

She hated picking up these stupid—

"Pick me up around two."

"Please be ready."

"I will—Aw, HELL naw! What the fuck! Mutha—"

"What happened?"

"No you didn't just piss in the bus stop. Hold up, Neon." She heard the sound of scuffling then thumping. Then a yelp and sharp groaning.

("A yelp? Niggas don't yelp, baby."

"Look, this is not a documentary, this is art. The whole point of this is that that entire way of life is artificial no matter how hard it's kept real. It's scary and it's fucked but it's violent and it's stupid."

"So Elaine's ass was better than mine, right?")

"Le'Mon?"

The groaning was him. He grunted. "Muthafucka hit me a little in the nuts! Crackhead muthafucka!"

A grizzled voice cackled, "Shouldn'ta woke me up, nigga!"

"Nasty—ugh, stankass mofo muhfukah!"

Neon listened without interest.

"Suck my dick, bitch, 'fore I come back and beat your ass again!" the scraggly voice shouted from a little ways off.

Then she heard a loud crack of thunder through his cell

phone. It was about to rain like a sonofabitch.

"Don't get too wet," she said just to hurry off the phone, seeing as being caught unprepared was, for him, par for the course.

Bela had bugged him all day to help move to his car a filing cabinet the company was throwing away. Barclay agreed to help for three reasons: the cabinet wasn't large; Savory had already been requisitioned for a new one, and lastly it gave Barclay the opportunity to stay late working on his manuscript since it didn't seem proper taking up precious elevator space during business hours. Not too late, only a half hour or so after general quitting time, but it allowed for loose lips to disappear and non-managerial stragglers to be ignored.

The cabinet was barely three feet tall and slightly less than a foot wide but it was old-school metal.

They penguin-walked the ungainly thing past empty cubicles.

So far they hadn't seen a single white employee, so they were fine. It was bad enough when something went wrong that the tree swayed their general way, but the mortification of being caught recycling office furniture like actual thieves was death by embarrassment.

Which meant that when they rounded the corner a white dude almost ran into them.

"Hey, Murphy."

Turned out they were all on their way to the elevator, which was right there.

"Hey, Barclay."

Murphy reached between them to hit the button. Murphy made himself blazingly ignorant of the fact that the other two men couldn't depress the button without one of them setting an office filing cabinet down. He stared at the grey doors.

Bela and Barclay stared mutely at the empty space of the

phantom dimension.

"Got plans for tonight?" asked Murphy, who had read one of Barclay's books and hadn't been impressed, so he didn't think asking whether Barclay was going home to write was important.

"Probably do some weeding," said Barclay, invisibly wincing at his carelessness. Murphy had probably already subconsciously taken the "ing" off.

Bela gave the noncommittal frown of no-plans.

The door opened. Murphy edged aside to allow them on first.

"What floor?" he asked.

"Basement." Which was only four floors. God willing, there'd be no stops. It was easier carrying things out through the service dock rather than fumbling with the lobby doors. Plus the service dock had a ramp that led right up to the East parking lot. The basement was best for carrying things out, not for sneaking. Murphy knew that.

Murphy hit the B, then the star for lobby. Both circles lit side by side and mute under a column of otherwise dead discs.

The elevator stopped at the lobby. They scooched corner-wise to allow extra room for Murphy to pass. All three men mumbled generalities about good nights.

The door shut.

Barclay looked at Bela. "You are one ignorant motherfucker."

Bela gave him the secret satisfied smile. He had two Snickers in each of his front pockets.

They passed the cleaning crew on the loading dock. Since the crew hated coming in while employees hung around because there was always some guest--the agency told them the employees were "guests" not assholes, even though the crew were the outsiders in the tower)--needing a special request, the dock was a good place to be.

Nito smoked; Farbman did crosswords; Irina ate potato chips and read the newspaper; Sandra obeyed the cell phone stuck to her ear. They didn't even glance twice at Barclay and Bela. It would have been more alarming to see them not carrying anything.

Irina had a thing for Bela. The short, ignorant motherfucker was actually kind of cute in a token-black-on-a-sitcom kind of way. Irina's straw-like blond hair and Russian stoicism didn't jump people as being pretty either, but she was. Barclay had made her smile once tripping over a "Cuidado, Piso Mojado" sign and had been amazed on his way to the floor at the difference in her face.

And he noticed she gave a tiny glance as they passed.

The sun spotted them. Being naturally inclined toward guilt, stepping outside put Barclay in mind of two dark blots trying to hide on a white sheet of paper, although the security guards didn't particularly care what anyone took out. Savory Controls was one of several tenants in the tower. What went out was not the responsibility of Point Guard Security. Inbound fools were.

Barclay reminded Bela that he was indeed an ignorant motherfucker.

The cabinet wouldn't fit in the trunk of Bela's shiny new car even if they dropped the seats. They wheeled to the side, pulled the door open as wide as possible, and stood a moment performing the complex calculations of men about to ram something.

"I'm thinking turn it on its side," said Bela.

"Angle it?"

"Yeah."

Barclay's phone rang. He held the cabinet against the jam with his knee. The only person who'd be calling was Marilyn.

"Hello?" he said.

"You hit them niggas yet? I'm just checking in with you," said Cross.

"Hooked up with them now," said Barclay.

"Give them niggas my love. Seriously. Crosshairs Books is in the business of crossing over. Niggas ain't reading my books in the numbers I want."

"That's all that buys your books," said Barclay.

"Black women aren't niggas. I'm talking about men. I need male readers, and not gay, before you open your mouth LOL."

"You just said 'lol'."

"Make sure you tell them you're a Crosshairs author. Let 'em think they'll be characters. Guerrillas in the mist. Hey, I'm thinking about doing a TV show with unknowns and we never tell the viewers who the actors are, that way people are completely immersed in the universe. You think it's legal to make actors sign binding no-billing contracts? Need clauses like 'you won't talk to Entertainment Tonight or piss with TMZ cameras around.'"

"I don't know anything about TV, Jim. You're sniffling a lot; you got a cold?"

"Just something up my nose." Cross went quiet for a moment. Jim Cross never went quiet. He believed in the image of the Type A go-getter who sat down to take a dump and laid down for his final rest, but other than that was constantly on the move. "Know what the goal in life is?" he said. "The goal is to get as far away from the most people as possible. That's why people work toward fancy homes in the suburbs. That's why people publish glossy magazines of high end ads with two pages of content. It's a lotto world, and that's sad. Sad, Royse. Sad things got to that point."

"I'll give the niggas your love."

Cross sniffed again. "I mean, y'know, I'm set and I ain't about to invite BooBoo to come chill with me, but it'd be nice if I felt able, y'know. Comfortable. Like I didn't have to count things after they left. That's my people. You feel like they're your people?"

"I got no people."

"Yeah, you're one of them Lone Wolf McQuade people. You're gonna finish this book for me, right?"

"Already in it."

"I'ma make sure Netta gets you your next statements on time. She's slacking off way too much, no matter how much I like her like a sister, know'msayin'? Yeah...Hey, Ok, I gotta let you go."

"First draft next week, two at the most."

"No, take your time. Crosshairs be here."

"Thanks."

"Maybe by the end of the month? I ain't trying to rush you but I know you can write your ass off when you're up against it."

"Long as I keep my mojo going."

"Hey, pussy goes a long way toward inspiration! No, your wife is beautiful, man, lovely woman."

"I'm writing for her."

"American dream, baby."

"Keep you posted, brother."

"All right."

"First time he's ever called high on coke," Barclay said. He dropped the phone into his chest pocket.

"You have got to get an agent," said Bela. "How long you figure before he goes out of business?"

"About a year," Barclay figured. There was no way he was the only author with dubious royalty statements with fanciful explanations waving behind them.

"You had a lawyer review your contract?"

"Not yet. Let's get this thing locked up." He gave the cabinet a good shove.

"Hey!"

"It's nowhere near the seat. I don't think Elaine would mind scratches anyway."

"I had to correct her about my name," said Bela.

"I'm sure you did."

"Lugosi was classy."

"Best-known Dracula in the world."

"So when you plan to lawyer up?"

"You think it's worth it?"

"It's your money, man."

If he'd have said, "They're your books, man," a lawyer would have been a given. As it was, a shrug was about all Barclay could manage in reply.

Chapter Three

"Loretta Devine was right."

Le'Mon interrupted Neon's reading of *Prada My Ass.*
"They 'bout to start up by that new school."
(*'Drugs,'* Marilyn *noted in the margin.* 'Pharmaceutical
entrepreneur?'
'Amway,' Barclay *wrote back.* 'That's the joke; the men are
always dope dealers on the rise in these books. What about
roughneck Amway salesmen? Any real difference?')
"Don't tell me that," said Neon. "Now I gotta turn your ass
in." She grinned and stared into his eyes, because people who
stared into eyes in books found shit out. Le'Mon didn't mind.
He loved her smile. Made him think about this girl back in fifth
grade who let him see her titty then smiled at him like she
knew something. He didn't recall her name but she hadn't had
to buy her own milk an entire semester after that; come to
think of it, there were a couple other girls he used to
automatically transfer food to from his lunch.
"The best thing though is I ain't gotta be nowhere near
them fucking damn kids. Fake Rome got the sales floor. I'm
back office."
Le'Mon's boys called themselves the Light-Skindid Thugz.
They operated in near-suburban areas where high yellow
meant they weren't chased off too quickly. Not a one of them
had ever been called nigga except by each other.
"How long ya'll trying to be there?"
He grabbed a couple fries from her tray. "Prolly till fall."
"At least it ain't a middle school."
"Shee-id, middle schools sell like a motherfuck."
"Yeah, but still. Let the kids be kids for a little while."
"Fuck kids. You plan to eat all them fries?"

She pushed the tray closer to him. He clawed up a handful and added them to the huge pile on his tray. A group of hard boys walked past looking dead at Neon; oldest one couldn't have been more than fourteen. She set her book down and ignored the hell out of them.

Le'Mon watched them amble down the mall. "Punk ass bitches," Le'Mon muttered. She caught him glancing to make sure they hadn't heard as he bit into his burger. "Can't stand them punkass niggas."

She shrugged. Malls were made to contain stupid people.

"Punk asses chased me out this food court one time."

Who hasn't kicked your ass? she thought.

"I'ma need you to ride me a little today."

"Where?"

"Quick business stops. Then we gotta go by Plenty Mo's."

Her mood plummeted. "That crazy—"

"Neon, it's a quick stop."

"You know," she said, and this time he wasn't too sure he liked her staring into his eyes, "you're all up in my day without asking how you fit in."

"When this money rolls—"

"This place is full of that money roll speech, Le'Mon. How many times I heard it from you? Seven? Eight?"

"Ain't nobody 'sposed to get pissed on by crackheads."

The only reason she was here with him was the sale was over today. She didn't even like this particular mall. The merchandise was crappy, food court pitiful, and the entrance to the stores smelled like socks. Something in Le'Mon's tone set off a hellacious revelation—and she hadn't woken up looking for a revelation but, dammit, there it was. "Know what happened to me this morning?" She had stepped out of the shower, brushed her teeth, popped her birth control pills, glanced in the mirror to see how she wanted to do her hair—

And saw that she didn't look like a fool. She'd woken up

feeling like a fool. Living here, you were supposed to be a fool. Even that crazy woman down the block had told her once she was living like a fool. But something about listening to Le'Mon getting his ass kicked by a crackhead in the middle of the night wouldn't leave her alone as she tossed the hot night on that lumpy mattress, and in the morning Neon stared at herself without any makeup, bare assed and alone in her bathroom where she didn't have to do anything for anybody for any reason—and alone in that bathroom there was no need to pretend.

Her eyes were pretty. She didn't have any major blemishes. She was beautiful without makeup, not gorgeous but pretty enough to make a man goofy *(Marilyn crossed off the y and added "ier")* despite himself. The only people gorgeous without makeup were people who felt alive inside. She didn't feel alive, and she would have been a fool to keep trying to convince herself otherwise. There was a tiny speck of a mole on her left earlobe, and her eyes—without the pale light-brown contacts—looked like the eyes of somebody real instead of a cartoon character. She hated the truth as much as anybody, but the longer she checked herself in the bathroom mirror, chin up, chin down, side to side—the more she knew she wasn't a fool.

When you looked at eyes in a mirror, somebody you knew well stared back.

She fastened her bra to raise her girls up. Locked and loaded, she left the bathroom like a new year was starting and a resolution was about to be made. That crazy woman down the block wasn't about to be right anymore.

Simply put: The woman in the mirror didn't look like somebody who was going to spend the rest of her life getting phone calls in the middle of the night, particularly not from Le'Mon.

Le'Mon, who sat across from her in a dirty mall, chewing

away and trying to scope passing women without getting caught.

"Know what happened to me? You woke me up last night from a good sleep," she said to him. "This morning I woke up alone in my head..." Was he feeling her on this? "...and damn if that wasn't better than dick."

"Whatchoo sayin'?"

"You've never told me you love me and you never will tell me you love me and if you ever do tell me you love me I'ma fuck you up."

"What the fuck we doing talkin' about love? Girl, how long we been knowing each other?"

"I ain't complaining, Le'Mon. Me and you are warriors, that's how it's supposed to be."

He liked that, agreeing with a nod of his head and tipping dangerously backwards on the legs of his chair. Le'Mon was twenty-seven going on fifteen. "Fucking warriors, muhfukas." No one around them paid any attention. "Ghet-to sol-djah!" he reggaed, grinning her way and tightening his doo-rag.

"Fuck ghettoes and fuck soldiers. Soldier nothing but a glorified punk under somebody's dirty thumb. You wanna get fucked up the butt by your government, you go right ahead. A warrior don't need other warriors to be a warrior."

His hand automatically reached for her fries again.

"Dammit, you still got fries on your plate!"

"Damn, girl, why you partin' my ass?"

"Brokeback thuggie ass," she mumbled but Le'Mon didn't really hear her. He softened his tone.

He frowned in thought. "You need to get some?" he said, stupid enough to actually sound concerned, which made her want to reach out and pop him. Like: *Oh, if only he had known he would have cleared the table with his thing and laid down ready for her, damn the mall cops!*

"You. Stupid," she said with the equation mark inserted

between the two.

"Who stupid sitting with stupid?" he said. "Our shit is tight, Neon, that's why you get to fuck with my pretty ass so much. We ain't in love but I ain't punk-assed not to admit I need you. Ain't nobody in my life like you and ain't nobody about to ride with me but you. I'm about to get paid to where what you want I will get you. That's real, not some Hallmark bullshit."

Why the ugly ones always think they're pretty? she thought. Granted he wasn't straight ugly, but still, Blair Underwood didn't have shit to worry about. *You got too many teeth, your head is blocky, and all those razor bumps on the back of your neck look like popcorn.*

"And I wonder why I feel like I ain't nothing but pussy most of the time."

"Since when? Talking about getting some bothers you now?"

"I might as well open up to this damn plate of French fries," she mumbled.

"Oprah Winfrey wannabee. Worrying too much about what niggas think will fuck up a beautiful thing."

"What do you need at Plenty Mo's?"

"Plenty Mo got something for me," he said, leaving it at that on purpose. "You still going by that computer store?"

She shrugged and looked away from him. People made her feel weird about her computer stuff.

"I got whatever you wanna get outta there. I got enough."

"When's the last time you were happy, Le'Mon?"

He grinned. "Had me some weed last night."

"Uh-uh, not getting high, fucked or doing nothing fun or eating all my goddamn fries."

"You ain't happy?"

"This place is fucked, Le'Mon, please."

"I'm happy." He tipped back in his chair again. "Ain't a mutha alive can do shit to me." He laughed and leaned close hoping she would laugh too. "I am a living, breathing, walking big dick squeezed constantly by the hand of God—watch out now!—my balls are the playground of life. Last of the poets, girl."

"But nobody knows it?"

An old lady walked by and scowled at him. He scowled back. "I'll fuck a old lady up," he said when she was two steps far enough that her hearing aid wouldn't pick it up. "I'm happy as I need to be. Tonight I'ma make you happy as me."

You'll fuck a old lady up? "You ever see *Waiting to Exhale*?"

He drew up a bit, instantly searching her face for signs of warning. "Movie with Angela Bassett burnin' shit up?" Women must have done some serious wrong to cavemen that it takes less than two seconds to move modern men all the way from content to prairie dog "watch yo shit!" "Helluva arms," he said. "You should get arms like hers."

"You too, ya doughboy bee-yotch." He drew up a little more but she rolled right over him. "I was watching that waiting for you to call me. See, and you just remember a crazy heifer burning shit up. Typical. What you blocked out is when they were talking at the birthday party."

"Come on! You ain't one of them bitches talking about you can't find a man. Leave that shit for them scrawny ass secretaries and shit."

"No," she said pushing her cold fries away. She looked him dead in the eyes and made him even more unsure where this was going. "I've been trying not to believe this about ya'll the whole time but Loretta Devine was right."

He gave her the *Who the fuck is she?* expression, then the expression immediately bloomed into him frustratedly saying, "What the fuck are you talking about!"

"I'll run your deluded ass by Plenty Mo's but I ain't getting out so he can play with himself later picturing my ass. Loretta was the one Gregory Hines liked. The fat chick. The girls got tight at the party and Loretta broke it down. She said, 'I'll tell you what's wrong with men: they all got little dicks and cain't fuck.'"

Well sweet damn. Le'Mon didn't say anything to that because what in the hell was there to say to that? Brother fell into that deep, Buddha hush.

"My birthday's next week. Did you remember that?" It was probably best not to move, so he didn't. This was like that mongoose story, Riki Tavis Smiley: "If you move," said the bitch-ass cobra, "I strike. And if you do not move, I strike."

Bitch ass cobra.

"That's what I thought. No, I am not fucking happy, Le'Mon. Go on and eat. You're gonna buy me that software, we're gonna do these runs, I'ma take ya dick home—to my home—and," she said this looking unblinking into his eyes so she noticed that his nostrils flared nervously a couple tics before he was able to control himself, "we are going to fuck till I sing Happy Birthday To Me and mean it."

"That's my girl."

"Yeah, you keep thinking that."

Mario didn't creep. He appeared. Barclay's 'Works' file was open. Mario pretty much knew all the house's codes and passwords. He kind of liked Neon as a character; she was funny, the kind of girl he wouldn't bother at a club even though he felt he should. He'd sip a drink and watch her a while, most definitely, before coming home to his room. Barclay's strokes were kind of broad though. Mario bit deep into his Reuben, holding the sandwich far from the keyboard. Bro-in-law would need to watch out for that. Easy to come off as unprofessional.

A shadow fluttered the window. He glanced. It was nice outside: clear sky with the afternoon birds coming in for what was left of the stale bread Mario had tossed out the kitchen window that morning, but Mario Rolls didn't truck too much with the sun. Way too much of it out there for his needs.

Chapter Four introduced the next key character with (Mario noted scooping a clawful of popcorn) not much in the way of lead-in. He wasn't sure he should care for this character yet but was willing, for his brother-in-law's sake, to give her at least three clawfuls to gain hold.

Then he reconsidered: it wasn't like Barclay not to foreshadow or presage in some way. Foreshadowing had been a crippling flaw with *Onion Roll*, so he scrolled back a bit and re-read. He didn't plan to stay in the office too long. It was a little past noon. He stifled a yawn.

Brother felt a nap coming on.

Chapter Four

"Pam Grier ain't got shit on me."

The crazy lady down the block wasn't crazy, but she was Plenty Mo's cousin, something she didn't want anybody knowing seeing as he brought trifling to a new degree, so she pretty much kept to herself. And she was actually a few blocks over, not down the block. Plenty Mo was trifling. Yvonne DeCarlo was not.

Trifling seemed to be the word when dealing with the men around here, even that one white dude who hadn't moved out of the neighborhood yet, the one that rotated through the same three novelty tees and had a cat that never left its dirt patch in the front yard. Trifling pretty, trifling homely, trifling thuggie, trifling yuppie and especially trifling-no-good-ass def poet wannabee coffee house wooly-haired artiste negroes. Artistes loved some tall Yvonne; what's the point of putting somebody on a pedestal if not to look up their skirt? Yvonne DeCarlo Paul didn't have time for trifling, but that was the thing about life: folks who had too much of it constantly tried to flick it on you. They were the dumb asses who hadn't yet learned about Kleenex.

Nobody bothered her much anymore, not after that night the police took her in for wandering her backyard naked shouting, "Pam Grier ain't got shit on me!" She wasn't completely naked; she had her dog tags sitting at attention right above her breasts. The police immediately thought Section Eight but Yvonne wasn't crazy. She was pissed and drunk and maybe off her meds a little, but crazy?

See, folks needed to redefine that particular word. *(Mario liked that part. She'd survived the three-clawful rule.)*

Crazy meant blasting porches with kids on them and thinking somebody gave an ignorant damn whether you were hard or not.

Crazy was the last man on earth with the balls to call the last woman on earth "bitch," which a lot of ignorant fuckers would do.

Yvonne DeCarlo was pissed and drunk and sick of trifling (and might have been just a little crazy) but she wasn't insane. She never took her dog tags off. The military had owned her for years; now she owned them, even if just a small part. That night it was hot as hell in her bedroom and nobody alive will say rain on bare titties is not the sweetest, most erotic thing in the world. Hell, she was trying to figure out why the two policemen were harassing her.

"It's dark. Nobody's out here but you two and me," she had pointed out for their benefit.

"Ma'am, you're creating a disturbance."

"These monkey bastards the ones disturbed they can't appreciate this body," she declared, and wobbled a little as the officers wrapped her in a musty green blanket from the trunk of the squad car.

And lady had the helluva body. Tall, strong body courtesy of crappy high school and easy Army induction. The neighborhood was full of Happy Meal asses and droopy tits but there was only one body had style enough came close to hers, that girl down the street, Lightbulb or Firefly or something. Granted Lightpost wasn't as tall as Yvonne (who stood five-eleven in flats) and soft and supple described her whereas Yvonne was toned and Amazon, but if Yvonne were ever to turn that way—and she wasn't saying she never would because she was nothing if not an inquisitive soul—then Flamethrower could be on the shortlist of potential things to do.

Now, Fireant's face was better, granted, but Yvonne was not unattractive herself. Matter of fact, her close-cropped hair and high cheekbones made her look all-American gorgeous.

Except for moisturizing lip balm, makeup rarely touched her face. "Fresh" is the word, provided fresh can be edged. Trifling Porch Negroes always scoped as she moved through their days, but wouldn't open their mouths seeing as she just might fuck a nigga up, which neighborhood rumor said she'd done. At least twice. And it's a scientific fact that there are just some women people instinctively should not—and sensibly do not— fuck with. Some kind of doctorate-level mix of pheromones signaling the high potential of ass whupping.

She wore bras that made her jugs so straight she could change channels with them. *(Note to Cross: focus groups of men six to eighty-three show consistent, across-the-board favorable responses to any and all mentions of breasts.)* She wore t-shirts that fit her form and didn't stretch out the other way around. Out of shape, stretch-marked, belly-rolled girls did *not* need to be showing off that nasty shit hoping to attract some dick. Parlez vous French sneeze? It was like showing rancid cheddar to rats. Hell, the rats are gonna eat it, but damn! What you wanna feed a rat for?

She entertained thoughts about her body currently because she was about to go outside naked again. No, it wasn't raining and it wasn't super burning hot. The weather had actually cooled a bit since yesterday. Her birthday was next week but she didn't give the least happy damn about celebrating. She had a job that was non-existent two seconds after quitting time. She was lonely as hell and hated admitting it.

So she wanted to run outside naked and scare squirrels. Squirrels were terrified of boobs.

Only thing kept her inside was it wasn't dark out yet. It was early afternoon on a summer day.

The lady wasn't crazy.

Tits plus sunshine made fools get beside themselves, and she was in no mood to lay healing hands on anybody horny enough to try peeping over her fence.

Yvonne did get naked, but that was because she had a tub and she had enough sense to simply run water in that tub, get in, cry for a while, get out, get dressed and hit the mall.

People hustled and bustled there, and the anonymity howled. *(What the hell?—Mario.)* The mall was a good place to go when you wanted to feel like you weren't specifically part of the saying "There but for the grace of God."

Le'Mon seriously tried Neon's patience by asking her every two minutes how much longer they were going to be. Thing was, they were a good drive from Plenty's and he didn't want to be late. He didn't know how fortunate he was to have Neon detouring into boutique after boutique. It was here at this moment at Locked Gate Mall that he saw Yvonne for the very first time in his life and—-being Le'Mon—-couldn't successfully try to hide the fact she immediately blessed his mini-me with an anxiety attack. If God had given men the goods his panties would've dissolved so he could fling himself ass up in the middle of the floor for her. From forehead to feet she was a comic book dream in brown leggings and green t-shirt. Posture straight out of perpendicular. He tried to think of a hellacious adjective for her but *damn!* kept getting in the way.

She and Neon acknowledged one another without a word and passed on. Thundra went into a candle store, Neon into Sector Zero Zero One, the geek store full of thuggies plus little suburban kids who already had too damn much anyway, crowded like ants to sugar around demo video games. Every head shot up the second Neon entered. The thing about teenage boys thinking they were men was to ignore the hell out of them since they were dumber than a dog's nut hairs. Space was tight in the software boutique. Le'Mon stayed close.

Dumb was easy to ignore. Stoopid, though—with double

O's—took more effort. A pack of boys sniggered behind hands and x-rayed her from clavicle to pelvic. Neon was twenty-five damn years old; there wasn't a damn thing these little boys could've done for her except wait with a warm towel and a cool drink.

"Babe, you found what you want?" Le'Mon asked. He stared openly at one of the boys until the boy looked away as the others elbowed and laughed returning to the game.

The store clerk, familiar with Neon from cleavage-level down, lived for these special discounts. Girl never missed a sale. He surreptitiously watched how she shut out the rest of the store to search the racks. He wished her fingernail trailed his pasty back instead of software spines. Black chicks dug smart white dudes, didn't they?

She approached the register to address his geeky butt.

"I didn't see the Image-It upgrade over there."

He smiled and pretended to acknowledge Le'Mon. "I think we got one copy left. Let me check under here—" on the way down linger on tits, on the way up linger on tits—"Here we go. Twenty-five percent off plus ten percent with member card."

Le'Mon pulled his wallet out.

"I didn't bring my card." Yes she had.

Le'Mon stared at the clerk till the clerk realized he waited for the total.

Clyde entered a code into the register. "I'll give it to you anyway. One fifty-five ninety-eight."

Holeefuk?! Le'Mon had thought it'd be like thirty bucks. He pulled out two hundred, keeping the wallet angled so she couldn't see what was left in there.

Three dollars.

Outside the store he said, "You're always doing stuff on that computer."

She didn't need to answer.

Leaving the store he hoped to glimpse Thundra.

Neon thanked him and swung her bag.

"You ready to go to Plenty's?"

"I thought we were going there last," she said.

"I want to speed things up a little bit."

To somewhat quote the prophet Rock (comma) Chris: "In the world there's black folk and then there's niggas... and niggas got to go!" A blatant referral to Plenty Mo, who was probably robbing one of Rock's entourage at the time. Plenty was a scary Kareem Abdul-Jabar looking mofo, came out of prison and admitted he'd fucked men up the ass. Looked folks dead in the eye when he said it. Whereas Yvonne doled her crazy out in bits, Plenty stockpiled it like the Federal Reserve, always ready to release it in case of recession. *(Can't mix politics with bitches, Mario thought. Everybody knows that.)*

Neon's ass was a particular target of Plenty's crazy. He'd palmed it once with his big basketball hands thinking she was just some ho Le'Mon would share, but the hurt and determined reaction on her face made him step back and say he ain't mean nothing by it. He'd palmed a major dead president to her.

"You're sorry, so it's all right," she'd responded.

Le'Mon had poked his head out the man's fridge.

"Retarded motherfucker, you at home?" Plenty had shouted at him. Plenty Mo looked at Neon and frowned toward Le'Mon, deciding then and there that when he finally had Neon it wouldn't be a fuck. Ass like that was fresh bread from the oven. You pulled it apart slowly anticipating the soft, warm insides; you buttered it up, and tasted it giving praise to most merciful High.

He'd whispered to her: "I'ma make love to ya, girl."

Ever since, if she (unfortunately) found herself in his presence, he became the clumsiest scary mofo, accidentally brushing against, across or into her ass; it was better for her to act like she didn't notice, and that made him respect that ass even more.

And now, while she sat outside with her windows rolled up and the A/C blasting over the radio detailing some mayoral scandal, Plenty stared menacingly at Le'Mon.

"What'd you do to her?"

Le'Mon glanced out the door at the woman sitting in the car and shrugged. "Female shit, man."

"Tell her I said hi."

That sounded weird coming from him. Le'Mon half expected Plenty to bust out laughing.

Plenty had a gold wedding band on every finger of his right hand. They gleamed when he picked up a backpack that had been sitting quietly by the door. "I'ma let you hold some shit."

"What is it?"

"Motherfucker, did you just ask me what this was?"

Le'Mon threw his hands up and jerked his thumb toward Neon's car, like this lapse was her fault, shaking his head like he didn't believe it himself. "Naw man, shit," he said.

"Le'Mon, keep up with me, man, this shit ain't hard." Plenty handed him the bag. "Some mysteriousness. You can handle that?"

"Scooby Doo ain't got shit on me."

Plenty Mo laughed. "Scooby a funky bitch compared to you. Look here, I gotta get with some peoples first, then I let you know where this gotta go. Put your cell phone in the bag."

Le'Mon's smile went on the decline. "I need my phone, Plenty."

"Nigga, my left nut is achin' to introduce itself to you! Why's she driving you?"

"Car in the shop, man," he lied. "Pick it up tomorrow."

"Ain't gon' be no fuckups."

"Not from me."

"Don't fuck with my left nut, man."

"Ain't touching yo nuts, man."

"What?"

"It's cool. I'm cool. Wherever you need this rode to I ride to." *You must have a lonely ass little right nut. Deez nuts, muthafuckahhh.* Le'Mon imagined his boys swelling up on cue. *Deez nuts!*

"Set your ring tone so you know it's me. Do not take the cell phone out the goddamn bag before that."

"But what if—"

"You see Rod Serling behind my ass? No. Ain't no 'what if' shit. You ain't got shit to do but make sure that phone rings four times by next Wednesday."

"And if you call?"

"Why you think I said set it so you know it's me?"

"But you said don't take it out the bag."

"Motherfucker, I'm callin', answer the fuckin' phone! Got my nut itchin' like a centipede in my draws."

"Just wanna be cool, Plenty," Le'Mon said.

"All right, close the fucking door, man; letting all the air conditioning out. Come in here and sit down, lemme explain some shit to you."

From the car Neon saw the front door closing. She cursed. Le'Mon was paying for this gas.

After a few more minutes he came out of the house, got in without saying a word, and she immediately headed out. Le'Mon noticed, though, that Plenty stood watch at the screen the whole time.

"I don't even wanna know what you're doing with him," she said.

"Ain't shit."

"First time you ever come out of there with a bag."

"He knows my shit's moving out."

"You're not as hard as you think you are."

"That's quite all right."

"A hustler's life, huh?"

"The world is a buyer's market. We gotta make some more stops."

"I'm staying in the car."

"That's cool."

There wasn't much to do later when they pulled in front of her house, so they wound up bumping uglies in the living room. He did her thinking about Thundra. The only times Le'Mon ever hit this neighborhood were for quick dips in Neon. He'd never seen Yvonne before because he'd never needed to, but damn if he couldn't feel her muscles against him right now, her thighs lock and loading him in till his spent manhood—that's right—couldn't do anything but hibernate.

Changing position, his eyes cleared and he saw Neon, slick, her eyes shut and her jaw clenched, but as soon as he was inside from the back it was Thundra's ass his palms rested on. The small of her back was like a steel cable twanging up and down. He reached forward for a dangling tit, its weight and warmth making him feel comfortable and secure in a mean, petty way. And when he came again, Oh motherfucker, he came with the thunder! Dick pulsed inside pussy till his lips felt chapped. *("Yes, yes, I been there!" Mario said. Bro-in-law brought the heat.)*

Ten minutes later Neon was ready for more. She didn't want his thing though, she wanted him to kiss her, so he went slower and gentler, letting her mix in his mind with Thundra so he could pleasure both women at the same time. He nibbled little kisses from Neon's ribcage to her curvy hips. If she moaned in a pleasurable way he echoed it with a growl of his own, wishing he could feel what felt so damn good to women. He kissed his way upward, licking her nipples till her left eye twitched. There was a spot along her right jaw that made her goofy. He kissed and licked it for a while and dropped his hand between her legs. It was like soaking in bacon grease. He could've slid his whole arm inside. With fingers treading, his redbone lips teased her neck till she went limp, got tight, shuddered, eventually started muttering His name, and began bucking against Le'Mon's hand to meet her second coming head on.

And then she pushed him to the carpet and swung pussy as if it was attached to a pendulum.

By the third time his dick was stupid, humming while it waited for the short bus.

Nuts gave out at number four.

She wouldn't let up. She kissed, licked, sucked and bit down his high-yellow back to his stubbly buttcheeks. Every time her breasts and nipples trailed solidly against his skin he received tiny jolts. Teasing a fingernail along his ass crack made him squirm. She maneuvered him like a chew toy. Men got off more than women when their nipples were licked. She worked his till his little man showed signs of life then gently jacked him off, never leaving the nipples alone. The power she felt over him was amazing. He was like a rag doll too pleasured out to know how much pain he was in. Neon squeezed him harder and pumped him faster but kept working slowly at his nipples and chest. It wasn't about making him come. Coming for men was like asking a cheap ho if you could buy her a drink: the answer came ridiculously easy and quick. *(Yes! The cheap hoes do that!)* It was better if Le'Mon stayed afraid of the fact that any woman—this woman—could fuck him past where his dick was any use...and have his ass keep coming back for more. Every man was a crackhead when it came to poon. The better the rock the more they danced for it. Ain't a woman alive ever came just because dick was inside her, but let pussy accidentally graze a man's tip and that's it, game over, man.

Game the hell over.

When Le'Mon finished off he could barely open his eyes.

Afterward he didn't complain when she sent him and his

backpack on their way to the bus stop. Some folks actually worked for a living, and she was riding less than half a tank. She settled on the cushions and treated herself to a bowl of butter pecan with the cool bowl resting on her belly. She powered up some cable TV. One station was doing a Star Trek marathon, the old Kirk episodes. Sometimes she watched Star Trek for hair ideas.

Another channel was doing a weeklong tribute to black cinema. She'd seen shit from back in the day she didn't know actual black folks had been a part of. Comedies quick and sharp as Groucho Marx; dramas that soared like huge Gone With The Wind sagas stuffed with morality and over-acting; musicals that showed where Astaire got his moves—Neon had gotten hooked watching. The station had made it to the seventies now. Scream, Blacula, Scream, about halfway through, caught her attention, and her first reaction seeing it was what the fuck is this, but then Pam Grier came onscreen and you could tell that the black vampire would have put on some sunscreen and said fuck it, just to be with her. She turned the volume up to block out some fool outside thumping bass from the rear of his car. *Drive your ignorant ass on,* she begged, while Pam oozed out that voodoo sensuality.

Neon gave a long stretch and decided that later on it was all about some silk, some lace and some more of that butter pecan.

The movie looked like it cost five dollars and some food stamps, but it made her remember her mama's pervert boyfriend—and what young woman hasn't been through her mama's pervert boyfriend, right?—telling one of his partners wasn't a man alive honestly thought anything in his pants was good enough for Pam Grier even though decent Christians would have smacked a Baptist to try. He was funny when he wasn't looking around the neighborhood for somebody else besides Mama Neon to fuck. Watching this movie, she could see why Pam Grier used to be the shit. Pam Grier had that expression that said I might be acting but don't think I can't kick your ass in the real, an intensity that guaranteed something dangerous and sexy at the same time.

But, as Neon got up for a quick shower so she could catch the rest of the movie, she thought to herself, *Pam Grier ain't got shit on me.*

Chapter Five

"No the #@!! you didn't…"

That night a blast of gunfire jolted her from a dream about ice sculptures. She had no idea what time it was, but it was definitely late. A silly infomercial on TV was telling her to buy *Ab-Solution,* the Amazing System to Pray Your Way to firm, flat abs.

The shots were right outside her front door.

She dropped to the floor.

Whoever was shooting needed target practice or was just mean. No voices, no footsteps, just that hard evil pop pop pop pop with breaks of even heavier silence that meant somebody was now dead or somebody had gotten away. She waited.

In three…two…one: the sound of a car driving away but not zooming. No real need to zoom away from the scene of a crime in the ghetto.

She hated the summer and hated the city and hated these stupid motherfuckers. Hated not being born white so she could actually enjoy weekends and really wasn't too fond of the fact that somebody as fine as her had to struggle so damn much. Vain, yes, but damn! She hated how often dreams about ice sculptures broke when things went pow in the night, hated how often her heart woke her up with a sledgehammer to the chest, even though a lot of the times she refused to open her eyes.

Neon waited a few seconds on the floor then went to the door to press her eye to the peephole. Her porch light didn't show anybody in front of the house. The Porch Negroes across the street had reemerged, so that meant it was safe. They'd be out all night shouting and playing dice by streetlight. She could just make out their shapes moving hesitantly and an occasional glint from a bottle. She couldn't pick up what they were saying but definitely caught bits of nervous laughter. Get scared enough, you gotta laugh it off.

Bullets don't give a fuck who you are.

She gritted her teeth and headed for the bedroom, killing the power on the TV without even looking at the screen. "Everything ain't funny," she said to her small, dark house. She took by its trembling silence that it agreed with her.

(This was a good place to take a nap, Mario decided. He shut Barclay's computer down, dusted a few crumbs off the desk, and made his way to the unknown that was Mario's room.)

Neon worked at *Bootísma!*, a clothes and accessories boutique in an office building almost but not quite downtown. Bootísma! specialized in jeans and dresses that emphasized or provided ass. Ass was vogue so skinny white chicks loved it. The office tower's security guards hated that the shop was on the ground floor. Women constantly adjusted bras and panties in elevators; only thing that would have made the show better was if they all smiled for the cameras.

In the subterranean monitoring room where the guards changed shifts, Neon was the untapped mother lode. The security guards waited daily for that one moment she'd have to ride an elevator to offer up thirty seconds of touch and fix.

Today, like every day, Neon refused to acknowledge the guards because they stared too hard when she entered Munday Tower. It wasn't like she was at a club. She was at work. They stared at all the women but since she was this cool breeze mystery, they stared even more. As far as she was concerned, though, she was one of thousands of professionals working around those rental bastards, and they couldn't respect that professionalism? She was *not* a stank ho. She wore flowy dresses every day to work, stylish ones, not tit and ass jamborees. Yes, the only way fabric wouldn't hit curves was if she wore a stiff cardboard sack, but still.

"Hey, girl," said the boss, a tall glossy woman that Neon imagined decorated her house with white carpet and knew the names of eight different mixed-wine drinks.

"Hey, Charlene."

"Good morning. Sweet blessings. I need you to sell your ass off today. Gotta get me a cruise ticket next month."

"You don't do cruises," Neon said, surprised because Charlene actually sounded serious. Charlene Beatty didn't do water unless it had a spritz of lime and a couple fingers of very smooth gin in it.

"Hell no," she said as she quickly arranged two mannequin displays at the same time. "Divorce present."

"She finally divorced his ass?"

"No. He's divorcing her. You know my sister doesn't have the sense to make bus fare. I need to get her the hell away from me for a while. I need," she said, "my house," she said, "to myself!" She twisted a mannequin very roughly. "Oh, and you're late."

"Five minutes."

"You say that like it doesn't make a difference?"

Neon eyed Charlene's display, frowned at it a second, turned the entire doll a slight angle, then nodded approval. "Hip should always angle out, not in. Better?" she asked Charlene.

Charlene nodded too. "So you see that a little makes a difference."

Charlene was the kind of older woman people are never surprised to find with a rotation of younger men. She was too grown to own a store called 'Bootisma' but made just enough money that she didn't care about anybody's irrelevant opinion.

"Point taken," said Neon.

"So why were you late?" Charlene asked. She was a nosy

woman. She nudged the mannequin back the way she'd had it.

"Haven't slept well lately." Neon stopped and allowed the pause. She waited for Charlene to suggest a wise, tried-and-true sleep aid.

"Hmf," Charlene grunted, then grabbed her pricing gun to mark up a new shipment of knock-off Gurrini purses.

"That's all I get? Where's the love?"

"Take your ass to bed. By yourself. A lot of people in the hallways?"

"Breakfast crowd," said Neon. "Kinda muggy outside. Stragglers."

"Sylvia won't be getting deluxe accommodations. Outfit's laid out in the room," said Charlene. The first half hour after opening, Neon always put on a fashion show based on whatever Charlene's displays pushed. Bootísma! even had a worn red carpet remnant they used as a runway, stretching a few feet away from the store entrance.

"Diva is ready," said Neon. Charlene put her in the mood to throw a little pop-locking in the routine today.

"Boom, bam and pow," said Charlene.

After a while lunch came around. Neon performed her usual exercise walk alone (in her own clothes again), which was good because every day you needed to be alone for a bit from whatever job paid the bills. Lunch was a salad and doughnut from the dirty restaurant that served their little downtown fringe; it was dirty but it gave serious portions and they knew her, so most of the time they washed their hands. The owners even taught her a little of their language, whatever the fuck it was. The cook's wife liked talking to Neon. She talked to anybody but especially to Neon. Neon guessed she was homesick. Salah Memsa was never boring and never overstayed her welcome.

"You heard what they did?" she said, sitting with two glasses: tea for herself and free lemonade for Neon. "Donbrough's crazy a—self," she corrected, in case of eavesdropping customers, "is putting the city on curfew. Somebody broke into the mayor's mansion."

Ha! "They steal his homemade porn or something?"

Salah shivered at the thought of their dumpy Mayor Donbrough and a grainy video camera. "His people aren't saying what was stolen. But he's putting the curfew on. Violent crime is up this summer."

"It's up every summer. And winter. And fall. And spring."

"Yes, but he used the kids from last week as excuse. Four shot in one week."

"Four shot in one week," Neon repeated, just to hear the words out loud. "I hate this city, and I hate this world." Neon surprised herself having said it. Lunchtime was for gripe sessions, not deep emotional revealing. "When'd they break into it?"

"Two days ago! And the news is only now reporting it. It's a Cheney all over again," Salah said, the esteemed vice president of the United States having accidentally shot a fool in the face (pop pop, mothafuckahhh!) and managing to keep it out of the press for a couple days. "Two days ago and the news is only now mentioning it. I watch the news every day. It came out as one of those reliable sources things with the mayor's office finally having to confirm it."

Once it's out, rats are quick with confirmation, Neon thought. Mayor Donbrough was a dumpy, weasely brother who tried way too hard to be charming. The running joke through the city was he used to be a pimp, that's why he fit so well into politics.

Salah's fourteen year old son—who never seemed to be in school—emerged from behind the restaurant counter, waved at Neon and half-dragged a rag over a table before heading through the kitchen's half-door. He was the kind of unmanageable kid parents enjoyed seeing leave the house every day, even though they knew he was screwing suburban girls rebelling against who knew what. Impregnating dumb over-privileged girls who would never admit they had granted all access immigration to his narrow foreign behind was one thing, but shaming them with the authorities for not knowing how to tell time was another.

And for Salah, shame was everything. They couldn't afford to move out of the city yet, which meant that a crackdown on curfew meant he'd be at home seriously hampering the Memsas well-deserved freak. The Memsas did it every chance they got. Stupid sumbitch mayor! (Salah had learned all the necessary cuss words.)

Serious freak. Like with butter and shit.

Neon read all that in the blink of an eye from the way Salah glanced at the kitchen door while unconsciously rubbing a finger along her pale wrist.

The girl was good at observing things. Hell, that was the best part of life. Why else had the Lord God said let there be light?

Check this: Neon had already made three of Charlene's freedom cruise sales just by observing three women that hadn't been laid in a while but hoped to correct that funky situation with a little spice at work. They were white except the last one, a black lady—of damn course, Neon had to say—and the black one spent the most money because she had the most to prove, mainly that she wasn't a bitch, which she was. Hello? Who wants to fuck hankty when you can get six hoes for free? That was probably in the Bible somewhere. Self-esteem daddy issues don't improve one bit in an aqua-knit double-slit dress. Heifer had the nerve to ask Neon to follow her through the store holding the clothes she might (Neon backed up on that word) want to try on.

This ain't the suburbs, ok? Hello? Recognize.

Each woman entered looking for casual but sexy, which was code for some dude at some upper level of management about to be fucked, fucked hard, fucked long, fucked in triplicate, and filed away for future fucking. The first woman came in the door just reeking of no-dick. It was easy selling her a bright red pencil skirt and a tight top. Second lonely cow touched things too much. Something lacy for her, a touch delicate so she could pretend she wasn't heading straight to hell. Black chick—Of damn course, fretted Neon—stubbornly maintained that funky disposition not a man alive wanted to be bothered with for longer than it took to jerk off. Woman either, for that matter. Dick wasn't the issue for her, getting attention was. Women can be invisible all over the world until titties and ass get in the mix.

Sad little office ladies didn't know that in the human arms race they were living nuclear bombs, tasers, and a can of mace wrapped around a barbed stick.

That's what started the war back when dicks left tracks in the sand.

Menz (big, sweaty menz) didn't want to admit that God…was a C cup at least.

Shee-id, need a pagan Negro to properly appreciate me, thought Neon, and then let Sister Buttstuck who wanted clothes carried behind her servitude-style know that she'd be more than happy to start a fitting room for her, as unfortunately there were other customers.

The lady had looked around. There wasn't anybody else in the store but her.

Neon pointed her toward a sleeveless tit and ass maximizer, and that was that.

Observations were pretty damn cool things when it came down to it.

When Salah got up she swiped the condensation ring off

the table a little rougher than she needed to. Other customers entered. "It's good you don't have young ones."

Neon sipped at her lemonade. She bet Salah and her husband videotaped themselves. "You ain't never lied."

On the return trip to work Neon observed three relationships about to crash, two men preparing to discover new and troubling things about sexuality as it related to their friendship and—as she entered her building and pushed her sunglasses into her flowing hair—one high yellow grinning asshole dangling a red and black backpack and looking like a carp in a school of office working dolphins streaming past.

Now, she hadn't seen that one coming.

She didn't even know he knew where she worked.

"What're you doing here?"

The grin cracked wider. "They told me you went to lunch."

She'd have a talk with 'They' later.

"I need you to hold this till the end of the day," he said, swinging the bag.

Neon laughed, drawing even more attention from the security guards who were trying not to laugh at the bus schedules sticking out Le'Mon's back pocket.

"For real. I got stuff to do. I trust you with it."

"Shoulda left it at home," she said.

"Shit disappears at home." Damn moms.

"I'm not in this." She stopped before they got to *Bootísma!*

"I'll be back. Matter of fact, before you get off work."

"What part of I don't deal with Plenty Mo in any way, shape or form is giving you problems?"

"Neon. Can you hold onto this bag for me a couple hours?"

"Naw," she said, grabbing the padded strap from him.

"Thank you." He was grinning like a retarded kid with fruit.

"I'm not taking this home."

"I'll be back. Three hours. Just let me know if the phone rings."

"What phone?"

"Inside the bag."

"Then take it with you."

He shook his head.

"Le'Mon..."

"You can't call me either."

"Why?" Not that she wanted to.

"That's my phone."

Obviously he didn't realize how stupid he sounded.

"Le'Mon—"

"I gotta be out. Bus. Listen for this:" and he hummed the ring tone. "Mostly that one."

You just show up... she thought. *Why am I bothering with your trifling ass?* Then she looked around at the seven ninety-five security guards acting like they weren't tracing the curve of her ass and she realized that in ten years three out of four would still be seven ninety-five security guards. If she were with any one of them she'd still be twenty-five years old coming every day to this building selling fake curves to heifers, hoes, skanks and librarians. Except she'd be thirty pounds heavier and one of her own best customers.

Le'Mon wasn't meant to last. He was circumstantial. A minor distraction in every way to everybody, only he was the only one who couldn't see it.

Le'Mon J'ello Arness would cease to exist the moment her circumstance changed.

"I owe you, Neon."

"I *will* collect," she said, and left him to finish out her time.

She didn't explain the bag to Charlene. She tossed it behind the counter and proceeded to whip out eight more sales before the end of the day. Four-thirty came around and Le'Mon bounced in trying to feel out whether he should wait around for a ride without actually coming out and saying so.

She gave him the bag, told him it hadn't made a peep (which it hadn't but he kept pressing her till he started suspecting it had), and she proceeded to whip her undivided attention back to the few last minute customers in the shop, shutting him down.

Lockdown, fool! Be thou gone from mine presence henceforth, you ignorant sumbitch.

He mumbled thanks and left.

Neon felt Charlene's eyes on her but as far as Neon was concerned no man had ever entered the store.

By the time she pulled up to her house the summer heat had cooled enough for a decent walk. She threw on a tank, jean shorts and heeled sandals. There was a chance of rain, and that meant the raggedy park not too far from her house would be mostly empty.

Two-mile roundtrip.

She set a goal of beating the rain.

Day City was always loud. Hell, every city was loud. Loud voices, loud music, loud emotions, loud regrets. She wasn't about to let this noise keep her inside. She carried her phone when she walked but never answered it. She liked to walk when she didn't feel like a full workout. Curves didn't maintain themselves by being chiseled by appreciative eyes.

She marched down Blossom Drive. Folks waved, she waved back. Past Four Mile Drive. Old lady worked the flowerbeds by a tiny porch. Three blocks down Hertford, which was a long wide-lane state road with the raggedy park at one end and a hospital several miles away at the other to treat the folks hurt fighting in that park.

The gold-rimmed Impala definitely following her came out of the side streets a block ahead of her. For the second time. It turned slowly onto Hertford and made another right down the next block.

By the time she got to that block the Impala was gone.

She reached Buckingham Park, a large grassy area that today was relatively quiet. There were always a few cars parked along the road that wound through it, the owners off somewhere either getting a drink, barbecue, or both on. The city actually cut the grass on a regular basis and had even thrown up new fencing around a refurbished play area. Up ahead a bunch of loud broheems convened with brown bags on the hoods of a couple Cadillacs and an old K car. Every now and then one gave a loud bark of laughter that the muggy air smothered.

Ok, you know it's coming so hop up and ride. Mama Neon's baby girl always walked the length of the park and back. She had no plans on making today any different.

Perched on top of a weathered bench looking at nothing in particular was the crazy lady from down the block.

Even though it was still hours from darkness the clouds made evening seem close. There hadn't been any thunder yet though. Neon might make it home without getting too wet. She had to wash her hair anyway, so why bother running?

Her bra certainly wasn't made for jogging.

She thought about veering away from Yvonne but something said don't. Two seconds to pass by and nod weren't going to hurt anybody.

The crazy lady didn't look up as Neon approached. Neon checked some details. She looked to be in her thirties. Worked out regularly. Real workouts. Her hair was in tight highlighted ringlets, short enough not to have to fuss with too much, and matted even more by jogger's sweat. Nice skin. Black gym shoes, grey leggings and tan sports top. Camouflage colors. She didn't want to stand out any more than she had to. No jewelry except for what looked like a light-fixture pull chain around her neck, and sapphire stud earrings. Strong jaw line.

Neon got closer.

"Hey," said Yvonne.

"Hey." Bodacious tatas. "Don't get rained on," Neon said.

Yvonne nodded thanks. After a second's hesitation she hopped down and caught up to the younger woman.

They'd seen each other in passing enough times to warrant brief conversation. "How long you lived there?" Yvonne asked.

"Little over a year."

"Yvonne."

"Neon."

Flashbulb, thought Yvonne. Her name would forever be Flashbulb. "You mind company a minute?"

"Naw."

"You know them niggas down there already know your bra size."

"Yeah."

Yvonne smiled a little, taking a quick glance over Neon. Ass to last in her little jean shorts, cleavage for several days, and shoes not worth a damn for even running for a bus. But she stood straight and she walked like fuck all y'all; the shorts weren't so tight you could see—and damn, how you gonna show panty line through denim?!—that you could see whether she had fresh draws on or not, and as for the cleavage: fat man shows a gut, skinny lady shows her ribs. Titty is as titty does. At least they weren't pushed under her chin or dribbling out the sides of her tank.

Yvonne couldn't stand hoochies. They were like combo meals. *"You want fries with that ho?"* She smiled again before catching herself. "I don't see you talking much to people."

"Naw."

"Where'd you get 'Neon' from?"

"Seventeen year old mama."

And the girl wasn't veering away from the men up ahead. Very impressive.

Then the ugly Impala sped up just enough to pull alongside them. Three Meh-hee-canos, definitely outside their usual turf but feeling the big nut, smiled at them under a blanket exclamation of "Daaaamn!"

Aw sweet hell.

"Whassup, ladies? Ladies? Whassup? ("Call em bitches, man!") Dora my explorah! You sisters? They must be sisters." The loco boys glanced up the road a ways, saw the gang of blacks milling around, and stopped the car a couple rolls ahead of the women before pacing them.

A shaved head leaned out the passenger window. "Where you going? We get you out the rain."

Yvonne stopped. "Do I look seventeen to you?"

"You could be ninety-four looking that good and I'd hit it!" said the driver.

The passenger, who was apparently the leader, dropped his smile. Yvonne had never seen such an ugly Mexican before. "Yeah, you got jokes," he said.

"Yo, bitch, whas up? Come sniff my balls," laughed the driver.

"Keep walking, girl," Yvonne tight-lipped.

"Two balls for two bitches," the driver said, laughing nervously at the obscure reference that nobody else got to an old gay-ass musical called *Seven Brides for Seven Brothers* that his moms used to watch all the time when he was little.

"Shut yo high ass up," the leader said. "Ladies? Ladies! Why you walking? It's about to start raining. Hair about to get all wet. C'mon in the car."

"It ain't a perm, it's a temporary," the driver said, laughing hysterically. Neon and Yvonne walked quietly on. The Impala crept forward.

"What what? You don't talk? Hooked on phonics and don't speak English?" The smell of weed coming from the car was 3-2-1-*contact.*

The driver leaned over to inform: "I got the jawbreakers."

"Punk ass!" shouted the leader, pushing him away. "Ladies,

where you going?"

The women had veered toward open ground. They were still a ways away from the Cadillac boys, who weren't paying any notice.

The car stopped abruptly. The one in the back seat was about to get out.

Yvonne came back in toward the car just a little.

The Cadillac's loud music undercut the scene. Yvonne knew both groups had guns and she did not want to get caught in the crossfire these stupid broheems would cause trying to rescue a couple fine black chicks.

"Ladies? We taking you where you want to go," the passenger said.

"Take those heels off," Yvonne side-whispered. She looked squarely in the passenger's face. "We're ok," she said with the most hard-eyed grin he'd ever seen.

"Get these in ya mouth, roll em round ya gums—Ow, bitch, don't be hitting me in fronta bitches!"

"Get your ass from shouting over me!" The leader glanced at the one in the backseat, who unlocked the door and quickly scooted.

Neon ran.

The leader tried to bust the door but Yvonne threw a hip against it, disappointed she didn't catch some fingers. She hip-jumped the hood and caught Balls-boy with a hard fist in the face. He folded so fast she was able to get in an elbow to the neck then knee to the chest before he was curled by the tire. Backseat Boy rushed a bear hug on her and slammed them both against the car with his dumb ass actually taking most of the force. She thrashed as wildly as she could, screaming "Get off me!" as loud as she could. Neon's running had caught the attention Yvonne needed but it wasn't about buying time anymore. She needed to finish this before any guns were drawn.

The leader hadn't gotten out yet so maybe she'd managed some fingers after all.

The Mexicans knew there was about to be a gathering storm of bum-rush. The leader hadn't gotten out because he was doing the math: two car loads of niggas plus his Impala currently running on a quarter tank of gas (damn, but gas was expensive!), plus two fine fine bitches, subtracted from three locos mexicanos, basically equated to a beat down of god-like proportions.

But if he'd had any mathematical acumen he wouldn't have been driving around harassing women like a hyena musk ox; he'd have finished school, got a cheap ass job with a bunch of other Pedros, and probably never developed the need to think of himself as a man.

'Cause if you got to pretend you are... hello.

So he got his tattooed ass out the car ready to whip a gun, since all the trouble they'd caused, this tall bitch was destined to become his personal pussy Pez dispenser. "Get her in the fucking car!" he ordered, but the lieutenant couldn't since he was getting his ass handed to him. Yvonne had wilded free, enough to drive two sharp punches to his nuts. In movies, a man gets nutted he grimaces and falls but gets up to keep fighting.

Shee-id.

Two solid knocks to the nuts and Loco Boy wished he was a girl.

The driver tried getting up. Yvonne kneed him in the side of the head on her way to meet the leader, who stutter stepped back before remembering he was the one with the gun. That hesitation was all she needed to scream out "Help!" and fall to the ground as though he'd hit her. He bent to grab her by the neck and managed to angle away from the nut punch. He kicked her hard in the side. She curled up ready to trap a foot with the next kick but instead was treated to a symphony of cussing telling his ass he was about to get fucked the fuck up.

Six dark versions of hell were almost on him, and Neon was right there like a general.

The leader ran. Six bodies flew past Yvonne in a rush of wind. Neon helped Yvonne up and away. The nut-punched banger was trying to crawl to the Impala. Neon ripped the keys from inside and threw them as far as she could.

No the fuck you didn't! the terrified expression on the testicular-obsessed one's face said.

"When you're paralyzed in your wheelchair," Yvonne said hot in his ear, "Think about how you shoulda let a bitch walk in peace." The leader got dragged back their way.

Nut Boy dug his nails into Yvonne's ankle. She jerked away and spotted blood. He looked up at her with his mouth pursed to spit.

"No the fuck you didn't!" she said.

She cocked back. Fist met him dead in the eye.

"Little bitch scratched me."

"Hey," Barclay asked, "Do you love Elaine?"

"Not yet."

"What about her?"

"I don't think she plans to. We'll see how far it goes."

"I love Marilyn."

"I know."

"It scares the shit out of me sometimes."

"That's your luck, man. Keep it close."

"Why don't you look for love, man?"

"Love scares the shit out of sensible folk."

Barclay never knew what was going to happen in life and hated that ignorance with a passion. Life was too random, and any deity who relied on Chaos Theory as an overriding operating principle was no benefit at all. Being part of "God's Plan" didn't offer the comfort contained in a single cup of cocoa. Back in tenth grade civics his teacher announced to the class that anything they could imagine happening was happening at that precise moment somewhere on earth.

That meant rape didn't just happen in filthy alleys in the worst part of the night; that murders didn't just occur for the benefit of television news; that somewhere right now a child was being strangled; a sad teen was slashing her wrists; a man sicced his dog on his girlfriend; somebody's husband changing radio stations at a stoplight looked in the rearview mirror in time to see who rear ended him at seventy miles per hour; bullies forced the weakest kid in the class to pee on himself; a knife entered someone's body; a friend did a friend's wife; a wife fucked a husband and hated him with a passion; on and on until the only sanity left fit in a thimble of love that had to be protected at all costs.

That meant that no matter what you thought of as good in life, it never superseded evil. It hid from it, a tiny marsupial to a leathery skinned Komodo dragon.

A life of fear held in check by bursts of creativity and profound, respectful love. As far as he was concerned, anyone envious enough to want to trade, welcome to it. Except the love part. Nothing would separate him from that. Love was the only thing worth worshipping.

Love was all you needed. Anything else was pure fear.

Chapter Six

"I hit him dead in the eye."

"That was some crazy shit!" Neon said while Yvonne handed her shoes to her. They dashed quickly across the park away from the two little dudes who'd stayed with the Cadillacs confused whether to watch the women or the beat-down farther off. But they weren't about to actually leave the cars. Damn thousand dollar speakers in there.

Yvonne breathed hard enough to crack a diamond.

Neon worked to keep up with her. She was glad the crazy lady didn't break into a run since there was no way she could've kept up, and this wasn't the best time to be alone. Even her insides shook. *Muthafuckas fucking with territory ain't got SHIT to their names but a goddam shit car and dumbfucked tattoos that in Spanish or English scream I ain't got shit else to do!* she screamed at them internally.

The ladies quickly cut across the park and made it to the safety of concrete.

Instinctively Neon headed for home. After a while she realized Yvonne—quiet the whole time—was still beside her, then it dawned on her that the house they were in front of was her own.

"All right," was all Yvonne said, then she turned around and headed home herself with a slight limp Neon was only now noticing.

"I should walk you home."

"Then I'll have to walk you back. That's an infinite loop."

"Let me get my keys out the house." She ran in, snatched up the car keys, and came back relieved to see Yvonne hadn't left.

She unlocked the door for Yvonne then got in herself, quickly glancing around to see who'd seen the two of them, but it was grey and gloomy and none of the usual Porch Negroes were out.

"Should we go to emergency?"

"No."

"He kicked your ass hard," Neon noted.

"Gym shoes." She'd been kicked by combat boots. Big difference.

"You got kicked," Neon uttered, half-believing it even having seen it herself.

"Somebody else is kicking a woman right now." Yvonne wanted the subject changed. "You drive a Neon."

"Yeah."

"Never mind."

Porch Negroes were in full effect down Yvonne's way with enough aluminum cans in paper bags to start a recycling plant. Neon felt about eighty-four eyes arrow in on her crotch as she exited her blue Dodge car.

"Yeah, they make my pussy itch too," said Yvonne, glaring across the street. She was glad Neon hadn't just dropped her off but got out and walked her to her porch.

"Look," said Neon, "if you need to go to the hospital—"

"I got a car right here."

"But still. Here's my number, you can call me." She rummaged a slip of paper from her sparkly purse and scribbled the digits. "You sure you're all right?"

Everything about Yvonne was far off and unattached. She murmured, "Motherfuckers were trying to kidnap our asses. That ain't no simple shit."

Neon didn't say anything, but, naw, that ain't no simple shit.

Life didn't truck with simple shit anymore.

"I hit him dead in the eye."

"Punched the shit out of him." Neon flashed a nervous grimace that was supposed to be an appreciative smile. The weird lady from down the street was all right. She paused. It was scary saying what she said next but she had to say it. "You saved my life."

"Just don't wear those shoes anymore," said Yvonne. "They thought we were pussy. Just didn't know we're pussy with a capital P. Being cute ain't worth shit if you get some primitive dick intent on a fuck. Feel me?"

"Yeah."

"At least get some mace."

"I will."

"Learn to punch a nut."

Yvonne opened her door and entered the house. Neon walked down the steps then turned around.

"You think we should call nab?"

"Nab ain't thinking about no dead Mexicans," Yvonne said from behind the screen door. Why bother the police with a moot point?

"Call me if you need me," said Neon getting into her car, hoping that the crazy lady would keep watch as long as she could from her screen door.

She did.

The first thing Neon did when she got home was cry, and she cried for a long time, holding tightly to her small teddy bear.

Then she took a bath.

Then she got creative.

She wrote the world's first Attempted Abduction greeting cards.

It was so so wrong what happened to you
Life's scary that way, not knowing what folks will do
I'm here anytime and always, you know it's true; anytime you need someone to trust
And run to.

(She kinda liked that.)

Opened up a can of prime whup ass
Good thing for you beat downs don't last
Dumb ass best take this lesson to heart
Punkasses who get beat down--
Ought know to hold their keys
And floor the gas.
(Maybe not so much.)

In her heart of hearts, Neon needed creativity. She designed greeting cards on her computer. *Neon's Brights* she called them. She was good enough with the graphics and arrangements that she didn't need to use the prepackaged software templates. Each card was original from concept to completion. She had business cards and everything. She mostly sold break-up cards to her girlfriends at two dollars apiece, but a few people from around the way came to her when they didn't care to send the very best. She did obituaries or invitations—if she could print it out at home she could provide it on the cheap.

Neon Temples, Graphic Temptress, her powder blue business cards announced, featuring a wavy line suggestive of feminine curves, self-designed, self-printed and—hell, no shame—looked a helluva lot better than the cards on the counter of Bootísma! for customers who couldn't make up their minds but planned to come back later. Simple bastards. Ass, no ass.

What?

She wondered if she should tell anybody she almost got abducted. It was weird as any Area 51 shit. Butt probes and everything, because those Mexicans were definitely not about peaceful exploration.

But if you need to wonder something like that then you really, truly have nobody to tell.

Next morning, when she slipped her feet into her sandals— noticing an angry grass stain from where she'd kicked them off—she decided today was no ordinary day.

She would definitely punch a nut today.

And what Yvonne DeCarlo did was work out like a mad mofo till her arms and legs were screaming but her head felt clear. After that, the longest, hottest soak with the tallest, most alcoholic drink. The bruise where he'd kicked her had already spread like a slow mushroom cloud; the hot water stung the ankle scratches. For a quick second she thought to tell Plenty about it, get his crazy people to find out which Latino gang was trolling for black women, because it was no accident they'd tried to get them both. They were trying to pull a doublemint. She'd noticed their car when she'd jogged to the park, big long-assed thing like a rusty shark.

Yvonne slid down and let the water rise over her lean stomach. Her knees rested against either side of the tub; it felt good to spread flat out. On her CD player the duo Wendy & Lisa played. A sad song called *The Life* fluttered against the mirrors and walls of her bathroom. When exactly had her life become a Lifetime Network movie?

When she arched her hips a tsunami rose and fell through her pubic hair. She did it again because it felt so damn good. She slunk downward till her breasts were islands and hot water lapped at her chin. Legs spread wider and she loved it. She wished she had installed mirrors on the ceiling. Pussy made men crazy and primitive and stupid.

God had to be a man 'cause only a man could create something so dangerous.

"This is fucked," she said to the Lord. "I can't even exercise without it turning into Wild Kingdom out there? Do I need to cut my titties off and shave my hair?"

She trailed fingers underwater till they touched a pearl. "Pussy under water is a beautiful thing, Lord. You shoulda been a girl."

The next day Yvonne's doorbell rang at twelve-thirty in the

afternoon. Yvonne looked Neon up and down, noted she was still wearing those shoes, and took a step back, allowing the younger woman to pass.

Flashpoint, why are you here?

Neon's eyes swept the living room. It was full of plants. "I like your house," she said because she was supposed to.

"You haven't even seen it."

"I like it anyway." Dammit. "I called in sick. I wanted to check on you." She looked around again. The woman had hanging pots, ferns, lilies and cacti. "I couldn't keep all these plants."

"I try to keep my blinds open as much as possible. Go ahead and sit down."

Neon's sandals click-clacked over the distressed hardwood floor (as in scratched up) till they sunk into a plush accent rug in front of sofa. Yvonne's glass coffee table held books and all kinds of candles with pretty holders.

"I didn't mean to bother you," said Neon.

Yvonne hadn't followed Neon. She was looking out her peephole at Putt, one of the neighborhood's lazy eyeballs. He saw everything since he was always where he wasn't supposed to be. She was sure he still had the afterimage burned into his bloodshot eyes of Neon's ass moving like school kids under that skirt.

She didn't like people who looked hard at her house. He was mostly crazy and harmless though, so she came away. Question now was, what to do with this girl in her house who probably thought they had shared something?

Besides whip Bubba out on her. That was just the devil talking though.

But Flashpoint was cute though.

"No bother. You ever think about martial arts?" Yvonne asked. She sat on the arm of a chair.

"Naw."

"I imagine yesterday gave you something new to think about."

"I brought some salve," Neon said and searched her purse. "It might be a little expired though. How bad is it?"

"Looks like Australia." She leaned toward Neon and pulled the side of her top up.

"That's nasty." Neon glimpsed part of a longer scar whipping around Yvonne's back before the top went down. For the first time she noticed the dog tags clinking at Yvonne's chest. They looked like the real thing. That meant she'd learned to fight in the service.

She placed the tube of ache ointment on the table.

"Scuffed up my heels," she said.

"Hey," Yvonne began.

"What I mean is thank you again."

"Some of us are made to look good and some of us can't help but look good."

"Yeah. I think. Ain't never had to fuck anybody up."

Supernova, why are you here?

She must have said it with her face. Neon blurted, "I'll pay you to teach me some Kirk shit."

"What?"

"You jumped all over the top of the car chopping niggas in the neck—"

I went through four years of army training and all it left me was some Kirk shit? Then Yvonne suddenly shot off the chair, exclaiming, "What the—"

Neon jumped back.

"No, somebody was looking in my blinds," Yvonne said. She peered out the window. She knew it wasn't anybody but Putt. She realized she was spooking Neon. "It ain't nobody. I know who it was."

"Curfew means people gotta get their crazy early."

"Not this old fool. And when's the last time you saw the

police through here?"

Came to get your ass, didn't they? she thought. She shrugged.

Yvonne said, "Crazy doesn't need a special time or reason around here. Crazy's just crazy."

"I can pay you for whatever you can teach me."

"How about I give you a couple cans of mace?"

"I'm gonna pick some up later; it's on sale. Just show me how to punch a man in the nut without caring that it's gonna hurt him."

"Get to that point it ain't even a question of caring. Lesson one, free of charge. And you ain't about to jump on the hood of a car."

"Well, no, but..."

"But my ass. Yesterday was a bullshit fluke. I know you're scared."

LIFETIME MOVIE blared across the scene.

But Yvonne was more a Cinemax girl.

"Scared the hell outta me," the older woman admitted. "Just because they had guns we were supposed to quietly get in the car? Nowadays just being born you're in the wrong place at the wrong time. I cannot teach you to fight like Captain James Kirk because you, my sister, would rather wear heels and confining skirts and walk with enough twist to snap a neck."

"True dat."

Truth was truth. Simple, clean and sugar free. "But let somebody corner me again," Neon said and held Yvonne's eyes, "and I'd whip yo ass."

"How sick are you?"

"About two, three days worth if I want."

"Ok," said Yvonne and returned to the arm of the chair again. "But you gotta do something for me."

"You're not as tall as I thought," said Neon. The way

Yvonne's hip muscles worked under her leggings kept drawing Neon's eye. Looked like she stored an Olympic runner under there.

"I don't know exactly what yet but I'll let you know," said Yvonne.

"I don't do crazy."

"You wouldn't be here if you didn't," Yvonne pointed out, challenging her dead in the eye.

Neon fidgeted. Was this about to get freaky? Yvonne held her gaze, and Neon had had enough women surreptitiously graze a boob or ass in the clubs to know...yeah, here came that spooky vibe, the nasty tingle, the lesbian tango, the—

"Hell yeah!" a scraggly voice shouted from the window.

"Your ass is mine when I catch you!" screamed Yvonne.

Putt crashed from the window and ran off.

"He must be high as hell trying to get shot like that," said Neon.

Yvonne waved it aside. "You threw him a curve." She kept holding her gaze.

Here comes that music, that waaka-waaka-bow wow, hey girl, I'm so bored...

"I think he's back." Neon pointed out a flicker of bushes at the corner of the window.

"Horny drunk must pay." This time Yvonne slid her feet into her house shoes, quick-stepped to the door, ripped it open on Putt trying to untangle his dirty shirt from the bush, knocked him through the bushes then put her foot squarely up his ass. And she defiantly looked directly across the street at the men who had watched the old drunk do his peeping Tom.

I hate this city.

She went back into the house without a word said, resisting the impulse to slam the door. Instead, she very calmly shut it, locked it, opened her blinds even wider, took a huge, deep breath... and speared Neon with her gaze, binding her into something they both knew—even though it was crazy, random and spontaneous—was necessary as hell.

Blitzkrieg, one or both of us is getting away from here. It's just that simple.

"This is turning out to be a crazy week," said Neon.

Yvonne didn't feel comfortable in the house. Her hard eyes softened. "What do you do for fun when you're sick?"

Neon brightened. "You ain't said nothing but a word."

*

It took thirty minutes to drive to Shropshire Mall. The divide between Day City and Shropshire Glade was immediate and painful, like one minute you're in downscale Iraq, and the next you've entered the beautiful Bermuda Triangle where Amelia Earhart jogs past ultra-green manicured hedges with all the safety a bouncing blonde ponytail affords.

Shropshire's mall was the Vatican of area malls. Huge glass panes everywhere. Tiling. Faux-marble. Even a cobble-stoned central fountain.

Plus the Gap and Cookie Barn.

In an ultra-bright store they touched and felt on silks and brocades and weird last names, tuning out the appreciative stares they got because, let's face facts: two fine sistas will get stared at by the Pope and a Rabbi on a good day and don't say the clergy won't nod together with a 'Can I get a damn!'—but this was the usual hoity mixture of *what y'all doing out here,* with *be nice if you were my mistress,* and overly seasoned with (from over-aerobicized wives who apparently had nothing to do but spend money they didn't make) *they ain't got shit on me.* Shropshire Mall catered to suburban wives with the quickness.

It wouldn't have been wrong to see Botox dispensers in the restrooms.

"This," said their salesgirl in the ultra-bright flagship store, "is one of our more elegant lines—" (Neon squinted to read the salesgirl's nametag; it was printed in tiny flowing script). Iris. Merci (known in the hood as Boocoop Bucks) was like a directory of designer labels and perfumes, expensive but not we-shall-overcome expensive (since the savvy marketer knew that the surrounding Shropshire Glade's husbands had to split their money between their wives and mistresses, and the wives usually knew about the mistresses, so the wives had to feel they were putting the bite on the man without going so far as to bite it off and spit it out; the savvy wife could load up some nice blingedy bleep at Shropshire Mall).

"I like that," Neon said, forcing Iris to pause her motion toward the less expensive items in the designer purse line.

"I like the stitching on it," Yvonne said just to say something.

Your ass is too big.

Scrawny bitch.

Black cow.

"I'm looking for something a little more versatile though," said Neon.

Big word for the day.

Commission hag.

"For going out?"

Say it, say it: to the clubs. I'll knock your ass out!

"Something that can go from work to dinner."

Grocery check-out to a forty and a burger?

Work, bees-natch, as in you are serving me. "Maybe something over there? These look good but they're like for going to a concert."

Those pay-my-bills tours you go to don't care what you're wearing. Legs'll be in the air and dress above your head by the end anyway. What, wait—WHY is Daniel looking at your ass! "You can browse over there; let me know if you find anything."

Oh, boyfriend wannabee checking me out? I do declare! Maybe I'll forget to pay for something so you can watch him grind my ass when he tackles me. Plainclothes store security Starsky and Hutch stalker bee-yotch!

Yvonne stepped into Daniel's clear field of vision. Daniel's heart skipped. Pants threatened to tighten. He leaned into the clothes rack he was supposed to be nonchalantly browsing until that sudden unexpected rush of joy died down.

Then Neon moved out. The young man's clothes became an unfortunate aspect of life, teaching him what it felt like to be oppressed by The Man. Iris didn't know it, but Daniel the plainclothes security officer was going to get deep in some Iris in the package pickup bays tonight, maybe even for the next couple of weeks.

But let's be clear, Shropshire: if you're fucking the store security, please check all attitudes at the door.

Neon and Yvonne pestered commission hags for a little while longer, then hit the fancy food court.

Another word to the seditty: if you work someplace where 'food court' comes up...

A pasty teenage boy dragged past wearing a wrinkled tee shirt two sizes too large that read *Now Back To Your Regularly Scheduled Program.*

"This place is huge," said Yvonne. Sunshine streamed from a vaulted skylight running the entire length of the court.

"I come here all the time. So, you gonna teach me?"

"Neon, if three men try to get you in their car, run the fuck like hell."

"I don't mean just that. Listen, I live by myself, I got no real man in my life, don't have a gun, I'm allergic to dogs and if I put bars on the house I might as well put 'for sale' tags on all my shit. I ain't trying to learn the five fingers of death and shit."

"How old are you?"

"Twenty-five."

"You should be a lot more confident then. There's no substitute for just living the simple life."

"What?" said Neon. Indignation at a moment's notice was a special skill.

"Stop trying to attract a man all the time! Every outfit you looked at was V-neck. You got great titties but I know when to air 'em out and when to tuck 'em in."

"Ok, you gon' talk to me like you know me. Ok." Neon pushed her chair out. "Ok." She glared at Yvonne. Or hoped it came off as a glare. "You done fucked around and walked home."

"Don't get embarrassed out here, girlfriend. I will nut up in a heartbeat. How old you think I am?"

"Thirty-four."

"That's several more years bullshit I got on you. Know when to put an ass down and listen. I'm saying you are a beautiful woman, so don't market yourself so much. Valuable shit sells itself. If it's crap they put it on TV. You wanna be a movie of the week or a certified block buster?"

"Obi-wan army ninja bee-yotch," Neon said, resuming her seat.

"Push some of them fries my way."

"I don't need these fries."

"And slide over the rest of that pop."

"Don't need this pop."

"You were saying," Yvonne said, popping Neon's straw out and sliding hers in for a long suck. Damn, but good lemonade could straighten out the short hairs!

"I don't remember." She frowned, looking at a good portion of her food across the table. "Look," Neon said leaning in so nobody could hear her, "I'm just a hoodie bitch so I'ma come out and say it: how'd you get that scar?"

"Desert Storm shrapnel."

"You fucked up a drill sergeant when he tried to rape you."

"World War II. I was about to kick Hitler's ass."

"You did like this, you went, 'Suck my dick!' after you kicked his ass."

"Iraqi Freedom."

"Not gonna tell me?"

"Shock and Awe." *Who comes up with this shit?* "Story of my scar ain't free yet," said Yvonne. She downed the last of the lemonade and grabbed up her tray. "I'm ready for some more elegant shit, how 'bout you?"

They whirled through the mall. Bought precious little. Annoyed quite a few.

Yvonne tried hard to enjoy it but truth was she hated shopping. Shopping involved people and somewhere along the way people had foresworn the ability to generate brain wattage. She loved to buy things, but shopping? Shopping made her hear Captain Kirk's action music and want to fling her body headlong at people. Chop a whole bunch of stupid fucks in the neck. Even throw in the real Vulcan death pinch.

Teach her some 'Kirk fighting.' *I'll teach you, all right. Throw all kinds of Shatner at your ass.*

"Why come way out here to shop?"

Because, Neon didn't want to admit nor did she, this was one place she was practically guaranteed not to run into anybody she knew. This one time with Yvonne was the only time she'd ever brought somebody with her.

"Something different," she said.

"I like my skinny, snooty white chicks closer to home." Something caught Yvonne's roving eye. "Ooh, let's go over there."

She didn't know the exact cause but Yvonne had partially lost her sense of smell in the service. Keeping her house filled with scented candles, incense, potpourri and oils was essential to keeping real life in front of her. And since it was her birthday next week she decided to treat herself out here at Shropshire nose-in-the-air Mall. She made purchases by name. Lilac Valley sounded better than Juniper Musk; Mango Breeze sounded better than Peach Flush.

And, for her money, Cosmic Orgasm had to be the best incense ever made, next to Money Burn and Spirit Rush.

She asked Neon if she burned candles.

"If I fry up some fish. I mostly spray."

"Leave that canned shit alone. Candles, girl. Earth, Wind and Fire: 'If there ain't no beauty you got to make some beauty'. Can't stare at a can of Febreeze, not without looking stupid. But light up a candle—time to meditate." She held a box of sea green tapers to Neon's nose.

"That's nice," Neon said. Expensive assed perfumy wax.

"I'll light this up when you drop me off, see if you like it."

"Ok."

"If you like it I'll give you one."

"Ok." Again, Neon had seen enough 'women in prison' movies to know, and she hoped this lady wasn't about to head where no woman had gone before.

Bumping in clubs was not the same thing as bumping uglies on a rug.

Please don't talk about oils, please don't talk about oils, please don't—

"You ever use the scented oils?"

Damn!

"Feel this. No lotions, no creams, just oils after the shower." She held her arm out. The muscle tone in her forearm was supple as warm ass.

Neon checked out the elbows though. Not a sign of ash. No lotion my ass. But on the whole her skin was pretty smooth for a rough ass Amazon army chick.

"Pick out some oil," said Yvonne. "I'll treat."

Somebody else might've said no thanks but what did Neon hear? Nothin' but a word. Sometimes she used the star and fish shaped oils that dissolved into gooey slicks in the tub, but this stuff here was elegant.

So despite feeling this affair was about to get freaky—the woman was treating! Hey!

She picked a scent she thought would mix well with boob sweat, a tiny vial of ginger lemon essential oil.

Maybe, thought our heroine, *I need some freaky shit in my life...cause for damn sure what I got ain't what I need.* "Is it all right if I pick out two?"

*

Le'Mon was selling it.

"Got that Amway. Amway, niggaz," Le'Mon said to the roughnecks heading into the corner store.

They ignored the hell out of him.

"Y'all cain't buy this shit in stores, I'm tryin' to hook you up. Am-fuckin-way, muhfukas," he said, grinning like he was talking to his best friend. The ones who didn't ignore him looked at him like he was crazy, which was all right. The ones looked at him like he was crazy were the ones usually wound up buying something.

Light-Skindid, bitchazz!

It was too hot to head out to the suburbs today, but suburban kids loved some Le'Mon. Get them in for a cut of it, they get their moms and pops on it, next thing you know, PAID.

One of his boys came up. "Muthafukcah. One of my boy's bitches saw your girl out at the mall with another bitch during the afternoon. Don't your bitch work?"

"Which bitch?"

"The big tittied one."

"Did I stutter?"

"Neon, muthafukcah. Always playing like you got a long dong."

"Punk ass, move on. What'd she look like?"

"Round titties, round ass."

"Who we talking 'bout?"

"My girl, right?"

"I'ma have your girl suck my dick while you take notes. What mall?"

"Shropshire."

"How she know Neon?"

"Fuck I know? Prolly that threesome we had. Muhfukcah, I

fucked her, my girl," he said counting off on his fingers, "while your future wife watched."

"Man, go ask a squirrel for your nuts back."

"How much you sold?"

"Ain't sold shit."

"That's 'cause you look like a school kid carrying that damn backpack. You're killing the Light-Skindid Thugz. Muhfukcahs think you're begging for lunchables."

"What," Le'Mon said, losing patience, "did the one with Neon look like?"

"Ok, see, my girl ain't into pussy. She got too much thickness to worry about. Tallish lady."

Le'Mon catalogued through Neon's known acquaintances. Unknowns were never cool. It wasn't like he knew who she knew, but he liked to think he knew who she didn't. He wasn't cool with surprise unknowns.

Unknowns tended to get each other thinking crazy shit.

Chapter Seven

"Happy Birthday, Bee-yotch!"

There was a bottle filled with rum and cola, shaken. The sun sent amber into the living room through the partially closed blinds.

A sea green candle burned in the center of the coffee table. It smelled really good.

There were a couple of big glasses that had been refilled several, several times.

Check off talking about men, love, family, fears, regrets. Check off Yvonne saying, "Know what? Let's pretend it's our birthday," and grabbing up drinks and a candle.

Check off Neon playing it close and saying, "Ok."

Now check off that heavy, punch-to-the-gut sadness that comes when you know you're forcing yourself to have fun to keep from thinking you could have died.

They sat on the floor and leaned against Yvonne's furniture. Yvonne had lots of woods and browns in her house that looked more expensive in the setting sun than they were.

"Those dog tags don't look good on you," Neon offered.

Yvonne had nothing to say.

"Is it true all y'all girls in the service is dykes?"

"I knew I shouldn'ta let you feel my arms," said Yvonne. She was hungry again. She crawled closer to where the nachos and salsa were, which was by Neon.

"Naw, naw—"

"Is it true every hoochie in the hood is a ho?"

"Yes!"

"Bad example—girl, move ya titty so I can reach my chips."

Neon leaned back. "A hoochie," Neon said slowly and studiously, "is by definition a ho, so ipso facto..."

"And domini domini vino sangria."

"By the powers vested in me."

"By these powers stomped on be." Yvonne said this as Neon suddenly swooped closer to her, frowning in her face like she was trying to recognize something. Something crucial. Something she might have lost but only suspected she had ever had. The crazy lady had nice lips that looked like they were always warm and soft and comforting.

Neon's rummy exhalations streamed hot from her nostrils.

"Don't step up 'less you plan to smak it up," Yvonne said matter-of-factly.

"Shut up. I don't wanna fuck you." Neon was pretty sure she was never going to see this woman again, so anything— she dropped back on her haunches and took another solid drink—anything in these walls was a blank slate. She swallowed hard, letting the liquor fuel anger at those dumb motherfuckers who had to mess THE WHOLE FUCK UP her day because pussy for them was cheap.

Pussy ain't cheap, you lack-ass motherfuckers! Pussy gold!

"Ever want to close your eyes and wait for one good kiss?" she asked Yvonne after another swallow. "Get kissed and not know where it came from, how you got kissed or who, and when you open your eyes it's like neither one of us knows shit about it." Shit, now she felt like crying. Poetics and shit! It is the knowledge of the doomed that tenderness never comes cheap. Unless you're drunk.

She forced herself to keep from crying but that sucked too because it made her feel like a kid. Rum and cola don't do shit but make you sad! All she'd wanted to do was take a walk. A simple little-assed walk on her planet. Shit was just always wrong! A woman wasn't supposed to be sad and always needing distraction. With the alcohol in her she couldn't really remember how she'd met Le'Mon since he blended in with Boo, Fake Rome, Andre the Step, Deez and every other half-off clearance sale bro-heem she'd dealt with from high school to now.

"I don't give a fuck anymore," Neon said and meant it. She closed her eyes and swayed her head to rhythmic music floating in a barrel on the rum in her brain. "I want somebody to kiss me when ain't nobody in this room but me."

"I keep secrets all the time."

"Then it's just you and me." She prayed now that God On High had warm, soft lips.

"I'm not going to kiss your ass."

"We know you want to. Fuck it. Go 'head. Blow out the candle," she said, looking at Yvonne, "turn out the lights, get down on this rug and let's just woman to woman fuck, 'cause dicks ain't doing shit but fucking things up."

"You're trembling like a little bitch."

Neon closed her eyes again and leaned her head against the sofa.

"Yesterday wasn't about pussy, lust, me or my body but I coulda died anyway."

"You think everybody wanna fuck you for some reason," said Yvonne, watching Neon go out of focus for a second. "Put that gratitude pussy away," she said, crawling forward till she was above Neon.

"Drunk ass Rambo dick hiding dyke," the younger woman slurred.

The first touch was tentative and almost ruined by a burp of rum. The second, Yvonne's lips parted just enough to take in the soft fleshy part of Neon's lower lip. Neon sucked in a breath of shock. Her eyes shot open and she jumped away.

"I need a drank, I need a drank." She fumbled for the bottle as though she'd been poisoned. Hoo damn! Crotch throbbing, nipples tingling, partly from fear and partly from Damn, she could kiss! It was more a psychic thing than physical. No tongue, just lips and a slight sucking pull—like a brightly colored fish wanted to know if her lips tasted good.

Tasty. That's what that kiss was.

Or like strangers on a train.

"You can do whatever you want on your pretend birthday," said Yvonne. "Ain't nobody but me ever in this house."

"What else you got to drink up in here?"

So we got two drunk ass, horny, lonely ladies, one of them can get dick like Chiclets, other one is strong enough for a man but nobody will pretend couldn't be made for a woman: "You're a slut but you ain't a hoochie," Yvonne hooted when they were on their second big bottle. She raised up a toast. "Happy birthday, bee-yotch!"

"Hold up. Hold up. Hold up." Neon slipped off the edge of the sofa. She bounced right up. "Hold up."

Yvonne waved her off. "Slut just dude without a dick. How many kids you got?"

"Shee-id."

"And can you conjugate a verb?"

"To be or not to be, bitches."

"Hoochies is dumb."

"Ignint mouf-breathin' basturds!" Neon hooted back.

"I'm glad you ain't dumb...but you still show them titties off too much." As she said it Yvonne reached across and honked a boob. "But, hey, you a slut."

"I don't fuck just anybody."

"You tried to rape me on my bearskin rug!" They laughed so hard they got tired. "Ok, when you kissed me—"

"I didn't kiss you!"

Yvonne nodded. "You done been there. You can't say you ain't done a woman yet."

Hold up, Neon thought, then realized she hadn't said it out loud. "Hold up. Yet?"

"Let me be the first to tell you yo daddy, yo mama, yo favorite math teacher, yo favorite baller and that ugly bastard down the street done at one time or another a gay slide.

Somebody done felt a tit or rubbed some hairy ass or looked extra hard and heard some thoughts. You peepin' me spladowed right here. Don't tell me you ain't wondered how they fit in a mouth," she said and tweaked her own nipples through the shirt. They immediately stood at attention.

Neon busted a laugh.

"Sex ain't but skin, girl, and skin knows what makes it feel good. Everything else," Yvonne said and gave both middle fingers to the air.

"I need to be going soon." Neon swung her head toward the blinds Yvonne had gotten too drunk to think about. It was dark out. The living room was cozy with that one candle and a small thrift store lamp on in a far corner.

Yvonne fumbled to the table. "We gotta do the candle." She blew out the candle. "All right, made my wish."

"Naw, we gotta do it together. You saved my life. I love you, bee-yotch. It's my pretend birthday too. You a good lady. I'ma—" Hoo, damn, where's the fucking floor?

Yvonne re-lit the candle. Neon hobbled to her knees. The women leaned toward each other.

"Blow on the count of three," said Yvonne.

Both closed their eyes and wondered if the other one was looking at pursed lips and thinking *damn if those ain't a bottle cap for nipples.* Attracting the opposite sex was an everyday thing; attracting the same sex was the double-whammy of fine that straight people all over the world secretly aspired to.

They leaned close to the flame...close to each other...

There was a sharp rap on the window.

"Y'all know I can still see you, right!" said Putt.

Yvonne shot up. Putt took off.

She thought about chasing his lunatic ass—but just for a second. She calmed herself with a quick, deep breath. Beating a crazy ass wasn't worth the police again.

She closed her blinds all the way.

"Y'know, I gots to go." Neon stood. Or thought she stood. Her head seemed higher than the floor.

She hadn't been this drunk in a long time.

Yvonne didn't want her to go but she knew when all the air had been let out.

"Crazy bastard," she grumbled. She went back to the floor and nodded at the flame. "Blow your candle out."

Neon blew but didn't make a wish. Wishes, she thinks it might have been Shakespeare, weren't, dear souls, for bitches. Not ones that somehow got caught up in crazy mofos peeping in windows telling the whole hood about yo gay ass. She just blew. She didn't even bother closing her eyes.

"You're too drunk to drive home."

"I know. Where my keys at?"

"In your purse."

"Where's my purse?"

"By the door."

"I be awright."

Smoke trailed from the candlewick into Neon's eyes. What was she doing in this woman's living room? Door dead-bolted, blinds drawn. Titty squeezed, for God's sake! Sitting around with some Lone Wolf Dyke instead of getting fucked by Boo or—or—

Dammit!

Yvonne caught Neon's confused grimace. "Happy birthday, girl down the block."

"Happy fake birthday to you too."

"I'll give you ten minutes to be home before I call you," said Yvonne.

In fifteen minutes, after Neon was home, locked in and shedding clothes on her wobbly way to the bathroom, her phone rang.

Neon smiled.

*

When she got ready for work after her two sick days, everything seemed pointless. Hourglass dresses with stomach smoothers and ass producers somehow weren't so vital to society's interests the more she thought about it, and she did a lot of thinking after the hangover and all.

She thought about her boobs. Healthy 36 C's built better than God made 'em, firm, Playdoh free and fortified with essential vitamins. The key to manipulating a man was knowing men never got over being breastfed. Thanks to Fake Rome, Le'Mon, Boo and everybody else, Neon's girls had twenty-thousand dollars more in their savings than anybody else's boobs.

Today she would consider not wearing as deep a V as usual.

Neon wiped fog from the bathroom mirror. She lotioned her upper body, cupped her full breasts to make sure they stayed in place, then drew her hands down the curve of her waist to the flare of her hips, and realized something: all her girlfriends either had stretch marks from kids or tattoos for niggas. She didn't. When she was naked she was naked. You couldn't tell anything more about her when she was naked other than that she was beautiful.

She liked that. Thought for the day: Be Beautiful When Naked.

She wound up being the most helpful she'd ever been at work, approaching solitary customers and spreading the Word.

"—You ain't got enough titty to wear that padded; he's gonna see you naked and wonder what happened."

"—Uh-uh, not that one. Michelin Man will not get you any play."

"—You got a nice body already. See that green one? Take the shoulder pads out, leave the top button open, Ok? Now, your face ain't ya best asset so all that makeup draws attention to it. No, I said the green one."

When she was finally pulled aside she had no idea why.

"You have obviously lost your mind. You come back tomorrow if and when you come across it," said Charlene from beneath one of the wide-brimmed, sleek hats she wore to make herself look sophisticated.

Neon frowned like a politician genuinely unsure what to do with a glory hole.

"Somebody don't need any more cough syrup," observed the owner. "Do you understand the words coming out of my mouth?"

Neon grinned a little. Charlene was a good boss. Didn't trip unless there was a big enough fall to cause a stumble.

"Go home and sleep it off. Insult somebody tomorrow though. I know you don't think my smile means job security."

"I didn't hurt—"

"Yes you did. You hurt their feelings. Lost me some money. Lost me. Money. Go home. If it's weed, leave off the smoke. If it's drink, dry thoroughly. If it's a man—" Charlene just shook her head at that.

"What about the truth?"

"Aw, hell." She felt Neon's forehead. "Baby, you on drugs? Am I sellin' that? Go home and come back. New day dawning and everything."

"New day."

"New day," said Charlene.

Hell, somebody needed the truth. Neon passed one of the ground floor security stations, thought for a second, and back-pedaled to the guy who quickly snapped his eyes to the floor.

"If we did, you couldn't do nothing but cry," she said and did the Naomi Campbell exit.

She didn't head home immediately. Neon drove past Le'Mon's house instead, seeing who was out, who paid attention, and who she might have known. A big yellow Bull Mangani woman in slippers and biker shorts was on his porch.

Moms didn't own the house, moms was the house. With peeling trim painted gaudy-assed bright yellow, porch steps too, Neon saw who would name their kid lemon Jell-O and think throwing apostrophes in it made it exotic. She knew his mama was like 'Ugh' but seeing her here on the porch like a piece of cold okra squishing between teeth reinforced it to the bone.

So here was the plan: take her hard-earned titty money, start her a business, a good one, because she could work her cleavage into the business world too, and most importantly start reading. She'd noticed those books scattered in Yvonne's living room, important for one reason: there were people saying shit out there that she wasn't hearing, and that shit was about to stop.

She drove off, saying to Le'Mon's part of the ghetto, *This I don't need.*

Her part got the same. So why, when she got home, was Le'Mon sitting on her porch resting back on that damn backpack like he was at the beach on a vacation day?

At, at (she looked at her phone) 2:45 pm? Oh. Hell. No.

She went up the steps without looking at him, went into the house without talking to him, closed her front door without acknowledging him, and stood in the doorway afraid she was gonna have to kill a fool Jesus God!

"You been trippin' a fuckin' lot," he said opening the door.

"I'm not feeling this," she said and stalked away.

Le'Mon grabbed her wrist and for a second tried to pull her back. Her jaw clenched and chest started to heave.

Don't let a woman build up no steam, you stupid fool, a little voice said to him.

He let her go and locked the front door. She marched off, kicking off shoes and taking off earrings.

Oh, shit...

"I was just—" he started quickly, then she pulled her dress

over her shoulders, still moving like a steam train. She unhooked and snatched her bra off in one smooth motion.

Oh shit with a smile...but maybe not, so he stayed put. Panties slid down and she stepped out without breaking stride.

Neon didn't even look over her shoulder at him. "Come on!" she snapped. But she was going toward the bedroom.

"We don't go in your bedroom," he said.

Hell, a naked ass tells you to follow you'll fuck on the spit-polished desk of the Oval office.

Shouts out to Bill!

Le'Mon followed.

Her bedroom was tiny. For some reason when men checked out a woman's bedroom it made them hornier. Half-opened jewelry box by the dresser mirror. Scattered makeups. Where the draws at? Couple outfits on the back of a wooden chair. Bra draped over the knob of the closet door. Pantyhose, yes! He'd almost missed that; they'd fallen on the floor.

Her body crossing the mirror focused his eyes on the bed's reflection. Full sized mattress for somebody who hated sleeping alone. One pillow. Unmade bed. Neon turned the floor fan on high. Thing sounded like a jet engine.

Then she closed on him, taking that silly backpack by the strap and flinging it to a corner.

Neon grabbed his balls and pulled him; leaned up and burned his ear with the dirtiest promises a true sinner would take the time to write neatly. She kicked the door closed. She knocked him on the bed, yanked his baggy pants to his ankles, and gave fierce head, knowing exactly when to stop and grab his thing like she was taking its pulse to keep him from coming. He twisted and fluttered like a southern Belle. His Johnson was taffy and his balls molasses.

Whenever he tried to sit up she knocked him down. Couple times she grabbed his nipple and pinched and he almost squealed. She went from the back of the scrot to the tip of the dick and slalomed over the top like a roller coaster. She wasn't slow, she wasn't gentle. She made him almost come eight times in the space of two minutes.

Then she left him nasty cold, crawled up the bed, straddled his face and just knelt there, pussy hovering right over the flared nostrils of his quivering nose, pussy that looked like it was about to drip acid and have little teeth shoot out and fuck him up, except she slid down and drew her lips and soft bush over his smooth chin—

Oh my sweet greasy damn!

--teasing the hell out of his lips with the salty musk of her own. He tried rising up again.

"Don't you fucking move," she warned. She pulled away a centimeter and he froze. Then she dropped three centimeters and lips were on pussy and pussy was not just wet and not just good and not just soft and not just hot but ultimately and satisfyingly a blessed, sacred thing.

Neon rode the clit back and forth over the tip of his nose till her teeth gritted. She remembered to let him breathe, but certainly dying in the service of a woman was an honorable death. She clamped down, feeling the rush build, jumping off at the last second and hitting the bed face down.

Ass up.

Le'Mon tore his shoes and pants all the way off and got in position.

While he was trying to figure the proper angle of thrust she reached back, grabbed him, popped him in, squeezed her cheeks so that he couldn't move if he wanted to, and alternated her inner muscles.

He became pure dick consciousness. Buddha dick.

Dick which was the coming and the becoming.

All up the ying yang.

Waaay too far a leap from sitting on some steps to

monkey-lovin' from the back. Brother nearly fainted but he kept it real, kept it strong. The small of her back was beautiful. He held on and closed his eyes.

She took off like a bronco.

He was a motorcycle passenger holding for dear life with all the twists and bumps she threw at him.

A true fucktress will keep a man hard for seven hours. She'd heard "Shit!" and "Goddam!" from him but was waiting for our Lord and Savior—

"Jesus!!!"

There we go. Neon suddenly pulled off and threw him on the bed. He'd never realized how strong she was. She was on him before he had a chance to rebound once; pinned his hands to the sheets; made sure her tits rubbed heavy across his chest as she went to work on his neck, leaving a huge starburst hickey there.

This man's dick probed the air like a divining rod. Yeah, he was ready.

She put it on him and snake-twisted.

Hold up.

Hold up a minute.

Ok. No, wait. Hold up.

Ok.

Damn.

He was knocked the hell out. There is sex and then there is sex. Folks in the back need to hear that.

Neon left the bed with a mental note to strip the sheets. She cleaned up, padded naked through the house, checked her email, then went back to the bedroom.

That red and black backpack sat there like it didn't have a thing to do with anything. She opened it up. Inner pocket: his cell phone and nothing else. Big main zipper, quiet, slow ziiiiiiiip—

Hello.

She smiled a smile that would've made the green, funky Grinch proud.

Chapter Eight

"All y'all do is suck dick and eat balls!"

"He had a bag full of money."

"How is it he don't know that?"

"Too scared to open it."

"And he's carried it around for how long?"

"Few days."

"He knows what's in there."

"You think he took some out?"

"Is he that stupid?"

"Basically."

"Where'd he get it from?"

"I don't know, he just had it one day."

"Wrapped or loose?"

"Loose."

"A bag full of ones is a bag full of money."

"Naw."

"How you know?"

"I ain't mess with it but I know. That's money, capital M. What d'you think I should do?"

"Stay the hell away from it. And him. Don't get shot for some dick and balls. They ain't that crucial."

"You ain't never lied."

"Yes I have, and so have you."

"I just wanted to see what somebody else thought about it."

"That's some foul shit, Flash—Neon. A trifling fool with a sack of money ain't Rubik's Cube to figure out."

"Huh?"

Yvonne let out a sigh of frustration. *Young ass girls ain't got shit to do but fuck and watch Povich these days. I swear!* "Rubik's Cube. Puzzle? Make you feel stupid but have fun doing it? I swear, all y'all do is suck dick and eat balls! Do a fucking puzzle sometimes!"

"Girl, it's like you've known me forever," Neon said. This early on and it was already easy to bait Yvonne.

"Kirk training starts at seven tonight," Yvonne informed.

"Neon?" Shondanelle said to Neon's voicemail. "Neon, where the fuck you at? You forgot how to call people back? Tickets, bee-yotch, to the hottest reunion concert of the month! Hello! Cain't nobody else go. You need to stop sucking dick and eating balls so much. Maybe you could call somebody back." Beeeep.

"Ok, I left you a message two days ago and I know you ain't been fuckin' nobody two days straight." This was Hiawatha. "If you ain't dead call me. If you're dead, that's some sorry shit. Whoever's listening to this message, let me know and I'll send some flowers." Then she called right back. "I know what you're doing, you're sucking dick and eating balls. Damn, girl, leave some for another bitch! Get to the point where you could suck the skin off a rhino. Ha!"

Beeeep. "Cabaret, ho! Tonight, one o'clock. It's me. Van Club cabaret. Van niggas, girl! From all around the state! We. Gon. Get. Fucked. Up. To-night." Sheela this time. "I ain't gotta take nobody home, girl, the van is right in the parking lot! Mama's already watching Devonne, I'm just waiting for you to call me. I need a ride."

Then Sheela called back. "It's almost eleven. Dick and balls, girl, dick and balls. And chicken. And drinks. Probably spaghetti. Where the hell you at? Where the—Mama, will you please put Devonne to bed, ok?!—Ok, call me back. Oh, it costs fifteen to get in and I only got twenty but you always got money. Hit me or text me, girl. Don't leave a bitch hangin'."

Some phone calls ain't worth a got-damn.

*

Neon tied the sash tight. She wasn't trying to have this robe pop wide open trapped in Yvonne's basement (finished basement and actually quite nice) with nothing but her young supple body as weapon. Hell no. It felt weird wearing Yvonne's clothes in the first place, but Neon didn't own a single pair of leggings, sweats, or Karate gear. She had a ribbed tank under the robe, but really, titties only looked more enticing covered up by ribbed tank tops.

And Neon didn't think the scrawny green mat on the floor was thick enough. She wasn't trying to break an assbone. Yvonne had on the same uniform except hers was black and Neon's red. And Yvonne didn't own anything but leggings. And army-green t-shirts.

"So tell me again why you gotta throw me?"

"Kirk-fighting was your word. Didn't you see *Charlie X*?"

"Malcolm's brother had a movie?"

For that, I'ma fuck you up special. "Episode where Kirk was pestering this little psychic boy; teaching him to fight. Told him he had to learn to fall before he could learn to fight." Trekkie and proud of it.

"I just need to punch a nut."

"Nut's probably trying to knock you on your ass. First we stretch out." Which they did. "Now a little calisthenics." They got the blood going. "All right, I'm gonna show you some basic moves, show you how to center yourself." Yvonne stood with her feet pointing outwards, knees slightly bent and arms palm to palm straight above her head. "Do like this and hold it."

"This hurts."

"Shows how out of shape you are. How the legs feel?"

"Wobbly."

"Tingly too?"

"A little. My arms feel heavy."

"You've got the upper body strength of a nursing home. Man would think you're trying to massage his nuts, not punch 'em." Yvonne brought her arms out to her sides and dropped her pelvis into a deep squat without moving her feet. "Change position."

"I can't go down that far."

"I bet if a diamond was down there you'd pick it up without your hands. Drop lower." They held that stretch a few more seconds then Yvonne bent with her head almost touching the floor and grabbed both ankles.

"Ow! Shit," Neon said.

"It doesn't make sense you're that stiff."

"You'd think," Neon said straining to get lower, "looking this—ow—good," she grabbed both ankles and pulled, "I'd be more limber."

"Shouldn't ass up come natural to you?"

"That was mean," Neon said but ignored her, focusing instead on getting into the same position as Yvonne.

"Drop your ass now but don't let go your ankles. Let it bounce, and bounce, now drop down to either side."

"This's like this position called Slippery Ninja."

"Is everything sex with you?"

"Everything *is* sex."

"Get these stretches right they'll improve your fucksmanship tenfold."

"My shit's already illegal in three states."

"How many boyfriends—change position, keep your stomach muscles tight and your titties pointing at the opposite wall—you got?"

Neon felt sweat already gathering between her breasts. This was like working out before working out.

"I got these two niggas I mostly kick with."

Yvonne rolled the sentence around in her mind. The best this girl could come up with was "two niggas I kick with"?

"They know about each other?"

"Hell no. Am I stupid?"

"You're lonely as I am, girl."

"Look, I don't mean to offend you but, you know? And don't be trying no more Jedi mind tricks on me, Ok?"

Next thing she knew she was finding out firsthand how much cushioning that mat provided. Yvonne had bum rushed her so fast all Neon had time to register was Whoop, but Yvonne didn't let her hit the mat with full force.

She hopped off Neon and Bruce Lee-bounced.

"Say you bent over to tie your shoe," she said while Neon rolled to her knees and got up. "Now some dude got you in an alley."

"I wasn't ready!"

"Ain't nobody ever ready for this shit, that's why you got to *be* ready. You think crazy just got violent the last couple years? We been perfecting this shit since day one. Jesus didn't leave of his own accord, girl, he got run the fuck out of town. This time watch what I do when I'm coming at you."

Neon watched. There was a subtle shifting of feet, a realignment of weight, a quick release of energy and she was suddenly back in Yvonne's arms being lowered gently to the mat.

"I'm supposed to stop you?" Neon said.

Yvonne looked at her like she was crazy.

Neon shot back a *then what the fuck* look.

"You saw how I went from relaxed to knocking you on your ass in two seconds? It's all about how fast you notice things," said Yvonne. She helped her up. "Defense is knowing where you are in relation to anybody else. Offense is being dumb enough to get caught in the first place. Centered person moves in any direction with speed and force. That's two things we got drilled at good. Finesse doesn't mean squat if you're slow and weak. Speed and force first, then finesse to embarrass the hell out of somebody."

"Yeah," Neon agreed. "Bruce Lee." She adjusted the robe, brushed herself off, and faced Yvonne a little more ready.

"Be Kirk. Kirk might look ridiculous and make you grin but he's beatin' yo ass while he's doing it."

"Keep coming at me," said Neon.

Yvonne smiled.

"What?" said Neon.

"Only heard you say 'can't' once."

"One thing to remember about me? Neon gets her money's worth. How much you plan to charge?"

Yvonne shrugged and set her stance.

Neon mimicked her. "Even better," she said.

Yvonne showed her basic blocks and dodges for thirty minutes; showed her how to control an opponent of any size with a few simple twists; showed her how to quickly dip and punch, since if you're going to punch a nut you'd best work that uppercut.

Then she spent ten minutes showing her how to use a fall to her best advantage. By the end Neon's hair was crazy but Neon felt something she hadn't felt in a long time.

Energized.

Controlled.

They bowed to each other.

Neon asked if she could wear the uniform home.

"I don't wanna put on my clothes all sweaty." Then she had an idea. "I'll pay for this one in food. Do some Chinese?"

Yvonne's stomach rumbled definite agreement.

"Ok then. My house. About thirty minutes for a quick shower. I got cable."

Cable didn't have a damn thing on. They wound up watching *Beastmaster* and sucking down Chinese, wine and cheesecake ice cream.

"Know what? That man got a nice ass," said Yvonne. Beastmaster ran around in a hide loincloth, boots and not much else. "Movie sucks though."

"But look at that white boy's ass! Them greased up thighs!"

"White boy got an ass."

"White boy nice ass," Neon seconded. "Probably got a little dick under there but that's all right."

Yvonne jingled her dog tags. "I've seen some huge white dicks."

"I figure everybody in Hollywood got little dicks. Kinda makes sense to me. You did somebody?"

"For the record, only person fucked me in the army was me."

"You did that sleeping next to people?" Neon asked.

"Girl, girl will get her freak walking down the street if her pockets are deep enough."

"You swing both ways?" she asked bluntly.

"I didn't tell you I swung at all," Yvonne said.

"You wanna kiss me again?" It was an idle question, not an invitation.

"We ain't drunk."

"But that was some weird shit, wasn't it? I ain't done that with nobody."

Yvonne headed to the kitchen for more ice cream. "You enjoyed it," she said from Neon's kitchen.

"I wasn't thinking that it meant you wanted to do me like if you'd been a man."

"What if I'd been trying to?" Yvonne posed from the kitchen.

"I still think it would have been a different vibe. Men put too much on my mind."

Yvonne returned with a huge Jethro Bodeen bowl of ice cream. "Man's first thought when he sees titty is what he's going to do to you, and he hopes it'll be pleasurable for you," she said.

"But knows it'll be for him."

"You can make a man come by looking at him hard; woman goes for what she's gonna do with ya. Big difference in the payload. If you find a man who can kiss you without his mental dick sticking up, hold on to him."

"What if you never do?"

"There's remedies for that too," Yvonne said with a smile. "Y'know, this's some damn good ice cream." She noticed Neon was smiling just as deliciously and with a twinkle in her eye. "What is it?"

"Follow me." They hadn't toured the house.

Yvonne got up with her bowl in hand. "What, you got some freaky shit in the basement?"

"That's too far to walk."

"I told you about stepping up to the plate. What's in your bedroom I need to see?"

Neon waved her off.

"I noticed you're burning that candle I gave you," Yvonne said around a scoop of ice cream, following. "You got a nice butt. Athletic, not a bubble butt."

"Bubbles bust and flatten out." She went to the dresser. "Since we're talking about men." She pulled what looked like a chocolate rope from her panty drawer. "Meet Bubba!"

"Oh," Yvonne tried to say around her mouthful of cream, waving her spoon in recognition, "Yes! Yes!"

"You got one of these?"

"Girl, Bubba is my best good friend! I know me some Bubba. Yours got the—yeah."

"And—" Neon flipped it over.

"Damn!"

"Deluxe."

"I guess so. Submersible?"

"What's the point if it ain't?"

High-fives all around.

"Yours a little bigger than mine though. I mean, damn," said Yvonne.

"Ain't got time to play. You saw *Waiting to Exhale*?"

"Yeah."

"Then you know me and Bubba have a special understanding."

"Go 'head, professor."

"I got different toys in every one of these drawers," said Neon. "I used to be kinda shy about 'em but they know me by name at the shop now."

"I order mine online."

"Not me. I want to hold that shit in my hand before I get it home. Test it for weight and balance."

"Now, I love a good dong...but why are you showing me this?"

"Because I'm not just about men—I mean about looking for what I need from, you know," she said, waving to indicate the neighborhood.

"Why fuck with them at all?"

"Sometimes you wanna hear another voice. Like these two I'm with now."

"The bag of money boy?"

"He's one." They took seats on the bed, Yvonne by the headboard, Neon at the foot. "One's nice but I know he's fucking other people, and Le'Mon—Le'Mon's just Le'Mon."

"You're doing the same thing."

"Maybe I do gotta have a man then."

"You couldn't convince a Catholic priest with that lie."

"Sometimes Le'Mon is fun. Most times he's confused as hell. He keeps it real."

Yvonne's exasperation almost made her smack her. "Keeping it real's another way of saying misery loves company."

"You know what I mean."

"I know. You mean he's dumb. Fuckers and their reality. Ain't nothing real about this shit. What about the other one?"

"Boo will do anything I ask him."

"No you are not a money bitch."

"Naw. Fuck, I gets mine, but they gets too."

"That doesn't make it cool." Yvonne leaned back on the headboard ready for a few justifications.

Which never came. Instead Neon playfully bopped her on the knee with the chocolaty rubber dick, accidentally hitting the switch and making its head twirl. "Don't be trying to make me into a ho."

Yvonne shrugged. She reached for the dildo. "Is that clean?"

"Of course!"

Yvonne took it and used it to emphasize her points: "One. You don't love them. Two." The chocolate head stared Neon in the eye. "You got better shit to do. Three. Money for pussy equals a cheap ho."

"I like to fuck."

"Fuck fuckin'! Start making love. You like to fuck but you got a roomful of kitty toys."

"I don't care what people think."

Yvonne almost whopped her upside the head with Bubba. "Activate a thought, girl. It's like prayer. You have any idea how many prayers to whoever you wanna call god were about fucking you today? There's been a train running on your ass since you walked outside your front door. Thoughts are actions. Ho with a hellacious body equals dick all up in it. You don't need to be thought of as a vehicle for dick all up in it. And dick ain't even that fucking good!" she said shaking the dildo. "I make the world a better place just by handing a free supply of Bubbas to every lady on earth!"

"I got twenty-thousand in the bank," Neon said simply.

You could hear the brakes slam. Yvonne arched her brows. "But ain't nobody said that's a bad thing."

"I am not a ho. Hoes don't save. And as a woman I admit to being a little manipulative but that's the only reason God made these. I don't take advantage."

"Neon, your curvy smooth ass has made you twenty thousand dollars richer than the med student down the block."

"We got a med student down the block?"

"Yes."

"Damn."

"Yes."

"So you're saying I got no self-respect," said Neon.

"No," said Yvonne, waving the head at her again. "You got it, you choose not to use it."

"What's your story then? Cause you're fine as hell—"

"Thank you, yes."

"—but you got just as many toys as I do. Am I wrong? You were in the army, came out a little fucked up, which is cool. Any of that shit would fuck anybody up. And you live alone in the ghetto."

"You know about that night too, huh?"

"Everybody knows about that night. What I'm curious about is, why are you still here? You don't fit. It's like you're trying to keep up a secret identity to fool folks from suspecting who you really are."

"Know what? Niggas pop guns here every day. This is a war zone. Rule one in war is keep your head down."

"So why you here then?"

"Why the fuck you here?"

"I don't know!"

"My titties ain't made me twenty thou'."

"Then yo titties need schoolin'. Hey, am I gonna be sore tomorrow?"

"Not a lot."

"You ever been in love with somebody? Not like me and Boo and them, but y'know, wish it coulda worked kind of thing."

"If it's woulda shoulda coulda it wasn't real. My 'keepin it real' is grounded in reality."

"And you don't go for women?" she said skeptically.

"Given the chance I'd split you open like a watermelon. Given the chance I'd ride Ving Rhames till his thang made a dent in my back. But I don't fuck nobody that's just a dream or fantasy. Shit, sex is sex, but I know you didn't bring me in your bedroom to see if you could seduce me into seducing you. It ain't like that. If you want to kiss me, take my top off, and suck my titties, I'll do it; stretch out and let you go to town. When you're done I put my shirt back on, finish my ice cream and we go watch some more movie. I wouldn't touch your tits at all, 'cause this is your curiosity thing."

"I'm not curious."

"Yeah."

"I'm not."

"Ok then."

"I suck dicks they need splints."

"Go 'head use that power for good." Yvonne truly liked Neon. The girl was funny.

"Don't you want to get out of here though?" Neon asked. "If you could go anywhere you wanted to and nobody was tying you down?"

"Misery loves company, girl, but you see I live alone."

Neon smiled. Simple words like that carried so much weight that it felt like Yvonne had given her the green light she wasn't aware she'd been looking for. Twenty thousand dollars was a lot.

But a girl could always use a little more.

*

Jim Cross had questions.

"Where's the shooting scene?" Cross asked. "The main characters haven't been shot at yet and I'm sixty pages in."

I only agreed to send you chapters because I don't care about this book, Barclay thought. "Most people don't get shot at."

"Yeah, but in these books they do."

"I'm keeping it real. And people with a habit of getting shot tend to be stupid. They're not reading my books."

"But they are reading Crosshairs books."

"No, you want them reading Crosshairs books so you're dumbing your list down."

"Sounds like we understand the business of this then," said Cross.

"Oh yeah."

"Then you'll have a good manuscript for me?" There was real worry in Cross' voice. How could one man have built from zero and potentially wind up with absolutely nothing? It wasn't as if there were that many black people of power in the publishing industry. Just like book characters, if you weren't specifically and clearly told otherwise, the default setting remained on white. Cross had built something that generated dollars, enough of them at one time to be on speaking terms with a major distributor. The second the larger publishing houses sniffed the amount of money Street Lit represented talk of a Harlem Rebirth was born. The Urban Renaissance was at hand.

"Are you giving me the book I asked for?" he asked.

"I'm giving you more than the book you asked for." Barclay felt good having said it. Neon could stand proud as a character now, somebody people wouldn't mind visiting again to catch up on things.

"I don't want more than what I want. Don't give me some overblown morality tale with deep meaning and delusions of grandeur. This book needs to ring my doorbell ass up and ready to make money." Cross laughed to drive his serious point home. "Sheet Rock Books just announced a subsidiary deal with Archway Ellison. Sheet Rock. The home of *Skanky Bitch.* That bitch Rowella Childs is now paid. I can actually write a book and I know Shakespeare meant for *Hamlet* to be a trilogy."

"No, he didn't."

"And I definitely know Rowella Childs and them sorry-ass wannabees at Shit Cock got no business outpacing me. Crosshairs Books is in it for the long haul. When hoochie bitch books are long gone and all these two-dollar 'publishing companies' have to ask MC Hammer for money, Crosshairs' authors will shift the proper gears and keep on moving. But for the next two years—and that's forever in our publishing— hoochie bitches are greasing the wheels. Ignorant thugs are greasing the wheels. Let me ask this before I read anymore: did you throw a white girl in there?"

"No. Why?"

"'Cause I'm looking to cross over. Do you have a clue how much *More Than A Mouthful* made?"

"They're making a movie out of it."

"Exactly, brother. That means fifty million skinny white chicks with lattes know that book inside and out but don't feel like they're as wannabee as they could be yet, so they need a movie. Hollywood does not fuck around unless dollars are about to get fisted deep inside asses. Ain't nobody making a movie out of *Ho Down!* And two ignorant niggas with a camera and their hooked-on-phonics skank girlfriends trying to act don't count as a movie. If you can get Neon in the hands of enough hip white girls who get it...do I need to go on?"

"No."

"Because we will explode the hell up so huge Colin Powell will be looking for shit to turn into presentations against us. I know you haven't been completely happy but I keep your best interests in mind, believe this. There's no Crosshairs without you and Wendy and PJ and Bea and Stefano and everybody else who trusted me to see their work presented like real books. I remember meeting you, what, five, six years ago? And now you've got three books out? Do you realize how huge a blessing that short span is? People go twenty-five, forty years before they're ever published."

"If they're published."

"Spoken like a soldier. Writing's a battlefield, brother. You gotta be willing to take it to the death."

"I'm starting a farm."

"A what? Anyway, you did your research. You know what these books need. I trust you."

"Netta's got those figures to me?" Barclay droned.

"I wanna say she put 'em in the mail Tuesday. They're on the way. Listen," he said and paused dramatically. "I want you to think on extending with me. You can be the flagship of Crosshairs."

How to put this without biting the hand feeding him? "I'll be honest with you," the words provided themselves, "I'm not sure how long-term I am for this."

"Don't give me that shit. I know me. I got into this because it seemed easy. You do this shit because you love writing. You've got an ink pen in your pocket right now, don't you?"

"No."

"You a damn lie," Cross said with that trademark laugh. This Negro made him smile in ways he'd forgotten how. "You've either got a small tablet in your back pocket or a few blank business cards in your wallet that nobody knows about."

This was why it was best to talk to Cross over the phone rather than in person. The man was shifty but he was as observant as a virgin at an orgy.

"You take notes," he continued, "because things come at

you at all times of the day. Most of what you write down you will never use, but you feel the need to write it anyway. Farm my ass. You had a goal when you submitted that first completed book to me...and that goal is not yet satisfied, is it?"

"It's a sin to waste people's time, Cross."

"It's a sin just being born, man! Where've you been, brother? The pope ain't rescinded those rules yet. Do what you need to do to get me this book. Fuck a skank if you got to. On the DL though, man," he said with the broad laugh. "Don't need a divorce messing with the rhythm. Just think about rolling with me a little longer. We can be on stabler footing. Don't send me any more chapters till you're done—because I trust you."

Life's all about trust, isn't it? thought Barclay. What you can trust, you love. What you're not sure of, you have to control. *Where do you put us in that mix, Cross?*

"I'll throw a white girl in there."

"And somebody gets shot."

"And somebody gets shot," Barclay appended.

"Then you can get all up in your subtext."

"The deeper meaning behind fucking skanks."

"There's got to be one."

He dropped in on his online community. Paradise Lost had posted another terrible, grammatically painful poem. Several folks responded enthusiastically to the topic Sell Your EBook Without Actually Writing One. WB Fields, a young woman with a picture of Mahatma Gandhi as her profile avatar, served up another thoughtful blog on the questionable state of global politics (there are no comments to this blog). Barclay knew she was a woman because they'd corresponded privately. Wilma Brown was twenty-eight, loved haiku, history and hemp (for clothing) (in that order), and operated on the passionate principle of the Higher Mind. Barclay posted under the name Loki Charm just to be a dick, but his posts were usually worthwhile and usually generated at least one response, at least until he posted the one that dashed the hopes and dreams of Nektar Sweet, Thong Song (the erotique postier), Philly Sax, and ABBA (angry black bastard attacks, but at twenty-three he was too young to fully register the raging irony of his chosen moniker). This post, being the result of bouncing around various online writing communities the past couple years, was gangsta:

If there's one thing we're pushed to do these days it's talk, and there are too many people who think writing is simply the physical equivalent of talking. I have no intention of being nice. Being nice means people who would be better off starting a garden or joining a gym are instead filling the world with useless, incorrect words. To ninety-nine percent of the ever-growing mountain of people considering themselves writers: you're not. If you're writing just for you, that's one thing, but if it's out there, whether blog or eBook or random post on Why My Dog Is My Lover *and it's all about how you have been passion to be a writer since high school and you feel that it is your opinion that in your words you are blessed to have peace that your writing...you get my drift.*

Main problem is writing is a verb, so people think that when they're writing they're "writing." No the hell. If doctoring became widely used as a verb, would folks decide putting a Band-Aid on constituted doctoring? Writing is a profession. It's not some grand, democratic, all-embracing activity that welcomes anyone with the desire to join the fold. A bad writer can't become a good writer. A good writer can become better. And a great writer, well, those are few and far between. There's the physical act of writing and there's the mental discipline of being a writer. Art used to be something special. Now it's American Idol *and everybody with a computer trying* to write Smak It Up 6. *How do we appreciate an artist's efforts when we wrongly say, "Aw, we can do that," when we can't?*

Dig out the album Around the World in a Day *and listen to* Pop Life *again. It's by Prince, you ignorant sonsabitches.*

We can wait.

I'm passionate about music. But I'm not about to stand up and make myself look a fool thinking because I can play the opening notes to The Beautiful Ones *I need to perform. I can air-guitar like a mofo, but put a real guitar in my hands and watch it spontaneously shatter. Somebody says to me, "You can't sing," I don't get offended; hell, I can't sing. But I do sing. I'll bop around my house trying my best to hit a baritone and melt my wife's draws off like the second coming of Barry even though I sound more like I need to take something for a cold and lie down. A lot of y'all out there cannot write. That ain't harsh, that's truth. And you don't get points for trying. That's what's wrong with the world, everybody wants the right to fail in flames of glory but get points for trying. No. Not when your lack of preparation guaranteed you were going to fail. Let's stop coddling ourselves, people. Do what you wanna do but be who you are. A writer is somebody whose words coil around your mind like somebody who's studied the* Kama Sutra *and is itching for his final exam. If they take you where you've been it's only to show you what you missed, but more likely a good writer is taking you someplace you might not have thought to go.*

I'm not trying to dash hopes and dreams. I'm trying to be honest. If you're more concerned about what picture you post or cutesy screen name you come up with in order to show the anonymous world that you have a fabulous personality, than with wondering whether you're offering anything to the stew by showing what you wrote, then, no, you are not a writer. President Obama had the word "elitist" thrown at him a million times. What's wrong with being elitist? The incorrect perception is that it automatically excludes ninety-nine percent of us (yes, I'm making up figures) from playing in the reindeer games. And if it excludes, it's bad, right, because that's how the Man keeps us down! Fight the power! Lovely people, to borrow the old expression, that's some fatback bull! Elite doesn't mean stay out, it means come on in, but wipe your feet and turn off the cell phone and keep your kid from climbing on top of the dining table and be prepared to be intelligent. And nobody out there (all three people reading this) better pretend America ain't the dumbest it's EVER been. Black folks, come here, come here: Listen. Enslaved. Yanked across an ocean. Separated from families. Split from their native languages. Getting the daily beat down in America. What the hell'd they do? They learned other languages—not the least which was ENGLISH—so they could communicate. What other languages do you know? Besides "Papi"?

But I digress.

I'm elitist. I expect a certain level. Not that I won't eat some fast food like it's Pam Grier on a summer day, 'cause I can tear the hell out of a Wendy's double, even when it's stacked up all weird by high school girls too busy flirting in the back to pay attention, but I will turn away from that in a heartbeat if somebody is firing up seafood peppers with baked sweet potatoes. Elite doesn't mean keep out. Elite means you ain't there yet but the door isn't locked. Like I said before, we used to appreciate good music. We expected Earth, Wind & Fire to pronounce from the gods; we heard lyrics full of emotion, metaphor, beauty—hell, damn near literature!—and we felt something. We felt the artist respected us. Artist brought his A game. Otherwise, it's an insult. You better not tell me Make Love In This Club *will be on rotation 30 years from now in the same block as the soulful anguish of the man singing, "I want you but I want you to want me too." I will kick you in the balls.*

Don't play with something you should cherish for life.

Love your art, and it will show love.

For those who want to learn about writing as a hobby, cool. Nothing but applause. Gardening, hitting the gym: same thing. Hobbies are the playground of the elite. (And for those of you thinking elite means money: I grew up in the worst ghettoes of Chicago; we moved around about four different times before I hit sixth grade; the neighborhood drunk—when he was sober—taught me to play checkers; I know poor and I know ghettoes, and I knew then—as I do now—that a ghetto ain't a place until it's a state of mind.) But don't write awful shit thinking somebody needs to see it. Write it, then put it away, then go out and meet somebody. Be a part of the world. Have no fear. Don't think you're a writer till you've put in the work to be a writer, same for any profession. Writer, doctor, musician, farmer, basketball player, film maker, reporter—do what you wanna do, but be what you are.

"I know I'm no poet, but I don't wanna blow it. I don't care to win awards. All I wanna do is dance, play music, sex, romance; try my best to never get bored."

If you feel all right let me hear you sing.

Nobody responded much anymore, even when he did his best bad-boy provocateur. WB did; they'd struck up an e-friendship (trademark, pat pending). Sometimes Paradise Lost asked a question, so she was trying. ABBA thought whining about how baby mama drama sapped him as a man elevated the poor decisions he'd made in life to art. Occasionally somebody posted a short story for critiquing. Mostly they posted to be congratulated for posting.

He checked on WB's progress getting a chapbook together. She answered him back a half hour later on his personal email while he was in the middle of rewrites on *Neon*. He switched over.

'Sad to hear you haven't had any time to write,' he typed. Commiserating with her was fun. He imagined she had the body of Sheba Baby and a library full of Joseph Campbell's mythology books. She was sharp enough to have been successfully published if she'd truly wanted, which she actually didn't. Online, among those who took themselves way too seriously and those unaware they weren't serious enough, WB Fields posted to play, sometimes Chutes & Ladders, sometimes checkers, and sometimes Russian Rules chess.

The office, washed with the tones of early evening, allowed for reflection and slow sips of beer. Various noises of a neighborhood winding down filtered in. This was the time of the day when he was no one but himself. Barclay wasn't a husband or a brother-in-law or Bela's friend, he was what his thoughts directed him to be, just this dude chilling quietly amongst thoughts and ether. WB wrote about her daughter's second birthday and how fascinating it was to see a blank slate taking on the mental twists and shapes of a bona fide person. Wholly untaught, the girl showed definite signs of a distinct personality. Granted the terrible two's were universal but Arielle Fields (nicknamed Strawberry for the thick tangle of strawberry-blonde hair plastered to her wobbly head) showed signs of intolerance toward stupid people—something most folks didn't learn till past thirty. People who babied her excessively with their baby faces and doofy noises got left in the lurch unless they had food. Having a child terrified her, not because she was a bad mother. WB knew she was an excellent mother because she was an excellent person. Simple math. She was thoughtful, considerate, and very engaging in person. She didn't romanticize the single mother experience because it was hell on earth; her husband had died of complications from pneumonia just before Arielle's birth. The woman in her died a little that day; the spark in her kept things going a little longer; and the mother in her upheld its nature: it stayed a mother. She suspected her daughter must have soaked up some of that in utero suffering and came out realizing time spent on fools was time unforgivably lost.

This afternoon she frowned at me in a way when I told her I thought both of us could use a nap that said, 'Please! Today I am a woman.' My mother never even looked at me like that, he read. *She seems to know that if mommy can't rest mommy won't write, and if mommy won't write, mommy won't cry. I don't cry around her a lot, but god bless the empathy of a two year old child, huh? I know you can't stand kids but you'd love her if you met her—[she'd wanted to meet him for some time now]—and might even get some new material out of it. The chapbook is on hold for a bit anyway. I'm auditioning for a play. I have never acted. Wish me luck. They say life is a dream and death is when you wake up. Just don't want to wake up screaming as I swap one identity for another.*

He typed: 'Maybe you're hearing a louder call for a reason. You're a talented wordsmith and you're a beautiful woman. Those pictures you posted of your daughter show she comes from good dirt. Poetry can come from motion (pictures) same as it can from an open mic. Transition that talent and beauty to the stage then the silver screen and A-list parties where you might remember me enough to invite me as one of the authors scavenging among Hollywood's elite. Please?'

He sipped his beer. It was starting to get warm, but he also had an appreciation for flat pop, so warm beer was ok. But warm beer made him have to pee, and he wasn't ready to leave the office yet, not even for that minor interruption. The separate world of the artist was a special thing, valued by the few and misunderstood by the many. It would be like going from a sauna to the arctic if he walked out of the office and happened to bump into Mario. Horniness in the case of the wife but same effect: a dislocated shoulder of the brain that he would have to pop into place Lethal Weapon style to keep functioning in their world. What he sometimes did, then, was to pee in the can immediately after finishing the drink, thereby returning the favor. There was no danger of anybody walking in and it wasn't as if he let the warm, High Life pee sit and congeal into green oily funk; the can got emptied immediately upon leaving the office. Nobody knew he did it, especially and particularly the wife, which added up to the perfect no harm, no foul.

He edged into his corner, looked and listened over his shoulder, and let loose the satisfying warm weather whiz that comes from loose shorts and sunny days.

Having an office was a good thing. At the old house he'd had to pee in the adjoining bathroom's sink to keep from losing that unconventional frame of mind.

He'd only stay in the office another half hour anyway. Early evening was the best time to take walks or get pulled into watching Wally and Terry play basketball. There weren't a lot of kids in the neighborhood. Most of the folks were older and settled. Barclay had made sure to research the beejeezus out of the neighborhood on that. And the fact that it was a cul de sac didn't hurt his feelings. He liked that most of the houses surrounding him were kept up and the neighbors for the most part had sense. The Royse house wasn't wealthy but they had enough to never have to worry about food, with enough left to donate to charities and save for their nebulous retirement. They'd talked about retirement often. They both knew they'd likely never see it. No free rides in America for longevity, if there ever had been. Old folks weren't working at Wal-Mart because they especially wanted to. When money came and went as it pleased, the first law of economics should have been There Are No Guarantees.

He'd married Marilyn in a church walking distance from their old three bedroom home. They weren't members but they'd had enough in their bank account that the pastor didn't mind. Walking home from their wedding in full tux and gown and having people giving them the nod, the car horn or the joyous laugh was the only thing he missed about the old 'hood. It was Marilyn's idea. They didn't live in the worst neighborhood in the world, just not the neighborhood they wanted to live in. Worse is always attainable; better takes finagling and a sense of defiance. A bride in white walking with train in hand down Clarion past front yard barbecues and dudes sitting on porches watching cars go by—and watching brides—definitely linked elbows with defiance in a march of 'we shall overcome.' Her chutzpah helped Barclay with the exceedingly high level of discomfort a man in a tuxedo walking through the hood endured.

They walked like the queen and king of England that long block from First Corinthians Church of Jesus the Christ Amen Lord Jesus God to their Clarion Street home.

The queen and king of England now lived on the eight thousand block of Axlawn.

The king, having relieved himself of the royal beer in the royal way, felt the usual momentary guilt for sitting in a nice office overlooking a very nice backyard that a lot of people not far from him would never get from life. With three books under his belt, however, the guilt barely pinged his radar before his brain ran toward thoughts of the outdoors with the fire pit, lemonade, and ahhh. Particularly the ahhh. The ahhh was like a woman with sex in one hand and silence in the other.

A second ping of guilt hit, expected on evenings like this when it was just too nice to stay indoors, related to the fact that he hadn't actually done any work yet. Ok, so Neon wasn't Shakespeare, but he still had an obligation to send the girl off well-dressed and smelling good.He promised the setting sun he'd get at least a few pages out.After he emailed WB a few more times. And maybe took a walk.

Mario appeared before him. "Your boy called."

"Bela?"

"Yeah. You were down the street."

"I've been home an hour."

"Not big on taking walks myself." Mario stood there. Barclay was used to Mario disappearing by now.

"Ok," said Barclay.

"Sounded like your boy had drama."

"New relationship."

"Yeah."

There must have been a malfunction in Mario's cloaking device.

"I was going to say 'women' but, y'know, my sister lives here," said Mario. "She's down the street. Citizen Kane's wife." Citizen Kane was a retired old German who cultivated about a hundred rose bushes on every available space of land at his home. His wife was even older and frailer and loved when Marilyn came to visit. They didn't do anything in particular, which was best for the old lady. She'd done enough living for both her and this funny lady who loved her cookies.

"Yeah, I saw her note."

"Yeah." Mario wanted to ask about the overarching theme he saw emerging in *Neon* of sexuality as liberation among diasporic peoples. "I think your boy might be gay, man," he said in one rapid burst then disappeared, leaving Barclay mouth dropped and unable to push 'What the hell—' from his mind. Barclay didn't bother calling after him. You don't call after smoke. He returned his attention to the TV. The writer in him, however, blithely threw out the undisputed fact that not every gay man tasted himself or overly talked with his hands. 'I'm just sayin',' the writer said. 'Hell, nobody really knows anybody else.'

"That," Barclay said aloud, wondering if this was cause for maybe another beer, "is for damn sure." He'd get back to work that night, definitely. Maybe. No, definitely. Maybe.

*

The phone rang.

"Hello?"

"This Plenty, muhfucka. Why'd you answer the phone?"

Le'Mon panicked. "Cause you told me to!"

Plenty paused a second. Then he laughed. "I'm just fucking wit you, nigga. How yo nuts be?"

"Tight and round."

"Mine loose and full of come. I'ma need you to bring that bag round here. Anybody else called?"

"Naw."

"You sure?"

"I ain't heard it ring."

"That might mean a lot of things."

"It ain't rang. When you need it tomorrow?"

"About ten thirty tonight."

"I'm on my way somewhere, Plenty man," Le'Mon whined.

"You think I don't know what the sound of bus brakes is, nigga? Betta get yo ass up and get a transfer and get over here."

"Naw, it ain't like that. My girl had to use my car to pick hers up from the shop and she got a flat, see."

"Ok."

"And her girlfriend with her can't help her do shit."

"Ok."

"So I'm on my way over now," he lied.

"So I see you 'bout ten thirty. Bring her by here."

Neon gon' fucking kill me!

"I got some dogs grilling on the porch. Hey!" Plenty Mo shouted off phone, "pop some more bottles in the fridge," then he was back. "You talkin' about Neon, right? She like chocolate cake? 'Cause I can have one of these niggas pop one in the oven right quick. I got some mix."

"It's hot and she probably—"

"Bring my bag by ten thirty. Now put the phone back in the bag and close that shit up."

Plenty Mo hung up.

Le'Mon looked at the old man sitting across from him at the back of the bus, but the old man wasn't paying any attention. If Plenty saw him walk his ass up to the house without a car around—a blue Neon—there was gonna be shit, plus it was too hot to be hopping bus to bus trying to get to Plenty's on time and then have to hop bus to bus to get home.

Everett stop was coming up. If he jumped off there and hustled to Kilpatrick he could catch the eight forty-five and make Neon's by nine.

She gon' fuckin' kill you.

He slouched deep in the seat. The backpack rested square on his groin and he reprogrammed intimidation into bravado, telepathically letting Neon know: Deez nuts! Deez big nuts. They were gonna run to Plenty's for a minute, head back to her house, break him off some, then drop him off at home.

Drop him off 'cause, you know, she wasn't gonna let him stay the night, y'know?

He reached under the bag and scratched his stuff.

Deez Nuts.

Nigga just might change his name.

*

The doorbell rang while Yvonne was in Neon's bathroom. She leaned forward and listened.

Man's voice.

Neon saying whadafuk.

Something about a quick run. Something about who you got over here.

Something about why you don't think to call, then him answering his phone was in the bag.

Hello.

"My girlfriend tryin' to have a ladies night," Neon said.

The exchange was a little heated but nothing Yvonne needed to break an ass for. Yet. There were some more mumble mumbles, a couple damns, then, right after she flushed and washed her hands, a little something dropped down about Plenty Mo.

She came out the bathroom quick.

Le'Mon's dick started speaking in tongues. Le'Mon's dick would've healed the sick. He stopped everything the second he saw her. His dick realized Le'Mon was about to say something stupid and stopped him by taking control, locking up everything except his eyes.

Ice cold, fool!

"Hey," said Yvonne dry as sandpaper. She went to the sofa, sat down and eliminated his presence in favor of the end of *Beastmaster*.

"Hey, how you doin'?" Le'Mon's dick said, giving her the nod. "Y'all got the eats on up in here, huh. Chinese huh?"

No, motherfucker, they put pizza in these little boxes!—this thought actually came from both women at the same time.

"Dang, I shoulda came over earlier," dick said, trying to be funny, with a grin toward Thundra but keeping one eye on Neon for danger signs.

"Listen," Neon said to Thundra, "I need to run him somewhere real quick."

"That's all right, movie's almost over," Yvonne said.

"Y'all doing a sleepover?" it asked. Le'Mon's right hand spasmed at an image of them naked. "I ain't see no car."

"You can wait for me if you want," Neon said hopefully.

"I think I will," Yvonne said.

"C'mon, Le'Mon." She snatched her purse and keys.

He rushed a handshake to Yvonne. She had to twist to reach, which smooshed her torso into cleavage a la mode.

"Le'Mon," he said. "Nice to meet you." He only gripped the ends of her fingers. *Nice one, nigga!* his dick complimented with pride. *Class all up the ass!*

Yvonne smiled at him with her eyes and nodded. She turned back round to see Beastmaster using ferrets as deadly weapons.

Neon barked from the doorway, "Come on!"

Le'Mon hustled out.

"I won't be gone more than a half hour," she told Yvonne. "More ice cream in the basement freezer. Make yourself comfortable."

Nothin' but a word. Door closed and Yvonne broke off the top and popped the bra.

Titties said thank ya, jeezus.

Titties wandered all around Neon's house after a while. Nothing better than checking somebody's shit half-naked and alone. The air was more invigorating, you were more agile, and damn if your eyesight didn't improve two notches or three. Yvonne made sure she didn't touch anything as she went through every room in the house.

Kitchen: tiny, cluttered, not a healthy bite in sight.

Basement: big enough for a washer, dryer, freezer and a pile of dirty clothes. Storage area in the back with a bunch of mish mashed stuff. Security guard uniform hanging up in there (make a note of that).

Bathroom: birth control pills next to the mouthwash; backup pack of condoms in the medicine chest; makeups and alcohol wipes. Shower and toilet were clean, toilet a definite plus (she hated being in somebody's house and there being the *need* to wipe down the toilet first—nasty bastards!). Lotions and hair products on the back of the toilet. One toothbrush: ain't got to go home but you got to get the hell out of here. Nice.

Computer area over in a corner of the living room: again, cluttered, sticky notes with cute handwriting (her name's Neon, she drives a Neon, she has cute handwriting: what are the odds?), bunch of papers and notebooks, crappy discount shredder, big ass dictionary (nice; spell check is for lazy asses who don't give a fuck if it's right or wrong), and an expensive-looking printer. There was a cutting mat tucked behind the desk table, and where there are mats there are blades. Yvonne spotted the handle and scalpel-sharp replacement blades under a sheet of cardstock. Good to know.

Small bedroom she used for storage: more mish mash, too many shoes, too many purses and a bunch of photo albums (save those for another time).

Another small bedroom she used for self: lived in and comfortable, dresser, chair, closet, mirror, TV, VCR, boombox and DVD. The closet door was partially open; she peeped past the clothes at things of more interest, like the brown box likely used for porn storage and the cylindrical hat box good for a variety of on the go fun. A huge print of a black woman dancing alone (ain't that the truth, sister) that she got from some mall (definitely not Shropshire) dominated the closet wall.

Where was the secret stuff that people who lived alone tended to hide in plain sight though? The revealing glimpses into their personality, besides the fact that her voicemail light blinked repeatedly with unheard messages?

Yvonne wondered about the people Neon didn't feel like being bothered with compared to the ones she did. Had to be some helluva losers. There were no photographs anywhere in the house, not family, childhood, friends, events or even just frames with those giddy white folks inside having more fun than anybody else ever will—which meant she was trying to wipe away a past. Not her past but a possible past that, if allowed out, might have possible repercussions on the possible present and foreseeable future.

Family will fuck you up, girl, I know. Get that denial.

The fact that Yvonne wandered the house half naked

gradually brought on a touch of horniness. Bubba was still curled on the bed but Nah, you can't do that.

And masturbating on the ground floor somehow seemed wrong without Neon there to give permission. Basement though? *Hey, gas man can do it, so can I.* Also? There were other flavors of ice cream down there.

Plus that light skinned Negro's essence still lingered in the living room, and she wasn't about to give even his essence any play. Essence couldn't sense a titty, but pussy?

Like a shark.

She went into the cool basement and leaned against the washer ready to work her button like she was launching the space shuttle. The second she was about to squeeze a nipple the phone rang. She stopped. She poked her head in the stairwell to listen.

"Hey, this's Neon. Holla back," then the shrill beep.

"Neon! You in there getting sexy? Happy birthday, it's ya birthday!" a deep voice sang out.

Yvonne found herself laughing despite herself.

"They got me covering another shift. I ain't forgot ya birthday."

"Ain't this some shit, we share the same birthday. It's my birthday too," she told the machine.

"I'll call you later," he said. The house was extra quiet after he hung up.

"She let me do that whole pretend birthday knowing her birthday was right around the corner," she accused this stranger's house, mounting the basement steps and realizing her hand was still down her pants. It was actually kinda sweet Neon wanted secrets. You never want anybody giving you all of themselves from jumpstreet.

When she got tired of wandering the house she put her clothes back on and settled in front of the TV looking for a show that might keep her horny till she got back to her own house.

*

He'd done quite a bit of writing before he went to bed. The brain ran around like a poodle after a treat. Barclay dreamed he was on the conservative arts show Words and Images. The interviewer, Diana Billiard, held an upcoming book as though afraid to get too much of it on her.

"Why'd yours," she was trying to get to, because the crux of the matter was this, "as a black man, have to be a black book? Isn't that restrictively limiting?" she asked, making sure the blank, earnest face was in place.

You're kind of stupid, he thought. "Is his book," said Barclay, nodding at G.P. Patterson, "a white book?"

Diana morphed the Botox into mildly charitable dismissal. "Well, no. It's just...fiction."

"Isn't he white?"

"I'm pretty white," said Patterson, best-selling author of *Primitive* and the soon to be a major motion picture, *Guitar.*

"Main characters white, G.?"

"Very much so, B.," said Patterson. He, too, thought the interviewer was kind of stupid.

"What makes his book fiction and mine ethnic, Ms. Billiard?"

"I wouldn't mind being ethnic," said Patterson.

"Sales aren't as good, man," said Barclay.

"Oh. What if I wrote the same book you wrote?"

"You'd get your ass kicked." When Barclay looked back at Billiard she was naked from the waist up. 'Obviously I'm not getting enough sex,' Barclay thought. Being a lucid dreamer meant tagging this thought for future reference.

Billiard hedged. "Well, your book is clearly informed by ethnic sensibilities."

"As is mine," said Patterson. Diana Billiard was an uptight

harpy both disingenuous and of questionable intellect but graced with a knockout body that guaranteed a sizable thirty-four to forty year old college-educated male audience. Wardrobe courtesy Dionysian. Career courtesy the foresight to have married a prominent cable news anchor.

Her nipples were slightly too tiny to be effective point guards for the reinforced troops behind them.

Dinged a point.

"So the basic question, then, is why am I secondhand smoke and G. here a fine cigar?" said Barclay.

"Cubano," said Patterson.

"G.P. Patterson is a respected author—"

"—of books featuring white folks who need the FBI to keep them from getting cut up in little pieces. Y'all some vicious G's, G."

Patterson flashed the three fingered W. It was the first time Words and Images had seen a gang sign.

"O.I.B.," said Patterson, the tufts of grey hair behind his ears matching his closely cropped grey beard. "Old Incongruous Bastard."

"My nig."

Billiard's neck went spastic.

"Is it because my characters are black? Or related to author? I'm not going to apologize for either."

"I wrote a book with a black character once. He got killed."

"Classic Hollywood syndrome. Incurable. Don't worry about it."

"What about being accessible?" asked Diana.

"Same question." She had a blazer on now. Didn't faze him. "How many books you sold, Patterson?"

"Rollin', B."

"Audience?"

"Milk and cream...with floaties."

"You, sir, restrict to a base most foul."

"A right bastard I am," Patterson agreed, crossing his legs and leaning into the deep slouch, white socks against a pasty ankle shining under studio lights.

"Black man writes a book with black characters, it's the second coming of Zulu. I denounce you on the grounds your nipples are too small, your logic shoddy, and your facial reconstruction fucked up."

"They expect you to write a book with white characters, man; show your gratitude," said Patterson.

"Y'all did teach me English didn't you?"

"Hell yeah. Show some love."

"Can I feature white characters?"

"No. Top billing," said Patterson, but at least he was apologetic.

Billiard positively preened. Why did he even bother with Words and Images? Sometimes the show featured interesting authors, but was that worth the anal itch that was Diana Billiard?

Clearly the wench thought there was safety in numbers despite G.P. Patterson thinking she was a shallow sow.

"If my premise is of universal appeal," she said and winked for the camera, "don't you think it's limiting to write in such a...focused point of view?" she said.

"Your basic premise is racist and childish." Barclay turned to Patterson. "Can I wax polemical for a minute?"

"Wax on, wax off."

"If a reader can't see beyond their own daily confines to embrace what is essentially a remedial primer on the comedic truths inherent to the disadvantaged—"

"Turtle Wax, bitchas," piped Patterson.

"—that reader condemns herself—"

"Watch out now."

"—to the limited sphere of second hand knowledge cursing the world today," said Barclay.

"Wax off?" inquired G.P.

Barclay sniffed. "Wax off."

G.P. gave up the fist bump.

Then an itch on Barclay's left nut abruptly changed the dream to a chase sequence featuring a Volvo, rabbits, and several varieties of pie. Just before he disappeared down the rabbit hole, Barclay awoke dazed, confused, and grumpy. *Bloody hell,* he thought, because at night after certain dreams one can be as British as one wants to be. G.P. Patterson was cool and a damn fine writer.

As he arose to scratch and pee, he tried to carry the fantasy of having actually met a real author into the real world. Barclay flicked the bathroom light on, blinding himself, hit the toilet with wild pee, did a quick hand rinse, then snatched a quick stare at the mirror, imagining Patterson winking from that reflective world. He turned his back to the mirror before flicking the light off, and quietly mused, *G.P., are ya wit' me?*

Hell yeah, Patterson reflected.

Barclay dropped back into bed with the thought *Cool* sweeping through the room as the sheet settled over his head.

Heroes made good companions.

Next day, back to work.

Thirty minutes after Le'Mon interrupted her evening she was antsy. It was like being at freaking work when she'd rather been at the club.

Forty-five minutes and she was tired of Plenty and his dinner guests hovering around her.

Forty-six minutes and she was about to embarrass the hell out of Le'Mon.

That's about three...two...one second out from: now.

She grabbed her purse from between her feet, blocked everybody's view of the flat-panel TV as she smoothed her skirt, finished off her hot dog en route, and headed right out the front door.

Le'Mon just kind of sat there in the glow of the TV and watched it all happen in slow motion. The weight of faces turning to him made it dawn that he just got the fuck left.

Yeah, that was her car starting up.

Oh, yes, she took off with the quickness. Yes, she did.

Here was Plenty coming in off the porch with another plate of dogs...

Heading straight for Le'Mon...

Dead in front of Le'Mon...

Frowning straight down his nose at Le'Mon.

"Say she ain't feeling good. Man, why you got her out here?"

Awwww, damn.

Somebody actually paying attention to the TV said, "Sit the fuck down, nigga, Bruce Lee 'bout to come on!"

Sometimes Plenty wasn't sure if he liked pussy or Bruce Lee better, just that pussy was a lot easier to get, head hang down rest in peace. He sat the fuck down and promptly forgot about Le'Mon who was wondering when and how he was going to get home since Plenty hadn't brought up that bag yet. All they'd done was talk shit, smoke shit, eat shit and drink shit.

And watch TV.

Plenty sat next to Le'Mon and damned if Le'Mon didn't feel this crazy bastard shiver with pleasure.

So he sat there watching *Game of Death* with his hands in his lap and that bag between his feet since Plenty took up most of the room, and at every commercial break there were loud discussions on whose ass Bruce Lee would've kicked.

"Bruce Lee couldn't do shit to Iron Man."

"Mothafukka, take yo drunk ass home!" the group said at the same time.

Plenty opened the floor for serious discussion. "Jet Li," he said.

"Steven Seagal." It was the little fool again. They ignored him this time.

"Ali."

"Yeah."

"Tyson."

"Hell yeah."

"Bruce'd fuck any nigga you put in front of him," Plenty said. "Be like, 'You have offended my family—Spla-kow! Get yo ass off the floor.'"

Everybody agreed.

"I miss me some Bruce," Plenty said and there was a moment of silence. "Only man ever lived who every man alive would brag he got his ass kicked by. Man say he got his ass kicked by Bruce Lee, what's a hard nigga do? Give that nigga a hug."

"Yeah," said Le'Mon, "if I'm gon get my ass kicked let it be by Bruce Lee."

Plenty turned to him. "See, I was talkin' hypothetical. Are you not aware that he's dead?"

"Yeah, um..."

Plenty looked hurt. "Yo tone wasn't respectful, man."

"Bruce Lee, nigga?" Le'Mon heard from somewhere.

"Plenty, who the fuck is this anyway?"

"And where them titties go?"

"You done fucked around and disrespected the dead," Plenty said staring straight ahead. "And when I take pieces of that sentence: you fucked around with Bruce Lee."

"Aw, fuck, Plenty, I coulda had my ass home now!" he said as Plenty took a deep sigh.

Plenty just chewed his inner lip while thinking of the best way to fuck him up.

Then proceeded to do it. Disrespectful mofo.

Cross leaned back after reading this. He'd told Royse not to send anymore but the man kept on. This was the shit. He'd definitely have to get him booked even though the man was not publicity-ready. Words and Images was always looking for the next Noble Savage; what better than the savage who'd learned English but went back to grunting and hooting for comedic effect? Barclay Royse and his savage irony would make Diana Billiard absolutely wet, and James Cross still had enough juice to make it so.

Tall, geeky writer mofo could thank him later.

Neon apologized over and over after she got home.

"I didn't want to leave your house open," Yvonne said, "otherwise I'da went home."

"He," Neon started to say but stopped. This woman didn't want to hear her trifling concerns. Le'Mon didn't own the Jaws of Life to force Neon's legs open so there wasn't shit to say. "You're probably ready to get home."

"Gotta work tomorrow."

Neon showed surprise. She'd assumed Yvonne was on disability or section eight or something.

"Fitness instructor at the Y," Yvonne answered her. "Every other day."

"Fat greasy people?"

"People wanting to make changes. I like 'em."

"How about our next lesson?"

"Day after tomorrow."

"Cool."

"Cool."

"Negro, what happened to you?"

"Not now, mama. Ma, why you still out here on the porch? Go inside."

"They're arguing down there again. Can't hear good in the

house."

He trudged past her, backpack in tow.

"Put some ice on your nose, but don't use the good ice," mama said looking at the result of Plenty's elbow to Le'Mon's nose.

"Mama, what the fuck is good ice!" He tried slamming the screen but she had installed a new pneumatic closer, so it stopped short and quietly shooshed the rest of the way. Paid one of Le'Mon's boys, Fake Rome's second cousin, twenty dollars to do it.

Always having to pull that door up? Too much like work.

*

Neon drove Yvonne home. She offered theories for Yvonne's quirky inclinations.

"I figure your daddy let midgets fuck you for money when you were little or something; or your boyfriend in high school gave you to a pimp to pay off some debts," said Neon. These were generally considered tried, true and valid theories.

Yvonne's face went white. "Who the hell'd you grow up around?"

"Some kind of freaky shit like that."

"Therapy is a beautiful thing, girl. Get you some."

"Y'know, I like talking to you. You keeps it real."

"So what's really up with your boyfriend and that bag?"

"I don't know. Fucking around with some crazy people."

"Seems like he got a little temper."

"Naw, only thing scary 'bout him is being with him too long." She got the feeling Yvonne was looking for more. "He ain't never hit me," she said levelly. "Niggas get killed for that."

"Yes they do."

Neon parked in front of Yvonne's house. Yvonne opened the car door and stepped out. It had cooled nicely. Be a pleasure sleeping naked with the windows open tonight.

"Next session cost you some barbecue, Neon."

"I know just the place."

Bedtime for the ladies, but later that night, instead of sleeping well, Yvonne paced. She had had the nightmare again. George Bush kept sending her into dangerous situations that he promised was the last time, and every time she'd complete one he'd say "Mission Accomplished" then send her out again.

War was a sumbitch. "Don't let me become a lucid dreamer," she muttered. "Fuck your ass up good."

(Back off here; Bush is no longer topical, Cross typed in red.)

Yvonne returned to bed. She flipped. She flopped. She rolled over. Who was up this late in the night? Hoes and drunks, but she wanted somebody to talk to. She always wanted somebody to talk to. Somebody she didn't have to think would laugh at what she'd say or try to calculate the clearance of their dick to the space between her breasts.

A lot of people woke up alone though. No big whoop. She dragged her pillow under her breasts, drying the boob sweat.

The undersides of her breasts hadn't been kissed in a long time.

She rolled quickly out of bed and paced a few more feet.

Even if she had somebody to call, it was too late if you actually cared.

She bet Napalm was up.

Midgets and pimps. She picked up the phone.

What if the girl was the type who picked up the phone during sex?

She put the phone down. Yvonne had called an army buddy once who'd done that, answered a breathless "Heh-lo?" Yvonne holding the receiver felt like she was jerking the unseen guy off with her own hand.

Nasty bastard.

Girls like Neon never had to wake up alone.

But even if all they wanted was to hold on to a man's sleeping Prairie Dog to realize it was the shortest choke chain ever, there was no disputing the physical truth of that leash in those hands.

Sometimes all a girl needed was a little concrete reality instead of dreams.

Whether Yvonne wanted to admit it or not.

Eleven fifty-six pm.

Neon groggily reached for the phone.

"H'lo?"

"Happy Birthday! I squeaked in under the wire!"

The automatic gloom brightened a little.

"That's sweet, Boo, even though you just wanted to see if I had somebody in here."

"Why you always do that? *(Fuck the Ebonics, man, just write this shit, Bela wrote.)* You ain't get my message?"

The red message light blinked angrily. Being full of bitches talking about sucking dick and eating balls, it was ready to purge.

"'Cause it's true," said Neon.

"You know you're my special. Feel old yet?"

"Boo?" She rolled on her back and stretched long and hard. "Yeah?"

"You need to know when to shut the fuck up and just say I'll be over to see you, and then come on over here with some flowers and even more chocolate."

"Oh? Oh!" he said, realizing romance and shit. "I don't get off till one."

"Booty be sleep then." She grinned and watched the floor fan's breeze play with her curtains. Making men horny was like playing jacks, easy, simple, and fun as hell. "Thanks for telling me happy birthday, Boo."

"Ain't no thang. Like I said."

"I'm your special."

"You need it, I get it. You wanna go out to dinner tomorrow?"

"Yes!"

Boo smiled. Booty booty, titty titty. "Dress up for it," he said.

"Oh?"

"Lobster Galley!"

"Oh." Every Negro in the world went to Lobster Galley as if it was something special. Hell, it was a restaurant chain, barely a step up from Ginny's but only because Ginny's didn't serve free biscuits and cheese.

"Lobster Galley," he said again in a sing song voice, "get ya biscuit on!"

"You need to do their commercials." A man taking her to dinner was a man taking her to dinner. "Booty got an alarm clock, you know." A fingernail had already found its way in the dark to a lengthening nipple.

"Naw, girl, I'll see you tomorrow, g'on get some sleep. We goin' to the movies tomorrow too. Hold on." She heard him talking to somebody off phone a second. "Listen, I gotta run out here and fuck a wino up. Pissin' all over the building."

Later on, he wouldn't want sex 'cause he got punched in the nuts.

Chapter Nine

"Let's get this party started right!"

Movie day, just like Boo had promised.

"How many?"

"Lemme get two," Boo said.

The skinny kid turned to his trunk and pulled out two CD cases. Neon thought about giving him one of her cards because she could definitely do better graphics.

"First run," the teenager named Springer said. He was the most non-descript white boy a stranger could ever meet, couldn't pick him out of a lineup two minutes after Nab caught him, which was how he liked it. Only thing constant about him was his car, and even that was grey forgetfulness on four tired wheels.

"These ain't even been released yet," Boo said. "Hell yeah!"

"Who ya nigga?" the boy said.

"You my nigga. Look at this, baby. I know you wanna see this."

Streptococcus 4.

"Zombies vomiting acid now," Springer said. 'Springer' because he was always ready to bounce up and out with the quickness. He was the best bootlegger the entire east side. Always knew what you wanted and somehow had it ready for you.

Boo checked the other title. "The Green Man! You got the Green Man?" Boo nearly danced.

Neon brightened and grabbed the case. She loved the Green Man. All that cosmic superhero shit tickled her draws off. And this was the director's cut. It hadn't been released theatrically yet but this was the director's cut. Springer was bad! Deserved much pussy for this, much pussy. Neon puffed her chest out for just a little bit of reward.

"Includes the trailer for *Green Man 2*," Springer told them. "Way they keep making movies at the same time I have the trilogy to you before the first one comes out." Oh, see, now Neon had to lean over into his trunk a bit so he could get a valley of tit. There was gonna be some furious masturbating tonight!

"Boo the fuck yeah!" said Boo.

"Hollywood hangs on my nuts, man, not the other way around," the lanky boy said.

"Look here, where you plan to be next week?" Boo looked Neon's way. "You wanna go to the movies next week?"

"Definitely."

Neon was happy but quiet on the drive home from the movies.

Boo kept trying to put his hand on her thigh.

She finally grabbed his wrist and dropped the hand in his lap, not mean but gently.

"You all right?" he said.

"Yeah." She bounced the DVDs on her knee. Boo was stupid 'cause he did things people told him to do. Right now he was driving too fast because the car commercials said so. City streets whizzed past but she wasn't concerned; nothing of interest ever happened out there.

She had a problem that amazed her how quickly and fully it settled. Problems were supposed to reveal themselves with a slow awareness because of how complex and huge they really were, the whole ant on an elephant's ass thing.

Nobody wanted to kill her. Nothing extreme like that. Nobody planned to sell her into prostitution. Selling drugs didn't mean fiscal responsibility. Hell, even Le'Mon didn't sell drugs. Le'Mon was a wannabe but not that stupid a wannabe. She hadn't witnessed a murder, at least not that she was aware of or that anybody would care about.

Le'Mon was not the problem.

Boo was not the problem.

The problem was, she didn't want to stay here. Day City hated its citizens.

It whizzed outside her window in the face of where she wanted to be. It was like the difference between accepting just a picture of Hawaii versus living in Hawaii. She was going to live in Hawaii one damn way or another.

"Why so quiet?" Boo asked.

"Nothing." She was bringing him down, and she definitely didn't mean to. "Hungry," she said.

"Biscuits and cheese!"

If I was a ho, she told herself at dinner, *I wouldn't appreciate this,* but she tore the hell out of some biscuits. She wished Lobster Galley would start stocking some real syrup like her grandmama—rest her—would sop biscuits and cornbread with but, hey, we shall overcome ain't for everything, right?

She spread butter and jelly on another biscuit while Boo sandwiched up some cheese.

"I'm not going in at all today," he said.

"I got you all day?"

"Well, y'know, later on I got a few sumpins to do."

"Oh."

"Not till six though," he added quickly.

That was Boo: the fringe man. She stared through the pattern of saucer crumbs.

"So what is it, birthday blues?" he asked.

"No blues today," she said, wondering who he'd pick up with once she was gone. She faked a chipper attitude. She smiled at him. "Life's a beach."

"And then we fry."

That was Lobster Galley's happily scrawled corporate slogan.

It hung over the salad bar of every one of their restaurants.

Ain't that some sneaky shit.

"Those have got to be the most ignorant passages ever written in human history." Barclay saved the file, shut the computer down, pulled a writing pad over, and spat redemption.

I sat. The evening sun faded. I knew the day would come when I would be found out. I saw it clearly: yanked from my home, marched outside with a crowd surrounding me for the last time in my life. I'd see men who had wanted to court me, men who did, and men I had loved; ladies who had confided to me their men had strayed—never knowing I knew exactly the length of each man's leash—and ladies who had invited me to teas and suppers. I would stand in the pouring rain, cotton gown torn, lemon breast showing, welts and scratches all over me as the rocks flew, and I would cry long and loud. Because that was my house. My dirt I was being thrown into, my hard packed dirt that did not want to be turned into brackish muck. Mine! And not one of them had the right to be on my land as if I had wronged them. You can't wrong somebody simply by being born. They would come for me because of some small slip somewhere. But I knew from where. Some things aren't a matter of time; some things are already over and done with, and we are slow to catch up. Abner had already said he wouldn't touch me no more. His words. "No more." I could have corrected his English ten times over but I didn't. I couldn't count on him staying scared to talk for too long. I know how fear always turns to anger in men. As sure as hell on earth is real he would be the one leading them, and none of them would wonder how Abner knew exactly where my bedroom was, and these things are always done in the rain when it comes to women. We are flung into the muck, slicked with filth and slippery, because that is the best revenge they get against us. I watched the sun go down. The only things I dreaded were the whips, because they were hot in the rain. I turned to the young stable boy, Abner's, who had snuck away from his chores to come see me. "The day is coming," I said to him, "when you won't be able to come over here anymore."

He looked up at me. Russet hair and hazelnut eyes, and those lips just like mine. I was the only one who let him sit in peace and follow the breeze sometimes, and didn't treat him like a slave.

"How old are you now?" I asked.

"I'm a grown man now, Miss Greer," he said, the timbre of his young voice growing into its final stage.

"Not yet," I said to him. "But you're about to be."

He wasn't smart enough to wonder what that meant, and I wasn't in a mood to tell him. I wasn't in a mood to do anything now but go into the house and touch things gently, the way my friends did. When the white ladies touched things it was always like everything in their world was made of glass. Sarah admired my red China vase, but she didn't know I knew she was the one chipped it. I stole it from the last person to ever hear "master" come out of my mouth—

Barclay stopped. That felt good. Then there was his favorite passage from *Onion Roll*:

Jerome was nice but she had learned not to trust writers, particularly poets. Male poets always struck Justine as men who never got enough ass. Too involved with romanticizing her faults after considering themselves lucky to have gotten to know her. Actually, having gotten to know a woman; poets are weakling misogynists, offering large houses with plenty of room to run around in; she usually found herself becoming exhausted trying to search out which room the artist truly occupied.

Martin, the first, she'd known in college. Sophomore year for both. Spent all his time trying to contemplate the entire universe until he found out she existed within it. Nearly brought the whole stack of cards crashing down.

   You see a woman dancing front of the fire

   The forest burns down

   The forest burns down—

Unfinished and juvenile, but she was actually dancing in front of a fire when he saw her. Fire in a trash can, sparks flying up into the night, paper glowing red, darkened at the edges, the air smelling of ash and beer. Justine out at eleven pm in front of a fire. Martin, the sophomore, sitting on the steps watching her. Four other students milled around the fire. It was chilly. The fire was more the alcohol's foolish suggestion than actual need for warmth. They could've simply gone indoors. They each lived in the old brick tenement upon which Martin outcast himself on the steps: Justine, her roommate, a mutual friend of both that roommate and Martin, and one other.

Whales were dying. That's why Justine danced October twenty-seventh in front of a trash can fire. College students needed causes, whether they knew this or not. In nineteen-eighty the fishermen of Baffin Island, following a three hundred year tradition, herded dozens and dozens of beluga whales shoreward where hundreds of family and folk waited with gaffes, tung knives and hip waders to meet the beaten animals inward. The brisk waters churned a bubbly red froth. Opponents said the whales screamed; proponents said the opponents whined. The whales were to be knifed left of the blowhole, severing major arteries and spinal cord. News crews filmed it, and because we are outraged by what we do, the news spread. Tiny thumb and index finger paragraphs in papers here and there for a day or two, forgotten for a little less than a week, then followed up in a few lines to show that those who concoct the news never slip up and forget the news. Justine had no idea what she would do about any of this. Whales were being killed. She danced aware. She danced specifically (but not intentionally) to draw attention to the facts of humanity, i.e., she was being ridiculous. To be out after dark on a chilly October night tipsy and dancing gracelessly to some private tune in protest to hundreds of nostalgic fishermen killing dozens of whales farther from Tedesco University than she had ever gone from one place to another in her life, with eyes closed to invite the universal mind (the audience she danced for), but being watched only by Martin who came up with those three lines of his unfinished Justine—that because she was out here being a fool as a direct consequence of those men's actions proved how ridiculous they themselves were, with their salty accents and crows-feet eyes...

The forest burned down. Publishing was a world of boulders and knives that crushed and stabbed with ease. Cross held Barclay's balls in his hands and massaged them at leisure. The cover of *Onion Roll* proclaimed itself 'A Barclay Royse Book' as if that meant something. There were no Barclay Royse books. Anonymity outweighed everything. For fuck's sake, he sat here writing a book home to the words "Boo the fuck yeah." Why? Because Jim Cross held his balls in his hands. Rebellion was excellent to dream by, but mortgage-wise? Not so much.

But calling a writer a hack was like calling out his mama. Unless the writer was a hack. Money then acted as an effective soundproofer.

Writing wasn't easy; getting published was harder; being lucratively published damn near impossible. Barclay recognized how fortunate he was to take up minor space in the major bookstore chains, a fortune shared with ten thousand other puppies in the window, but that didn't mean becoming a sell-out. True music had little to do with Pop radio. Barclay didn't need the online community that shunned him. Octavia Butler, rest her soul, wouldn't have wasted time calling herself Exotique Mynde. Harper Lee would have thought a blog required medical attention. Even G.P. Patterson admitted the last thing any writer needed was attention. "We are the unnamed soldiers, our books our shields, the world forever at war," Patterson wrote. "We die by the thousands, for liberty, for truth, for the godhead itself."

People forgot that almost every creation story began with the world spoken into being.

The word. Writing was hard freaking work, even when nobody particularly paid attention to the man behind the curtain, but it had to be done. Worlds rose and fell on words.

Heaven and Hell were simple matters of diction.

It wasn't fun having your balls in someone else's hands.

Barclay left the words in favor of finding Marilyn.

"You need to stop being a pussy," said Bela. "He's essentially paying you to write a book you could write drunk and drugged? Shut the fuck up and get direct deposit. Nobody's worried about those higher ideals but you."

"Shouldn't they be?" asked Barclay.

"I love you like a brother," said Bela, "But you're stupid. Listen, I need to call you back. Elaine's telling me I need to keep pads over here."

"Pads?"

"Wings and shit, man! She's riding my ass."

"I didn't mean my ideals. I—"

Bela hung up.

Elaine exited the bathroom pulling the door closed tightly behind her and saying, "Leave that be for a while. That him again?" She adjusted the elastic of her panties between the butt and thigh crease with an audible snap that irked Bela like a gaggle of tweens popping sugary gum. "He calls every time I'm over here." Which, counting this evening, made three times she'd stayed over. She plopped heavily on the bed and stared at him.

He stared back.

She stared with greater intensity.

It dawned on him that he was supposed to decipher this. He spoke quickly and without thinking; in situations like these, thought slowed a man down. "You still on what happened at dinner? Look, the white girl flirted with me. You think she flirted with me. Even if she did, it ain't the end of the world. I can't help who I get flirted with. I was just trying to find the cooked pieces of my steak." He should've known not to order well-done in a high end restaurant. That meant hold it over a lit match.

"You looked straight down her cleavage," Elaine said through tight teeth as if she didn't want his bedroom to hear her out of embarrassment for the relationship.

Elaine was topless. It's hard for a man to exhibit the proper concern under those circumstances. She could have told him she had malaria, tuberculosis, and eyebrow herpes and he would have managed, "Ok."

"And then gave her your business card!"

He threw his hands up in the air. The left hand still held underwear. "She had an MBA and was looking for work! That's all our company does is accumulate strings of letters. We don't create anything but XRPs for GNLs to cross with MCMs," he said, "performed by BAs, MBAs, CPDs and PAs. Hell, I'm ECGTS."

"Which means what?"

Like I know. "I don't have time to tell you what it means. It means we went to a damn good restaurant."

"So you could look down a white girl's pasty titties."

You don't even know what kind of cereal I like and you're gonna accuse me of peeping? But since the human race is predicated on men not saying half of what they think, he remained silent. He watched her pick up his remote and change channels without actually looking for anything. *Put that sumbitch down you can't respect it.* "You ready for me to take you home?"

She flipped.

"I said—"

"I ain't deaf."

If he'd known two weeks ago she'd be on her period he'd never have made the stupid reservation at the stupid expensive restaurant in his stupid basketball kicks with his stupid friend to impress this stupid, technologically-enslaved girl!

She kept flipping. Damn cable had two hundred channels. They might be at this all night.

"Then maybe—" Bela started.

"Can you put some clothes on please?"

Dammit, hell naw, I'm in my bedroom butt nekkid. He'd have to tell Barclay later about what he did next.

He put his hands on his hips Superman-style.

Buck naked.

Then he gave her the level, grown-ass man voice. "The woman bent to give me her card. I was seated. She's a client looking to jump ship. I turned to face her. Don't act like I slid a dollar down there. You showed a lot more than she did."

"Was she your date?" She gave him that stare again.

For some reason you're under the impression we're in an actual relationship and why do women put on makeup while driving? Park your homely asses in the back of the lot and take care of that! Hell, now he was angry at all women. "Elaine? There is no way you're jealous. I'm sorry. That cool for you?"

Women generally said more than half their mind. "I don't appreciate that kind of disrespect. You think I got dressed up so you could smile down another woman's tits?"

"I didn't disrespect you! That dinner cost me two hundred seven dollars."

"So I got a price tag?"

"Let me throw some clothes on so I can take you home."

"I'm not going home."

Fuh duh?

She pulled the sheet aside, stretched out, pulled the sheet over her, and kept flipping.

You better put a towel up under your ass! Brother literally sputtered for a moment. Awkward at being angry naked, he grabbed a robe then popped fists back on hips. The Superman pose was also good for utter disbelief.

"So what'd he want?" she asked.

"Book stuff."

"He really thinks he's a writer?"

"He's got books in the store."

"So does Lifah the Writa. His ass works at Wendy's. He works with you, doesn't he?" she said. "Y'all are like two high school girls."

He realized right then that she was one of those Black Hole chicks, the ones whose lives sucked so deeply that time dilated and stretched so unrealistically they could seriously believe a man loved them after three dates, and they were an old married couple after a month. That was the only reason to account for this stranger in his bed calling a grown-ass man WITH HIS HANDS IN THE SUPERMAN POSE a high. School. Girl.

"You don't write. Why's he calling you?" She caught what she was waiting for: that fire flash in his eyes. Superman pose all you want; ladies eat kryptonite as breath mints. She patted the bed, not invitingly but commandingly. She softened her eyes to let him know it was Ok. "I accept your apology, but that was still wrong, man. I mean, damn."

"So if she'd been black you'd have been cool?" he said taking his seat.

"Naw, you'd be in a whole 'nother world of it. Sista girl too."

"If you're feeling up for breakfast in the morning we'll head out. You ain't got a thing to worry about from nasty ass diner girls." Bela crinkled his eyes a little at her, a move he'd learned from Barclay. The crinkled maneuver itself wasn't new, but the Barclay Maneuver added that tiny lip smile to the edge of it while maintaining that smidge of perfectly devilish eye contact that made serial killers deliciously charming.

Of course, the following Monday, in the elevator, Barclay told him so.

"I didn't want to tell you so. Psycho Booty Trudy. So was the woman at least attractive?" he asked Bela, whose crooked tie showed he hadn't gotten much peace over the weekend.

This hurt Bela's feelings. "Of course she was. Tanned, freckled cleavage."

"You used peripheral?"

"Peripheral only."

"Brother, you win your case."

"Restitution and damages."

"So your girlfriend is crazy. Don't lead her crazy ass to my house. Your midlife crisis must be a bitch, huh?"

"Brother, you have no idea." The elevator opened on three. Bela stepped out.

"Ms. Royse?"

"Yes?" She had to look down. The speaker was just under four feet tall.

"My ivy hurts."

"Know what? You and I are going to find a nurse right now," said Marilyn, leaving the wall chart she'd been trying to decipher. She immediately made her eyes compassionate and cheery. Something was inherently wrong in a six year old dealing with anything more serious than two favorite cartoons airing at the same time on different stations. Six year olds did not belong in hospital cancer wards. That was wrong. Quite simply. And unequivocally. The kind of wrongness that needed to be seriously accounted for. Not being particularly religious, Marilyn nonetheless kept a running tally for if she ever actually met God.

She volunteered the last Monday of every month as she'd been doing for the past two years for ICU outreach at New Heights Hospital, in the various children's wards. She interacted with everyone: the kids, parents, nurses, even doctors—once the doctors had seen her enough to crack their primadonna shells—in the mundane ways ICU doesn't generally allow. She found she had a hidden aptitude for touching the backs of people's hands.

But she was there for the kids, not to make herself feel better, but because they needed to feel better. Most of them liked her immediately. A few couldn't stand her. A teenager had touched her butt on the sly and she'd let him get away with it. She kept a bookbag of books over her shoulder. A reading voice soothed all kinds of ailments. The cancer ward of New Heights needed that soothing.

"You're wheeling that IV like a pro now," she said, steering the small body with a gentle touch to the shoulder. The nurse's station was down the hallway and around the corner. "Are you even supposed to be up now?"

"Pop went downstairs," he explained. "It's burning."

"Eight Twenty-two South, right? Let's go stretch you out, and I'll be right there with a nurse."

Eight Twenty-two South contained about thirty stuffed animals bunched haphazardly along the window sill and all seeming just a tad afraid. The child's father was under orders by his son to bring at least one every day. Aaron hated stuffed animals. In that one word that encapsulated so much of a six year old's coming future, they were stupid. But a room full of stuffed animals would make his body want to leave the hospital sooner. So giraffes, monkeys, bears, elephants and several kinds of lizards cowed against the windows never knowing when or if they'd make a trip to the garbage but trying their absolute damndest to make Aaron cheery.

Where the hell were all the nurses? She hadn't spotted a single one the short trip back to his room. He climbed on top of the covers and went straight for the remote, changing the channel from one bright, chaotic commercial to the next, not worried now that his burning hand was in adult hands. She set her bag on the bed. "I'm gonna leave these books with you, Ok?" The boy loved to read.

Janitorial always knew where everybody was. Outside, she searched briefly until she came upon Ada. "Hey, baby," she said.

"Hey, hey," said Ada, pushing a waste container two times wider than she was.

"Where'd all the useful people go?" asked Marilyn.

"Eight Fifty. Birthday."

"The Baby?" There was a three year old with pancreatic cancer everybody called "The Baby." Cancer in kids seemed due to being born with too old a soul, because every one of these kids had the most wizened, soulful eyes, like the eyes of dead grandparents trying to keep a foot in the door. The Baby looked at people and made them practically want to kiss the hem of her gown. There was no way she was three. Peace and beneficence didn't come off three year olds in waves the way it did this girl.

Marilyn checked her list of regulars for birthdays every time she volunteered, and it was not The Baby's birthday. She moved off to Eight Fifty.

Four nurses crowded between equipment and family members, and The Baby beamed at every one of them. The Baby held a helium balloon's string in one hand and spastically jerked a bright green balloon up and down like a bobber. There were toys and there was food (of a fashion: blue cake with white swirls, which, to her delight, The Baby hadn't been stopped from gouging); people's smiles at her were so full of permission that The Baby couldn't help but gleefully smile back having decided there were things in this room due to be seriously messed with, and this looked like a good start to do it.

Marilyn got the attention of Nurse Flotila. She had excellent calf muscles; she was the shortest of the nurses but somehow always managed to find herself on the outer fringes. "Aaron says IV's burning," she whispered.

The nurse was out of the room immediately. Marilyn followed her, and whispered even lower when they were a good distance from the party room, "How bad is it for The Baby?"

Normally Flotila wouldn't answer, but this was a volunteer she had seen personally berate a father for abruptly stepping out of his kid's room for a cell phone call and taking a good twenty minutes to return. Hospitals, no matter how bright or cheery the walls were painted, were inherently scary places to children, especially children who, through the glances and codes of adults, knew they were very, very sick.

The father's blond hair had aged to grey by the time Marilyn was done with him. It had taken less than twenty seconds and three turns of phrase. Certain women are good at that. She'd gotten in serious trouble for it, but she kept coming back.

"Very bad."

"All right." Marilyn stopped walking. She ran a hand over her face. "Let me get myself together then."

"I'll tell Aaron you'll be right back."

Flotila walked away. Marilyn marveled at the resilience of some women, the efficiency of some women, the sheer femininity of some women, and wondered why in hell she didn't have some of that herself. She'd never be the woman

Isabel Flotila was.

She took a deep breath, ready to return to Eight Twenty-two South.

Maybe she couldn't be her, but she could follow that woman's footsteps, of that she was damn certain. She held to the smile on The Baby's face, readying herself for Aaron. A smile and a floaty, bouncy balloon.

The Baby's world was all right.

Even still, Marilyn cried in the shower for just a little bit that night. It's what real women do.

Neon went back to work.

"Obviously you think showing up to work is an optional thing," Charlene said the instant Neon stepped through the door the next day. There were never customers first thing in the morning. "That man came looking for you again yesterday. Apparently he didn't know you were sick at home. I don't like him."

"I called in."

It actually was where she was thinking of going to work as an optional thing.

"That doesn't mean I'm telling anybody who walks in where you're at."

"No, I mean—"

"I know what you mean. And I know he ain't attending community college with that backpack. Don't bring any craziness in here."

"I'm not about to."

"And these sick spells?"

"Charlene," she said, "I'm feeling much better."

"Um hm."

"Getting better every day."

When Neon got home she made cards for all her girlfriends and her boss, sweet goodbye cards (except for Sheela, who got the raggedy inscription, *Hawaii, Bee-yotch!*—Neon had never liked the way she treated her son) that she would likely never send (except Sheela's) but it felt good printing them out and licking the envelopes sealed. Even did one for Yvonne on the spur, out of a sudden happy feeling. She was just about to slide it in an envelope when the phone rang. She dropped it.

"Oh, I see you're at home now." It was Le'Mon.

"Inconsiderate ignorant rat bastard, don't be callin' me like you're wronged."

"Where you at yesterday?"

"Le'Mon?" she said as patiently as she could. "What'd I just say?" She sign-languaged over the phone. "I was out for my birthday," she said pointedly, ensuring he wouldn't say anything for the next few beats. "And the day before that I was actually trying to have some company. Next time you decide to just show up, don't. If you can't act like you respect me at least pretend you don't openly disrespect me. Why do you sound so funny?"

"It wasn't your birth—" he started to say and realized it was the dumbest thing he could've done but too late since, before he could work the tip of the tongue for the letter D, she went:

Click.

And left the phone off the hook.

Then turned off her cell.

Let him drop by now. There'd be a foot meeting a nut real soon.

WHY THE FUCK SHE GOTTA HAVE A BIRTHDAY! he railed at himself, swinging around ready to go to his knees.

Ok, shit was going downhill fast. His nose looked like a marshmallow, this bitch was trippin', Plenty had called twice since day before yesterday chatting as though he hadn't elbowed him in the face ("Anybody called yet, man?" "Naw." "Why you sound funny?")—and it wasn't easy carrying around a sack of fucking money without dipping in it!

Kot-tam sons a bitches, this was the ticket but why'd the ticket have to have a crazy sumbitch attached to it!

Of course he knew he had a sack of money; he'd been in it the first night he got it. Ran up to his bedroom, shut the door, zipped it open cautiously at first (in case of booby-traps), then quick while his nerve was up, and beheld unto him: a whole bunch of loose fuckin' money.

No, correction: fat fuckin' money.

A bunch of fat bills, and his cell phone, in a backpack.

"Goddamn sons a bitch!" he said again at the corner of Bono and Partridge. People looked at him like he was crazy, especially since he held the dirty public phone's receiver down by his knee and knees didn't have conversations.

Then a supreme calm settled over him.

Granted, he couldn't walk off with the money.

But he could hide it in plain sight. Why not instead of him disappearing with the money, the money disappeared with him? He could tell Neon somebody'd been following him. He disappears with the money. Plenty gets with Neon to see what's up. Neon tells him everything she knows. That somebody had been following him.

He smiled. Yeah.

When a man gets to thinking magic just opens up.

Take a memo: Neon trippin', make that shit up to her, mo better for you; go get some pussy from Ramona—she'd see the nose and the general shittiness of your being and lay draws on you, and yes, sympathy pussy is pussy; take ma's car (naw, I ain't gon' ask); pay Plenty a visit; let Plenty think all is well, I'm on top of this shit—wait, back up...

Pussy.

Thundra.

Thundra was over Neon's house.

Thundra knew Neon.

Thundra and Neon hung out at the mall.

Le'Mon's fumes of heavy dicktitude made women walking by quicken their pace away from him.

Realistically, Thundra was a long shot.

But, realistically, ain't that what a long dick is for? he asked himself.

And the little pocket preacher said *Preach On.*

At home he took the keys from his mama's purse and drove away before she even managed to rise up from the lawn chair.

He drove to the nearest mall. What did Neon like? Women liked chocolate. All righty. He walked into an elegant chocolatier, saw the price tags ("Got-damn!") and walked out. A pack of BabyRuths and a pat on the ass be more like it.

Naw, now, when poon is mad, gotta turn that particular frown upside down.

Think, fool, what the hell does she like?

A woman with a nice round ass appeared before him.

(Testify, Brother!)

He found himself in Tiddly Bits pointing out for the salesgirl titties and asses that looked close to Neon's size. He purchased a bra and panty set, dainty and delicate blue lace, sexy as hell with (preacher stomped the ground) zip front closure at the bra—

Say it again.

Zip front closure at the bra, so you'd never have to fumble at those teeny clasps at the back.

Preacher dabbed sweat off his brow.

Jet off to Ramona's. It was poon, it was tang, but it wasn't Neon. And he did wear a condom. Neon's one rule from the get go: you gon' fuck me without a condom means you gon' fuck everybody else with a condom.

Some people just make an art form out of ass. Brother got to respect that kind of honor and craft.

Ramona had a slightly lazy left eye and her lips were too big for her head. This would've been a good thing 'cause ugly women will screw dirty rough, but she didn't know a thing about sucking dick, which is an integral part of a man's spiritual well-being.

He made up a story for her about getting jumped by some bitch-ass mofos who he fucked up but, shit, brother can't catch a break; all he wanted was some peace in his life and not have to fuck up niggas all the time—naw, you can't see what's in the bag—and you know, hold up, just sit with me a bit, lemme put my head on your shoulder, rest my head on your bosom (Ramona loved the word "bosom"; it was lady-like)—and of course once he cupped her left tit it was on.

Bounce outta there a few milliliters lighter and on to the next point of business.

Le'Mon kinda felt like a politician.

Yeah.

Stay the course, baby.

"Yo, Plenty man, wassup?" They slapped hands and Le'Mon went right to it. "Listen, man, I need some back outta you. I been seeing—"

Plenty cut him off. Plenty never let anybody speak.

"You holding onto that bag tight for me, right? Look here, my cousin reminded me her birthday just come up and she don't get out much, y'know, just all up by herself, lookin' to meet some folks now so I'ma throw a little sumpin for her this weekend back in the yard, do it right, she ain't goin' for no porch shit and I ain't having all them niggas up in my house from before, I'm inviting real folks, so you and Neon come on by. Six o'clock on. Phone ring yet?"

"Naw."

Plenty slowly chewed his cheek. Le'Mon eased a step back.

"Couple more days, man," Plenty told him.

"I'm cool, man."

"Nigga, you just think you cool," said Plenty and slapped

him on the shoulder. "Stand back, give my nut some room. Styling and profiling on the hairy tip. Cool like a motherfucker. Oh, don't bring no foil to the party; ain't shit leavin' with nobody."

"I'm thinking I wanna help you out with some shit after this."

"What shit I got?"

"Yo shit."

"What shit?"

"The shit."

"My shit?"

"Who the shit 'round here? Kickin' is cool for you but I'm your man to get it done."

Plenty regarded him a second.

"That's some deep shit," Plenty said.

Le'Mon waited quietly.

"Let me think on it," said Plenty.

They slapped hands again.

Le'Mon left smiling.

Stay the course.

Boo was not Michael Clark Duncan big but Michael Clark Duncan's little brother big. Kinda favored him in the face in a puppy dog Green Mile Magical Negro kind of way. He was beefy enough to make that security guard uniform look like it actually meant something.

Ok, and he was stupid as hell but not in a mean way. Wasn't knowledge stupid; Boo knew shit. He was life stupid, surface comfortable.

He had two kids that he never saw since their mamas tripped way too much when he was around.

When it came to females Boo had one mantra: Fuck the Dumb Shit. Dumb shit from any direction interfered with the flow of juice, and James Beaurics Radley definitely preferred the flow.

(*"Fuck, fuck, fuck!" Barclay shouted, then immediately regretted it. Marilyn, in the backyard, looked up, and he was sure the kids were right on the other side of the fence. He sipped his beer, lowered his head, and kept typing.*)

Neon hadn't offered up the birthday draws after dinner. Granted, he would have had to decline (on account of taking that blow to the nut) but still though...

And she didn't want to tell him what was wrong, which was cool. Wasn't like he wasn't able to find out for himself. She'd told him to come by later in the week and they'd watch the Green Man.

Looked like Baby could use a little heroic-ness. Boo puffed out his chest. Whoever was bothering her would be found out.

Let a fool learn his mantra.

Thursdays were wander nights. Bookstore. Video store. Grocery store. Never after anything in particular; just generally reaffirming his place in the world. Tonight, bookstore. He'd told himself he wasn't there to check out the urban table, which made him inevitably feel like a paroled molester in a playground every time he glanced its way. No one circled the table for a change. He noticed a white girl in her early twenties considering it as she ambled along a nearby aisle. Very rarely were there white people at the urban table. There'd be a white girl every blue moon and a young white guy after a high-profile rapper had gotten shot, but other than that it was strictly a young black girl's scene. Or their older mamas or aunties. Wearing expensive, ill-fitting things on both their bodies and their heads. The weave hadn't been born that wasn't inherently ridiculous.

Barclay figured once she was assured there was no scent of predators this white nursing student would zip to the water's edge, peruse quickly, then disappear maybe with a sip, maybe two, into the thicket of self-help and romance where not even the most desperate predators tread.

He moved a little deeper into the bargain books section, still within eyesight but far enough away for a fawn to feel bold and safe. She moved in, straight for the table, circled once unhurriedly, grabbed from a stack, then departed. He immediately went to see what she'd taken.

Nigga, What???: A Thug's Poem by Bakon. *Dantay ruled the inferno of South Central, but what happens when B'Nydril breaks all the rules?* (B'Nydril, as depicted on the cover, looked precisely like the word 'fuck' if it wore high heels.) *The rings of hell are about to bust wide open. The new hood allegory from the red hot author of* Nigga, Please!

Bacon. Dante. Francis Bacon. Shakespeare. All within the same family. This was no accident. And since this was no accident...why was the young man writing this shit? His author photo on the back was standard hard life fare, but Bakon, whose book began "For a man to cry he has to be alone" but ended the same paragraph "...B'Nydril hated the banging he did in the world but loved the banging he did in her thighs," Bakon knew there was more to the world than thugs and hoes. Everyone knew this. Ignorance was not bliss; it was ignorance. A fast food diet created an indolent, decaying body. Same thing for literature, music, television, film and human interaction: just because what went in the brain was invisible didn't make it any less important than the morsels of food consumed. Barclay imagined Bakon might have written a true allegory about people and not paint-by-numbers cartoons; the young man was talented compared to the rest of the urban table; he clearly could create and control where he wanted his words to go in the minds of his readers, but he was opportunistic. He had the opportunity to write a book; this book sold.

His name was right there in print: *Nigga, What???* by

Bakon.

The creation of a world was an intoxicating thing.

And what are you doing, Mr. Royse? he asked himself.

I'm writing a hoochie book because it will get published, he answered. *But I'm not serious about it,* he defended.

Whatever gets you home, Mr. Royse.

Thursdays were wander nights.

*

"Bela?"

"Yeah."

"Road trip."

"What're we looking for?"

"Blackness."

"I'm on it. Be there in sixty."

"I want to come too," said Marilyn.

"You're already plenty black, baby."

"So are you."

"I'm not black." *Brother Black,* he thought, *Blood even.* "Wally told his friends this neighborhood is quiet 'cause it has so many white people in it. Depressed the hell out of me. I like quietude."

"You're black, baby," she reassured.

"Not anymore." He pointed out the window behind him. "When a kid equates blackness with noise and chaos, I give up my card."

"You can't turn the Race Card in."

He opened his hands to the air. The invisible weight plummeted. "Done. I'm through. Let everybody else be black, whatever the hell that is. I'm not even African-American. I've never been to Africa. Angelina Jolie is more African than Compton and Detroit put together! African-American my ass! That's just to make us feel good. We don't know what we are. We're mutants. Might as well call us the X-Men."

"Get your rant on, babe," Marilyn said, peeling the husk off a large ear of corn and dropping the yellow torpedo into a pot of boiling butter water.

"Something ain't right about a kid thinking black means loud and stupid, Lyn. And if just one kid thinks it, the human race is doomed. And it's not like this neighborhood is full of white folks. They're the minority here. If I'm booshie, let me be booshie right, move out to Fuck You Heights and only see another black family in the bathroom mirror."

"Will you two eat before you leave?" she asked, knowing he didn't want her to come and fully OK with that. If her man needed Sancho Panza in a moment of Don Quixote, it was cool. She'd be home waiting for when he was Barclay again.

"You doing the pineapple glaze for the chicken?"

Marilyn nodded.

"Yes," said Barclay.

"I bought you some more writing pads. They were on sale. In the foil drawer."

"Sweet."

"And don't be too late out there."

"We won't."

"Can you check the chicken for me?"

He peered in the oven. Chickens remained dead and browning. All was good.

"Honey?" she said.

"Yep?"

"Call me when you find Black America."

"I will."

"First thing we need to do is hit the corner store," said Bela, eager for doofy distraction. "White America has no corner stores. That's significant."

"What about poor folks?" Barclay pointed out.

"If they're poor they're not white Americans even if they're white. Says so on their shirt labels. You gotta pull the tag out.

How many corner stores you had in the old 'hood?"

"'Bout six."

"How many now?"

"One."

"One that actually sells food, man," Bela pointed out. "That's a market, that ain't no corner store. Corner stores are the first measure of blackness. We go there."

They drove the shiny new car to Action Market, about ten minutes off the Boulevard. Several cars more expensive than his were outside, so Bela was cool. Even factoring in random chaos theory, there was a hierarchy to theft.

A woman with droopy breasts and the nastiest tee shirt they'd ever seen—and don't forget they were some nasty men; Barclay peed in cans, and Bela, Bela was a crying shame—sat on an overturned metal trash can beside the building where an overflowing dumpster emitted visible stink into the alley. She stared at the ground and didn't stir at all. Her tee shirt was the once popular 'Don't Ask Me For Shit' model from the nineties, the one replaced by 'Ghetto Fabulous', then a whole bunch more printed shirts and clothing till it was cheaper just to tattoo something on your neck and forget about it.

She could have been anywhere from twenty-five to fifty under her life, and the sun had baked her the consistency of coal dust.

Three teens and a thirty-something stood opposite the store's entrance. A cinderblock kept the door open. All three teens' hands moved idly under their floppy shirts. Itchy bellies were epidemic in the black community, as well as sudden ass deflation (SAD—as evidenced by the pants hanging off asses). Droopy britches pooled at their knees like a Looney Toon squished by an anvil. Resigned to their condition until a telethon showed up, the boys held their faded pants precisely below ass-line, showing the necessary amount of boxer shorts to illustrate their righteous displeasure at the United States' unwillingness to replace its outdated socio-economic system with a more agrarian, cooperative mode of commerce.

"Got that weed," the one nearest the door mumbled as Bela and Barclay passed.

Etiquette prevented responding verbally; either money was exchanged or you kept moving. Which they did.

That feeling of stale humidity from stepping into somebody's musty, poorly-lit basement with bare feet was exactly the feeling Action Market nailed. And Barclay was sure chocolate bars and candy weren't supposed to smell like cheese.

The sheaf of Plexiglas protecting the owners from the customers hadn't been cleaned in a while. The two Chaldean dudes operated the store in a haze of Vaseline, and both were actively involved in arguing with an old man outside the lottery window who repeatedly told them, "Two seven two! Fuck you don't understand about that! Two seven two!"

"Check your numbers before you leave!" the fat one (whose name was not Laurel, but hey) said.

"I told him, I told him," said Hardy.

Barclay looked at the display showing what that evening's winning lottery was, pulled a half hour ago.

Two seven two.

"I didn't ask you for two seven three. You heard me! Two seven two!"

"Check your numbers!"

"No, no," added Hardy, "write your numbers down. Slips! Slips right there! Whole stack. Nobody uses them."

The old man knew from experience that once either shopkeeper's hands went up the entire matter was over and they'd quickly put him out before he had purchased his bottle, which meant a double wasted trip.

But those winning numbers would have been five hundred

dollars, and five hundred dollars demanded a definitive and clear statement of an elder's assessment of their customer service policies, as well as the promise of overt hostility during all future interactions.

"Fuck you!" the old man said, flinging the non-winning ticket at the window. "Gimme the Cutty."

"Which one?"

"Dark!" growled old Grizzly.

Laurel slipped a squat brown bottle from the wall-to-wall behind him into a brown bag and the bag into a turnstile which he kept his hand on until the belligerent old fuck slid money into the tray. Laurel plopped change into the silver tray. A plastic cup joined the brown bag, and both items spun their way to the old man.

The elder further clarified that, under the rules of civility, this was, for immediate purposes, resolved but far from over, by loudly proclaiming "Motherfucker!" He left the store.

"Yeah, yeah," said Hardy, then said something that didn't require a Rosetta stone to figure was "fuck you," while watching Bela move down the canned goods aisle and Barclay the freezers.

Action wanted two dollars and fifteen cents for a small can of soup, and black folks paid this.

Expiration dates were more suggestion than caution, and folks accepted this.

Bela rounded the aisle. The ripped linoleum was unsettling. A couple kids fought over how much money one had and why she wouldn't buy chips to go with the honey bun.

"Why you gotta be a bitch all the time?" her skinny younger brother whined, not caring one way or another about Bela standing there.

She turned away when he tried to force the chips into her arms.

"I know you got enough!"

"No!"

"Just get this!"

"No!" She spun, leaving him and the chips on the sticky floor. They might have been eleven and nine. The boy stomped after his honey bun. The chips stayed on the floor till Bela returned them to their home in the "reduced for quick sale" rack. He went to the front of the store. The porn magazines with pouty, sultry, fuck-me faces peeping above plastic covers and black bars (by law) lay under the register counter, the ultimate impulse buy. The kids paid for their stuff, desensitized to the porn whereas Bela snuck a peek where somebody had tried to rip the black plastic off one. They ran out still arguing. Having an older sister himself, Bela knew the boy would get smacked a good enough distance before they got home that by the time they got home he wouldn't bother to tell on her. Siblings calculate such things better than a supercomputer.

Laurel and Hardy wondered whether Bela and Barclay planned to buy anything. They pretty much knew the faces in the neighborhood. Unknowns simply perusing the store were rarely a good thing. They didn't look like robbers, but Laurel and Hardy didn't look like they could field strip an AK-47.

Which they could.

Barclay met Bela up front.

"How you doin'," Laurel tossed at them through the glass. Hardy was on a cell phone call.

Barclay nodded, thought about buying something for the sake of it, saw an injured roach trying to crawl to safety, gave Bela the nod, and they bounced.

They passed the three teens and the older guy. Nobody said anything. It was understood: they still got that weed.

Next store, Pioneer Express. Then Mr. C's (because no matter where you go in the world, even tiny Chinese provinces, there is a store called Mr. C's, none of them affiliated, but all of them having pizza and hot dogs). The one thing about corner stores is that none of them serve any actual useful purpose whatsoever. Doctoral theses could probably be written on the fact that every single one advertised liquor, beer, wine, lotto and food, in that order, on blinking signs or crude but colorful storefronts. Inside, cheap, carcinogenic individual blunts were sold to anybody who had pocket change. Every poor black neighborhood they went into, only one out of four corner stores were run by blacks; in the white neighborhoods, whites ran them. In the search for Black America, Barclay made a mental note: Black America didn't own much of anything. Near the more affluent neighborhoods, where corner stores became convenience stores or markets and the liquor sold there was for "entertaining" rather than knocking back, ownership was representative of the racial makeup, the stores had better lighting, and the porn section was smaller and behind the counter.

Poor neighborhoods tended to be loud, about equal to club night at one a.m. Most rap was crap (most anything mass-fed was crap) but why was all the crap concentrated in the poorest areas? Music that sounded like somebody trying to punch a head repeatedly was not cruising music. Cars blasted beats that sounded like giants slamming concrete. One car actually made Barclay's fillings vibrate.

Kids of all ages traveled in packs. Teens traveled in packs. People stood on their front porches and talked loudly to people standing right next to them. Nobody described a dream they had. Nobody practiced a musical instrument, unless they did it in their basement. Barclay was sure there were some kids out there who'd love to learn to play guitar. Hell, he'd love to learn to play guitar.

He and Bela counted how many young men they saw with shirts either off or pulled to hang inexplicably off one shoulder. Black America was apparently too hot for its shirts. And twelve year old girls wore shorts that back in the day he'd masturbated to on grown women. Black America didn't get its share of fabric. The Man was capricious.

At East David Village they got out and walked a few blocks. *Black America's kids cuss better than I do,* Barclay noted:

"Bitch, get the fuck back!"

"Fuck you, motherfucker!"

"Suck this! Suck this, ho!"

The arguing group of boys and girls parted ways, still arguing loudly, but a Hanna Montana marathon was about to begin on one channel, and Gundam Fighters on another.

"How deeper you wanna go?" asked Bela, stifling a laugh.

"Heart of Darkness, man."

The dice corner. Thugs didn't play dice as much they used to but there were still those diehards, meaning which they hadn't been shot yet for winning, so they played it extra hard.

For all the hand twisting, there really was no skill involved. Dice bounced across pavement and you hoped for a favorable number. Black America embraced chaos theory.

Money, hands and dice shot out in flurries of motion. Bela and Barclay stood far enough away so as not to be a threat but close enough to warrant being looked up and down by the boys on the fringe, whose quick assessment was the game was more important than these two. They immediately returned to see whose boy was about to lose how much money.

Which apparently was a lot.

There are ways to say "Fuck!" that convey the absolute despair forced on a man whose options have left him a course of violence so clear it grants clairvoyance to those in range of the word. Throw in a sudden reach for a gun and it became obvious that Black America was still number one in sprinters.

The small crowd busted.

Leaving Barclay and Bela standing there.

With a dude with a gun. Who saw them, ignored them, returned the gun to the pocket of his baggy jeans, and stalked off to where his boys waited.

"Your wife will fucking kill you," whispered Bela.

"Get the fuck in the car," said Barclay. The car was down the street. They would have to pass some of the scattered folks to get there, but it would look too stupid going way down another block the long way.

The problem was solved when somebody from the gunner's crew shouted, "Punk ass bitches!" at the sprinters, negating any sense of caution on the runners' parts, who had guns themselves and decided to show them to the other crew. Who ran.

There's something inherently comical in seeing two groups of aggressors trying to run fast while holding up pants with one hand and trying to keep their guns from jangling too much with the other, looking like penguins trying to hop and powerwalk at the same time. Nothing inherently comical, though, in inadvertently catching a bullet in one's ass, so Barclay and Bela exited with the quickness.

Black America supported the NRA.

They drove a ways, parked, and waited for their hearts to catch up to the car. Deep breaths in and out, and the shared thought that it was due time to head home.

A huge pit bull walking a guy brushed the car. This was the sixth combo they'd seen like that.

Black America loved animals if they were big and mean and reflected the potential to consume small children favorably, seeing as it took a real man to control a beast like that. And Black America was hard, of that there was no doubt. Hard like diamond, but the analogy, sadly and for far too many, pretty much stopped there.

There's no beauty in being poor, Barclay wrote later after reporting to Marilyn that they "Drove around." *Being suggests totality. We can live in poor circumstances, but we are not poor. Shouldn't have to search so deeply for beauty when poor. It should be right there, because there is where you are.*

And you damn well deserve it.

The search for "Black America" bothered him until he finally had to lie down, grab the remote, and turn on the TV.

Cross was pleased with where the book was going. He'd reached the section where Yvonne removed the dog tags when she meditated: It was the only time the metal didn't nestle at her breasts.

Yvonne drew in the small cleansing breath and held it till the deep breath beckoned. She held the deep before releasing it slowly and without effort in exchange for improved Chi. Her fingers folded themselves for proper channeling. The interior of her hollow was fertile.

She planted the seed.

Plenty's people.

Plenty's people.

Plenty's people.

Trifling people.

A party at cousin Plenty's house when she'd rather have her clit circumcised by a pro-life Klansman.

Ok, start over. Small—no, hell with it, deep ass breath and hold it till you pass out.

Plenty had always shown a weird kind of regard towards her and she'd never known why (it was because she had developed quick and he'd overheard his daddy talking about her titties like he wanted cake).

According to Plenty (Steve—Plenty Mo was the dumbest shit a Negro'd come up with yet) he'd developed quick too. After his first run to prison people would have thought jails were some kind of secret Holiday Inn that provided exotic poon at the right password. That's how Plen—Steve told people he became a man.

Dumb motherfucker.

Ok, obviously meditation wasn't going to do it.

She opened her eyes and slipped her tags back on. They clinked before settling at ease above naked boobs. Yvonne ascended the basement stairs with a determined look.

Where the hell was Bubba?

For the party Yvonne decided to wear a dress so she'd feel like a different person going over there. Later she could tell herself all about the craziness and she'd laugh and say *Well, better you than me.*

It was a simple orange summer dress that hit her at the calves and flowed with her hips. She wore white sandals. She dropped her dog tags into a slim white purse and strapped the purse over shoulder and neck so it wouldn't have a chance to walk away. She'd styled her hair the night before into fresh ringlets. A little spritz and a little mousse and she walked out the door with that just-showered look that always makes a man think of pussy.

And she could read a flared nostril better than anyone.

Plenty had one of the larger houses in the neighborhood, all brick and all secured, with a large backyard a landscaper could have had fun with. Escalades and Hummers dominated the parking along the entire street. Joe Chevrolet made do wherever he could.

It had been a surprise hearing from Cuz. He kept his ears open to the neighborhood for her, but to actually hear directly was a special treat. And on top of that he was expecting the finest woman he'd ever seen to spend an evening of shrimp and barbecue with him.

And there she was. Neon.

Plenty didn't care how he'd done it but Le'Mon had gotten Neon in all her tank-topped blue-jeaned glory to come supp in his abode.

Basically, the boy had begged like an orphan, holding the dainty Tiddly Bits bag in hand.

"Plus," he'd said, "When you're ready to go, you go."

"How about I don't want to go at all."

That's when he got religion and begged forgiveness for his sins. "I'm a man, y'know," he said sadly. "This world hard on niggas," he kept on, as if the last thing in a perfect world he would ever do was forget her birthday or treat her with anything less than queenly respect.

Let it be known that the sun tended to glint off his yellow skin.

"Le'Mon, you're lighter than a white boy!"

"I'm trying to say," he said levelly, "you're gonna have a nice time. We eat, do some horse shoes, get some drink and we're out; he said he's having the thing catered. After, whatever you wanna do is what we do, wherever you wanna go is where we go."

At the party he managed to pull Plenty's leering ass aside and said, "Look here, Plenty. She said she wasn't going nowhere with me I gotta carry this bag around. You got someplace up in here I can kind of rest it a bit?"

"Keep the phone on you though?" Plenty said, craning his neck for a view of jeans.

"Definitely, man. Vibrate on my balls."

They weaved through people, through cancerous pockets of gas station cigars and through snatches of weed.

"Guest of honor is on her way," Plenty rambled through the house. "Had to make a stop, got stuck in traffic. She's the one told me to start the motherfucker on time too. You got Neon sumpin' to drink didn't you?"

"Oh yeah."

Crowd density thinned deeper into the house. An empty cheese tray rested on a hall table. "Who ate all the goddamn cheese already? Somebody betta fill that cheese tray back up." To Le'Mon: "Cuz loves her some cheese and crackers." Coughing came from the kitchen as they passed. Plenty backed up.

"Get yo coughin' ass away from the food, nigga!" he told a boy about nineteen wearing a dirty smock. "One of my boy's niece's boyfriends," he explained to Le'Mon. "Trying to have a catering business. I'll throw a muthafucka some help when they need it. You washed them hands, didn't you?" he called back to the kitchen.

"Man, why you trippin'?" the boy shot back.

Plenty moved on.

"You know I don't wash no hands," he didn't hear the boy say.

Nobody went upstairs. Ever. Plenty never said anything but it was understood: put your foot on that step and he'd put something hot in ya ass.

Now you could take that two ways.

He led Le'Mon to a small back bedroom and shut the door. The room was full of unmarked cardboard boxes. Le'Mon dropped the bag on the bed, quickly unzipped it and removed the phone, re-zipped it and handed it over to Plenty, who chucked it on the twin bed before leaving out, saying only, "Lemme know when you're fixin' to leave."

Neon fought a losing war to sit off by herself. They were four deep on her, steely as sharks. She'd managed to deflect them so far with little bops to the snout but it was only a matter of time before one became bold enough for a bite.

She noticed Plenty approaching and actually felt relieved for a second.

The sharks veered off.

"You out here in the sun," Plenty said to her.

"Need anything, babe?" said Le'Mon.

"I'm good," she said. As soon as this dumb ass cousin came along for Plenty to round up his drunk/high friends for this sorry Happy Birthday she planned to bounce like Tigger.

"Let's go see if them skrimps is ready," Plenty said to Neon with a playful nudge on her bare shoulder. Creamy skin. All lotioned up. Warm and naked, probably got the thong, left nut stand up, break into a song—

She made sure to catch Le'Mon's eye before rising to follow Plenty, who immediately snailed up.

She passed Plenty and her ass brushed the back of his hand: innocent elevator contact: he ain't even notice.

Left nut clap your hands!

Birthdays were so good. Plenty Mo was a kid at a carnival and he could eat everything he damn well pleased.

"It's cooler in here," he said when they got to the kitchen. "Jahmone? (Named for the noise Michael Jackson made) Shrimp up?"

"Not all of 'em," said the boy, and wiped his forehead with his smock's sleeve.

"Put what you got on a plate. Me and the lady need a nibble. You had some drink yet?" he asked Neon.

"Some pop."

"I mean some drink. I got champagne." It was champale.

Jahmone handed Plenty a plate of fat shrimp. Plenty passed the plate to Neon, telling her to find a seat while he hooked up real drinks.

He had Jahmone mix champale on the rocks with a vodka and lemon twist in two big tumblers.

Jahmone had noticed the roundness of that ass.

Plenty popped out then poked his head back into the kitchen.

"Jahmone!"

"Yeah?"

"Dot dot dot diddly daa da!"

Chapter Ten

"The Fucking Bridges of Madison County!"

Two times. That's how many times she refrained from introducing knuckles to Plenty's famous left nut. He managed to tap her ass on the sly twice before she'd even downed three shrimp.

It's too loud over here, let's move over there.

You wanna get by the fan?

It was a huge tower fan set on high. It blew her tank top against her in all the right ways.

"It's always good when you come around, y'know; I don't see you too much."

She smiled a little and shoveled shrimp in her mouth.

"He all right with you?" he said, nodding toward the invisible boyfriend.

"Yeah."

"Everything cool? You come 'round here anytime you feel it," he said, not even trying to hide the tone of voice that licks nipples.

She knew his eyes were trapped in her cleavage. She hated feeling short and small next to his tall ass.

"My boy is supposed to be along with some new movies today. Cuz likes the oldies. Pam Grier and shit."

"I saw Grier last week."

"Blacula?"

"Yeah."

"I saw that too. Pam was the Absolute Shit in the day."

"She ain't now?"

"I'd still bust a nut, but you know that one new girl—" He couldn't think of the name. "She was in that crazy ass black and white comic book movie—"

"Sin City."

"That was some sick assed shit!" Plenty laughed around a mouthful of shrimp.

"Rosario Dawson," Neon told him.

"Yeah, that's some crystal ass. No-ass havin Jolie needs to sit the fuck back and let a girl step up. All right," he said, bobbing his head, "I see you like movies, all right."

"I already got the Green Man," she said, wishing she'd shut up.

"White boy?"

"Springer."

"That's my boy! Devious little nigga. I got that one too. Shit, I got boxes of shit upstairs. I got horror, I got science fiction, hell I even got the fucking Bridges of Madison County 'cause my boy Clint's in it."

"You cussin' in front of a lady, muhfuckah!" somebody said passing through.

"Nigga, we speak French up in here!" To Neon Plenty said, "Don't mind my mouth."

"Parlez vous."

Plenty laughed. "Punk ass probably ate all my cheese." He took the nearly empty plate from her and set it down.

Le'Mon weaved his way to them.

"Get you some shrimp, man," Plenty told him. "We're about to head upstairs, check out my collection." He moved off without checking to see that Neon followed. He knew she did.

"I got hipped to Springer a while ago," Plenty said, letting his words bounce off his back to the top of her head as he mounted the stairs. "Nigga gets the bootleg of movies in pre-production! What ain't to love? Excuse the mess, girl, we gon' go back here."

He pushed open the door and let her pass, holding off on getting an ass brush this time. Man gotta be cool sometimes; pussy by itself was simple and common enough; conquest of same was cool. Any woman just gave up the draws was no more useful to Plenty than a lotioned up hand, which ain't to say a brother neglected keeping his palm supple every chance he got, just that sometimes you wanted to feel like that newly dropped testicle which ruled the world.

Party noises from below gave Neon a bit of comfort. Granted this was Plenty Mo's roost, but even the pope would receive the keystone beatdown if a woman screamed with the two of them alone in a room somewhere.

"All these boxes movies?"

"Mostly."

Black and red bag.

"Know how fools talk about retiring to read books? Fuck books. I'ma watch movies. I ain't seen none of these." He pointed out a column of boxes stacked three high. "Close to two hundred movies right there. He usually brings me ten at a time. Know what his real name is? Thomas Jefferson! Tell me that white boy ain't black," Plenty hooted.

Somebody shouted up to him, "Yo, Plenty man, your cuz is here!"

"All right!" he shouted back. "Go on look through. Be back in a minute." He left.

What in hell am I doing in Plenty Mo's upstairs bedroom, Oh, Lawd, I have taken leave of the last of my senses.

She sat on the edge of the bed.

She nodded to the bag. *How you doin'?*

She glanced at the open doorway.

She quickly hit the outer and inner zips, grabbed a handful, stuffed it into her purse, rezipped/repositioned the bag, and jumped off the mattress like it was a leaky waterbed full of AIDS.

Damn, that felt good!

She smoothed the bedding out.

No, a woman isn't going to stand up to go through these

boxes. She would grab some and sit down.

So Neon took a few from the nearest box and placed her buttcheeks back where they belonged.

Then she bounced a bit to leave a better impression. Misdirection was the key to magic.

She spread a few movies out, picking one that looked interesting so she could pretend to study it as he came up the stairs.

But he didn't come up.

She waited another minute, listening hard. Must have been with his idiot cousin.

She could pick out tones moreso than content:

Plenty introducing his cousin to somebody.

Le'Mon's voice.

General party noise, then Plenty again, sumpin' sumpin'.

Le'Mon again, a little excited.

Somebody booming *Let's get this party started right!*

Plenty saying hold up, hold up, then his footsteps running halfway up the stairs before stopping, where his voice called, "Hey, come on down. We're gonna do this birthday then you can swing back," then his heavy footfalls back down.

Plenty hugged Yvonne. "Cuz, this is the good shit. Family, bitches!" he said for the benefit of all. "Cuz and me, we used to be the shit. Ok," he told Yvonne, "head out to the backyard. I'ma round folks up and we do it right."

Yvonne walked through a mass of stares—

"Mothafucka, get out the goddam cheese!" Plenty shouted.

--and into the sunny dirt patches of Plenty's backyard where the wolves moved about hungrily. It was mostly the young asses in the backyard, teens to twenty-somethings. Race go forward, race go backward. *Step Back: the Next Generation,* then literally, "Step back," to a youngblood too high to realize he'd come to a party just to get fucked the fuck up.

And not in a good way.

"I ain't mean to, oh, I'm sorry, I ain't spill nothing on—no disrespect, I'm just, y'know, a bicycle pants wearing freak of your multitude (she'd changed at the last second, blouse and leggings—why mess with a classic?), y'know," and he started laughing hysterically and suddenly stopped. "Awiight? Somewhere close. Do a little sumpin', whatever yo sumpins is."

First she bent his arm behind his back, then she twisted hard and bent him double after the angry word "Bitch!" came out his mouth.

All after the fool tried to casually lay a hand on her waist to guide her.

"I can have your ass in a wheelchair three seconds after I let you go," she told him. "You thinking about that?"

He struggled. People snickered.

Yvonne twisted.

"Ow!"

"Not thinking hard enough." She turned him around and saw Plenty approaching fast.

She let the boy go. He spun on her.

"Fuck you doin', nigga!" Plenty thundered.

The boy pointed. "Nasty bitch—"

Which was all he got out. Since he was still mostly high he'd wonder later why his mouth tasted like dirt.

Plenty's knee pinned him face down to the ground.

"Say 'Happy Birthday,' bitch!"

The boy's lips made dirt angels.

A knot of folks surrounded them. Neon, finally making it downstairs and outside, had no idea what started the commotion and tried to see, then had a jolt of common sense: Plenty's people tended to have guns. She disappeared back into the house.

Plenty jerked the boy's head off the ground. The boy was

crying!

Oh snap!

"Haffy Birfd—"

Plenty got off and let him get up. "Take yo ass in the house and sit down, ya ignorant bastard."

The boy's eyes were red with weed but he nodded. He dusted his chest and walked with his eyes down.

"Don't say shit to nobody in there either," Plenty said with Neon in mind. "Yvonne, damn, damn, I'm sorry—y'all, what the fuck? Walk your asses somewhere."

The knot broke up.

Plenty searched Yvonne's face.

She looked stonily back at him.

He knew enough not to say anything.

He walked one way; she went the other and found herself something to drink out of one of the coolers scattered around the yard.

The music playing was Parliament Funkadelic. *Flashlight* blasted out the speakers. Youngbloods didn't know shit about it, but for the older fools in Plenty's yard that song was the national anthem. Heads immediately bobbed in unison; arms got thrown in the air, and they waved 'em like they just didn't care.

Standard procedure.

Plenty kept all kinds of uncut funk on his personal mix discs and that's all anybody was going to hear at this party. None of those fucking young-ass no talent kids hooked on phonics that tried to spell funk with a 'Ph'.

He'd chosen a Brides of Funkenstein track especially for Yvonne. When they were kids he used to tease her all the time about being Eddie Munster's momma.

One of the partygoers picked up *Flashlight's* chorus:

"Everybody's got a little light!"

Several people shouted back: "Under the sun!"

Yvonne wondered where Le'Mon had wandered to, then felt eyes on her ass. About fifteen yards due south behind one, two, three people. Peepin' like a weasel horny for chicken grease.

Plenty emptied the house, packing the backyard with people who gave a fuck that it was a free party but not much else. Shrimp, ribs, hot dogs and beer.

Shee-id.

Jahmone trotted out a cake. Neon, behind him, carried paper plates and forks. No candles on the cake; it was enough that Plenty knew Yvonne saw it.

But not in the way Yvonne saw Neon, who saw Le'Mon see Yvonne.

And Neon, well, Neon froze.

Prince's *Party Up!* cued up.

"Happy birthday," Plenty said and everybody kind of nodded in Yvonne's direction.

Now that the ceremony was done with...

Plenty walked around taking Polaroids.

"Negro, they don't even make Polaroid film no mo!" the little drunk muhfuka said. *Who the fuck was he?*

Plenty fanned a picture and studied it.

"Niggas don't smile no mo? What the fuck's wrong with y'all?"

"Keepin' that shit hard and real, nig—"

Smak!

"Who else gots to talk? Boy, you bet not start crying. Take your ass in the house too."

Neon wasn't sure what to do. Plenty intercepted her. Le'Mon knew precisely what he wanted to do, which was head over to Yvonne, but he couldn't because Plenty was handing him the camera.

Do I look like Jimmy Olsen, muthafucka?!

"I'ma give all these to Cuz," Plenty explained as Le'Mon

framed the shot. "Scrapbooking is some serious money now. I'ma get me a piece of that. Big cheese," he said, hugging up on Neon.

Flash!

Steve loved his cousin. She was the one showed him his first tit (in a magazine, pervert; she'd found it outside school one day) and told him that's what hers would look like. Seven year olds were so precious. She didn't care that he couldn't ride a bike. She taught him the difference between saying something and meaning it.

They drifted apart more or less when he said fuck it to the world at large. Nothing dramatic. Slow and imperceptible like icebergs riding a different current. When word got around to her what he'd become, she simply and literally didn't know him anymore.

Except he knew she knew him.

"I'm older than her by two years but I used to be this little shy assed backwarmer, wouldn't do shit 'less somebody did it first," he told his captive audience. Neon hadn't exchanged a word with Yvonne yet, and vice versa.

Le'Mon was busy trying his hardest to do math.

"And she didn't take shit from anybody even then."

Yvonne smiled a little. "FTDS," she said.

"Preach it, girl!" Plenty took a long drink from his tumbler of iced champale. "Quote scripture." He explained to Neon: "We used to make up pretend bible verses. Book of DeCarlo, Cuz."

"As it is written," said Yvonne.

"So shall it be."

"DeCarlo sixteen, verse three," said Yvonne. "Fuck the Dumb Shit."

"That's my motto too," said Le'Mon. He had this stupid way of grinning out of his whole face that irked the hell out of

Yvonne.

But she ignored the impulse to ignore him. "How can that be everybody's motto and we're always fucked up?" she said. She waggled a finger between him and Plenty. "I didn't know you were tight with my cousin. You here all the time?" she asked Le'Mon.

"Hell naw," Plenty answered. "Where y'all met before? Hey, remember I killed that rubber snake for you? Girl still hates snakes to this day."

"Not all of them," Yvonne said.

"Retarded boy had this rubber snake he was always playing with named Mike. Thing looked like a long skinny black dick! Crazy ass white boy playing with a fake black dick. Left it in the grass on purpose behind her. She screamed like hell when she saw it and I chopped the muthafuck in half with the shovel. That was some funny shit. Retarded ass cried like a girl when I popped him upside the head with the pieces."

"Your ma made you buy him a new snake."

"My wild ass made her look like she ain't know how to raise anybody. Pissed me off she made me use my bottle money to buy that shit and give it to him, but I ain't fuck him up. Hell, he was a damn retard."

"He was not retarded."

"Why'd he always act like he didn't know the difference between shit and cheese? What's that line, 'Stupid is as stupid does'."

"Don't listen to him," Yvonne said to Le'Mon. "Crazy white boy was in Steve's backyard every time I went to visit."

"Dennis. Dennis the menace. Good times."

"What happened to him?" Neon asked Plenty.

"Like I know. You think you might want some kids, Neon?"

Her eyes popped.

"I ain't got a single kid," Plenty said proudly. "What kind of sick fuck brings more fools into this world? And all these white bitches adoptin' these oriental babies, what the fuck? That's some crazy shit. Like collectibles and shit. If Dennis had any sense he'da took his ass off to a corner somewhere and still be hiding there now."

Yvonne lightly grazed the back of Le'Mon's hand. "You wanna help me get these," she said. Ants converged on their paper plates on the ground. Plenty handed his over. Neon followed same.

When they were gone Plenty leaned in and tapped Neon friendly-like on the knee.

"Lemme know when you're ready to go back upstairs."

"Ok."

He sat back and smiled a broad smile. "God, I wish I had a woman like you!"

She hoped her squirm wasn't too visible.

"You kinda remind me of Cuz a little bit," he said.

"I think I'll start quoting the Book of DeCarlo myself."

"I'm gon' show you the tip of my dick," he said, buzzed just enough not to realize he'd said it out loud. "You'll see Plenty Mo." Then he clicked back to reality as though he'd never been gone.

Neon didn't say a word.

"So what you do when you ain't toleratin' him?" he asked. "I bet you write shit. You got that secret look. Like Alicia Keys, all Twilight Zoney and shit. Only thing I did every day—" he shrugged, "yeah, I got locked up for a bit—"

No!

"—was watch *The Twilight Zone*. At five fifty-nine somebody was changing the channel! Six o'clock my ass was there."

"I write sometimes."

"I might get my ass into some publishing too. I'll hook you up. Punk ass holding his dick over there?"

She looked. Yep, drink in one, balls in the other.

"Took my publishing title. Deez Books. He's got four writers but they ain't sellin' shit. *Two Thug Honeymoon*—who the fuck wants to read that? Better throw some lesbians or something in there. He even told me he don't read that shit when they send it. Don't nobody read it, just get it printed. Me, I'd treat it like a bakery; you gotta sample shit so you know what's good and bad. You could probably sell some shit if you wanted to."

"I'm not a book writer."

"Neither are they. Look, I'm deciding right here and now: I'ma throw some dollars at my own publishing company. Plenty Mo Deez?"

"Uh-uh."

"Frontin' Pages?"

Neon rolled her eyes.

"Gimme something," he said.

"Use something simple."

"SDW Press. My initials. What's that, a ghost name?"

"Pseudonym."

"Naw, not just 'cause he stole my idea. Hate lawyers." Speaking of hate, where was Le'Mon? Plenty was well aware of him sniffing out Yvonne. Turned out to be good interference, true, but Cuz wasn't leaving outta here with a trifling redbone.

Le'Mon deflected Yvonne's questions about his nose and tried to appear rico suave nonchalant. If you let a woman know she had the upper hand she'd be all like, One Ring To Rule Them All, Ha, ha ha!!!

Get all Sauron on a man's ass.

So Le'Mon reeked out the vibes *I want you...but I ain't got to have you.*

Which was a damn lie. Yvonne made him want to pee her name in the dirt.

Glancing up, he caught Plenty's glance. Both men nodded across the yard.

"Neon's over there with Plenty all happy," Le'Mon pointed out. He sniffed to show it hurt but he was a man. "Long time me and her. Y'all almost share a birthday." Now let a little pain creep into the mix. "I couldn't do a party so I brought her here to celebrate too."

Yvonne looked horrified...and just a touch disgusted.

Score! he thought.

You ignorant (she thought)—*How you gonna tell me you brought your date to share my birthday!* "A lot of people wouldn't do that," she said.

"Well, you know..."

"I haven't known her that long."

He perked up. "No?"

"Got out the service not too long ago."

"Takes a while getting your groove back, huh?"

"Only reason you see me. Meet new people. Know what, can you hold onto my drink for a minute? I need to run out to the car. I brought something for Plenty I need to give him."

"How about I walk with you?"

At the car she made sure he couldn't see in the top of the large mall bag she pulled from the trunk.

"Want me to get that?" he asked.

Yvonne swung it to show how light it was.

"Anything in there for me?" Le'Mon joked.

"Depends on what you like."

One ring to bind them...

"Let me get this to him and I'll see you back over there by the grill."

Yvonne strode up to Plenty and Neon, swinging her bag just as sweetly.

Plenty raised eyebrows at the bag.

"I didn't figure on presents so I stopped and got myself a little something, but I need a woman's opinion to see if I might need to take it back." She looked at Neon. "Do you mind? Just a few outfits."

Neon stood up feeling somewhat like when Yvonne had told her to kick off them shoes, like there were dark clouds coming fast.

"We'll be upstairs," Yvonne told Plenty. "Don't let anybody up. What's a good room? I ain't tryin' to see anybody's draws on the floor."

"I'll show her," Neon said.

"I woulda got you a present," Plenty said behind them.

Yvonne threw a smile over her shoulder. "You already did."

This time it was Neon's turn to let words bounce off her back and on top of somebody else's head as she led the way up the stairs. "What other family you got I need to know about?"

"You know, you look good enough in those jeans to make this kinda easy."

"Get off my ass. I bet he doesn't know you're a freaky ho."

"When he corners you and mentions his Little Bo Peep, bow-leg back to me and talk about freaky."

The crinkle crinkle of that handle bag was damn near irresistible.

Yvonne set the bag on the bed. Neon closed the door.

Yvonne pulled out a white linen dress, a beaded mesh cardigan with a taupe skirt, a hellacious blue shirtdress with a plunging neckline, and a black and red backpack identical to the one sitting dumbly on the bed.

Which she then sat beside the one on the bed.

While looking innocently at Neon.

"No the fuck you didn't!"

Yvonne hand-modeled to point out the fact her new bag was similarly stuffed.

"He's your cousin!"

"Le'Mon's not." She gauged Neon's reaction and deemed it perfect.

But then, "I don't want him hurt."

And they both knew that meant killed.

"He won't be," said Yvonne.

"I don't want anybody to be."

"Let me be real: nobody at this party deserves to walk away from this party. Murderers, dealers, rapists and abusers. God's Grand Plan is a bitch to figure out and I ain't received a memo in a while, so far as I'm concerned this is a blank slate. Le'Mon's gonna stay so tough on me that Steve—Plenty—won't think he did it. Sorry if you haven't noticed your boyfriend's dick raising my skirt."

"He ain't my boyfriend."

"Strange world you live in. Know what? The only way somebody is gonna get killed is if they're stupid enough to set the bullet in motion themselves. And if they're that dumb, the bullet was already in motion before you and I ever met."

"God's plan."

"It's helped many a fucker sleep at night. Notice this bag is just a touch worn and doesn't have that new bag smell? Did the girl not think of everything?"

"How'd you know it was up here?"

"Observation and applied logic. Get you some."

Yvonne picked the real one up and checked it for weight. Hers matched closely enough. A few alterations on the paper stuffing for shape and consistency—

"You're not gonna put any money on top to make it look like a full bag?"

"That's cutting into profits, girl."

—a check for obvious identifying marks: none—

"Plenty knows we been up here."

"He's not gonna think we took it," Yvonne assured.

"How'd you find the same bag? You only saw it for two seconds."

"I know where Steve's cheap ass shops for garbage. Back to

school sales, girl; they got eighteen more of the things."

Yvonne put the money bag in her handle bag.

"Why you doing this with me?" asked Neon.

"No. You're not a part of—"

Neon flashed open her money-stuffed purse.

"Ok, damn." Yvonne looked Neon square on. "No reason me and you need to stay in this city. Steve threw this party for you, you know that by now. Your man is currently doing the math on how to kick you to the curb for me, and he's probably thinking the same thing as us: a bag full of money is a serious enticement. Mayor got broken into last week? I have it on good authority—since I eavesdrop at work—that one of the mayor's security detail did some robberies of all the mayor's after hours titty bars—"

"Knew I shouldn'ta voted for his ass!"

"—and folks are talking about pointing fingers. Quiet's as kept till somebody shines a news crew on you."

"Exactly how do you know?"

"Chain of secrets. Somebody always tells somebody else. What you think is secret, ain't."

"What about us? Somebody always tells somebody else?"

"I might tell Bubba but other than that nobody needs to know."

"I just want to get away from here."

"So we're cool. The mayor is keeping his shit quiet since him and his boy go way back."

"You picked out some damn nice clothes."

"Aren't they though? Don't think I can't razzle. One of the chain links is in our host's backyard now." She answered Neon's next question: "You hear and see people looking at your ass; I hear and see tactical information. Mayor's security and Steve crossed paths during one of Steve's civil vacations."

"Which one is he?"

"The little one that keeps shouting at him. You'll know

when you hear him."

"We really want to do this?"

"We don't know what's in this bag," said Yvonne. "What do we care about some nigga's bookbag? I'm up here to try on clothes." She started to undress.

"You're really trying them on?"

"Hell yeah, I might have to take this shit back."

Yvonne flowed downstairs looking pretty and innocent as a child after a bath, swinging her bag and happy at how feminine that white linen dress made her feel. The upper was gauzy with a built in half cami but if you looked hard enough you could make out the firm naked muscles of her stomach. The bottom flowed into a pleated skirt. She marched right outside, Neon right behind her.

Plenty saw them and hurriedly sucked the barbecue sauce off one hand while holding up the other to stop his cousin.

"Hold up, I don't want any of this to hit you."

He sucked the fingers of the other hand and iced up a napkin.

"Happy birthday to you! Look here, in ya southern finest."

"Other stuff didn't hit me right," Yvonne said with a disappointed frown. "I'm taking it back." The dress had silver beads at the scoop neckline that caught the waning light. She offered just a hint of cleavage.

"I'll run that out for you," said Le'Mon.

"That's all right," she said.

He was already up.

She fished her keys from her purse.

One of Plenty's boys trespassed up to her the second Le'Mon headed off; Le'Mon hurried and tossed the bag in her trunk then trotted back not wanting to look like he rushed.

He made straight for his two ladies but Plenty deflected him.

"Why don't you bring one of them boxes down?" It didn't look like Springer planned to show; that was cool, though. Sometimes the boy overbooked but his clientele understood. "We can watch a movie when you want, Yvonne. Hey!" he said standing. "Who all wants to watch a movie?"

Nobody said anything.

Then: "What you got? Ain't nobody tryin' to see you bust a nigga over Bruce Lee!"

Plenty pretended to chase him and the little drunk ass laughed.

"Muhfucka always got something to say," Plenty said, but he was smiling.

Le'Mon, prudently, shuffled off.

The trespasser moved back in on Yvonne. "It's ya birthday, huh?"

Then the little drunk ass joined in, beer and a sausage in hand. "Get yo no-line-havin' ass on. 'It's ya birthday.' Baby," he confided to Yvonne, "you are surrounded by some of the most retarded negroes you'll ever know. And white girl Wendy over there."

The only white person at the party held up her drink.

"She can dance her ass off but she—You stupid as hell, Wendy!"

"Fuck you!"

"Why you think you at the party?" She gave him the finger; he caught it and put it in his back pocket. "I'ma save that for later. Look here," he told Yvonne, "Lemme know when you wanna go to the clubs, I getchoo in any club in the city, niggas know—Plenty, why you trying to rush me, man, this is a good line—niggas know my velocity when I roll."

"Life's gon' scare the hell out of you when you sober up," said Plenty.

The first trespasser nudged the drunk on, but Plenty cock-blocked both.

"Get the fuck away from my cousin." He'd told himself he wasn't going to cuss so much with Yvonne there. "I ain't even invite yo dumb asses." He didn't usually listen to himself.

"Nigga, we live here," the mayor's drunken security high school buddy said. His head swung toward Neon. "Baby, I live here." Suddenly he got so close to Neon there was just tit room between them.

"Fuck you doin'?" two male voices said in unison.

Nobody'd noticed Le'Mon returning behind Plenty and taking one step forward.

Tyreese's little drunk ass tossed some grim toward Le'Mon but backed off, making Le'Mon's balls swell two sizes too large, but it was the lion behind the mouse Tyreese responded to. Plenty's disbelieving, zombie-eyed crocodile stare forecast pains Tyreese wouldn't want to admit made Tyreese less of a man.

"Go fuck the white girl, please," Plenty said, shooing his dumb ass on. His left nut was about to act up, so he knew Yvonne's hair trigger was less than a few seconds from kicking some ass in her white lacy dress.

"Why all your people actin' like they ain't had none in four years," Le'Mon said under the influence.

"Don't get fucked up, Casper—again," said Tyreese. Then Tyreese made a fake karate motion at Le'Mon, who of course flinched. "Damn, you a pussy."

All right, fuck it, Yvonne thought. She went for the drunk.

Wrist lock (but step close on him so he feels the titty crush); warm breath on his ear (try not to breathe; ain't nothin' worse than forty ounces on the mouth on a hot day); let him think he powered loose (step back so he can remember the house never loses); and finally say to him sweetly, "Respect my birthday, sugar."

Tyreese grinned it off. "Baby got skills."

"Yes, I do." Hold his eyes so he'll think you're flirting with him. "Steve, let's go watch a movie."

Later, in the living room, she whispered to Le'Mon, "I'm tired of people disrespecting you with your lady. I didn't plan to step in front of you."

"No, it's cool."

Neon came back from the bathroom.

"A lot of men wouldn't be able to step back," Yvonne whispered.

Plenty got off the floor from popping in a second, unscratched DVD. The first one, *Drive It To Death,* had stopped a quarter of the way through. He'd be sure to mention this lapse in quality control to Springer.

"I ain't tryin' to mess up a party," Le'Mon said.

They all watched *The Color Purple* together...

Elaine was on the rant again. She'd had a dream about Bela and her sister.

("I didn't even know you had a sister!")

She'd expended the rounds of major artillery and fell back on what she had left: close range firearms: "'Bela?' You sound like something out of a damn Disney movie! Need dancing pots singing to your ass."

"You know what? You know what?"

"You better move your finger," she said under her breath.

He didn't move his finger. This was the finger that got held up when somebody needed a lesson. You didn't just move that finger simply because somebody told you to. Obviously they needed that finger. "Look here," he said.

"You don't understand shit about this relationship," she said.

"Your psycho ass dreamed I was doing your sister!" he shouted. "Dammit, girl, get some therapy for that shit!"

Which was pretty much the end of that.

Once the weekend was over Bela hit Barclay's cubicle.

Barclay was in full edit mode. He barely looked up.

Bela had a notepad.

"Hey," said Bela.

"Hey," said Barclay.

"What's the worst smell in the world?" Bela asked.

"Fresh pee on top of old pee," said Barclay, the majority of his mind focused on a particularly tricky turn of phrase. "In a urinal."

Bela jotted this down. "Worst feeling in the world?"

"Worst as in mortality or worst as in a sorry damn?" Cross wanted crossover, so White Girl Wendy had to step up.

"Let's do damn first."

"Finger piercing the toilet tissue when you wipe your ass."

"You nasty bastard." He jotted.

"Mortality, a kid dying either figuratively or literally under your watch."

"Worst sight in the world?"

"A loved one sad because of you." Barclay continued typing.

"Are you really paying me attention?" said Bela, writing away.

"No."

"Worst use of time?"

"Talking to salespeople."

"Phone or in person."

"Telemarketing bastards. Worse than damn mimes. Useless bastards. Get a job masturbating horses, at least there's some dignity in that."

Bela skipped that part.

Barclay mentally squinted at the screen in front of him. Be lunchtime soon and he began to realize White Girl Wendy might need her own book.

"Worst thing a woman can say to a man?"

"The friend thing." He glanced Bela's way. "Sometimes I'm

actually busy, man."

"When the hell are you busy at work? Be friends or think of you as a friend?"

"Think."

"Yeah," agreed Bela.

"Yeah."

"Hate the shit out of that. Wouldn't hurt them to add, 'But we can fuck anyway and I won't talk about you.'"

"I know," said Barclay. He added a little extra impatience to the glance this time. "What's this for?"

"Elaine. The break-up talk. She hit me with I got a little dick—"

"Aw fuck naw."

"Yeah. So I wanna be able to come back with the thunder."

It was better to face down the no-dick-having rant instead of the little dick beat down. No-dick was easily shrugged off as vengeful exaggeration, whereas—unless the man was obviously hung—the little dick hit with the explosive force of an improvised nuclear bomb to the eyelids.

"When's the official break up?' asked Barclay.

"Soon as that fuc—"

"Lower your voice."

Bela resumed their contained monotones. "Soon as she brings back the spare key she stole from me."

"You gave her a key?"

"I can't find my spare."

"Change the locks."

"We argued two days ago and she ain't been by."

"Motion detectors too."

"It ain't like that," said Bela.

"Yes it is. She left a lot of her stuff, told you everything you didn't understand about her, and left out without looking at you."

"...Yeah..."

"Crumble that paper up and go to Radio Shack. Y'all won't be playing the dozens."

Resigned, Bela closed his pad. "Damn."

"Flirt with Irina on your way out today," said Barclay.

"I can't go out the race, man."

"You masturbate thinking Jessica Simpson might accidentally join you in the shower."

Bela flicked his chin at the computer. "What're you working on?"

"Trying to figure out this one character. You bring lunch?"

"No."

"What're you feeling?"

"Chinese." It was pretty quiet for a Monday; they hadn't been interrupted by prying eyes or ears yet, which was unusual before lunch. "Scoot over," said Bela, "let me see what you've got."

"Aren't you supposed to be at a meeting?"

"Got an intern to do it." Bela picked papers off Barclay's desk to hold while appearing to read intense Savory Controls business over his co-worker's shoulder.

White Girl Wendy had never danced for her father, which was good because that would have been weird as hell. She was a third tier dancer at the Sweet Tease, which meant the other ladies only let her come out when the only dollars left were those in her most needy, gossamer dreams.

"That ain't working," said Bela.

"That ain't working?"

"That ain't working. Make it gritty."

Barclay backspaced. His fingers tossed out: only let her come out when stragglers had to choose between bus fare or begging a ride off somebody when it came to that one last peep of the night.

Plenty and that stupid light-skinned boy in the backyard were tripping over their own two feet following the tall lady and the knockout, and Wendy wondered why the two ladies were trying to pretend they didn't know one another.

And since there was no way Wendy could compete with the Amazon Bitch, her dreams of cornering Le'Mon—Wendy knew how Plenty worked: get somebody goofy to do something goofy, like shuffle around a bunch of dollars stolen from the Sweet Tease, Tata For Now, the Brown Round, and the Crotch, some of the foulest scratch and sniff titty bars outside of fallen Mormon country. Every person at this party she'd seen at one point or other at the Sweet Tease, except for the dude with the backpack.

"Sucker" blinged off him like a neon light.

Ever since that party at Lil Lil's house (regaining consciousness to not one but two dicks? Come on!) she made sure to notice everybody in attendance since the police didn't see the use in "Fucking nigga motherfucker" as a description.

Even drunk-ass Tyreese sniffed around Wonder Woman, little pygmy-dicked bastard. He owed Wendy eighteen dollars in lap money! Eighteen dollars!

That was a quarter tank of gas.

Wendy might've danced at the Sweet Tease, but unlike six of her coworkers she didn't have a single kid, so she figured that put her smarter than them right out the box. Those two ladies were up to something, and anytime you have to say "up to something" it means you need to bust a Sherlock Holmes on somebody.

Plus it meant there was money involved.

Wendy would figure out how to wedge herself in the mix even if it killed—

"Wendy!"

Oh god. "Tyreese, why the HELL do you keep shouting after me? I'm trying to think."

"No pain no gain. Why don't you run in the house, bring some more beers out here?"

Wendy sputtered a moment. She wanted to come back with a snappy pa-dow.

"Fuck! You!" she said, trying to hit it with a little Meryl Streep Oscar-worthy inflection.

"I'ma still want my beer."

Wendy rolled her eyes. She tried losing herself behind a few dudes playing dice against their ladies and losing. One girl was using the fingernail cheat but, hey, you do what needs be done.

She watched a few minutes to give herself time to come straight to it: she'd go directly to those two and find out exactly what was going on. If her suspicions were right, she'd threaten to drop a dime on them if they didn't cut her a slice.

She waited to catch Yvonne alone. "Hey," she said, walking up on her.

"Wendy!"

Fuck!

"What! What?!"

"Damn, girl," said the little drunk. The exchange took three seconds.

Yvonne was gone in two. White trash with an idea was never a good thing, and it was clear in the white girl's approach she was a squirrel searching for a nut.

Wendy flowed with it. Neon, then—If she could peel Plenty off her.

Better yet, maybe she'd just mention to Plenty that there was some underground shit going on. That kind of favor meant he would owe her maybe one or two back. She wasn't greedy. Women are never greedy.

Fuck that, yes they are.

But she wasn't.

Well, she was. But not in this instance. Outside of vaguely wanting something that had nothing to do with her. As the only white girl at the party she had a unique vantage point:

she was invisible. Conversations didn't stop when she came around. If anything they got louder.

Neon stood by the stereo looking around for her tall friend.

Neon didn't dance at the Sweet Tease. For this reason, Wendy immediately considered her a friend. It was hard enough living off Taco Bell as it was, I mean, Taco Bell cheese? Come on! Bowel movements were rare and beautiful things.

Wendy could fuck and suck with the best of them, but she didn't pretend she could turn heads. She wasn't pudging yet, but she would. The mushroom top over the jeans was on the way; an expanded belly would swallow the navel ring. Light glinting off that navel was a major attraction at the Tease.

Maybe she should go straight to Plenty's mule. Le'Mon. Especially after the way he came busting back to the party like he'd just found out somebody'd given him a sex change operation. She'd probably even hear something else at the Tease that would help her case.

Plenty led Tyreese away and she couldn't do anything but praise Jesus; in addition to owing her money Tyreese thought his dick was a shiv when it came to fucking, sticking it everywhere a hundred random times. He was rough and didn't care about anybody and had slapped her. Hard.

She imagined the conversation: "I can help you get that money back," she would say, maybe meeting Le'Mon in the last place anybody would think to start some shit, like the library, and hoping to hell she'd seen enough movies that saying it came off seductive.

"Girl, go the fuck away," imaginary Le'Mon dismissed.

"Ok." She walked away.

Girl had a nice ass.

"Wait."

She glanced over her shoulder. He finger-flicked her back. Up close, he realized she had freckles.

If white girls were the black man's kryptonite, then white

girls with freckles were kryptonite dipped in honey butter and grilled to perfection.

To dream the impossible dream...

A white girl with freckles was the ultimate white girl. And not the ugly-assed leper colony freckles, but the ones that look like a Hollywood production complete with lily white skin and red hair.

Wendy was woman enough to imagine naked, so maybe there was truth to her outrageous claim. Le'Mon would listen.

Le'Mon, in her imagination, did listen.

So she'd say: "Big Dick Willie down at the Sweet Tease—"

"Big Dick Willie or Sweet Dick Willie?" Le'Mon interrupted.

"Big Dick."

"'Cause there's a Sweet Dick works the clubs too."

"That's east side Sweet dick. West side Sweet Dick Willie's in the hospital."

"Just to be clear."

Proceeding: "Big Dick was getting head near the dumpster. Manager and Tyreese—the little dude at the party—come out talking shit, but they don't see Big Willie. Somehow or other the mayor's involved in this shit." Not that she gave a fuck one way or another; she hadn't voted for him.

"The mayor of Day City?"

"Yes."

"The mayor."

"Big Dick Willie said—"

"Wait, I'm still on the mayor. Let me put this delicately: you's a crazy bitch."

Generally, in her imagination, that's where people fucked up.

"You stole from Plenty," he'd say, because by then the money would be gone.

"Do you have any idea how many times Plenty has eaten this pussy? Why the hell would I risk him using teeth?

Obviously you think we're all as stupid as you are."

"You know about the money," he'd say.

"Ignorant dick, I can add two and two together. You left that party ready to piss. If it'd been anything more than a piddly amount of money you wouldn't be here now, but what's piddly to Plenty ain't what's piddly to you and me."

"How can you help?"

"I'm a crazy bitch."

"Stay on topic."

"If I keep my ears open at the Sweet Tease, what can you do for me?"

She could tell that Le'Mon had never in his wildest dreams—except for one that likely involved Lindsay Lohan—done a white girl. The possibility of hitching this trailer park along as backup poon issued orders too sensible to ignore.

She imagined he would chew his lip a moment. "You and me go straight up with Plenty, let him know he got fucked, point the fingers and get paid."

"Why?" she said.

"What?!" he said.

"Plenty Mo doesn't offer rewards," she said, contradicting her thoughts of two seconds ago. "And I'm not about to open my mouth and lose my job at the Tease. Cable and phone bill's due next week." Wendy was a junkie for some Lifetime Network. There wasn't a suffer-porn movie made she didn't identify with. "Sniff around the Crotch tonight and see if you don't hear something about Plenty's party," she offered, deciding why act as a golden retriever for this fool when she could send him on a wild goose chase instead, and while he was out of the way maybe she could approach the two ladies again. The best work is done on the fly.

I mean, come on, right? They'd listen to reason. Plenty wouldn't want to kill his cousin, but nobody wants to eat carrots either, right? And getting some from Neon was a simple matter of putting her final call on hold till after the deed.

Wendy wasn't even looking for a three-way split. She would quit her job for five hundred dollars and two dinners at Ginny's.

"You got jokes," Le'Mon would say, nodding and grinning with what he hoped was a knowing air.

"I do?"

"You and me, we're headin' to Plenty."

"I said—"

"I don't give a fuck what you said. I said—"

That's when, sitting in the library, she would reach into her purse, pull her cell phone out, and drop it loudly on the table in front of her.

With the noise reverberating through every shelf.

"You think you can dial him faster than me?" she said. "I'll be with him before you can reach into your pocket to say hello to your little friend. What've you got, a thirty-eight? Lugar, asshole, don't let the freckles fool ya." She kept a free hand inside her purse.

"We ain't gotta do all that," he said.

"I approached you in good faith."

Le'Mon re-evaluated. This was crazy poon, and some things simply weren't worth that kind of trouble.

"Take your Fantasy Island ass on, girl, and don't follow me no more."

And that'd be that. She'd stand up in the library, look him square on, and say, "Then I'm out."

Then she'd leave and not be a single inch closer to all the money out in the world floating a fingertip away from her grasp.

But she for damn sure was getting that eighteen dollars out of Tyreese.

"I wanna see her at the titty bar," said Bela.

242

"I'll work on that later," said Barclay. "Let's eat."

*

"You're breaking up with me?" she said, incredulous at the tone in his voice that said he even for a moment thought he was the one initiating it. She thrust a hip out that would have hurt a small child. "You're gon' stand here and tell me my selfishness and immaturity is why you're breaking up with me? I. Don't. Think. So. I was done with your ass last Friday and I'm still done with your ass. See, this is what I need in my life: a man. Not some dude who thinks taking care of me means listening to me after we do it or trying to talk to me about shit I don't give a damn about. What I need—Hello? Let me call you back. What I need," she said, then stopped, because he was doing something so unexpected it broke her rhythm. He held up a finger and cocked his head to the side, the most polite of interruptions. She widened her eyes impatiently at him.

"Sweet Nut Flakes."

She frowned deeply because this was the stupidest thing she had ever heard, then prepared to speak as though he hadn't said a word.

This time he held the finger up and added *Aht.* Nobody speaks when somebody says *Aht.* "The blueberry kind," he continued.

"You crazy sumbitch," she pronounced summarily.

"Where's my key?"

"I don't have your key."

"If you didn't you wouldn't have said I don't have your key."

"Look, I just came back for my shit. After this, fuck you isn't even a memory."

"Right by the door. You didn't even have to cross the threshold. 'Everything you own in a box to the left,' right? Spread your wings and fly away," he said, nodding at the box containing the feminine products she'd smuggled in. "It's a small enough box; you don't even need my help carrying it to your car."

"Your monkey ass will be calling me back in a week."

"If I do it'll be with a list you really don't want to hear."

"Trick."

He bit his tongue. The temptation to hurl an insult squeezed his gonads. She waited him out like a cobra ready to strike the instant he opened his mouth, her body tensed to release the sista inside. He saw the tiny squint narrow her eyes and matched it with the flat, dead stare of his own, avoiding the enticing bait as though it held no enticements whatsoever. Watching her stress level erode like the Wicked Witch pushed straight into a hot tub gave the gonads a pleasurable rub though. As she snatched up her box and left wordlessly, flinging a key over her shoulder, Bela felt an almost religious experience at this psycho chick relenting so easily, not church religious but definitely Yogi Mahareeshi-ish. And it was well known that getting off easy was about on par with malehood.

Let the church say amen.

"That was it?" said Barclay.

"Your imagination gets the best of you," said Bela. "Like the thing you've got with mirrors at night."

"Nobody looks at mirrors at night."

"That's because there's no light to see, not fear that something might look back."

"You look at mirrors at night?"

"I shave at night with a Ouija board widget." He didn't look at mirrors at night.

"So take Irina to a movie now."

"Can't do it. And why are you pushing her on me?"

"Because she likes your ignorant ass. This day and age, particularly with the end times coming and all, that matters a hell of a lot."

"Likes me likes me, or likes me likes me?"

"I will beat you like I don't know you."

"Seriously, man. She's cute and all, but number one: she's Russian or something. I don't know how to sex in Russian. Two, she's cleaning crew, which means she'd be deeply offended at my house. Three, does she just think I'm cute or is she open to doing me, which means she really likes me. I need to know where I'm positioned from, not that I plan to proceed."

"Uppity negro mofo, ask her to a movie and make her smile."

"All right. Maybe. I don't take advice, though, from a grown ass man afraid of the Bloody Mary."

"Go home and smile at yourself in the mirror tonight," said Barclay.

"I'll do that."

"Then come to me and tell me you didn't pee on yourself, you ignorant, tiny dicked pussy-less bastard."

"A memo about language did go out," said Bela. "Don't act like you didn't read it."

"I think I wrote the goddamned thing." Christine in HR knew he was a writer and constantly pawned assignments on him in exchange for not wondering how much company time his paycheck actually reflected. "Let me ask you this: you emotionally torn up?"

"No."

"Then why you got four of my Snickers in your pocket?"

"Courage food for when I ask Irina out."

"Bela with the white chick," Barclay sang. "You uppity negro."

"We shall overcome."

"You're not going to ask her out," Barclay said.

Bela just looked doofy.

"Ignorant negro."

*

Mario, after the third hour playing *Doomed In Death* (M for Mature), figured it might be time to get up and do something vague, like maybe walk from one room to another, or better yet, since it would take his mind off that damned video game, finish bro-in-law's book, it being about as vague as vague needed to be. It was a very good thing that Barclay never thought of passwords or security—not that Mario would violate the sacred trust implicit in snooping through Barclay's things—but a grown ass man in the age of the internet who didn't password protect his files, let alone his porn (which, thankfully, did not include Marilyn; otherwise Mario would have had to kick Barclay's ass) was a man who needed the invisible guardian angel that was Mario when Marilyn and Barclay went to work.

For a first draft it wasn't bad. Mario had scrolled to where it said "The End" and whipped his attention back several chapters where entire sections were highlighted above Barclay's italicized gobbledygook writer's notes.

Somehow or other Le'Mon wound up pointing a gun at Neon? Granted the book was a sellout, but did brother have to do a sell out within a sell out? White Girl Wendy had, thankfully, been dumped, but a gun...in the hands of a thug...was just so... pedestrian. A slow, tired walk at that.

Mario read on. The game was on pause and he'd already been in the kitchen. His day was pretty much done except for cashing in his lottery ticket and getting around to boxing up his stuff. Barclay kept a million spare boxes in his basement. Weird man. But Marilyn liked him, so he was cool. Mario stuffed a handful of potato chips in his mouth, then noticed a beer can in the lee of the desk, probably placed there to keep it cool, not too far from the air conditioning vent.

In the car:

Barclay to Bela after the break up: "Was the sex worth it?"

"Why would you even ask something like that? Of course it was."

"I forgot pussy was above mitigation."

"That's what marriage does to you. 'Making love' makes you forgetful. Get back to where you once belonged and feel my pain for a change."

"Sorry man."

"Ignorant bastard."

"Who's buying lunch today?" asked Barclay.

"I bought last time," said Bela, knowing full well he didn't.

"No, you didn't."

"I did."

"Boy—"

"Fuck it, I'll buy."

"And fuck your pain too."

"Oh, I fucked my pain."

"All right then."

"Ok," said Bela.

"I want pizza."

"I'm asking Irina out."

"No, you're not."

Bela thought a moment. It wasn't that she was unattractive. It wasn't that she was somewhat Russian-ish. It was that she was smarter than him. Every time he saw her the intelligence in her eyes practically slapped him. Bela knew in a few years he'd be considered trifling. It was a set course on a ship that sailed for reasons only his therapist charged for. What Barclay and Marilyn had was lovely as hell, and free sandwiches tasted excellent under such a roof, but Matthew Bela Hills was—for the moment but nowhere near unchanging—not about to waste a smart woman's valuable time. Bela wasn't a religious man but that had to rank up there with the upper sins.

'Thou shalt not trifle a woman with more sense than you.'

Actually, it was rather gallant of him to deny himself the undeniable attraction between chocolate and peanut butter. If there was an open forum and the question was, in an ideal world, did he want to do her, the answer was any man would want to, the way she swished that mop around with those figure eight hips and wore those dowdy tops to cover modest but curvaceous boobs.

On the other hand, what did they have in common besides him being a man and her being a woman? Common sense locked deep within answered, 'Isn't that enough?' A simple enough question.

"Do you like Irina?" asked Barclay.

"Try to date a white woman who's seen me sneaking out office furniture? I see her five seconds every couple days."

"A spark's a spark. What do you figure she weighs?"

"One forty-three."

"Clothed?"

"Naked."

"Ok then."

"Would you say I'm simple?" said Bela.

"Very much so."

"This is precisely why nobody likes you, man."

"Everybody likes me."

"No they don't. They like me."

"You ignorant bastard."

"I'm not the one that got married," said Bela.

"I'm ignorant for getting married?"

"My shit is complex because I didn't. And ignorant as in simple."

"You heard me say I wanted pizza, right?"

"Yes."

248

"But you're driving toward chicken."

"I know. Let me ask you this: if Marilyn wanted to leave you how would she go about it?"

"She'd change the locks and tell me if I rang the doorbell one more time she'd come out and kick my ass."

"No, I mean like an affair or get hooked on weed or hide money in a secret account. Enough money for a pool boy."

"Didn't want chicken today." Barclay watched the city a moment. "She'd tell me I never really made her laugh."

Comedians and insecurity, Bela thought. "See, no faked orgasms—"

"Hey, can't do anything about that, can I?"

"—no cussing you out. You never made her laugh. You simple bastard." The car pulled into the lot of Mama Stack's Chicken.

"I had chicken yesterday," said Barclay.

"What am I missing out on, in your enlightened opinion?"

They got out of the car. Barclay held the restaurant door for Bela. The place was packed and noisy. It smelled like heaven.

"Brother, you've tapped pure ass. I can't do shit but salute you," said Barclay.

"I'm missing something, man," said Bela.

"That, brother, is the statement of the ages. Let me know when you find it," he said.

"She's always reading *The New York Times*," said Bela more to himself than Barclay. "What am I supposed to do with that?" He noticed Barclay wasn't paying him any attention. "Get the Mac and Chick combo. You always get the Mac and Chick combo."

"I get that I gotta get extra cornbread biscuits," Barclay reminded.

"So?"

"Don't want the itis this afternoon. I need to finish editing and send this book off."

Bela remembered high school book reports and college papers. "How do you write an entire book in less than two weeks? You need to thank Savory on the dedication page."

"All we do is look for what's missing," Barclay said, still on Bela's previous statement. "Why is everybody missing pieces? That's the root of all suffering, that struggle to fill holes. What if the holes are there so we can see through to other things?"

"Don't get deep at lunch."

"Sorry."

"I'm getting some of your cornbread," Bela said before making his order.

Marilyn hadn't read the book in a few days so she was surprised when Barclay placed the ceremonial manuscript box on the kitchen table and looked at her with that expectant air of a man awaiting recognition. "Last edit," he said.

"Sooo?" she said, prompting his opinion.

"SDW lives!" The phone rang. Barclay had emailed Cross the manuscript that morning. "Hello? Yes. I hope so. Let me know. No, she's right here. Thanks, I'll tell her. Just about to head out. Ok. Seriously, let me know. Ok. Bye."

"What?"

"Cross wants to take us out."

"Why?"

"Something about nitro glycerin."

After a book is written there's no time to sit back and rest. Writing is always a struggle to control eight dogs chomping for the same bone. Writing begets writing. The next book had a title and a theme. What it did not have, not concretely yet, was a publisher.

Its theme was loss, its theme was loneliness, the theme

was horror, horror at the indifference of life and God to life's pain. It was about a child born knowing who would be the instrument of her death, and going through an entire lifetime never knowing when or where she would meet that person.

It would not be considered an uplifting romp by any stretch of the imagination.

Neon, however, was poised to bounce her happy ass the length and breadth of the entire United States.

The week went by. Then another. Nothing from Cross. Which meant that just as Barclay set his office phone to go straight into voice mail, Cross called his cell phone.

"I finished the manuscript two weeks ago," said Cross. "Got time to give me your thoughts on it?"

"I finished it."

"You finished the hell out of it. Boy—this is the shit. Grits, cheddar cheese, bacon and biscuits."

"What do we need to change?" said Barclay.

Cross scoffed into the phone. "I don't even wanna think about that right now. Had to shut down my netbook at church, you had me laughing out loud. And what finally happens to Le'Mon?—Precisely where he needed to be! Damn. This is street."

"But is it street enough?"

"It's more than street. It's funny. Welcome to ground zero, my literary friend, because you are about to be at the epicenter of a nuclear blast. Netta's trying to get Pam Grier's endorsement. We get a blurb from her—"

"You sent this to Pam Grier?"

"—hell, get an autographed picture. Doesn't take but a day to get some galleys done; yes, I sent it to her. Her, Judge Joe Brown, Maury Povich, Martha Stewart, Harpo Productions— that's Oprah spelled backwards, know that right?—Tyler Perry, Mike Baisden, all the morning shows, Tyra Banks. Sent it to Ann Coulter and told her to contact me for copies for her friends. Only ones who don't have this are Sasha and Malia Obama, but wait a few years, Neon still be around." Cross frowned. "Brother...you're a little quiet on the other end of the phone. Did I not tell you there'd be explosions and car crashes and hot nude scenes? Crosshairs does not play. I'm behind you pre, during, and post. Know that."

Advance copies of this book roamed the streets telling everybody he was their daddy.

"Did you leave a copy on my mama's gravesite?"

"No, but I mailed one to your daddy. I'm joking, man, no disrespect. Two weeks after this book hits stores be prepared to be on TV. But we're gonna make 'em wait a little bit. SDW is a big dicked tease who puts it in you but draws it out slow. See? Got me thinking like him. I like how even the author is a character."

"That's nothing new."

"There is nothing new. Nothing new with fucking but a billion backs are doing it right now. It's what you do with it and what you invest in it. A man can halfway fuck but if he invites his lady out to nice restaurants he gets laid twice as often. That's physics, economics, and psychology rolled into one. I know I've said this one or two times but I wish I did what you do. You pull out the gristle without making it seem like work."

"Stroke me too much I'ma come."

"Hey," Cross said, opening an arm out and raising his chin. "Break out the camera. A writer's lucky to get even part of a money shot. You're about to skeet skeet all over the place."

"Skeet skeet."

"Skeet skeet skeet."

Barclay genuinely smiled.

"I'm gonna wanna meet with you and your wife soon. Netta will get to you on that."

Barclay frowned. Again with the wife.

"We do this right your other books will get a nice boost. Maybe I can kinda keep you thinking about writing a little longer. There are a lot of stories in this book. White Girl Wendy deserves a book all to herself. And Fake Rome and his boys? People know them. Hell, bounce them off the League of Nab! You're sitting on potential gold."

"All that glitters."

"Don't discount laughter. People need to laugh."

"Without laugh tracks it ain't easy."

"Remind 'em. Did they consider Shakespeare highbrow in his time? No. He was Tyler Perry's cousin. He did drama but he did comedy. You're a funny man. Hell, the best comedians speak truth to power. Nothing lightweight about that."

"What about the sex?"

"If a woman is laughing with you and not at you while you're fucking, what do you care that you're wearing clown pants and a nose? You managed to get the Alien movies into a sex scene and you made it work. The sex is good. Sex is where it needs to be and with who it needs to be." Netta entered Cross' office, flipped him the bird, and walked out. "I plan some changes here and there but nothing major. Matter of fact, nothing I'm even going to bother you with. Trust me to do it right." Would he bite? If he bit, Cross knew he had him; Neon would then become a viable property.

He bit. "Ok."

"My daddy used to say 'Hot damn' whenever he hit the numbers. I think this calls for those very words. Hot damn, my brother."

"With cheese," said Barclay.

A bit of time passed. Between the book arriving to him and the final copies arriving in stores a tsunami happened, an earthquake happened, scores of humans died horribly, wastefully and unnecessarily all over the world, and a mega sports star was revealed to be a mega adulterer. Nobody was surprised. About anything. After a while he couldn't keep the news on. Instead, he tended Marilyn's garden.

The day the courier service had dropped off the book he was so excited the eye crinkles nearly glowed. There was a baby inside that bubble-wrapped package. A misshapen, ugly baby but a baby nonetheless. His. The Crosshairs Press logo was crisp against the white packaging, and Barclay's address, complete with his middle initial, felt like the home of God. There was nothing to the world but this child in his hands, this small, paltry thing that he took care to open. It couldn't have weighed more than a pound. It didn't make a sound as it slid into his hand.

A baby with a half-naked woman tattooed on its belly was wrong.

The photograph of the model looked like a blue negative. Her hair, eyes, and highlights glowed ghostly white. The photo was positioned at the very right edge of the cover, split down the middle leaving half to view and half to the imagination. Her face—the one eye, one nostril and half mouth—was expressionless, but the long strands of beads strategically draped around her neck to obscure her nipples (but not the perfect curvature of her breasts) drew the viewer's eye straight to her body.

What stood out, though, was the emoticon.

The title was hot red shadowed in electric blue; replacing the 'o' in Neon was a yellow smiley face, slightly larger than the fonts beside it. The face's eyes bugged and its tongue drooled at the woman to its right. Beneath the title, in white, funky script: The New Novel by SDW.

Basically, a comic book.

Cross got it.

Barclay hadn't expected anything but he hadn't expected

Cross to get it.

The cover was practically a whispered perfume commercial a la Bugs Bunny. All this against a stark black background. This book was not *Mama Cap, Around Deez* or *The Skeeze And I*.

What Barclay had to admit to himself holding the slender volume in his hand and nearly oblivious to Marilyn and Mario standing there waiting for his reaction, was that this ugly water-headed baby conceived from a mean, petty whim, this child that deep down he refused to claim, this thing knocked out in record time...looked like a book. It was a water headed baby but that didn't mean it wouldn't play with the other kids.

Barclay flipped it over, read the beginning of the blurb, got pissed, and immediately flipped it back. There'd be time later to beat the living hell out of Cross about the blurb.

Mario couldn't say he'd already read it, and Marilyn never actually read his books anyway; hell, she'd married him, what more did he want? They waited for him to hand it over.

He presented it to them.

"You need *The Lion King* music playing in the background," said Mario. "One more for posterity, huh?"

"One more for the shelf, brother," agreed Barclay.

"*Neon*," said Marilyn. "He kept the title."

"It had to stay simple," said Barclay.

"The new novel by SDW." She flipped, thrilled to see sections she'd helped edit. It was like secretly knowing Da Vinci had originally sketched Mona Lisa blonde.

"You getting more copies?" asked Mario.

"You want one?" said Barclay, somewhat surprised. Mario never seemed a reader.

"If you sign it."

"Cross always overnight's one copy first. I'll have more by the end of the week."

Marilyn handed it off to Mario. "You glad it's over?" she said to Barclay, meaning she was glad it was over. Living with a writer writing something he didn't want to write was as fun as catching a colostomy bag.

"It's out there, babes. Train's moving. I'm moving on."

And that was it. The rest of the day was spent doing rest of the day stuff. He showered, went outside for a bit to watch Wallace and Terry play a round of one-on-one in their backyard (their mother and father always made sandwiches and drinks whenever another adult came over; they were starved for grown conversation), then he went home, brushed his teeth, copped a few feels off the wife and finally, when night had fallen and there was no way to postpone his head making contact with the pillow, he clearly heard the word of God: *It's out there.*

Bela, upon seeing the finished work? "Damn. That a real woman?"

He came home a few days later and almost had a heart attack as Terry picked up the book from his hammock.

"Whoa now!" He smoothly whipped the book away.

"Ms. Royse said I could cut the grass."

"Ok. Get to cuttin'."

"Ok." Terry tried x-ray visioning Barclay's hand blocking the cover.

"Ok," reiterated Barclay.

"Ok," Wally assured him.

"Ok," Barclay said, hating resorting to that kind of authority.

"All right."

"Ok then. Glad we had that conversation." Barclay left, keeping the book glued to his side, and went inside. "Baby," he said, "You cannot leave this out in public."

"Our backyard's not in public."

"It is when there's a kid in it. Since when do you read my stuff anyway?"

"I helped this time. I'm skimming. I never knew you wrote good sex scenes. Learn something new every day."

"Ow!"

"What?"

Through pained eyes he said, "Stubbed toe."

"Does Cross consider himself your agent?"

"I don't know. I suppose he does. He can think what he wants."

"Don't be sensitive."

"I'm not sensitive."

"I'll smack that ass."

He took the book with him. "You can't read this anymore."

"By the by, hi!" she shouted. Limping made his butt switch.

"Howdy."

He plopped on the bed. He raised his neck to regard his crotch. *You knew you had it in you, didn't you, son?* No writing, he decided, at least for a couple weeks.

Then a better thought: a quick vacation would be a damn good thing.

He went back downstairs.

"Is it too soon for you to put in for vacation for next week?"

Marilyn dropped the dish rag and grinned at him. "Ain't nothin' but a word. Beach or cruise?"

"I'm thinking I feel like a gambling man. Does what happens in Vegas still stay in Vegas?"

"Yes."

"Pack some liniment."

The gods didn't smile often but in Vegas they practically brushed their teeth and gargled for him. The first day there he won five thousand dollars. During the second bout of lovemaking one night Marilyn, first time ever, shrieked with delighted surprise his entire name (although "Fucking" was not his middle name). They even managed to eat three meals a day together without worrying about middle-aged weight gain. Simply having breakfast, lunch and dinner with somebody you loved was a damn good thing. The food tasted better and conversation became important.

"If I tell you I love you in Vegas it comes home with me," he said.

She tipped her mimosa to him. "Keep it in my carry-on bag."

Chapter Eleven

"Until you do right by me…"

They all watched *The Color Purple* together.

It was hard as hell to watch a movie with a party going on without wanting to kill someone.

By the time they got to the part where Celie gave Mister the finger mojo nobody was actually watching the movie anymore; they were just glancing for highlights and making plans for the nights and days to come.

Plenty was going to be inside Neon. That's just the facts of it. Fun's fun but nobody wants to play Pac Man forever, that's for damn sure.

Le'Mon was going to steal Plenty's money…and say it got stolen at Plenty's party. The trick was in the timing. Oh, and Le'Mon and Yvonne: boots. Strong boots. Timbalands with a two inch layer of mud on the soles, because the only thing better than Neon…was Neon's friend. It wasn't like he wanted to settle down or anything with Thundra (would she let him call her that? Aw, hell yeah!), but to get to fuck her about the same amount of time he'd been with Neon would be cool. A baller's life ain't but a tsetse fly:

Fuck hard, little fly. Fuck often. Fuck strong.

Neon was no lesbian. Had no plans on experimenting with sweet-n-low, wasn't changing her name to Thelma and/or Louise, and was not, under any circumstances ever, the rest of her life, going to find herself in similar circumstances such as surrounded her here and now. This qualified as absolute batshit. Her dream was to make it big doing greeting cards? Who in fuck cares about greeting cards?! Even two-dollar hoes owned their own computers now to fire off get-over-your-STD cards to friends. Maybe Plenty was on to something with this book thang. No-talent skeezes were out there making big money off sexual fantasies their tame asses couldn't pull off if Neon loaned them Bubba, a can of lube, and a supply of Chapstick. Neon envisioned the title of her blockbuster debut: *I Got Ya Fantasy For Ya.* Start her own publishing house with the seed money she was about to come into, get some hoes who had actually fucked more than once to write some hot sauce with sticky grits, and maybe, just maybe, start to feel like she was living real life.

Yvonne DeCarlo Paul knew one thing: out of the thirty some-odd fools up in here, not a one would miss her when she was gone and she'd miss not a one of them.

And, yes, that included family.

Taken as a whole, that, for the uninitiated, is how decisions got made.

Le'Mon's cell phone rang for the second time since Plenty'd given him the job. This time it wasn't Plenty, as Plenty was sitting right next to him.

The women had gone off to wait in line again for the bathroom.

Le'Mon's heart thumped.

"What number is it?" Plenty asked like a man with his finger up a supermodel's ass pausing to take a business call: cool as shit.

Le'Mon read it off.

Plenty told him not to answer it, got up, came back with a small notebook and made a couple quick, small scribbles, glanced around to take mental note of who was in or around, and—of those—who was nosy, put the pad right there on the coffee table for all to see, then went outside and didn't return for twenty minutes.

By which time Neon was ready to go.

So Le'Mon searched Plenty out to make his goodbye.

"Y'all 'bout to jet," Plenty said. He left his conversation

cold. "Let's run upstairs so you can pick a movie," he told Neon.

"That box is still down here," Le'Mon pointed out.

"I'll bring your bag down," he told Le'Mon. To Neon: "You get enough to eat?" He led her. "Take you some dogs home."

"He kind of burnt 'em."

"Ain't barbecue without a crust."

Up the stairs.

Into the room.

She sat on the edge of the bed while he hefted a box for her.

She got up nice and slow.

Ass cheek impressions.

His eyes went straight to it.

"When you gon' let me tap that?"

Nasty motha. "You've been doin' that all night," she said plainly.

"You're the finest skittle ever gonna be around here. With them China girl eyes. Get with me, you'll be legendary. I'll make sure of that."

This is Le'Mon's long lost daddy, she thought.

"I don't do fuck and tell anymore," she said.

"You think about it. Le'Mon still be there when we're done."

"Ok."

He made to grab the backpack.

"How many movies can I take?"

"Whatever you want."

She fanned a few on the bed then bent over to peruse them.

"Le'Mon all right with you?" she asked over her shoulder.

"He's cool," he answered offhand. "Le'Mon ain't got nothin' to do with me and you for a few nights though. No disrespect though."

"None to me?"

"I don't disrespect a lady. You're like the *Close Encounters* UFO over the mountain next to these hoodie bitches. Whale tales and tramp stamps. Niggas get tired of seeing draws and tats every female walks by." His eyes were dead on her ass and the small of her back. Didn't help he was positive she was like that on purpose, RSVP-ing to the left nut's hand written invitation.

Calligraphy and everything.

Neon found a couple movies she wanted.

Plenty grabbed the backpack.

Neon raised partway up, fingers splayed on the mattress. "Go ahead," she said.

"What?"

"You better rub it before I walk away."

Nothin'.

But.

A.

Word.

He palmed that ass surprisingly tenderly, slow like a mind-meld but with a sense of newfound ownership.

Neon walked out of the grip.

"You might need to stay up here a minute," she said.

"Shee-id. Niggas better duck."

"Thank you for the movies. I'll bring 'em around."

Plenty Mo was a happy-ass scary something.

Oh, and Yvonne was now officially what she was in the first place: an afterthought. Plenty bounced down to the party and partied up.

Merry Christmas to all and to all a good night.

"It wasn't so bad, was it?" Le'Mon asked her.

"I got movies and shrimp."

Nuff said.

"How'd you and her meet?" Le'Mon asked casually.

"Mutual friends."

"Good to have friends."

"Yes, it is."

"Plenty ain't get on your nerves?"

"Not much."

"How much?"

"Nothing," Neon said. "We been gone ten minutes, party's over. Why are we talking about Plenty? I came like you asked and I was cool."

He remembered the cell phone still in his pocket, regretting that he hadn't gotten the chance to carry out the vague notion he thought was a plan. He grabbed the pack from the back seat. Bag didn't feel entirely right, so he unzipped the inner compartment.

Oh...fucking...shit. "STOP THE CAR!"

Neon swerved across two lanes.

"What the fuck is wrong with you!"

"We gotta go back to Plenty's."

"What'd you forget?"

"Now!" he snapped. "Take me the fuck back to Plenty's!"

She whipped the car into a U-turn and got him there without another word from either of them.

"Wait for me."

"I should come with you," she said.

But he was already out the door, reading the party's currents to lead him straight to Plenty, clutching the pack like those squirrely men with briefcases in spy movies. He almost knocked Yvonne down getting there, but she might as well have been ugly Ramona with two bad eyes for all the notice he gave her.

Neon flew past Yvonne without a glance.

Plenty studied the sunken look on Le'Mon's face. He saw the way Le'Mon held the backpack.

"Plenty, we got a problem."

Plenty left his negotiating session with Wendy, re: the blowjob commissioned for deliverance in a few minutes.

Le'Mon didn't even wait for Plenty. He went straight inside and upstairs.

Plenty exchanged glances with Neon. Neon shrugged.

Yvonne sidled up. Plenty recruited her.

"Cuz, keep Neon company a minute."

Then he was off.

Le'Mon held the bag out and back-stepped into the room as soon as Plenty came off the landing. Plenty shut the door.

"Somebody fucked me, man," said Le'Mon with a nod at the bag.

Plenty opened it, didn't see what he was supposed to see, set the bag on the bed and scared the shit out of Le'Mon because he was calm.

"You been in the bag." It wasn't a question.

He answered Plenty dead on, staring him straight in the eye. "Fuck. No."

"Who knew what was in the bag, Le'Mon?"

"Nobody."

"No, somebody knew." Somebody at this party was about to—Ok, picture this: his big ass with his big dick fucking Smurfette as if she was the second coming of Vanessa Del Rio.

Pain aplenty for somebody who was too stupid to think Plenty Mo wasn't in the know.

Niggas done ate my shrimp and gon' thieve from me? Son of a bitch!

"I put a lot of work into that bag, Le'Mon."

"I know."

"Some clever shit went into that bag."

"I know."

The wheels were turning, the wheels were turning, and then a light popped bright.

"Where the fuck Yvonne and Neon?"

"I don't know."

"Leave the bag," ordered Plenty and went off for them.

They were in the kitchen eating cake with Jahmone.

"Anybody go upstairs with y'all?" he asked.

Neon questioned Le'Mon with her eyes.

"No," Yvonne answered for them.

"And nobody was up there?"

"Not that I saw," she said. "Some nigga with a camera phone sneak a picture of me?"

"No—"

"I see my tits on the internet—" Yvonne said.

"Thong too," Neon reminded her.

"—thong too, I'll act a fool up in here."

Le'Mon was briefly in a better place. Titties and thongs and Thundra.

Oh my.

Wait, and Neon was there to see it? That was almost like a three way the longer he thought about it.

Which totaled point eight seconds before the heat off Plenty's body melted all but reality aside.

Plenty stared hard at Yvonne.

Yvonne stared back at Plenty.

Plenty quickly swerved.

"Ain't nobody do that to you," he said.

"I'm not playing, Steve. They do that at the Y all the time. You'd think with more women in the world than men there wouldn't be so many horny bastards."

"Somethin' ain't where it's supposed to be, that's all," said Plenty.

"Nobody else up there when we went up," said Yvonne.

"Not that I saw," said Neon.

Jahmone stood in the background memorizing every word.

"Jahmone?"

"Yeah?"

"Get the fuck out."

There was a swig of champale left in one of the bottles. Plenty downed it while everyone looked on, faces showing different levels of confusion.

Plenty set the bottle down.

"I hate losin' shit. Cuz, you taking this cake with you, right?"

"You can leave it."

"Take it home. I think they ate enough out there." He opened the drawer for the foil. "Le'Mon, I'll call you later."

And that was that.

Party was officially over.

*

"Neon, why is shit always happening to me?"

Because you're stupid, Le'Mon, and you know you're stupid, and you celebrate it.

Because, Le'Mon, stupidity is not a way of life; it is not a religion.

She didn't say anything. Better just to drive.

"The Light-Skindid Thugz don't fuck with nobody, ain't no beef with nobody, but somebody wants to see my ass fucked. Twelve niggas have to hold me down, fuck my ass. Fuck that. Ain't nobody fuckin' me. This shit ain't on me. I ain't do shit he ain't tell me to do. Every one of them niggas probably out the pen. He just gon' leave the bag up there by itself. I ain't even know what was in it! Mothafucker thinks he's the shit too much. Everybody in the world don't give a fuck that he's Plenty Mo. You get yo nuts stomped just like everybody else, nigga. Yo dick get Bobbited just like everybody else's." He sniffed and swallowed hard, staring out her window at Day City.

"Why don't this place love me?" he asked, and turned to the soft body next to him for answer.

"The city's a fool, man. Run by fools for fools. Ain't you sick of the zoo?" said Neon.

Le'Mon nodded.

"What was in that bag?"

"I don't know."

"Was it drugs?"

"No."

It ain't a religion, Le'Mon. "So I'm stupid now?"

"Bi—" He stopped himself. "Neon. Not now. Shit!"

Neon took a deep breath and relaxed it slowly, and when she was done she didn't feel the presence of Le'Mon in her life anymore.

So *Waiting to Exhale* had gotten that right; it was all in how you breathe.

She dropped him off with a token and sullen titty suck in his dark driveway then went home and counted her purse full of money.

Chapter Twelve

The Werewolf

She realized she hadn't written Boo a note. He was the one who might actually miss her and it was only right he feel like she was happy somewhere.

Her whirring computer made the house seem much safer. The minute she had gotten home she immediately stashed six hundred and eighty dollars, and those bills pounded away at the proverbial floorboards like a tell-tale heart.

"My dearest Boo," she typed (she'd always wanted to begin a letter that way)... then hit backspace and watched the cursor gobble the sugar.

She typed: *I'll miss you, Boo...but I'll love Hawaii!* (Here she'd draw a happy face.) *Sometimes a girl needs to change more than her doo to set things right. I would've told you in person—*

Wait.

She *would* tell him in person. She deleted everything and shut the computer down.

She grabbed a business directory and looked up movers and storage. A girl was going to need a bunch of cardboard boxes in a minute.

After a half hour she got antsy. Phone hadn't rung. Door hadn't been knocked on.

Another half hour, and it was the Bubba invitational in a warm shower for the soothing of nerves.

Yvonne's hankty ass finally got around to calling when Neon was on her second bowl of ice cream and potato chips.

"What happened?" Neon asked.

"Mayor's security did it."

"That's what Plenty said?"

"Didn't need to say it. Didn't move outside three feet from him the rest of the night."

(Plenty put his arm around Tyreese's surprised shoulder. "You're my best friend now," he said.

"Fuck you talkin' about?" The smaller man tried pushing off.

Plenty held him. People edged away.

"Friends talk to each other, right? We 'bout to find someplace to talk right quick.")

"Watch the news tomorrow," said Yvonne.

That meant somebody was likely to end up dead. That was the one aspect of Day City Neon hadn't let in yet, that easy acceptance of the local news being nothing but on-air obituaries.

"This is some evil shit, Yvonne. You're going to let Plenty think that? What if he blames somebody else? We're going to hell. This is some crazy shit."

"Fuck an orphan; you'll feel better. Short answer? I don't give a fuck. Nobody at that party will be missed 'cause nobody at that party wants to be missed. And I talked to that white girl some more. That little drunk fuck has done some shit you don't want to know about. Don't believe that shit about everybody deserves to live. Don't you dare believe it. Ever hear the one, 'Men go crazy in congregations, they only get better one by one'? You and me, one and two. Steve is irritated now but it's not like he needs this, and it's for damn sure not his to begin with."

"But family..."

"My cousin ain't been family to a soul in this life since nineteen eighty-two. If you don't want any part of this I can get amnesia right quick."

"No, I wants. Strings?"

"We can divide it up butt nekkid. No strings."

"What if he finds out though?"

"I've talked about moving away since the day I was born. The service was supposed to take me away, but guess what?" she said, indicating by her presence on the phone that she was still here. "I wanted him to do the party to get Le'Mon over there. He did it to get you over there. If you want to guarantee he won't suspect you, let him fuck you. Make sure you take some Bactine with you."

Neon shuddered at an image of him gripping her ass like a pomegranate.

"That'll happen when you let Le'Mon in you."

"That's a thirty second detail, girl. I'll be by tomorrow to divvy things up. You near a calendar?"

"Yeah."

"Pick a date three Wednesdays from now."

"Why?"

"That's when we're leaving. Can you stay cool that long?"

Neon summoned up bravado she didn't really feel, but the second the words came out, she embodied it:

"I'm James Kirk, bitch."

Yvonne smiled on her end. "Kirk the fuck out."

Yvonne divided up the money the next day.

The day after that, Neon invited Boo over for movies after his shift.

She was preoccupied.

"Neon?"

"Yeah?"

"You're preoccupied. Been that way lately." Boo grabbed a handful of popcorn from the bowl.

That's because I got a hundred thirty-two thousand, six hundred eighty dollars in my basement.

"Ever think you'll get married, Boo?"

Backdafuckup—

He coughed out popcorn. "Baby, I ain't got that much

sense." A couple husks more. "Where'd that hellaciousness come from?"

"I'm getting soft, Boo. Tired of living edged up." *We fuck and you're nice to me, but that's all we do,* she almost said. "I've been thinking about moving anyway."

He groaned. He dropped his head back on the sofa and stared slack-jawed at her poorly painted ceiling.

Neon undid a uniform button and fingernailed the hairs peeking out. "Boo?"

"Yes."

"You gotta go when the spirit takes you."

"You ain't no church lady."

"I just wanted to let you know."

"This is fucked up."

She popped the next button on his uniform.

He took her wrist before she moved for the third.

"This supposed to be the last time we do it?" he asked.

She aimed the remote at the DVD player. The Green Man froze just before the Power Phantasmic infused him.

"I've always wanted to do this," she said. She jiggled her hand free and gripped his shirt at the collar.

"What?"

She pulled hard with both hands. Buttons pinged off her chest and forehead. A musky odor coated his broad neck and shoulders: his scent mixed with cologne, of muscles and hair and the hard places and crazy things men like to do.

And she couldn't lie: it made her wet.

"You care about the buttons?" she asked his surprised eyes.

"I ain't got sense but I ain't stupid."

"Do something you've always wanted to do to me."

He kissed her. Slowly and tenderly, full flesh to flesh, lips munched like berries the way lovers do, a kiss like they'd never done, one that wasn't rushed, that wasn't 'preciate it, the kind that drew life, a first and last kiss that was practice for the real thing. His hands trapped her face and she let him; fingers tangled in her hair and she sighed into the whole thing. They kissed past breaths and swallows into one long, winding kiss that she allowed him to break off in his own good time.

When he did, they drew simultaneous inhalations and just stared at each other.

Hey, who knew passion could be a slow thang?

"So where you goin'?" he asked, voice even more husky. His eyes reflected in her eyes.

"You goin' in in the morning?" she asked.

"Naw."

"Then let's take a shower and go to bed."

"Ok."

Anybody that hasn't just laid up on a woman's warm booty while she's dreaming God-knows-what but feels safe with you—we weep deep, 'cause that's some sadness there.

If Boo'd been a crying man he would have cried at the loss of something so warm, soft and pure as a spooned derriere.

But he wasn't a crying man. He lay there with her body nestled into the length of him and he thought thoughts. Like who was fucking with her and why?

He had a good feeling he'd find out before she was gone. Might not be enough to keep her from leaving but at least she'd leave a little lighter.

Yep, he was going to do some Scooby Doo, and old Mister McGreevy was about to get his costumed ass naturally kicked.

But for now, he was nestled in the warm sun where ass met thighs, and just reminding himself of that fact made his wee lad jump. He pushed the horniness aside.

They hadn't fooled around in the shower (not beyond him giving a nipple a quick vibrato suck and her soaping his ass), and they hadn't made love in the bed.

Sometimes it's better if a man just falls asleep.

Morning came—

—and, cued by fate's cruel embrace, oh pernicious harpy of life that delivers a man to such dire fathoms, so did Le'Mon.

The first thing Le'Mon thought to do when he saw this huge Bigfoot mofo from a distance stepping off Neon's porch in such early hours was bumrush him, except he'd get his ass kicked.

That's why he went around the block, cut through a backyard, and came up a little ways behind Boo. *Security guard, huh? No you ain't touched Neon with yo dick, punk ass. You 'bout to get some shit fired up on you! Light-Skindid Thugz, bitch!*

Now, it's one thing to fuck and doublefuck; it's another thing from a whole different part of the world where they don't even speak your language and the only way they have to communicate is to give you the middle finger...to physically see the dude you're dipping it with.

That's precisely why Le'Mon was walking around with a gun he'd bought off some suburban kid. Suburban boys had shit up to and including missile launchers; the untraceable gun in his pocket was more than adequate to pop somebody for trespassing on the poon.

Plus Plenty was still unusually calm; no good could come of that.

Boo, though, didn't notice the light skinned guy down the block veering away from him. Boo hadn't wanted to park his car so far down the block but sometimes you had to take what was available.

After he drove off, Le'Mon waited a minute then about-faced to Neon's house.

Her doorbell ringing that early in the morning meant it was somebody looking for her, and that meant one thing.

Sitting in the kitchen with buttons to sew, Neon cursed.

Fake Rome hadn't even been as troublesome as this boy!

And if he was only now coming up that meant he'd seen Boo. Neon thought about hiding the shirt but instead said fuck it. She threw on a robe and opened the door with the shirt hanging at her side, regarding him through the screen.

"Where you been the last couple days?" she asked.

"You thinkin' about letting me in?"

She unlocked the catch and stepped back.

"Saw your boy leave out," he said.

She closed both doors but didn't lock either one.

Oh, everybody was cool as dry ice.

"I might need to stay someplace for a little bit," he said.

"Did I not tell you from the get-go I was not in this?"

"I need you in this."

She threw her hands up. Her robe opened. His eyes settled on bush. She brushed past him for the kitchen.

"You sewin' a nigga's shirts?" he said.

"You got the pussy you wanted from me."

"Yes, I did."

She brought the slap from way down there. It whipped his head so fast to one side he didn't see the mess get knocked out of him.

Le'Mon returned with the ready fist but the look in her eyes stopped him dead. It was one step short of psycho chick.

He wiped the sting off his face and tried to laugh.

She advanced on him with fists of her own.

He stopped laughing.

"I've been sitting here the past couple days wonderin' when somebody was gonna do a drive-by just 'cause I was at the party. Whatever the fuck you were doing with him and that bag has got me inside it and that's...some...shit! If I'ma have somebody over here to make me feel protected, you shut the whole fuck up! This is your fault!" Tears rimmed her eyes. She whirled. "Where my fucking knives at?"

Oh, shit—

He intercepted her away from the cutlery drawer. She didn't even struggle, just let herself be moved like a limp doll.

They stopped at the sink.

He was in her hair, smelling it, horny despite himself, the cave man in him probably thinking her skin was still flush from doing Job Security. His wrists crossed over a tit. He wanted to werewolf the shit out of her, straight up bang till skin, blood and bone came off. Rip out Plenty's throat. Track that security guard bastard down.

Eat a motherfucking baby in front of its mama.

Then eat her too. The good way and the bad.

"When I let you go—" his voice was a low, calm murmur in her ear (he swore she was pushing her ass against him on purpose)—"I'ma pour me a cup of coffee. I ain't ate yet, so I'ma have me some toast. You'll be done trippin', and we're gonna sit down and figure out what the fuck is wrong."

He let go, ready to tense up, but she simply walked out of the kitchen and sat hard on the sofa.

Le'Mon puttered at the coffee pot and toaster.

Neon got up, went into her bedroom, closed the door, and got dressed.

He crunched into his second piece of jelly toast by the time she was done.

Jeans, a loose Betty Boop T-shirt that fell past her ass, hair pulled back in a tail and a pair of gym shoes laced up tight.

"I left you some coffee," he said.

She poured it and sat across from him.

He stared hard into his cup. "That's the first time anybody ever slapped me like that. Shit hurt."

"I coulda punched you."

"And we'd still be rollin' on the floor." He looked at her. "I ain't taking that shit from nobody."

"Le'Mon..." She sighed, feeling very old and heavy. Her

palm hurt where she'd caught his jaw. "You're trying to take me someplace I don't want to go."

"You don't know where you need to be!" He waved his hands in the air, flustered. "So who is he anyway?" he blurted.

"Just somebody I met, same as you."

"Just some more dick, huh? This is what I was gonna do with that money."

"What money?"

"I was gonna go somewhere."

"You were going to buy some shit."

"After I went somewhere," he said.

"Anything you got from Plenty is all about fucking you up more than you are."

"Ain't never liked that you cuss so much. You're supposed to be a fucking lady."

"Le'Mon. I think the first thing I said when we met, and stop me if I ain't remembering right, was fuck you."

"Yeah."

"Didn't I keep my promise?"

"Your club-ho friends laughed their asses off too."

"So now you're done with Plenty?"

"Naw."

She pushed away from the table and stood with arms folded. "Till you are, you are with me."

That was the simple thundercrack snaps a man in two.

He tried to shuck and jive her, motioning squiggles on the table with his spoon, grinning his grin as if something—to him and only him—was funny.

He said: "You wanna fuck right quick?"

He had never seen anybody stone up so quickly. Le'Mon ran his hand over his soft wavy hair. He caught her eyes following the motion. It was the first time she noticed he didn't have his usual doo-rag. "Yeah, I'ma let this shit grow. I'm sorry, I'm sorry, I'm sorry—that wasn't right. I fuck up everything, don't I?"

"I wish I would pity your ass. You've seen *Scarface* one too many times and you've got dreams of runnin' an empire while having these draws by your side to smooth things out no matter how rough it might be on me. That ain't got nothing to do with nothing."

"I guess it ain't. Niggas gotta hit it and quit 'cause y'all always be ready to bust on us. I ain't about to spend good time chasing bubbles that just pop pop pop. Cain't nobody be doin' that. Shit ain't right."

"You know, you're handy as hell with what can't be done."

"Fuck you know?"

"I ain't dumb enough to think every man is a zombie for pussy. Hell, most of 'em ain't. But I got you and yours doing the Night of the Living Dead for me, don't I? So, yes, I do know something. I know that there's shit in the world that actually makes a difference in me being happy. I don't need a man, Le'Mon, but when I do it's gonna be paradise 'cause his ass will love the shit out of me. You know that feeling when your finger punctures the toilet tissue and accidentally hits shit and you gotta wedge soap under your fingernail: that's where I'm at right now with you, man."

"Fuckin' talking 'bout love all the time now..."

"Oh, you ain't got to hear a word from me," she said. "Matter of fact, negro, guess what?"

He stared blankly at her, waiting.

"Get the fuck up and go."

The edges of his eyes hardened.

"Go on home, man."

"Can I finish my coffee?"

"God. Damn." She wanted to float away from him and this house and be done with tiresome shit.

"That how it always was?" he said, thinking about whatever they'd had to call a relationship.

"Here's a tip: anybody you meet in a club? They ain't interested in living your dream."

"You shoulda told me that back then."

"You chased me," she said, putting emphasis on that me to let him know this was gold he'd been dealing with. "What part of 'fuck you' didn't you understand?"

He drank the last of his coffee, stood, and stretched. She tensed up, ready to knock him on his ass and go George Washington Carver on a nut...but he walked by without even looking at her and left the house.

Question: Who was coming up the block as he hit the corner?

"Hey!" Le'Mon faked a big smile. "How you doin'?"

Yvonne tried to think of the quickest way of avoiding him.

"Just getting a little walk," she said.

"I just left from there. She musta went to work. You got time to talk a second?"

"I don't do street corners."

"You wanna go sit on her porch?"

"Not if she's not home. Walk to the store with me."

Every time he saw her he wanted to trust her with his thoughts. *You make my dick wiggle.* That shit was distracting as hell. As antidote he thought of fat women and the way they chewed.

"I'm worrying about her," said Le'Mon.

"Why?"

"Choices she makes, y'know?"

"Your face is kinda red over there."

"I slept funny on the bus gettin' here. I ain't had much sleep since your party."

She held a hand up, stopping both their motions. "Ok. I don't want to hear anything about whatever you and my cousin are doing."

"Know what? I got no plans doing anything with Plenty." He

held his own hands up, showing they were free and clear.

A man a little younger than Le'Mon bicycled past with a heavy load of books.

"I'm thinking about school, y'know, get me somethin' that's good for me," said Le'Mon.

They resumed walking.

"Neon just be sittin' around on her computer a lot, though. That ain't cool."

"How old are you?" Yvonne asked.

"Man don't tell how old he is."

"No, that's women."

"Y'all get better with age. Be hittin' them peaks. Men just get old."

"I'm over thirty, Le'Mon. Say what's on your mind."

"I think you're the finest plate of gravy I'm ever going to see in this world and all I wanna do," he said, suddenly having to furiously picture huge lady fingers tearing into sopping greasy chicken, "is make you feel good."

"And you feel good."

"And me feel good, 'cause, fuck, life is a bitch, Yvonne, we both know that. A gangsta fuckin' bitch. You know? When I saw you in Neon's house I said, 'Know what, this the kind of woman she ought to be with.' Not some silly-ass gigglies don't do nothing but drink and," he hesitated. Using the word here was too close to the real word.

Yvonne brought it. "Fuck?"

"Ain't none of 'em got sense. You do."

"Dog tags don't mean I got sense."

"You live like this shit never touches you."

"You know that already?"

"Like a light. I didn't know you lived around here."

She shrugged and said, "You're probably just in and out when you visit Neon," and forced herself not to smile but he didn't catch it. They entered a corner store where she pretended she wanted snacks.

She definitely didn't need him trying to follow her home.

She broke out missile-to-man artillery.

"Tell you what," she told him. "Let me think about you," which came out with the definite tone of leave now or be forever holding your piece when you think about me.

"All righty," he said, nodding to the beat of a slim possibility. "Ain't nothin' but a thang, right?"

"About it in a nutshell." She smiled vaguely his way. He smiled back, nodding again, and left the store.

Yvonne remained in the filthy corner store another few minutes. It gave her time to think.

Le'Mon was like the doof who thought everybody was as dumb as he was so he felt clever, not realizing everybody saw straight through his dumb ass.

She bought a pop, some Fritos, and two stale honey buns for the birds and went back to Neon's house, munching chips as if it was just one more summer day.

*

Mayor Donbrough fiddled with the earlobe that had the diamond stud. He hummed when he thought, but always told people he didn't when they pointed it out, which pissed his wife off so much whenever he said it to her that last week she'd slapped the fi out of him. She'd had a humongous headache.

"If you weren't humming I wouldn't have SAID to stop humming same as you need to stop pissing in the sink and keep your goddamn face out of titty bars!" She was a small-boned woman so it didn't hurt that much, but still...and she wasn't supposed to know he pissed in the sink.

Dennis Donbrough was squat and round but knew some shit about politics, main shit being appease the wife if you want a second term. Fastest way to go down in flames in public was to fuck with the wife. She was bourgeoisie as hell, but booshie didn't mean she wouldn't nut up on him straight into the Gospel if he pushed her far enough.

Day City was mostly black and so was the mayor—mostly but not thoroughly, not in the ways that mattered—so his excesses were justified far as he was concerned. Getting titty-bopped across both cheeks at dives at three in the morning was about right for keeping the Mack Avenue to Springwell bus line going.

That's just how a fresh mayor of a crumbling city rode.

He stopped his tuneless humming. He finished thinking, and knew exactly what needed to be said to Tyreese who was waiting patiently on the other end of the line.

"I said not to fuck with them in the first place," he reminded Tyreese, whose worried breathing came clear over the phone even though he was trying to pretend he was cool. "I said, 'Nigga, you at a whole 'nother level now rolling with me,' didn't I?"

"Idea seemed solid."

"Ain't shit a good idea unless I'm in front of a news crew

saying so. This penny ante shit ain't about to touch me."

"Man, we been knowing each other since high school."

The mayor planned to hang up in five seconds to go have dinner with the wife. "Tell you what," he said, "take a mop to this shit or I'll be seeing you at the reunion in five to ten."

Click. Lydia loved dinners together, made her feel whole again instead of just part of the Donbrough package.

It's all about appeasing the wife.

He said this to Plenty who, in crisp slacks and golf shirt, was across the room squinting at fundraiser photos.

"I'ma need glasses soon," Plenty muttered to himself, then agreed with the mayor's statement. "You ain't never lied," he said.

When Plenty left the residence, he did so out the back door.

(Leave chapters here in body of text, Barclay had noted to Cross, to create runaway train effect.)

Chapter 13

"The Domino Theory, ya ignint bastard!"

Yvonne had always wanted to try sewing...until now that she actually tried it. How was she supposed to spear a piece of string through a teeny-assed needle that couldn't sew up a mosquito's thong?

"Twist it," said Neon.

"You said wet it."

"Wet it and twist it." Frustrated watching Yvonne fumble at the hole, she said, "Leave it. Just leave it."

"So where you plan on going?"

Neon took Boo's shirt and dropped it on the kitchen table. She got up.

In the movies this part is simple! This is where shit comes clear and I say goodbye to the old with the sun coming up and a crane shot.

She felt trapped by wide-open spaces.

"Everybody says Atlanta is nice," she mumbled.

"You ain't going to Atlanta," Yvonne said.

"Fuck Atlanta."

"Fuck Atlanta."

"Going to Hawaii," said Neon.

"Go to the Philippines, girl."

"Ain't enough of us there."

"Exactly my point! Step off that plane and they'd start a cult around your fine behind. You'd be their god."

"I don't know if you've noticed, but God takes it in the ass these days," Neon said. "I wouldn't be a god for shit these days."

"Just avoid stupid people worship."

"That's like avoiding a white girl at a basketball game. And I still ain't changin' my name to Thelma. I ain't up for any crazy ass road trip shit."

"I've never particularly liked the name Louise."

"We've got enough money to move."

"That's all I need."

"I want a new life."

"Whatever life you have follows you, girl, unless you cut the cord. Money won't roadblock it."

"Screw you, Ilyanla."

"Dr. Phil, bee-yotch."

"Look, not much is gonna make me feel better today."

"Neon, this is money you found on the street. Keep some perspective." She toyed with the shirt. "Who owns this?"

"Just a friend."

"A lot of your friends keep extra clothes in your house?"

"Messy eater." Which he was. Boo couldn't keep salsa on a chip if you beat him.

Neon nervously paced from the counter to the sink to the stove, fiddling with things. Yvonne almost felt sorry for her.

Except for that hundred thousand dollars in her basement.

"Flashlight, I hate to say this but: how stupid you gonna be?"

"What'd you call me?"

"The main thing keeping you here is the lack of money endemic—look it up," she said to the puzzled flash across Neon's face, "to our social class. Armored car just lost a fat sack in front of your house. Paper-man just tossed it on your porch. Jehovah's Witness is ringing your doorbell and handing it to you with a copy of the Tower. Now, if you ain't took it up in your house yet, that's on you. Simple math, girl, one plus one is two, especially for a black woman. Me and you. Ain't shit else simple in our lives. We need some simple arithmetic, and when you find it you grab on like Sweet Dick Willie has come to town and plans to take you Hanukkah shopping. In other words, appreciate this rare, beautiful thing. Let it ride over, through you, in you, under you, as long as you ride with it. Personally, I like the sound of Hawaii...and I like you. It'd be cool if we weren't too far apart. You still ain't Kirk. I could put you at Chekov, but not Kirk. Who else you know can hang with the Trek?"

"I've got Wrath of Khan."

Yvonne stood up decisively.

"Then we need to be watching that shit," said the woman with the dog tags.

When the movie was over they made some calls, got online, did some research, and set a few things in motion.

Neon hung up from one call, thinking: Motion is easy, and the dawn of it lit her face with the most beautiful smile.

Yvonne nodded agreement.

"Things have to fall into place," Yvonne reassured her.

"Yield to the logic of the situation."

"Why do they have to?"

"The Domino Theory."

"Ohhh," said Neon. "If I'd thought it was that easy..."

"Shut up."

Yvonne stayed at Neon's till about two in the afternoon. Her stomach had been increasingly shaky after eating the corner store Fritos, but now it was really bad. Gurgles and churning twisted it to where she couldn't ignore it anymore. She was getting both the empty spitty mouth and that sudden hole-tightening that said ignore me if you want.

"Thelma?" Yvonne said.

"Yeah?"

Louise knew her body well enough to know she had enough time to get home in order to tear a bathroom up.

"I gotta go."

Neon noticed the green around Yvonne's gills. "You need the bathroom?"

"Some things you just don't share."

True that. "Need a ride?"

Yvonne was about to decline, but one plus one is two.

"That might be best." She rubbed her stomach gingerly. "Something's not sitting right."

"Probably something at Plenty's."

"Damn shrimp."

Dot dot dot diddly daa da!

Neon dropped her off then returned to her own home with a sense of purpose she hadn't felt since she was twelve and planned to win the Hemsley Middle School science fair. She'd been ahead of her time detailing the scientific properties of weave glue. Some skinny fool won, though, with a dinosaur/volcano diorama his daddy built.

Everybody knew about dinosaurs. Not one in ten folks knew how weave glue worked.

Volcanoes.
Volcanoes in Hawaii.
Neon in Hawaii.
Neon in bikinis.
And Yvonne.
Thelma and Louise.
Hell, Lilo and Stitch.
Just as long as we're together.
Sisters. Just like Shug sang in *The Color Purple.*

*

"I swear to God, if you don't stop pissin' on this building I'ma kill you." Boo was sick of this dirty-nasty coming around making him have to get up and work. The uniform wasn't about working, it was about sitting on ass.

"Best call me 'Sir', bitch. I kicks bitches inna nuts on a daily basis. Where yours at, bring 'em over here. I own you, bitch. Watch me fall down, yo ass just kneed me in the side. Tazer and shit. Your name on this building? 'Cause I will sue. I will sue a motherfucker."

"Just go home, man, I ain't got time for this shit tonight."

"Fool, if I had a home do you think I'd be peein' on the side of this building? I think not, you ugly sonavum bitch. I'd be pissin' on a ho who I done gave five dollars. Like a rich motherfucker. My mind's telling me noooo," he sang off key, "But my bod-day—"

Boo slipped his rubber gloves on.

Seeing this, Homeless Joe said, "You done fucked up now, nigga, you done fucked up! I know where yo nuts is; I'll pop them bitches again."

Boo advanced on him. He was aware of exactly where the cameras were and what they could see.

"You're about to believe your name was Osama at JFK," said Boo.

He went back inside Greenleaf Plaza feeling just a little less stressed and a little clearer-headed.

There was a reason for all this all-of-a-sudden shit, somebody who had gotten in her hair grease and was itching the shit out of her scalp.

On his next break he called one of his boys, a laid off police officer who'd read Walter Mosley's *Easy Rawlins* mysteries and thought he was a private eye.

In the Easy Rawlins mysteries, there was Denzel Washington, who'd played Easy in the movie. And there was Mouse.

Joe Nab was not Denzel.

He sat around his house most days thinking about how many people on his block he could arrest on sight.

Nab's response to being asked to put some eyes on Neon's house for a couple days: "What kind of trouble she in? Is she fine? You jealous of somebody? Don't involve me in any reality show shit."

"Somebody's messing with her. I need you to tell me what you see."

"It's cool."

"Eyes only, man."

"Did I not say cool?"

"No jack-off pictures."

"You just killed my inspiration."

"But any dude go up in there that ain't me?"

"Yeah?"

"Kodak quality."

His boy's name was Joseph Jermaine Nabal.

Joe Nab.

The original undercover brother.

Leaving the Escalade at home, Nab parked far enough from the corner drug house that his presence on the block could've gone either way. In his nineteen ninety-four Dodge Shadow he was as invisible as Ethel next to Tiffany.

The whole joy of surveillance was scoping female bodies with the full knowledge that the scope both served and protected. Boo's lady had a nice enough house, small and cute, bare minimum of landscaping and shrubbery since you know a sister ain't trying to fuck up a nail. It was a brick house that a woman could walk into and walk out of comfortably on a daily basis.

A blue Dodge Neon zipped past him and pulled in front of that little brick house.

That was Joe's cue to open his door and get out. He pretended he was on a deep phone call, but damn, she was fine. Actress fine. *The Princess Bride* was right: there was a shortage of perfect breasts in the world (rent the damn movie, dammit), and here was a new and vibrant species yet undiscovered.

Joe Nab fell in love.

But he'd told Boo 'cool,' and word is bond.

But damn if the ass was not just two smiles put together.

The way she headed straight up the steps without looking left, right or at anything at all told him not all was right in her world.

He slowly made his way down the block, still pretending to be giving advice to his boy on how to treat a lady right (never knew when the right words might snag up a honey's ear).

He passed her house and noted the relative security of the windows and doors, the general income level he was dealing with, emotional maturity, likelihood of her getting herself involved in some deep voodoo, possible reasons why she'd be fooling with Boo, general relativity theory (as in, there weren't a lot of oil stains along the curb by her house, which meant not a lot of male relatives visited, and the two stains she did have were concentrated in about the same spots, so that meant Boo and who else?)—and knew that a clever man would've found a reason to go up to her door and get invited in, and Joe Nab was clever.

But word is bond.

So who or what was bothering her?

Joe'd find out. Boo wasn't generally violent, but everything an elephant stomps on doesn't necessarily mean he's mad.

Joe Nab, on the other hand, was violent. Couldn't be a decent cop if you weren't. The best accepted the necessity of kicking ass and shaped it into a tool to use. In the world of Nab, big difference between brutality and violence. Ask Rodney King. He got violence. Brutality, and he wouldn't have been around for his fifteen minutes of fame.

Joe Nab knew some violent motherfuckers, and he was willing, for her, to bring 'em out on the covert tip.

He made his way back to the car.

It was two-fifteen p.m.

He came back at four-twenty. Memories cycled on an hour schedule. After two hours, he was brand new again, on the opposite end and side of the block this time. The blue Neon hadn't moved.

A Putt approached. You could always spot a Putt, the raggedy fucks that looked like patched concrete and knew who knew whose business. This wasn't Yvonne's peeping Putt, it was Neon's puttering Putt.

Putt One and Putt Two.

Never address a Putt, just start talking to them.

"Who do you see going up in this house, man?" Joe asked, flicking a finger toward the house to get Putt Two's attention. His other hand pushed into his pocket in the universal symbol for cooperation.

"Yellow fool Neon cain't stand." Putt hit Nab's pocket with spider senses tingling: some change, some keys, and there was a five dollar bill about to rise up out of there.

"Silver Jeep?"

"Purple Cutlass, but he ain't rolled that for a while. Pull up in a white Caprice one time. Woman's car. Got floral tissues on the dash."

"Probably his mama's car?"

"Prolly."

"Awright." The five exchanged hands.

"How often you see big fella?" Nab asked.

"Don't see the Hulk as much, but he's in that ass—" Putt had already pegged Nab as nab, with no romantic interests. Yet. Neon was a nice lady, didn't need any extra bullshit. "He comes outta there loving everybody!" Putt said, gazing at her house like it was Mecca.

Then Putt Two moved on, not sensing any more money.

Le'Mon didn't know, but The League of Nab (Joseph Nabal, Giuseppe Nabloni, Josiah Napstein, Tiananmen Jo Na and Harry Smith) was about to get all up in it.

Never fuck with laid off policemen, boy!

*

Sales started off sluggish but picked up because several groups Cross targeted precisely for that reason got offended and the United States had once again declared war on somebody. Folks were tired.

Barclay reviewed the figures Netta sent and ignored his heaving sense of ennui.

The Light-Skindid Thugz gathered in Le'Mon's mama's basement.

Le'Mon had to be judicious with info. Any one of them would have turned him toward Plenty if they smelled two dollars.

Fake Rome's second cousin, Rialto, stopped Le'Mon before he could get started.

"Look here, man, you never call us all together unless some

shit 'bout to hit."

"Ain't no shit."

"No shit?" Rialto's pale hands adjusted the silk scarf tied around his hair. He favored a wavy neo-pompadour and brotha'd had his hair done not two hours ago.

"I might have a little drama comin'," Le'Mon down-played.

"Who's got your back?" Rialto asked.

"Y'all do."

"No, seriously."

His mama's heavy voice smashed down the stairs.

"Le'Mon!"

She paused.

"Y'all better not be down there smoking weed!"

"Mama, damn!"

"Grown ass niggas down here," muttered Fake Rome's cousin.

"Smokin' my shit up," she said, threatening the first stair with the weight of her foot. It creaked in submission.

Mama, ain't nobody smokin' a god-damned thing! "Mama, ain't nobody smokin' a god-damned thing! We talkin'."

Everybody stared at him. Whatever the shit was, was some serious shit. The kind make a Negro shut up and watch the Discovery Channel.

"Ain't none a y'all too old for the army!" she snapped. They listened to her footsteps track away from them. She fussed the whole time. "Shoot each other up around here so much, go on somewhere and shoot somebody like a patriot. Whichever one was yo daddy, you sure ain't like him..."

Wish we could say Le'Mon's mama had been elegant and pretty once.

She ain't.

Jabba the Hut from the get go, mind, body and soul, which lets folks know the mind of a man who would hit that: his dick was a mole, tunneling away blind and happy in the dark.

Le'Mon Marcus J'ello Arness was just like his daddy.

(Le'Mon told himself No Fat Chicks, but if Kentucky Fried Pussy opened up on a dark and stormy night...)

He vaulted the stairs and closed the basement door. He thumped back down and inventoried his boys:

Rialto Rome.

Big Julius. Big faggot ass.

The Wookie (on account of the gargling noise he made when he laughed, and his huge bushy redboned fro).

And this little dude named Peanut (because every gathering of men had to have a little dude named Peanut).

Light-Skindid Niggaz all.

And not a single one of them had Le'Mon's back in the least pretense.

"Come on, y'all!" he whined. "Just let me hole up if I need to."

"This ain't like when them Jetstream Brothers was after your ass, is it?"

"Nothin' like that!"

"'Cause that shit was foul."

"Hell yeah," the Wookie agreed

"Them mothafuckers lost in the Bermuda Triangle somewhere; this ain't got shit to do with them!"

"What the hell is it, then?" It was Peanut. Peanut had a sharp little knife. That's all you needed to know about Peanut.

"I was holdin' somethin' for somebody and somebody got it."

"Cain't stand vague niggas!" Peanut said, causing the Wookie to wookie.

"Shut yo Chewbacca ass up," said Le'Mon.

Wookie shot back, "Then where the who, what, when, where, why and how, girlie-bitch?"

"Plenty had me hold somethin' for him—"

Four sets of hands flew up in the air.

"How's his dumb ass get to fuck Neon but my girl got three teeth?" Big Julius asked Rialto.

"Nigga, you ain't got no girlfriend. Sound to me," said Rialto Rome to Le'Mon, "like you need the False Prophet Buford."

"That nigga in the triangle too!" said Le'Mon, knowing just how much somebody like the False Prophet Buford was needed at a time like this.

Brothers Jetstream and Buford were mystics. Niggas in the hood know all about mysticism. They just ain't got time for it.

"Why is yo crack baby ass fuckin' with Plenty!"

"I'm just tryin' to work some politics," said Le'Mon.

"Politics is for pussies, man!" said Peanut in his high-pitched man voice. "My uncle be seein' Plenty with the goddamned mayor! At the Sweet Tease. The nastiest fuckin' place in the city! Why? 'Cause bitches will suck a dick there for a Cheeto. The mayor knows don't nobody in there give a fuck he's the mayor; Plenty the one thinkin' he's up there 'cause he's on the mayor's tip. Donbrough don't give a fuck about Plenty Mo! Donbrough don't give a fuck that niggas see him at the Sweet Tease! They keep their mouths shut, he's cool. That's real politics."

"Break down the system for this—"

"Oh, I'mo break it down," assured Peanut. "You fuckin' with street shit," he informed Le'Mon, "and have become a victim of the Domino Theory."

"Shut yo ignorant ass up," said Le'Mon.

"The Domino Theory, ya ignint bastard: If you ain't the nigga pushin' the first domino you ain't got shit to say," Peanut finished.

Big Julius threw the co-sign, "So shut the fuck up."

Rialto Rome stood up. "And we out," he said.

On the way out the Wookie shook his head solemnly at Le'Mon. It took less than thirty seconds for Le'Mon to be the only one standing on his basement floor.

Looking around.

Chapter 14

"You didn't know we wuz comin back like that, did you, my brother!"

While it's true that ain't nobody got time for mysticism, and white folks think mysticism is like Merlin and Buddha, that doesn't mean mysticism ain't there.

The same time Le'Mon was getting played, the Brothers Jetstream were fighting spirit wars.

The same time Neon was packing Bubba and her toys away, Raffic the Mad Buddha was rescuing his wife Sweetness and her brother Light from the Thoom, a dumb cult that didn't think Scientology went far enough.

The same time Yvonne was throwing up in her toilet again, the coroner was closing the freezer drawer that now held Tyreese Shears in it.

That was a long time to be cold, brother.

Plenty let Tyreese go back to the Sweet Tease, had let him get sucked off by Wendy, then they drove out to Antloo Commons, a huge wooded park on the west side of the city. Hoes stayed three deep at Antloo Commons till the sun came up. You couldn't grind out a blunt without stepping on a used condom, and women don't know this about men, but after a man gets sucked off and has recharged for a minute, he needs to get fucked. The dick skin needs to feel pussy. It's not sex. It's a biological imperative. You throw water on fire; same principal on a Rollo just got expertly blown. Tyreese spotted the extinguisher he wanted over by some trees and went for it. It was dark as hell in the park but everybody knew where their undies were and exactly how they slid down. Plenty waited in the car.

The money didn't matter all that much to Plenty, but he'd be damned if he was going to let the nigga he'd coached through it play him for dumb. They'd hit every major titty bar in the mayor's circuit to get that money—and after hours titty bars ain't nothin' but money machines—and they did it quiet as kept while the mayor was in each titty bar. Mayor Donbrough was a black hole in bar security; all eyes were on him since he spent money, moreso than on dudes everybody knew, dudes part of the mayor's detail who knew it takes just a minute to walk out of somewhere unseen with a bag full of back room money.

Multiplied by four.

Donbrough liked his titties.

In the park, Tyreese had paused halfway between the car and the extinguisher.

Plenty was still sitting in the car.

Tyreese trotted back to him.

"You sure you don't wanna hit any of that?" he asked Plenty as the window rolled down. The car's air conditioning cooled Tyreese's face.

"Naw, man. Go on, get you some. Don't be all night, motherfucker."

"Cain't rush the trick."

"Your thirty second ass."

"Fuck you," Tyreese said, but he was grinning happily. The window quietly slid upward. Tyreese trotted back to the poon.

Beep zip tang and he returned to the car, walking slow and mellow.

The tinted window rolled down. Tyreese could just make out the red flare of Plenty's blunt. Didn't see the gun, but he felt the bullet hit him square in the chest. Splayed on the ground, the view above him was nothing but treetops, night sky and a couple stars. Off to the side he heard footsteps on dry grass, then something hot and hard traveled through his head.

Didn't see or hear anything after that.

Did the mayor know about the thefts?

Yes.

Did the mayor give a fuck?

Not till the shit got stolen from his house. Where better to hide a couple hundred thousand dollars when you and Day City's youngest-ever mayor (Donbrough was all of thirty-four) used to fuck around with hoes in the freshmen drama club?

But then it hit the news—and in politics, that's called Crackdown on Crime. Curfew as diversionary stall.

Everybody knew Plenty had had the money stolen from Donbrough's house in the first place, but not even Donbrough was going to come out and say it. Once enough noise had been made, though, and club owners let antsiness get the better of their judgment, one had best believe Plenty, as his own personal mission, had "gotten" the money back.

The plan was four phone calls to make everything all better before anybody decided to get too detailed in front of a microphone. Four little calls, call in, we note the call, we call you later at a prearranged time to pick up most of your money at a prearranged place. Anonymous and everything.

Only thing was, Plenty watched too many movies. Had to go and use a little nobody to keep things moving like a shell game to scatter any blatant trails back to him or Donbrough.

There's always a double-cross, and it's usually a friend doing it.

Simple politics.

So Tyreese was dead. That meant maybe a mayoral photo opportunity about a valiant, dedicated member of his security detail and another crackdown on crime. Tyreese was one of those irritating dudes who constantly reminded you of your past with him anyway, no matter that y'all hadn't been that tight. Extremely irritating.

Donbrough smiled, not knowing the specifics but definitely knowing that Plenty had gotten the job done. Politics, baby, politics. Nothing cold about it. To be good politics, it couldn't be personal.

So while Tyreese was stretched frozen in drawer eight four nine of the morgue, Mayor Dennis Donbrough was cool.

Joe told the League of Nab how fine Neon was, and they agreed she deserved to be protected.

Ain't that some shit.

But it was like this: one day she might hook up with one of them, screw the odds.

The League of Nab had a lotto club, and they played it regularly.

Harry Smith was the only one to actually come out and assess the situation when they met for lunch. "There's something seriously wrong with five grown men taking this so seriously."

"Harry, shut up," Josiah Napstein said, beating everybody to the basket of warm bread. "Ain't like we got shit else to do."

"Fucking layoffs," said Nabloni.

"I'm just saying."

"Harry, were you sitting on your ass before I called? I was for damn sure on mine," said Joe.

"You charging Boo for this?" asked Tiananmen Jo. "How many times has he failed the entrance exam?"

"No, I'm not charging him. You were on your ass too."

"Fuck all y'all," Tiananmen said, a Chinese black man in spirit if not by skin.

Funny how you can't even sell mayonnaise these days without somebody rapping.

"Maybe after I've had some drinks in me. Business at hand: we got a damsel in distress and we are the League of Nab.

Now Napstein, we know you can't do surveillance worth shit, so keep your Jewish ass from over there," warned Joe. "West Bank, ok? Don't make me go Palestine on your ass."

"You know that's anti-Semitic," Napstein said.

"Man, just 'cause y'all got your own damn word, shut the fuck up. 'You're anti-Semitic, she's anti-Semitic'. Know what? If it wasn't so easy to mock you the League wouldn't have shit else to do. 'She didn't give me kosher head' —"

"And that's the good shit there."

"Nigga, count me Anti-Catholic, anti-Christian, anti-Muslim—" said Joe.

"Anti-freeze," Harry kept it going.

"Anti-liberal, anti-Republican—"

"Anti-dumbfuck."

"Anti-pussy ain't directed at me—"

"Got a foundation set up."

"And anti-class system, so shut the fuck up. Of which you got none. So stick to what you know."

"Complaining about shit," Harry elaborated.

"And pretending Jews ain't in control," Joe said.

"You done laughing at me yet?"

"Naw."

"You didn't know we wuz comin back like that, did you, my brother!" said Harry.

"I see llama lick him," Tiananmen said, tossing some dap Harry's way.

"Fat back shellac."

"How 'bout we put a scare on the fucker and be done with it?" This was Giuseppe Nabloni.

Napstein hadn't gotten laid in a while though. "We split this up," he said flatly. "I'm tailing the tail," he said as final word.

"You're gonna fuck it up for us," said Harry.

"Oh, he'll fuck it up royally."

He fucked it up.

Neon got to wondering why this slightly shabby Jewish dude kept following her. At first she thought IRS because, y'know, a sista ain't paid her taxes, but then she remembered Oprah had a lot more money than she did.

So she worried that Plenty had gotten involved with the Jewish mafia. Was there a Jewish mafia? Hell, everybody had a mafia.

The first time she saw Napstein, he was on her block. Unusual, but he could've been a landlord.

Second time was downtown that same day after she gave notice to Charlene and assured her she was all right. Charlene didn't believe her but, hey, Neon was a grown-assed woman. Neon hugged Charlene under the brim of that hat, with Charlene whispering, "I know some peoples," and that's how it was left.

Third time: parking lot of Prescription Conscription, where she purchased medicine for Yvonne. The lady had gotten sicker and sicker the past two days, losing her insides from both ends. Not even considering the karma they'd twisted up, this was bad timing no matter how you looked at it.

So she faced Napstein dead on. *Oh, you're gonna pretend you don't see me this time?* Neon headed straight for Joe Napstein, who had no choice but to fake it and keep walking as though going into the store.

A can of mace rode her waistband under her shirt.

Napstein smiled friendly-like at the pretty lady in his path and made to move on.

But the pretty lady stutter stepped.

"When are we getting married?" she asked.

Shoppers passed by in and out of the drugstore.

Neon steamrolled him. "We must be fated seein' as I keep seein' you. We don't need a big wedding but you best believe I'ma cost you some money." With him off guard she tried to assess how dangerous he was. "And you'd better be good in bed, 'cause I certainly am—"

"No the fuck she didn't!" the other Nabs hooted at the later telling.

"That's not all," said Napstein. "Then she goes:

"'Give me a single reason to scream,' looking like Rambette but eyeballing the lot for how many might run to kick my ass. So I pop off a 'Ma'am,' takes a little edge off, tell her I'm Detective Joe Napstein—"

"You ain't a detective."

"I am now. And she bolts. Wasn't even a cool bolt. Girl just ran. All arms and legs. I'm standing there like Charles Manson just asked her to French kiss, so I make quick to my car too."

"Hey," Harry asked. "Boo ever just flat out ask her what was wrong?"

"Harry, what'd your ex-wife used to say when you asked?"

"Nothing."

Point answered.

"She kinda reminds me of Lela Rochon, only a little softer, rounder," Napstein said.

"Diana made you watch *Waiting to Exhale*, didn't she?" Joe Nab said. That was the only reason Napstein knew who the actress Lela Rochon was. Napstein's wife was black.

"Yes," said Napstein.

"Jew-boy?" Harry said.

"Yes?"

"You suck at surveillance."

*

Neon Temples whipped her little blue car through traffic... but that's how she always drove.

She left that drugstore parking lot not thinking who, what, when, where or how; the word detective rang way too loudly for clear thought. Detective was police, police was trial, trial was jail, jail was girl showers and thigh ear muffs—

Shit, this was definitely a *James is dead* moment: black folks that watch Good Times, show the white folks:

Damn! Damn! Damn!

She slammed the dashboard at being stupid enough to screw around with some Plenty Mo shit! Granted, Yvonne had made it seem as easy as taking money from a baby, but still. Crazy fuckers plus loser boyfriends plus cool-ass psycho dykes don't make for a laid-back retirement.

And how the hell's she gonna get sick now!

There was a reason, Neon reminded herself, you called her the Crazy Lady From Down the Block.

She whipped from behind one car, rode another, got just enough room to squeeze ahead of the first one, jumped back over, and kept doing the car length shuffle till she got stuck behind two pacing SUVs. Of course, the cars she'd passed passed her.

She did an illegal left, a wrong way down a one way and a hard right into the hood, where she kept waiting to hear the jangling squawk and bullhorn of "Neon driver, pull over."

The normal thing was for there to be generally few to no police around the neighborhood, but did she not just run into a detective? Yvonne was about to get half this bottle of Pepto down her throat. Diarrhea was fun compared to the shit they were in AND WHY THE HELL WAS PLENTY WALKING UP TO YVONNE'S DOOR?!!

Her blue Neon acted like it didn't have a brake pedal it zipped on so fast.

She got home acting like a corporate fraud, getting shit shredded with the quickness.

She wasn't about to become a daily plunger for some ugly man-woman whose lovin' had backed up.

Farewell cards? That meant you had plans, didn't it? Nab come to visit her, she wasn't going anywhere. She shredded the thick cards two at a time till the beat-up machine jammed on her.

She immediately shoved boxes and bags into her closet. Charitable donations. *I got saved last week, Officer; have you accepted sweet Jay-zus in your life?*

The money bag was in the bottom of her clothes hamper. She'd even left a few panty shields stuck to some draws to discourage curiosity.

No need to bother that.

She cracked the bottle of Pepto and took a hard swig.

Ok, calm yourself.

Is the door locked?

She went back and checked.

Yes, it was, but that's why they made battering rams.

Another swig.

The thing was, you don't just get rid of a hundred thousand dollars without wanting to slit your wrists afterwards. Be nice if she was one to give it all to charity, but she'd hate to have to hunt a hobo down.

The money could stay, it just couldn't stay in this house.

Ok.

I need my thong.

I need my push up.

I need my heels.

Battle ready.

The rims on Plenty's black truck spun lazily in the summer breeze, making the Hummer seem even more a ridiculous, oversized toy. He'd parked it directly under a tree to show he didn't give a fuck if it got shit on—birdshit didn't have half a damn to do with the high level of Plenty Mo's cool, son. Did you not know?

Neon rang the doorbell.

Plenty stood six three.

Neon was five eight.

Five nine if the extra lift to her bosom counted.

The cocktail outfit was made of a thin material that in key places forgot it wasn't skin, mocha colored against her body for a seamless blend of fabric and fantasy, mid thigh length, perfectly framed on her thirty-six, twenty-four, thirty stack.

It took her a split-second to roll scene. "Plenty, hey! I ain't know that was your car behind Yvonne. Can you get this bag? It's not that heavy." She bent to grab the duffel's rope tie.

Plenty fell straight down her cleavage. He bounced up soon as she straightened.

She handed the duffel's rope to him.

"Ain't no thang." He held the bag aside to let her pass.

Her thong thwanged with each step like a rubber band.

"My washer's out so Yvonne said I could use hers."

"Yvonne's upstairs layin' down."

"Yeah, I brought her this," she said and shook the Prescription Conscription bag.

"Y'all hit it off pretty cool then," he said.

"Doesn't take girls long to know each other. You know anybody selling washing machines?"

"I'll get you one," he tossed offhand. The duffel bag actually had a little weight to it. "This bag is packed."

"That's why I had to wear this."

"You look nice."

"Thank you. This's my favorite club dress. You should see me dance."

Big negro stumbled.

"Oh, so you know you look good," he said.

"I wear this, I ain't the only one. Where's her bedroom?"

"Upstairs straight."

"You carrying that in the basement for me? I'll be right back." She bent for one ankle. "Let me take these shoes off though." She shifted for the other, squeezing her body like playdoh. "This dress only looks good in these pumps." Her calves and thighs whispered in the gartered panty hose.

"Can't be wearin' no sneaks with that dress," he agreed.

"And I got laid off," she said.

"Aw hell naw."

"What you gonna do?" she asked rhetorically. "If you ain't rich you're fucked. That's probably what that Latin means on money."

"Nah, you ain't fucked, just gotta prioritize your expectations. You need a little somethin'?"

"I could do a twenty for some gas."

He fished a fifty out. She tried to protest. "Nah, it's cool," he said, sending her on her way. He hefted her packed laundry bag with one hand to impress her then headed for the basement.

Neon tossed the Pepto on Yvonne's bed.

"I just got fifty dollars."

Yvonne gave her the universal *Why are you being stupid?* look.

"Testing a theory," said Neon. "We've got problems, girl, get out the bed."

Yvonne sucked down a couple swigs of the pink goo.

"Quick short version: my money's in your basement and the world's about to think I'm blonde."

They heard Plenty thudding quickly up the basement steps.

"There was a detective following me," Neon said fast.

"There's no detective following you," moaned Yvonne.

"I see the same white man three times and he calls himself 'detective' I think I'm inclined."

"Neon." Yvonne sat up. "You've got some pervert wondering if your pussy lips look like the front or back of your hand, that's all." She groaned.

"Maybe you need to go to a doctor."

"I don't need any damn doctor." She shouted downstairs,

"Steve! Can you bring me some ginger ale?"

His footsteps halted and reversed for the kitchen.

Neon went to the landing. "You know what? She probably needs some soup."

"That's a good idea," he shouted back.

Neon waited to hear him rooting through cupboards.

She returned to Yvonne.

"Three glasses of Malibu is keeping me calm, but we've got complications and troubles," she said.

"Why'd a detective be following you about this?"

"When you put it like that you make me sound stupid, but I know what I saw. He looked like nab."

"And that disproves my pervert theory how?"

"Yvonne, you promised me this shit wouldn't get crazy."

"No, I didn't."

"You should have! This ain't simple math, this is algebra."

"Trig."

"Ho."

"Huh?"

"I'm leavin' my money till a little while."

"Fine. I'll be here."

"That's all I needed to know. Do you even have any soup?" asked Neon.

"No."

"Let me go down there." She turned back to Yvonne. "The money's in my dirty clothes. I'ma hide it in your basement but I won't tell you where. That way, when you meet my pervert, you can be blonde down to the roots."

"Will you bring up some ginger ale?"

"Sure. Why is Plenty over here?"

"I'll tell you later."

Plenty, on his tippy toes looking in the back of cabinets, said, "She ain't got no soup."

Neon laid a hand on his shoulder. "I'ma pour up a little

ginger ale, then get these clothes started. I don't wanna be here too long, you know? Seems like things just ain't going right for me right now." She pulled the ginger ale out of the fridge.

"Whassup?"

"Things ain't that good with me and Le'Mon." Lather it up, but don't lay it on too thick. "I get tired of him not wanting to fuck when I do, and do when I don't." Qualified use of a blunt object.

Plenty Mo accepted the invitation. "I fuck when the word fuck comes up," he said levelly into her eyes instead of her cleavage. "Fuck's wrong with him?"

"He kinda told me what happened with y'all. He's worried."

"Nigga ain't got nothin' to be worried about. Situation is resolved."

A little bit more. "Still though. He fucked up. He doesn't know exactly what he fucked up. So he's even more fucked."

"And he don't wanna fuck?"

She gave a shrug.

"Dumb motherfucker. Don't be fuckin' around with nobody with manhood issues. I'll take you out tomorrow—wear that," he said to the dress, "We hit some dancing and get some eats, and later you feel like it..."

"We fuck?"

He smiled.

"And if I don't feel like it?"

"We still fuck. I'm just kidding." He smiled even broader, mouth full of alligator teeth. "Plenty got jokes, girl."

She looked him in the eye. "You don't even wanna joke about that, Plenty. Pussy hates to be confused."

"Pussy seeks clarity."

She gave a nod.

"Shaolin Temple pussy," he said.

"Exactly."

"You one of them don't nothin' happen to you if you don't want it to happen, I can tell."

"Except for losing my job and having to wear my best dress to wash my draws?"

He stepped a little closer.

"You smell good," he said appreciatively, using his most potent seducer voice.

"Body wash, lotion and spray," she said.

"So you smell like that—"

"Yes, I do."

Sweet damnation. There was a Lilac Breeze in the Valley of Gwangi.

"Here, let me get this drink up there," Neon said.

"I'ma handle things for you. Don't worry 'bout nothin'. I'll handle him for you."

Oop, might've lathered it on a little much.

"It wasn't that serious," she told him. "Let me know about tomorrow."

"Where the digits at?"

"I'll give you a business card."

"All righty then. Business."

She walked away with a little extra swivel.

"Before pleasure," he said, deeply admiring the view.

Yvonne, leaving the bathroom from having thrown up again, trudged past Neon and fell on the bed.

"You look dehydrated," Neon said. Neon felt her forehead. It was warmer than it needed to be.

Yvonne reached for the Pepto again.

"Won't too much of that make you sick?"

"None of it left in me."

"Sip this first." She passed Yvonne the drink. "Your cousin plans to fuck me tomorrow."

"That's nice."

"I don't want to be fucked by your cousin. Why is he over

here?"

"Throwing him a bone away from your boyfriend. I told him I heard something at the Y that reminded me of his party."

"The Y is the place to be."

"Who you tellin'? Brand new downtown location, girl, we get all the traffic through. State of the art too. I can make up anything about anybody in this part of the city and at least twenty-five percent of it'll be true. So I tossed him some vague hearsay—"

"So long as Le'Mon stays over here—" and Neon pointed at the imaginary side of the yard where the two imaginary dogs sniffed toward each other.

"Plenty's runnin' over there. Go tell him you think I might be contagious."

She did. Plenty hollered up the stairs, "All right, Cuz, I'm out!" When he turned back to Neon she had a powder blue business card between her fingers and half a smile on her lips.

"'Neon's Brights,'" he read. "Business and everythang!"

"If I'm lucky, business will boom soon. Otherwise I might have to move in with family."

"Oh, things 'bout to definitely pick up for you."

"Bye, Plenty."

Seeing as they'd openly discussed fucking it seemed perfectly legit for him to eye fondle her and grab a sliver of ass to go. He palmed her left cheek. Each finger was like a foundation holding up the flesh of her ass.

"Girl, if you wanted to be a dancer..."

"I just might. Career options are open." Grab her ass? Guess what.

She tugged a belt loop on his baggy jeans. He instantly got hard. Er.

She glanced at his tent. "Damn, Kemosabe."

"A dick ain't nothin' but a compass for joy. I'ma say it again, muhfuckas better duck."

Then he was out the door, erection pointing the way to the slowly spinning rims on his flashy black truck.

Plenty Mo had a big dick. He walked slowly so that everybody could take respectful note of it. He entered his Hummer.

He closed his door.

He shifted his dick in his pants.

He drove off.

The birds in the trees could finally stop holding it.

A single plop of bird poop fell just after his gleaming bumper cleared the space.

Life does *not* get better than rolling the streets with a public hard on.

She hid the money. She washed the clothes. Dried the clothes. Took her fuck-me dress off and threw shorts and blouse on. Sat with Yvonne in the living room and slowly returned to a sense of reason.

Napstein, after listening in from his van, tried following Plenty.

Joe Nabal reported the pertinent findings to Boo: a roller and a wannabee, with Neon in the middle.

Boo decided it was time for a conversation.

He parked that night across from the wannabee's address Joe Nab had called in a favor to get, and waited.

And waited.

And waited some more.

Le'Mon, meanwhile, was off fucking Ramona again. Used properly, sympathy pussy was like fine grit sandpaper, polishing away life's imperfections.

Boo finally drove off. He hit the cell phone. "Joe? He didn't show. How 'bout you do what you do next time you see him?"

Joe yawned into the phone. Joe Nab was about to get violent.

"Ain't no thang," he said. "I'll let you know," and he hung up and buried his head back in his pillow.

The League of Nab converged on Le'Mon's house the next day...but Mama was on the porch.

"Hell y'all want? Le'Mon, get yo ass out here, you about to get arrested."

"Ma'am—"

"Ha! Knew your ass was police. What'd he do? Le'Mon! Knock that air conditioner out the back window I'ma beat your ass!"

Le'Mon came warily to the front door, seeing five men he'd never seen before.

"Yeah?"

"We need to speak with you."

"I ain't seen no badges."

Five sets flashed in the afternoon sun.

"We can talk in front of the neighbors or we can enjoy the backyard."

"Ma?"

"I already took their pictures with my cameraphone. Go 'head."

"We're just going around to the backyard," Joe told her amiably. Scraggly bushes along the fence made it semi-private.

As they crossed the hard packed dirt at the side of the house, Harry advised Le'Mon, "That gun you think you're hiding better not see light of day."

"What the fuck is this? United Nations shit." Le'Mon's heart jackhammered. "I ain't done a goddamned thing."

"It's one in the afternoon and you're still at home. Naw, you ain't done a damn thing at all," said Harry.

"That gun clipped?" Joe asked.

"I ain't got no gun."

"If I search you I plan to fondle your nuts."

Le'Mon clasped his hands behind his ass and held them

there.

"That works," said Joe. "Last night I was thinking I should just stomp your trifling ass, but this morning was French toast. Cinnamon. I loves everybody right now, and I hope appealing to reason will keep us both on the road to a good day."

Le'Mon's eyes twitched between the five. With his back to the house, they semi-circled his front. Two niggas, a Chinese dude, an Italian and a Jew—What the holy hell'd he step into?

Aw hell, international Mafioso. He could tell from the way this nigga loved the sound of his own voice. *Fucking Illuminati!*

And nobody talked but the two black dudes.

"We've got mutual friends who you've put in a shitty position," said Joe.

"That's fucked up," said Harry.

"That's fucked up," Joe agreed. "You're gonna back the fuck up and make things right, with us never having to meet again, right?"

"Huh? Fuck y'all talkin' about?"

"I'ma have to punch you in the nuts," said Joe.

"Dammit, I'm tired of that!"

"Ok, without mentioning names—'cause we both know—here's how it is. Certain people you know: get amnesia. You got people running away not of their own choosing."

"Punch him in the nuts," said Harry.

"Oh, I'ma do that anyway. You got the safety on your gun?" he asked Le'Mon.

Le'Mon nodded.

Joe Nab hauled off and sent a Hail Mary to Le'Mon's nuts.

Le'Mon rebounded off the house and rolled on the ground. Pain strangled him to the point he couldn't even moan.

"Get amnesia, fool," Harry said. "Nobody you know needs you around."

"Get your ass a whole new set of friends."

Le'Mon couldn't see through the tears, but those could

have been blurry sets of feet walking away. His ears were just a rush of pain so he didn't even hear Tiananmen Jo ask regarding the other three, "Were we intimidating enough?"

Afterward his ma came back and helped him up. For a change she didn't say anything, just led him into the house, plopped him on the couch, and left him there shaking her head.

Sometimes you just get tired, and you want everything to go the fuck away.

Mama and son shared this thought in different ways and for different reasons, ending up on separate paths that went deep in the woods.

Yeah.

Poetic on an ass.

"Mama, I ain't done nothin'," he managed to groan out before she was gone.

She stopped a second, sighed, and shuffled back outside.

Chapter 15

"One plus one plus one is three"

Le'Mon balanced a gun on his knee and stared deep through the floor into the black-as-night underground. There was shit buried that he had to dig for, and he thought hard now while his testicles unlocked:

Punkasses had to be Plenty-related with those fake-ass badges, but it had a Neon feel to it.

It had a definite Neon feel.

That's what they were saying: leave her the fuck alone.

But Neon loves my beefcarver dick and the fact I'm the only one can keep up with her.

Except for Job Security.

Aw hell naw.

Don't tell me she had some muhfukas come punch me inna nuts for him?!

No, no, shit was not adding up. Pieces didn't click. Close but no click.

All right, force the pieces.

Neon being funny.

Job Security on the scene.

Fuck up with Plenty Mo.

Muhfukas sweating me.

Only two people upstairs were Yvonne...

And Neon. Who Plenty had a Jones for.

And Plenty had started the entire thing in motion...

Le'Mon dropped the gun on the bed because his hands were shaking.

Yvonne was the only one innocent in the whole thing.

Ok, but they don't think I know shit, so I be cool. Amnesia like a bitch.

Neon. Job Security. Plenty.

One plus one plus one is three.

He popped a Darvocet from mama's prescription stock and settled back to wait for it to kick in. Didn't take long for him to feel drowsy and loopy, and his nuts just flowed away down the drain. While he slept he ran through some dreams that, when he woke up, he believed were plans.

Somebody shoulda told him you don't act on a dream.

One of the dreams was particularly energizing: he and Yvonne found Plenty's money and she loved him all the more for it.

That got him off the bed and headed toward Neon's.

Neon half carried Yvonne's stubborn-ass and took her home with her. The woman was weak and slightly feverish but refused to go to emergency, plus Yvonne didn't want to stay home because one visit from Plenty was enough, and with all the Neon pheromones lingering around her house it was too likely he'd come back.

Now if Plenty called Neon for their date tomorrow Neon had the perfect excuse to dodge his wiggly dick.

She decided, though, watching Yvonne spread herself on the sofa, to retrieve the money from Yvonne's house. Yvonne was right, perverts come in all colors and creeds. What are the odds that a detective would be following her? And it wasn't right putting that weight on Yvonne in case for whatever reason somebody decided the money was in her house.

She got Yvonne's house keys, told her she'd be right back with the sack but wanted to pick up some soups first, so just relax and chill. She tossed Yvonne the remote.

Yvonne dozed and after a while woke to the doorbell, thinking Neon's hands were full. Rolling off the sofa made her stomach churn even more, which kept her from noticing Neon's car wasn't out the window. She opened the door.

"Damn, girl, you don't look too good," he slurred.

"Le'Mon?" She squinted through the sunlight behind him for signs of Neon. "Neon's not home."

"I know."

"But you rang the doorbell."

Neon hadn't even noticed his ma's car parked a little off from her house after she'd first pulled up.

His eyes were glassy and he swayed slightly.

She kept her hand on the door handle.

"Can we talk for a minute?" he said. "There's some real stuff goin' down and she might be in it."

"I don't want you catchin' what I got."

"I get a little what you got I'm set for life. Lemme in."

She let him in.

He talked and walked, trying to pretend he wasn't looking for something.

She noticed he was walking a little funny, but she had more

pressing concerns. She had to get him out before Neon got back.

"She done a little more cleanin' up," he noted, but the computer area was still messy. "But see?" He went over there. "This's what I was sayin'. She's on this computer too much." He glanced at a sheet stuck halfway in her shredder, one of those cards she was always making for her girlfriends.

"Gotta have hobbies," Yvonne said innocently.

He pulled the half-eaten card from the machine's jammed teeth.

"You sure she wants you messin' with her stuff?" Yvonne asked.

Crazy Lady, that kiss was something. I'm not saying we're ever going to do it again, but damn! ☺ Life ain't nothing but a clit party anyway. Those that hit it get bliss, those that miss get dissed. Thanks for being part of my crazy shit—

Whut. Thee. Fuck.

Ain't but one variety of crazy shit happenin' in the Twilight Zone, and Le'Mon Marcus J'ello Arness submits this for the world's approval: Thundra and Neon watched too many movies, 'cause damned if this particular one wasn't at cineplexes one, two, three and four.

How long'd it take to get to this point in the time/space continuum?

Let's see:

Not long at all.

And here, with Thundra watching the change come over his body like snow avalanching through bone and muscle, and him advancing holding the card with its twisted paper hanging off the bottom, him laughing at the mental image of something he'd dreamed about since first putting eyes on this Amazon goddess: her and Neon getting it on under his handycam direction. Worth two nuts! And here they were under his nose.

The Darvocet made him feel like Superman but right now that didn't mean anything. Feeling like Pee Wee Herman wouldn't have stopped his hand from doing what it did.

When she reached to take the mangled note from his hand to see what he was laughing at, he slapped her.

A little tap at first. Like, Ha, the joke's on me, good one, but she looked stunned as hell.

Like no the fuck you didn't.

Then he realized those five rent-a-cops had just played with him because it was broad daylight and Ma was there. The next time he saw them he was dead.

"Y'all told Plenty I did it." That slow chill went through his body again, but quicker this time, snapping wires to gather the speed it wanted. "Don't fuckin' open your mouth."

"You lost your damn mind?" The angrier she got the more her stomach twisted.

Next thing he knew he was slapping her and liking it, 'cause Darvocet is a muthafuckin' genius at wiping away pain. She stumbled back, surprised by the blow, which gave him time to fire off a third. By the fourth he realized his hand wasn't open anymore.

And there was blood. She tripped over the fan and fell hard.

Suddenly he realized the sweet simplicity of why stupid people throw their lives away: because they're stupid.

He was able to do the math. He'd just popped Plenty's cousin, who'd set Le'Mon up somehow to take the fall for money Le'Mon had planned to take anyway, and Plenty would kill him.

There's no man so hard he wants to die. Anybody acting fearless is a scared kid. No pretending against that.

Le'Mon clipped the last necessary wire in his brain, the one that kept shit together, especially shaky shit. The red wire was the one made shit blow up.

Clearly, now, there was an urgent need to choke a bitch.

He got to her quick before she got up, put his knee in her stomach and bore down. A hiss of air shot from her lungs. Her abs tried contracting; he punched her in the tits.

In his mind he pissed on the Mona Lisa, gave the finger to Nefertiti, and screamed "fuck it" to the world. "FUCK IT!" he shouted for courage, letting that last wire snap, watching himself reaching for her throat and feeling somebody's thumbs squeezing the flesh of her neck. Hell, Plenty was going to kill him anyway.

Le'Mon scooched to pin her arms with his knees. Sweat and heat clouded his eyes; vision got so murky he thought he was the one dying.

You are a pussy, Le'Mon, on a sick woman, and you're gonna disappear your pussy-ass as far as you can, motherfucker, no possibility for you to ever exist again, is what he told himself.

Which actually made him feel pretty good.

Another wire clipped, and he steadily increased pressure.

She goes unconscious, I can get up in it, said his numbed dick.

'Cause no matter what else, Le'Mon J'ello hadn't sunk down to fucking dead people. Knocked out was cool.

Hell, only rich people got to tap ass like this every day. Call it one for the road. Knocked out pussy is dry, but enough Vaseline would turn the Sahara into an ice rink.

A car door slammed.

He jumped up and dragged Yvonne into the bedroom toward the closet. A wall of woman-shit blocked him. Shoes, clothes—he couldn't squeeze a midget in there if Jehovah Christ had commanded him.

They'd be at the door by now.

FUCK IT! shouted all the clipped wires.

He pulled the gat.

Yvonne rolled on the floor like a pet toy, trying to cough her way to her knees. He grabbed her head and slammed her forehead into the barely carpeted floor, then sprang out of the bedroom, black metal in hand and pointed straight out for whatever was coming straight in. He rounded the corner into the living room and froze Neon in place.

"Why in fuck you got so many clothes!"

"Man, put that goddam gun down!" Neon's eyes darted. Nothing seemed out of place. "What are you doing, Le'Mon?"

"You fucked me."

"You wish I had a dick."

"You gotta be a bitch to the end? Shit, bitch, you fucked Plenty! I woulda hit you up with some of the money."

"Like I need anything you have!" she shouted but kept her eyes level on him. "I will do for myself."

"What?" he said incredulously.

"Put that muthafukin' gun down!"

"Neon." He closed his eyes, still keeping the gun level on her chest. "I ain't gon' do shit to you," he mumbled.

"Put the gun down."

He willfully clipped another wire. He put the gun to his temple.

"Le'Mon!"

"Just wanna see what it feels like," he said.

She put the moneybag and the bag of soups down. He glanced at both without interest and looked at this girl who he'd been inside on more than one occasion.

Neon took a tentative step forward. He was high as hell; she just had to ride his ass out.

"Guess I don't know shit about you," he said, arm frozen with the gun to his head. He felt like he could pop the arm off, step back, and just watch it float there.

"Homatic tramp," he said.

"Le'Mon, why you doin' this?"

"You gon' pull some Brokeback Mountain shit on me. You shoulda kept your ass with Fake Rome."

She went into utter submission. "Come on, baby. You know this ain't us."

"I ain't been hit in the nuts so much in my life. That's a sign from God. God don't fuckin' like me. Naw, this ain't us. One of us 'bout to be dead in a minute anyway."

"Well, hell, keep the gun to your head then." *Shut up, girl!* "Come on, man, why you doin' this?"

"Neon?"

"Yeah?"

"Shit scares you, don't it?"

"Yeah."

"Me too." He quickly leveled the gun back on her, letting the avalanche rush to the finger on the trigger.

A sudden chop bent the elbow of his outstretched arm. His finger never hit the trigger. Yvonne's weight carried them toward Neon, who side stepped then timed a sweep with Yvonne's release.

Le'Mon went down hard.

Yvonne grabbed him in a sleeper hold.

Neon screamed "Motherfucker!" in his face with tears streaming.

His eyes rolled glassy for a second then lost all focus.

"Don't kill him."

Yvonne elbowed him in the top of the head, bouncing his head off the floor and back into her sleeper hold.

"Next time you try to knock somebody out," she hissed, "make sure you knock 'em out! Head is fucking *killing* me!"

She rolled off quick and flipped him to his back, laying full out on him and holding his hands pinned above his head with her feet hooked into his ankles.

"Tie his ass!"

Neon scrambled to find something.

She didn't have to hurry, because Le'Mon was just lying there wondering why he wasn't getting a hard on with Thundra on top of him.

And he wondered why in the hell his mama named him lemon Jell-O.

And he'd heard theories about there being infinite possibilities across infinite universes, and whatever you could think of there was one of you doing it somewhere.

And then he was unconscious, because Yvonne DeCarlo Paul had to choke a bitch.

Neon returned with her silk robe's sash. She tied his limp wrists. Yvonne looked like she was about to throw up on the carpet.

She did.

She rolled onto her back. Her nose was bleeding and she hoped she hadn't bruised much. "Tie his feet."

Neon hustled out again, coming back quickly with another silk sash.

"You're a pussy to the end," Yvonne said to him as Neon tightened her silk knot. "God, I don't feel good."

"You going to the hospital now?"

"No. Stop trying to make me go to the doctor!" She was crying. Neon hadn't thought she cried. "Oh, my God—" she started but coughed and hacked so hard Neon put aside her icky feelings and held this vomity, bloody, bruised woman like the friend she was.

"I don't want him killed," she said again.

"We'll ask him what he wants to do when he wakes up."

That particular conversation was strange, because they gave him the option of the jealous boyfriend scenario, wherein Boo would administer a thoroughly genuine ass kicking to the point that Le'Mon would leave town (with a hushed up ten thousand dollars), and Neon would explain to Plenty that shit just hadn't worked out and she was about to move to be with family anyway; or, they told Le'Mon, "you can have the option of being fucked up the ass by Plenty while he chokes you from the back."

When you're tied up on somebody's floor there's no option to be too stupid.

So it later turned out Yvonne had accidentally gotten hurt trying to break Neon and Le'Mon apart.

Boo came in a hurry and without any qualms after assessing things about whupping the ass of a tied up man.

Le'Mon, though, took the beat down rather well.

Darvocet ain't but federal crack. Motherfuckin' genius.

"This is why I gotta leave, Boo." Yvonne was in the bedroom with a cold compress on her head. Neon'd cleaned up the vomit and had stashed the gun well before Boo'd arrived.

"He appreciates what's gonna happen to him he messes with you again," Boo reassured.

Le'Mon, meanwhile, was stretched unconscious across the backseat of his mother's car across town in the parking lot of a cheap strip mall nobody went to, untied, with nobody knowing the sack in the trunk was his ticket away from the Light Skindid Thugz.

Boo had driven Le'Mon's mama's car; Neon had followed, and she wasn't surprised to realize she didn't really feel anything seeing him dumped off like that. There was ten thousand dollars in the trunk of his car that he'd quickly nodded his head in agreement to; like she said before, she wasn't about to pity his ignorant ass.

"I was here for you, though. You know that."

"I know, Boo."

"Ain't neither one of us got no sense."

"Nah. Shit, you might as well go ahead and fall in love, Boo."

"Yeah, I might."

"I need it to be me, myself and I for a while."

"Let me know where you'll be, I'll come out there and hit it." He grinned when she shoved him away. He pulled her into a strong one-armed hug.

She thought about telling him something like keep looking, something meaningful with levels and depth, because, hell, this was it, but then she thought why be fake, it wasn't that important.

Like she'd told him, you either find something or you don't.

"Y'know, sometimes I would think you could read my mind."

"I can." She stood up and glanced toward the closed bedroom door. Yvonne wasn't coming out of there anytime soon.

She leaned over Boo with that look in her eyes that made sinners the world over sing hymns of praise.

"One for the road, Boo?"

She undid a button on her fresh blouse.

Boo reached up and held her slender fingers with his big, bruised hands. "Naw. How about we finish watching this movie?"

Neon bent low and planted a soft kiss on his forehead.

She popped *The Green Man* in and settled beside him.

It was near dusk; the last of the sun was about to give out. Which was cool.

Her name was Neon. She could afford to shine on her own.

THE END

With relatively few modifications, the book turned out to be a huge success by Crosshairs standards.

"Brother, we have got to get your face on the website!" Cross gushed. "I'm lining you up for some interviews." Cross had sent published copies to all the black weathermen on the morning shows. Sunny Side Up was the first to bite because ethnic flair sometimes boosted ratings.

Barclay looked at Marilyn. Cross had wanted them both there for the meeting. The confused frown on Barclay's face was close to becoming a permanent thing. It should have been obvious, but Barclay felt it best to say it anyway. "I don't want...to talk about this," he said hesitantly, because there clearly had to be a deeper meaning to Cross' statement.

"You're gonna tell me you haven't dreamed about getting on Words and Images? Your book is stupid as hell and people love it. You've got this country laughing at itself, man. That ain't easy. You don't throw your line in the water without setting your hook and reeling them in, y'know? Ain't nobody going fishing to give the fish a taste. You've hooked something big."

"I thought I was going to blow up."

"Then blow up, but you don't blow up quietly. Ok? Crosshairs doesn't do sissy Anthrax. Alien mutant babies are gonna still be suckling off our nuclear fallout. Feel me? Marilyn?" (because he felt he could call her Marilyn) "How do you feel about your man touring?"

Marilyn just smiled wondering why the hell she was there.

"I could probably get you on Words and Images," Cross said to Barclay.

The Noble Savage Pens A Satire, Barclay thought, adding the trenchant guffaw of the Englishman outfitted in huge mustache and monocle. Jolly Bloody Good That.

Cross dropped back. "I'm about to give you two a check for five thousand dollars toward the next Neon adventure."

"Jim..."

Cross held his hands up. "I know, I know. Write what you need to. This is your home. But keep that girl in the back of your mind. You do some serious work, you come back to Neon. I wouldn't book you till later in the year. Right now there's still enough anonymity to work in your favor. People are starting to really want to know who SDW really is. Hook's in their mouths; early November, I set it. Website. Interviews. Tug that line so hard the fish jerks out the water."

"Would that push his other books?" asked Marilyn.

"Yes, it would." He looked dead at Barclay. "You've already made three times that ten thousand on Neon sales to date. In a minute Simon & Schuster or somebody is going to come knocking. I can serve as your agent because we've got it like that. I've heard the big boys' knock and I know what to listen for." Cross ceremoniously placed the envelope containing the Royse's newest deposit toward their retirement account into Marilyn's hands.

"Thank you," Barclay and Marilyn said automatically.

Cross came around the desk. "There's business and there's why I brought you here, which is to celebrate. Come on, let's go hit some lunch and spend some of that new money you just made."

But at the next meeting: "Listen, I think we need to bump up peeling the layers," said Cross. "That bitch Rowella Childs is prepping a rip off of you. Rowella Childs writing as I.M. Fine. That is bullshit!" Cross shouted into his end of the phone. "Don't ask how I know but I know. Your man behind the curtain is working hard for you. She does that, that'll cut into your figures. People need to know Sweet Dick Willie is the Real Deal Holyfield. Accept no substitutions."

The conversation ended with various assurances and the renewal of Cross' ironclad resolve. Barclay pocketed his cell phone, put the finishing touches on the ENS report to CBI that he'd been working on, emailed it with review attachments to Assurance and Certification (separate departments that other departments silently laughed at for having only one name and thus no acronym), then considered whether or not to turn in his resignation, walk out onto Manny Avenue, and kiss the front of a moving bus.

"He didn't tell anybody that's what 'SDW' stands for?" Marilyn asked. Death from mortification wasn't covered in the insurance. They'd be screwed if either one of them kicked over. "That's only supposed to be me."

"I didn't tell him. He just made an educated, coincidental guess. It's a man thing."

"So every man on earth calls himself 'Sweet Dick Willie'?"

"Yes," he said, clearly having forgotten that.

"You need to stay up on your memos," she said.

"Y'all call your thing 'Susie'."

"Yes, but it's a separate entity."

"Willie is the god of Swerve. We embody him."

"Don't bring religion into a sensible conversation. You're going to be interviewed, baby," said Marilyn, half believing it.

"I know."

"You've never been interviewed before."

"I'm kind of stupid. What'm I going to say?"

"As long as it's not about me, anything."

"They're gonna wanna know why I wrote it, baby. 'Cause Jim Cross told me to' don't sing."

"Let's watch the morning shows. They've always got somebody hawking trendy crap." They'd decided as a couple never to watch morning shows anymore, as morning shows had no shame. "I'll record 'em and we can fast forward over the weekend," said Marilyn.

"I'll start having dreams about killing the weathermen again," he said.

"I'm fine with that. Do the co-hosts too. But my baby is not about to be interviewed on national TV and all he has to say is 'I like cheese'."

"Thank you, babe."

She patted his butt. "Now go get your pad and pen. Mama's gotta help you get pithy."

Of the four major morning shows, Sunny Side Up was the most ignorant. To reach inane it would have had to upgrade. The "anchor" smiled like a car salesman nervously shy of quota and the "co-anchor" sported eighties hair as though time, for her, had no meaning. Eighties hair didn't even look good in the eighties, and environmentally speaking, that much spray mousse didn't do anyone a bit of good.

They made sane people want to slap them hard.

"Who're they interviewing?" said Barclay on the off chance he might have been familiar with whatever young, white, trendy author was about to pretend they'd written something monumentally worthwhile, some yuppie piece of obvious crap even dead people shouldn't waste time on.

Non-fiction was the worst.

Why Your Baby Hates You: When It's Wrong to Show Affection to Your Baby's Father, followed by an über-earnest discussion where the interviewer adopted that just-fell-off-the-turnip-truck fascination and the author jumped at every opportunity to grasp at self-respect.

"Greta Millings," said Marilyn.

"Don't know her. Fiction?"

"Chick book."

"Damn."

Marilyn cued it up. Greta Millings, all twenty-eight years of her, summed her literary appeal succinctly with the practiced crossing of slit-skirted legs that very slowly and clearly pronounced her beautiful calves as worthy of being jizzed on. And, by extension, people should buy her book, men because they might one day run into Greta Millings, and women because they really ought to aspire to be Greta Millings.

Her uppermost buttons were undone that professionally sexy way that said 'I'm naked under here but it'd take a huge stock option for you to see.'

"Coming up," said Lacey Caplan, "Greta Millings, author of

the runaway hit *The Secretive Knees*, but first these messages and your local news," while Greta nodded at the camera with that look that said she regularly had fabulous morning sex and you should too.

Marilyn skipped these messages and the local news.

"We're back with author Greta Millings, whose runaway hit *The Secretive Knees*, about a nun's sexual awakening at the hands of a priest, is taking not only the literary world but the religious community by storm. Greta, good morning."

Barclay spazzed out, paying more attention to plotting out the size, weight and shape of Greta's breasts and ribcage based on her fabric's points of contact.

Which isn't to say he wasn't able to follow the interview. A dead worm could follow the interview.

"Good morning, Lacey."

"Right off the bat," said Lacey, leaning and reaching as though she wanted to swipe at the other woman's knee, "where did the inspiration for this book come from?"

"Well, I've never been a nun," and both laughed at such a hilarious notion. Nuns didn't have regular morning sex. Greta swept a non-existent mis-swept lock of hair back in place. "No, y'know, I wrote this book because sex, no matter who you are or how we'd like to pretend against it, is everywhere. I mean, there's no such thing as a non-sexual being."

Tie your book into sex, the teeny tiny part of Barclay's mind that actively analyzed the interview noted.

"And the last taboo is the sex life of the Catholic Church," said Greta.

At least The Thorn Birds had a movie with Rachel Ward. Rachel Ward is hot. Probably get Jessica Alba for this one. Can't stand Jessica Alba. Do her, though. I should try to look down Marilyn's blouse...

"Couple that," said Lacey, "with the nun in the story attempting to have a career—"

"Sister Clarice. That's the thing now, people within the church are encouraged to have a life outside the church, but how do we have it all?"

"That's an important question to women."

"Yes, and—" *(Get her to state the obvious, then get me to affirm the obvious,* Barclay thought. The wife's blouse was too high-necked to look down.) "—I think right now we're at a point in history—" (Inflate importance.) "—where a woman's sexuality is firmly in her hands *(Hee hee,* thought Marilyn before Barclay did)."

"Now—your book has as many detractors as followers."

"I'd like to think more followers."

Laugh, laugh, laugh—but seriously, "Didn't that worry you? As you wrote it, didn't you worry 'This might be pushing the envelope a little too much'? I mean, you don't pull any punches. The book opens with a pretty graphic depiction of sex between Clarice and Father Anoint, as he likes her to call him during their trysts. Was Father Anoint based on clergy you currently know?"

"Of course he was," Barclay's imagination provided, complete with Greta turning to directly address the television audience. "Father Douglass Rapp, Saint Benecio del Toro, one one five eight Exan, Church Rectory. Rather tall, did me once—roughly—diddles boys on occasion. I have a list of their names and addresses on my website."

"No," she answered, leaning away with her hands up for comic emphasis. "Actually, one of the fascinating things about being a writer is synthesizing, imagining, if you will, how this or that character might be, drawing on any number of sources."

"Imagining."

"Exactly."

Lacey crinkled her brow and nodded sagaciously.

"And it's Father Anoint who forces Clarice to confront the

question: is a woman defined by her sex...or the sex she has?" Greta paused to let the audience catch up. "Even today in America—"

"And we're both women," Lacey pointed out.

"Yes, so there's this expectation that we don't question sex. We control it—women—and are the objects of pursuit, but are we connected at all as women to the more spiritual aspects of it, which is entirely what Clarice's journey is about?"

"Do you feel that people perhaps are missing that point, the Church?"

"And there's that whole subplot about the fashions of the church."

"Yes!"

Sex and the Piety, thought Barclay, stretching it. Sex and the City, Sex and the Piety, disdain—he let it drop.

"And, as I'm sure many people already know, your book has been optioned for a movie."

"Oh, God, this has been such an amazing ride. I don't know many details about the movie—"

Authors never know anything about the movie.

"—but Jackie Lernerman is a fabulous director who, I'm sure, will bring a fabulous sensitivity to this project."

"Let's talk about Father Anoint. One reviewer described him as the ultimate father figure—"

Duh.

"—sort of a religious 'Mr. Big'."

"I was going for that familiarity with the character. I didn't want to fall into the trap of presenting this alienating character to the readers. Father Anoint had to be humanized, and, you know, Chris Noth is such a wonderful actor."

"Loved him on *Sex and the City.*" Lacey feigned the knee slap again. "So tell us, next project? What should we be expecting from Greta Millings?"

"A romantic comedy about two people who may or may not be werewolves masquerading as vampires to keep from being outed in an exclusive vampire community."

"Vampires are so hot now. Can't wait to read the next Greta Millings offering. Excerpts of *The Secretive Knees* are online at Sunnyside-dot-laceyreadsup-dot-com," she told the viewing audience. She gave Greta a hugely exaggerated smile, the kind that women who are strangers in porn movies share a minute before seriously getting it on. "Love to have you back." The camera immediately locked solely on Lacey. "Coming up, what to do when your toddler won't get off the supermarket floor. How tantrums affect parents and what children can do about it; the Sunny Side Up Family Project, when we come back."

Marilyn stopped playback right before the slew of home deodorizing commercials blared. America recently had become an extremely funky place.

"I'm telling the interviewer I like cheese," said Barclay.

"I didn't catch too much pith in that," Marilyn conceded.

"Not a lot of pith."

"We'll de-pith some of your comments."

"Cheese does a body good."

"Tell 'em you like string cheese."

"Good one."

"But don't mention me."

Epilogue:

Dear Sheela: This is me. This is my bikini. These are the horny beachmeat. Do the math, bee-yotch! Say 'Hawaii'.

Aloha.

P.S.—Get your tubes tied, you trifling no-mama being two times four eight dollar ho. Devonne deserves better. You need (and here she underlined the word three times) *to—*

But that's when Yvonne told her the cruise bonfire was about to get lit so she said fuck it and figured it didn't matter if she sent it finished or not, so long as she sent it. Hawaii was just a vacation stop. Expensive as hell living there.

In two weeks, Manila.

The worst thing about being on a show like Sunny Side Up, even though it was the lowest rated of all the morning shows, was he wasn't there to talk about *Onion Roll* or *Rambeau* or even *Fairy Tale*. A black dude had written a book from the point of view of two black women, full of sass, sex, and laughs. Neon wasn't about to be up for a MacArthur Genius grant, but the feeling was a lot of white chicks were about to start writing ethnic chick-lit. If a man was the flavor of the minute writing about black chicks, the novelty of white chicks writing as black chicks for white chicks was pure gold. Bridging the racial divide by way of shameless marketing.

"Street Lit hasn't quite seen anything like what you've done," said Lacey, whose eighties hair dared him to say something about it.

Cross had told him not to say he didn't think of it as Street Lit. "A sense of humor goes a long way in harsh environs," Barclay said. Nervously. Everything he'd said so far was nervously. There were a hundred people scurrying around behind those cameras, not to mention the crazy people outside the studio's huge street-level windows. And they'd put makeup on him! He'd never had makeup on his face his entire life. Except that time that once with that girl in college.

"But I didn't think sitcom humor was appropriate," he explained. "There's humor that seriously addresses something, and then there's that which makes tragedy palatable." *De-pith, man, de-pith.* "There's nothing whatsoever acceptable about anyone living in a ghetto."

Lacey looked on with concern. "So true, so true."

Back off the angry black man, Cross thought directly into Barclay's brain. He was one of those faces behind the cameras.

Barclay being on TV created sort of a mini-family reunion nationwide. His daddy in Alabama watched; his sister in Arizona; in-laws scattered throughout Florida; a couple co-workers at Savory, and a group Marilyn culled in front of the TV in her job's break room all became extended family. Elaine, he was sure, even watched, because he felt stupid peoples' eyes on him from the great void, not unlike little red target lights dancing over his body.

"Now—do you feel your book will have served the Black community in any way?" asked Lacey.

"The government never gives out string cheese. Why is that? No, this book exists to serve any community of readers with laughter. Satire—"

Don't explain satire, don't explain satire, Cross mantra'd fiercely.

It took. Barclay veered. "—well, let me say this book has such crossover potential that—" *(This was for you, Lyn, and that retirement sunroom you wanted.)* "—no matter what somebody calls their hood, they'll have fun riding with Neon and Yvonne."

"So this book opens minds and communication?"

No, it does not. "It might."

"Because dialogue is so important. Tell me, what's response been from the community?"

Real niggas like it. "Positive reviews so far," said Barclay, crossing his fingers in hope.

"And this isn't your first book," she said.

Props to the research department! "No, there are three others but this is my first tackling the genre."

"Do you see us poised on a new urban renaissance?"

He thought of telling her Havarti was his favorite cheese but smartly decided against it. "I think," he said, "there is the sincere chance that publishing as a whole will grow up."

"Do you anticipate any kind of backlash or controversy?" she said, referencing this last statement.

Was there book beef, like in rap? He didn't think so. Cross would've had Netta let him know if he needed to bust a cap in somebody's ass.

"I mean," she continued, "this is pretty raunchy, negative stuff."

Turn all negatives into positives. "Not so much raunchy. I mean, take *The Canterbury Tales,* which is now considered pretty high-brow stuff. Raunchy conjures up letters to men's magazines. Anything that starts 'I never thought this would happen to me' is pretty much gonna be raunch. Not to be too indelicate."

"Because this is a morning show."

"Exactly! I seriously doubt there'll be backlash or controversy. So far people are smiling. They get the joke."

"Or they want to get the joke," Lacey pointed out.

Barclay acceded with a nod. "Desire is the first step toward change."

Lacey faced the camera. "When we come back, more with street author Barclay Royse. First, these messages."

The broadcast cleared. Barclay allowed himself the most miniscule of slumps in his seat. He smiled at Lacey, who looked quickly over a sheaf of color-coded notes from a production assistant. "How am I doing?" he asked amiably.

She smiled at him over the notes.

"Should I sit up more?"

"What was that about the cheese?" Lacey said, an edge of warning in her voice. Lacey hadn't been doing this since just yesterday. She set the notecards on her off-camera table. Ever since the teleprompter had broken down during her one interview with Jennifer Aniston she kept at least one set of back up cards in easy (off camera) view.

He didn't answer.

"Live in fifteen," announced the floor director.

"I want to wrap up with how you got into writing," said Lacey. "Maybe something inspirational about how anybody can get into it these days." She stopped. "I didn't mean for that to not come out right."

He deflected her with understandingly pleasant eye crinkles.

When they once again beamed live to America, Lacey reintroduced Barclay as the newest literary star on the urban horizon, to which he could be nothing but gracious.

"Any thoughts of expanding *Neon's* universe?" asked Lacey.

"I'd like to see several other stories come out of Neon." Cross beamed. "The Brothers Jetstream, League of Nab..."

"Slightly interrelated?"

"Well, they're mentioned in the book as these fantastic characters within the black community. Black culture has always excelled at the fantastic. I think about John Henry, or George Clinton, Bootsy Collins, Hendrix—no matter what, we've created either in fiction or of ourselves these otherworldly yet utterly human characters, so there's a chance we might see the Jetstreams or the League."

"Tell us about your path to publication."

"Years. Then some more years. And then a few years in

between that. I'm here now because I caught lightning in a bottle, but before that it was just fireflies."

"For a lot of our viewers who aren't familiar with urban fiction, I want to read this section: 'The first thing Le'Mon thought to do when he saw this huge Bigfoot mofo from a distance stepping off Neon's porch in such early hours was bumrush him, except he'd get his blank kicked.' There's a lot of playfulness to that even though it's a potentially very violent moment. I mean, he's essentially running into the other man. What do you think when you hear that out loud?" she asked.

"That life is but a dream. Seriously, some of us dream in Technicolor and some of us are straight black and white. You can't read Neon without intrinsically knowing—even if you've never read anything like it before—that most genres are about as ridiculous as modern religion." Ok, maybe a point dinged off for that, but it wasn't like the church folks were going to buy it in droves anyway.

"Any chances of Neon making her way to the big screen?" asked Lacey.

"I can hope."

Cross jizzed.

"I have to ask: your other three books are considered somewhat literary; does that pretty much destroy your 'street cred'?" She playfully leaned for the knee slap, swiping the air a few feet from him without managing to rustle her hair at all. "You're not exactly the image of a gritty street chronicler."

"That particular street doesn't exist."

"Interesting."

"My hope is that everybody comes over to the new street."

"Lastly, the pseudonym. SDW."

"That was to give people time to know Barclay Royse."

"Is there a story behind that?"

"Just a pet name," he said, flashing the Barclay Crinkle

again but thinking really and truly that he was a soulless beast whose every utterance offended the ears of God and Man.

"Well, I found myself laughing out loud throughout this book. Any truth to the rumor—" (started by Cross) "—that the first copy of this book went to Martha Stewart?"

"I'm sure she likes a good laugh too."

"So street comedy is here to stay?"

Cheese, cheese, cheese! "Listen, and I say this as something my daddy used to say to me: Nobody is as funny as black folk trying to tell the truth. And we use the word 'try' because nobody is trying to hear the truth, they'd rather think truth always applies to someone else. Nowadays, though, everyone is so ridiculous we can't pretend truth doesn't hit us with a pie in the face. The best comedians—of which I'm not one—are prophets. Lenny Bruce, Bernie Mac, Mooney, Pryor, Engvall, Underwood—they don't tell jokes, they tell the truth. People are laughing at this book. If they were laughing with it because they identify, then I utterly failed to keep it real."

"Well we certainly wish you much success. The novel is *Neon*, available through Crosshairs Books. Choice excerpts online at our website, and we'll be back."

Fortunately, a lot of young black women didn't see the interview, and weren't so concerned as to bother searching the YouTube footage, but they heard that one of their own—a street author—had been on TV, so sales shot through the roof. The legend of SDW as the man who popped the deep street cherry on not only Martha Stewart but Oprah as well lent Crosshairs Books fresh relevance. The HaterRaters website—run by a group of hankty chicks with aggressive screennames, known to rip the weak to shreds—gave it three out of five stars, saying that it really wasn't that funny but it had the hot nasty like you wouldn't believe, which, when it came to it, was why a book was in a hand in the first place. And 2muchAzz4U said five out of five for this goofy, sexy, cool wasn't enough. They were sick of two dollar hoes trying to write three dollar books. Plus—and this gave Barclay the twinge of hope he needed to believe in humanity again—they mentioned Barclay had three other books. They hadn't read any of them, but he had them. In the world of writing that counts as a grand slam.

"Mario?"

Mario paused the knife in half-cut of his sammich.

"We're about to come into a bit of money. You think you might be able to move out now?" said Barclay.

"Moved out last week."

"Oh."

"Yeah."

Barclay frowned. "Where's the key?"

Mario's face lit as though he'd realized Fermat's Theorem. "That's what I've been meaning to do." He fished inside his pocket. "Here." Then he finished cutting the sandwich and offered half to Barclay. "Good work, Broheem."

"Thanks."

"Y'all cut the pie any way you want to, man."

"What're you going to do?"

"I got options."

"As long as you've got options."

Mario took a bite. "Another Neon book?"

"Maybe the Jetstream Brothers."

"That's an art so lost it was never found. Black sci fi adventure."

"Hey, they say Santa Claus is a black man," said Barclay and they laughed. He didn't think he'd ever actually seen Mario laugh.

When Barclay mentioned this to Marilyn later she said, "He's always laughing at you. He thinks you're funny."

"That can cut a number of ways," he said.

Marilyn kissed his forehead, turned him around, patted him on his butt, and sent him on his way.

"Daddy?"

"Yeah," his daddy said that way old men have of confirming who they were to people who already knew them. "Up on TV there."

"You read the book?"

"Gave it to Lou, she read it."

"Auntie Lou all right?"

"I'da bust her teeth out long time ago if she wasn't my sister and they wasn't false."

"This book is selling pretty well, Daddy." Fathers, sons and writing were always precarious. Always would be. "What'd Auntie Lou say?"

"Said black folks done turned black folks into white folks, 'cause she can't stand niggas either!" he said, making it tonally clear they would have been his words too.

"No, that's not—"

"I like how you got your mama's name in there."

Pam. Meaning Pam Grier. Pamela Diane Royse. Daddy Royse was the only man in the entire world who didn't know who Pam Grier was. When Pam Grier routinely caused national emergencies of four day erections in men back in the seventies, Bernard Royse had either been under a car or under a sink or under a car jury-rigging a part from a sink. He didn't have time for movies. The one time he went he asked if somebody could turn down the sound, then wondered why everybody would want to see a movie about a white man with a red 'S' stuck on his drawers and announcing he was simple with a bright red cape. Of course he knew who Superman was, and that's how he'd always described Superman.

Superman, when Daddy Royse broke it down, was just the Magical Negro in reverse, and the only Magical Negro anybody needed was the one putting in sixty hours a week on top of side jobs and the occasional numbers win.

Barclay wouldn't tell him he would never put Mama's name in a book like that—not that Daddy knew precisely what was in the book. Auntie Lou was one of the nastiest sex women in the South but she wasn't about to talk sex with her brother if it meant telling him the book's more salient details.

"We're thinking about coming down there late fall," said Barclay, time enough for all book hubbub to have faded.

"Let me know so I can make sure to head to the cemetery."

"They cut the grass there, Daddy. You don't need to be trying to load that lawnmower into the truck."

Daddy Royse grunted him off. The old rotary mower weighed less than a hundred pounds. What kind of man went to his grave not able to heft less than a hundred pounds?

"This book makin' you rich?" asked his pops.

"Nowhere near."

"Buy yourself a TV or something." Everything was better when you bought a TV. "You talked to Baby Girl in a while?"

"Not recently."

"Call her up, make sure she ain't in no foolishness." Barclay's baby sister Tandy was a session player for a small creative agency specializing in commercial jingles. She was usually on the outs relationship-wise, so Barclay usually timed his calls for the happy zone of her six month intervals. Great with the guitar, lousy with the heart strings.

Plus, and he could say this because he was her brother, she smelled funny.

"I sent her a book," said Barclay.

"And you're still married, right?"

"Yes, sir."

"Your cousin ain't and ain't told nobody. Divorced close to a year."

"Lyn says hi."

"You sent me those other books you wrote too, didn't you?"

"They're in the house somewhere."

"I'ma have to dig those up," said the father. Daddy Royse read; he was just particular in what he read.

"Talk to you again, Daddy."

"Bye, boy." Daddy Royse hung up. Last he'd seen those books, they were out in the garage somewhere. Too hot to go out there now, but he had plenty of time before the boy came down to visit. Lou had mentioned to him that this new book had a lot in it about sex. Daddy Royse missed sex. The older he got he steadily and increasingly regretted he wouldn't be around by the time the sex robots came out at Best Buy, which was a damn shame.

*

Essence ran an article on why Street Lit mattered, basically saying hurray for reading.

If people ate McDonald's every day nobody would crow, "At least they're eating." They'd fifty-million-pound-challenge their asses in a heartbeat.

"Will you shut the fuck up?"

"They're using the book as an example of what Street Lit can be!"

"What's not cool about that?" said Bela.

"Might as well have said *Gilligan's Island* is an example of what an adventure series can be."

"You're complaining because you're doing well?"

"I didn't think the book was going to *do* anything. I figured it would give the Barnes & Noble returns department something to do. It's bullshit."

"No, it's not. Don't argue with me, I'll slap you silly. You wrote a book you didn't want to write, but you wrote the book. You're actually pretty good sometimes. Credit where credit is due. It's like Prince or Mozart: their worst is somebody else's best. Except you're not that good. Plus you had fun writing it, you contrary bastard. Yes, every other one of those books is crap, but maybe now they'll at least try to write more than two compete sentences in a row and use spell check once in a while. 'In every revolution,'" he quoted from the *Star Trek* episode in which the Enterprise crew encountered their evil mirror universe, "'there is one man with a vision.' You're the captain of this Enterprise."

"For the moment."

"That's all you get. But I swear to God: keep whining while you're walking your ass to the bank and I will knock the DNA out of you. It's over, it's done, people like it. Check that huge ego at the door and act like you're pleased."

"I am pleased."

"Good, you ungrateful negro. Now it's your job to get an agent and start writing what you need to write."

"I've gotten calls since the interview."

"Good."

"Asking: Is there a planned sequel to Neon?"

"Fuck it, you know what? From now on I'm your agent. I didn't get to be ECGTS for nothing."

"Actually you did."

"I can negotiate my ass off, plus I don't care about writers or publishers. I'm the perfect outsider."

"What am I worth as a writer?" Barclay challenged.

"I get sandwiches at your house so you're worth a lot to me. Think about it: how much worse could I be from having nobody?"

"Friends don't do money."

"Don't believe that shit. If I fuck up what money represents, that's one thing. But if you're cool and I just fuck up money, me and you are still cool. What's the going percentage?"

"Fifteen."

"I do it for one. To cover the overhead expenses of working

from my cubicle."

"The sticky notes and staplers you take home," Barclay clarified.

"If I'm your agent here I don't need to take 'em home. We got a deal?"

"Shut your crazy ass up."

"Know how 'really' is the new disbelief for white folks? 'Shut your crazy ass up' will be my catch phrase for unbelievably great deals. Nowhere near as annoying. I've seen *Jerry Maguire.* 'Show me the money' or 'Shut your crazy ass up'—clear choice."

"Add 'What you talkin' 'bout, Willis?' and you're nearly there."

"You questioning my flamboyance?"

"Among other things. Can you get out of my office before you get us fired?"

"Maybe that's what you need to live your dream. Gotta have a dream, brother."

"What's yours?"

"Let me just say," Bela said around a blossoming wide smile, "that me and Irina are going to see a movie next week." Bela got up from his perch on the edge of Barclay's desk. He slid the candy drawer open and snagged two bars.

"You don't know a damn thing about being happy, Lugosi," said Barclay.

Bela grabbed another bar. "Plenty time to learn. Ain't like I'm doing anything else."

"You plan on contributing anything to the stash?"

"Just my love and gratitude, brother. Love and gratitude."

At The Book Expo:

Neon shared the table with Wendy and *Lost Inside;* PJ and *What you Won't Do;* Bea and *Gloss;* Stefano and *Utility Pole* (a blatant attempt to blaze off Cross' career), and others. She took up most of the available space, and it was a long table. Cross' decision to keep the identity of SDW an open secret paid off: when readers approached the table and recognized (vaguely) Barclay Royse from the backs of other Crosshairs books (even the readers who hadn't finished the books) or the interview a couple months back and put two and two together (he wore a tailored black t-shirt with a single thin blue neon line across the chest; Cross had wanted red but neon red was just another name for hot pink, and one look at Royse's face let Cross know not to push it), curiosity grabbed them like gravity. Barclay, at a table full of make-believe pimps, skanks, hoes, thugs and ne'er do wells all delivered to mass market heaven like terrorists to their seventy-two virgins, was—In a weird, engaging way—the sideshow geek. The eighties had Vanilla Ice, the late nineties got dealt Eminem, the two-thousands had Street on one side...and Barclay Royse waaaay on the other. Cross had one of the other Crosshairs authors write several blurbs. 'Neon doesn't just raise the bar for Street Lit, it snatches that mug up and sets its nasty ass on fire!'

Which was a bit much. Barclay would have been happy with "A Fun Read," but the other Crosshairs authors seemed genuinely pleased with his newest success. He always answered their emails with as much help as he could and, more importantly, returned the favor by asking it of them. It was nice being needed.

Across the way, Thor M.F. Jones, author of the relationship book *Can A Brother Get A Blowjob? One Man's Journey to Love,* enjoyed a line twice as long as Barclay's and skank-fortified to the maximum daily allowance. A few men punctuated the snake of a thousand cell phones, but young women absolutely dominated the quest to find out what it was the contemporary broheem really wanted. They called their sisters, lovers, friends and others to let them know they were in line with *the* M.F., about to get a signed copy of that shit. "And he is fine. Like roughneck at a good restaurant fine."

And he was fine. Barclay saw a younger, buff, more handsome version of himself had he ever been handsome when younger or been buff. Black t-shirt hugging muscles, fatigue pants (the excruciating metaphor "Love is a battlefield" was the opening line of his book) created the perfect image of the ghetto soldier with a pen. There was no poet like a down thug poet, and no better lover at keeping it real. *Can A Brother Get A Blowjob?* was as raw as an ashy fuck (Chapter Two: Fuck Ashy And He's Yours For Life – Sex vs. Maybelline). It was billed as the only relationship book you needed a condom, cigarette and private time in the bathroom to handle. Nobody else was saying the word "fuck" with such nonchalance in relationship books, and for damn sure Oprah wasn't making sure blowjobs attained the level of importance they were due. *Can A Brother Get A Blowjob?* was the book to beat at the Diaspora Jones (not related to Thor) Africanized Spelling Bee and Book Expo featuring none other than Diaspora Jones herself, keynote speaker, authoress, and 1972 spelling champ of Wagoner Middle School. And authors who knew they couldn't beat it were there to study it. Thor M.F. Jones, all six feet three inches of him, had opened the market wide open like the toned legs of a woman under Billy Dee Williams' knowing gaze to frank, raw, street self-help with its finger on the real and its mindset on the now.

Barclay imagined the conversation with Cross would go pretty much like this, with Cross pitching a book title:

"*Bitch, Please! Communicating With Your Man After The Tripping Is Through.* Guaranteed best seller. Last one, I promise."

"Street self-help."

"Nobody's talking to that market in their language."

"What the fuck language is that? Are they aliens with a third tit and sentient dicks? This subculture thing is a trip."

"Don't get upset."

"I'm not."

"You are highly upset."

"I have a right to be."

"Felt and respected. Can you honestly say the money to be made doesn't entice you?"

"I could've made money selling crack."

"And why didn't you? Because you care. You want to help."

"Because I'm human, dammit, and poisoning Sesame Street doesn't seem the best use of my time!"

"You're upset. Barclay? I've upset you."

"I'm Ok, man."

"One more, then we're done."

Fat people say one more piece of cake. Drunks say one more shot of Jack. It's always one more until something is used up.

Like Barclay's patience.

Thor Jones was an opportunistic punk using his penis to massage snake oil into the stiff emotional muscles of no-standards having women. That line over there was yet another round of idiocy and excuses. Well, no more. The woman handing Barclay her book for signing was barely seen or heard as his decision to march over there and overturn Thor's table fought to spread to his legs. He would stand over there and maybe rattle loose a few women, shouting "This book is bullshit!" at them...until Thor came around the table...

The lady took the book from his hands and stood there an additional second. Her voice was soft and demure. "Barclay Royse?"

"Yes, I'm Barclay," he said, because clearly she'd wandered into the wrong line. "Thor's across the way." He looked at her now to shoo her on.

She had the reddest freckles and hair he'd ever seen.

"You live here?" he said, astonished that he automatically knew who she was.

"Close enough to drive." She was the brightest, whitest person in the entire hall.

He flashed a smile at the ladies behind her. "This is an old friend. Y'all don't mind me coming around for a hug?" He came around and hugged her. "W.B. Fields, you read this book?" he said, standing apart and beaming at her.

She wrinkled her nose. "Hell no. Listen, sign a lot of books. I'll be here awhile."

He tried to banish happy thoughts from seeing her out of his head because Marilyn might pick up on them and zero in on his position. "Ok," he said, and she walked off, hippie linen skirt and all. He went back behind the table, made sure Marilyn wasn't paying attention, and ignored the Mandingo appreciation Stefano and PJ were surreptitiously giving him.

Lunch break was coming up. He wanted to sit with her and be a real person in this cyclone crowd of ambitions. He signed dutifully for the next twenty minutes, told Marilyn about W.B. and how he wanted a few minutes alone, got the wife's blessing, and was off. It wasn't hard finding her.

She wasn't tall, she wasn't gorgeous, and her curly hair could've done with a good leave-in conditioner, but the only words that came to mind as he stood behind that rash of hair were: "You didn't tell me you were beautiful."

She turned immediately, nothing but smiles. Gums and teeth. She was so white she nearly glowed.

"I try not to speak on the obvious," she said, locking happy eyes with Barclay. "What's SDW stand for?"

"I can't believe you came to see me."

"Why not? You had a line of people who came to see you."

He had, hadn't he?

"This would've been my anniversary," she told him. "Well, next week. My husband. Vincent. I decided to get away."

"Be among your peoples," he said, gesturing at all the writers inside.

"Be among my people." She looked the length and breadth of the spacious hall. "An army of one."

"There might be five of you out here. Ten if you count the boyfriends that got dragged along."

"More men than I thought would be here," she said.

"Not that you actually thought about who'd be here."

"Except you."

"There's gotta be someplace to sit." Most of the open tables were taken, but here and there individual seats popped out. The poets' corner was the least crowded. A short, close-afroed young lady gave a reading of her collection to a small group. Other poets watched her from paltry tables, hoping the group wouldn't disperse.

Barclay and Wilma found seats far enough away from the action so as not to be rude in conversation. Face to face, finally sitting down, the first thing to get out of the way was Wilma telling him, with an emphatic shake of her head, "I'm not a weird stalker chick. I actually only live a half hour from here," she said, pointing over her shoulder. "Had to come support you."

"How'd you even find out about this?" he said. It wasn't the biggest of venues.

"Black folks aren't the only ones reading urban books," she chided. "I get all kinds of network emails. 'SDW himself, Barclay Royse,' on not one but two email blasts." The familiar cover of *Neon* emerged from Wilma's oversized woven purse. "So, setting nasty ass on fire? You know you have to sign this."

"You actually gonna read it?" he said, taking the book.

"Honestly?"

He nodded.

"No. But it'll stay on my bookshelf forever. Until Strawberry gets to where she can reach it, y'know, fourteen, fifteen. I did flip through it. Then it's straight to mama's private stash."

"Are you writing?"

"No," she said without even a hint of remorse. "There's nothing I need to say."

"I might have two more books in me after this," he admitted.

"Six books is nothing to sneeze at. Harper Lee only put out one."

"I'm no Harper Lee. *To Kill A Mockingbird* will be read a hundred years from now. *Onion Roll* and *Neon?* I'm not thinking."

"I completely forgot to say it's a pleasure to meet you."

"Me too."

She extended her hand. "Wilma Brown. And her invisible daughter."

"Barclay Royse. Mrs. Brown, you've got a beautiful daughter. Does she know that?"

"I tell her every day."

Ten minutes was not enough time to talk. She told him he seemed more out of place than she did. "Because," he said, "I haven't had a chance to meet anybody. I'm sure there's some great work out here."

The poet concluded her reading to polite applause and a quick scattering of non-buying feet. She scratched at her afro a minute, then set about straightening her table for the next round of cheap bastards.

"Come by my table later," he made her promise.

"You have to inscribe me before you leave," she said.

He wrote: *The theory of relativity states that you and I can only be as close as we believe. I will never let you down. That, my friend, is the gospel truth. Peace and be well, Barclay.*

WB left to wander the tables and aisles. Barclay returned to selling *Neon*, finding that in his brief absence his wife had hooked a line at the Crosshairs table with a book in each of her hands and the sure voice of a snake oil practitioner telling folks she had what they needed.

It wasn't what they needed.

Trees died for a blow job manual. And bad poetry. And terrible fiction. Minds withered. Dreams deferred. Money was, and always would be, made.

The circle of life, except no animator would set a cheesy Disney song to it.

Now what? he asked himself on the floor of the Diaspora Jones Book Expo. Diaspora was the reigning queen of urban contemporary and hip hop romance and was rumored to be close to a deal with a major production studio. It was good to be Diaspora Jones.

Barclay Royse could walk out the door, get on a bus, and nobody on it would know he was Barclay Royse.

Marilyn handed books off to two women waiting patiently. She grabbed up two more and swung down the line, tired but smiling the entire time.

He was so lucky his wife had his back.

Across the way Thor still did a bang up job.

The next book just might need that matrimonial perspective.

About SDW: It's true.

SDW's note:

This is a work of fiction, but hell, it's got a picture of titties on the cover. If you thought it was a work of political analysis and historical depth, you scare me. To those same trifling asses who thought I was gonna mention them, no, your ass ain't in this book! Where I'm from is where I'm from, and no, this ain't your damned city! And Neon's name actually came from her grandmama who thought it was so fascinating that folks could take nothing and fill it with bright, colorful light. She wasn't her real grandma, but she was the old lady she thought of as her grandma. Junebug or something.

The Brothers Jetstream? Neon and Yvonne ran into them on the Hawaii cruise. Jetstreams bought 'em drinks, glad to be in civilization again. Didn't let on that they were the Brothers Jetstream, same as Neon and Yvonne didn't let on that they (the finest women on the boat, including that skinny-assed supermodel wannabe who everybody kinda maybe thought they'd seen in some catalog but weren't sure since everybody was shooting collagen in their lips and ass these days)... were Neon and Yvonne.

Pam Grier?

Shee-id.

www.ingramcontent.com/pod-product-compliance
Lightning Source LLC
Chambersburg PA
CBHW070200260626
47160CB00002B/404